WHAT IT MEANT TO SURVIVE

A NOVEL

MALA KUMAR

2024

For Cybel

AUTHOR'S NOTE

My life forever changed on April 16, 2007.

That morning, an armed student fatally shot 32 Virginia Tech students and faculty and injured 17 others. Then in my final semester at the university, I wasn't aware of what had happened until I drove up to the campus 20 minutes after the catastrophic event ended. My first memory of the shooting was of a fleet of ambulances and the devastated look on the faces of the EMTs.

It would take several days to confirm the identities of every victim. In that agonizing period, I found out about the members of a student organization I ran, the International Relations Organization of Virginia Tech (IROVT), who died. We lost three members that day. In total, I knew six of the people who died in the mass shooting, which was later dubbed the *Virginia Tech Massacre*.

On the 10th anniversary of the *Virginia Tech Massacre*, a friend and I visited the parents of our friend and former IROVT member, who lost her life in one of those classrooms. It was during our visit that her mother told us that we too were victims of the shooting.

After years of processing, it took her words for me to understand how deeply every single one of us in the Virginia Tech community was affected by the gun violence that day. While I had always known it on some level, I felt guilty claiming myself as a victim since I wasn't physically injured—in some ways, finally admitting the truth was cathartic.

I met my now-wife Cybel just a few months after that conversation, and I don't believe the timing was a coincidence. In the years since, we have created our own wonderful, stable, and unique existence. This has given me the courage to write this novel, which explores so many of the hypothetical situations that had always lingered in my mind: what if the shooting had happened two years earlier when I was in that same classroom? What if I had been shot? What would that trauma look like? What would it have meant to survive?

I don't know if there was one moment when I decided to write *What It Meant to Survive,* but I do know that every day more and more Americans are becoming victims of gun violence. In the same way the *Virginia Tech Massacre* and every other instance of gun violence haunts its victims, it was time for me to explore these dark questions. I can only hope this novel manages to lead us all to a safer, fairer, and more equitable world.

CHAPTER ONE

 Ramya

 February 5

 Ghana

THE GROWING PRESSURE from a decade of mistakes threatened to crush Ramya. She stared intently at her phone, knowing that a wrong choice could permanently screw up her life. Usually a decisive person, she flipped twenty times between two pictures of herself, carefully examining the lighting, the background, her body language, and her facial expression in both. While each picture had its merits, she needed to pick the one that properly conveyed her nuances as a person. The chosen picture had to be a glimpse into her soul.

"My God, this is so stressful," she whispered.

"Go with that one," Carl casually said, peering over her shoulder and pointing.

"Why that one?"

"Uh duh, this is a *Tinder* profile. You can't use a photo of you

1

in a suit! Save that for LinkedIn."

Ramya sighed and selected the picture Carl recommended. She clicked on the "Save" button and tossed her phone on the table where they were sitting. The phone bounced a few times as though ingesting the new profile information.

"Fine! Picture uploaded. Know-it-all."

"You're welcome. I'll ignore your tone."

"Sorry, perhaps I was a bit dramatic."

"Ramya, dramatic? Never!" Carl joked.

Ramya rolled her eyes, deciding not to react to Carl's exaggeration. She needed him to navigate the treacherous world of online dating.

"Thanks for the help. Dating profiles are the worst."

"Good thing neither of us look a day over twenty-two," Carl replied.

"It does help that we are aging well. Yet I feel old not having had time to do anything except work the past month," Ramya said, motioning around her.

"Seriously, this trip has been a major buzzkill. To us, for surviving."

Carl raised his glass up in a toast, which Ramya met before sipping her pineapple juice.

She glanced around the hotel restaurant and immediately noticed that for the ninth day in a row, she was the only non-white person downstairs eating breakfast. Were they in a remote corner of Poland, she would give the situation a pass. Being they were in the middle of Accra, Ghana, however, the composition of the room emitted the strong stench of colonialism. An American woman of Indian origin, she never quite knew where to place herself on the spectrum of oppressed <—> oppressor.

"Have you found anyone yet?" Carl asked.

"Ha, no one light enough to 'suit my interests,'" Ramya replied sarcastically.

Carl scrunched his face in disgust and said,

"That guy was awful."

Ramya and Carl had flown directly to Accra from Kampala, Uganda, where they had met a guy also working on their program. At first, the guy appeared to be a good-natured Italian staff member. Ramya liked his energy, and she and Carl felt uncharacteristically comfortable sharing intimate life details with him.

"Isn't it weird that he also had a near-death experience? From what he said, another minute and he would have drowned..." Carl said.

"I don't know how the subject came up."

Ramya rarely spoke about the most horrible day, the event that changed everything for her. That night, the words had flown freely. She learned that like Carl and she, after the guy nearly died, he had an epiphany to use his career for a greater good. Over their first two drinks, the three of them discussed how they had turned their personal tragedies into something positive.

After three drinks, the subject turned to their love lives.

"How is dating in Uganda?" Ramya had asked.

"Ah, it's ok. There are a lot of European and American women based here," he replied.

"And Ugandans, of course."

"Yes, but Ugandans are not light enough to suit my interests."

The guy had said the last part so casually and with such a big smile that Ramya thought he was joking. He wasn't. Ramya cringed thinking back to when she first started her career in international development, back when she wouldn't have considered going on a date with a Black African, either. Comparing herself to that guy was painful. At least now she recognized working to empower Africans in Africa without considering Africans as possible life partners was hypocritical.

"That guy didn't even see the problem," Ramya said.

"Screw that guy."

"Yeah, screw that guy! May I find my soulmate soon,

regardless of skin color."

"That's the spirit! You didn't answer my question though. Did you find anyone?"

"Oh, no. I'm terrible at online dating."

Ramya hadn't found anyone she was attracted to, except two people who were so good looking that she figured they were *catfish*, fakes. She still swiped right on those profiles.

She grabbed a piece of flatbread from her plate.

"Shall we go?" Ramya asked.

"I suppose. Let's get this boring day over with."

They made their way outside, the juice and flatbread sloshing around in Ramya's stomach as she walked. Despite their hotel being about a mile down the road from their office in the American Embassy, the taxi drivers made a spectacle of zooming in and out of the neighborhood to inflate their fare. Now in her ninth year in international development, that would normally piss off Ramya. Today, she sank in the backseat of the car and checked Tinder for the fifth time since she woke up.

"Oh wow!" she exclaimed at her messages.

"Who is it?"

Ramya flashed Carl her phone, careful not to show the driver that she, a woman, was looking at other women on a dating app.

"Wooooow!" Carl exclaimed.

They pulled up in front of the embassy and got out of the taxi before Ramya showed Carl the full profile of her latest match: Juliet. She was *gorgeous*, well dressed and,

"Deeeefinitely a catfish. And even if she were real, she's way out of my league."

"Please, Ramya. You're pretty, but you've got to let go of this insecurity you have. That is definitely not attractive."

Ramya scoffed. Carl had been lecturing her about her negative outlook on life since he met his boyfriend in grad school, before which, he had been equally bitter.

4

"Ah yes, you're right. There is, after all, a small chance in hell that this woman who looks like a supermodel and who is staying exactly four miles from our hotel messaged me and said I have sexy eyes."

"Well, I guess your profile update worked. Isn't this what you wanted?"

"Whatever, I'll delete the message."

"No! Message her back. Who cares if she's fake? You need a fantasy playing in your head to get through today."

That was true. Ramya had a knack for daydreaming, yet still managed to look engaged during the driest work meetings.

"Fine, I'll reply."

> **Juliet:** Hi. Ur eyes r sexy. R u in Ghana?
> **Ramya:** Hey, thanks. You're sexy and hot, too. I love your dress. Yeah, I'm in Ghana. You?

"You write like a nerd. Who puts a comma in a message on a dating app?" Carl said, peering over Ramya's shoulder as she typed.

"Well, it worked. Look at what she wrote back!"

> **Juliet:** U write well. Thanks. I made the dress myself. What r u doing today?
> **Ramya:** Wow, you're talented! I have to go to work. It sucks. But I'm free later. You?
> **Juliet:** Nice. Do u wanna meet me?
> **Ramya:** I do. Do you wanna meet me?
> **Juliet:** Sure dear.

> **Ramya:** Ok! We should voice verify
> first though.

Ramya's heart fluttered seeing Juliet's proposition at the word "dear." She loved that Juliet was being so direct. The women of online dating who dragged out the conversation or made wishy-washy halfway commitments were the worst, because Ramya never knew if she should push them to meet up, or back off. It was easy to misconstrue conviction as aggression on dating apps.

She slowed down to a crawl, praying she would get a reply before they went inside. Though this embassy let them keep their phones inside, the data reception was awful. Ramya wanted another taste of Juliet before entering.

"Damn it," she whispered under her breath.

Nothing more appeared before Carl pushed her through the security check point. She'd have to write the rest of the hot story in her head.

Ramya and Carl entered the familiar cramped conference room in the basement of the embassy, where they had spent the better part of a week discussing minute details of behavior change in public health. While she found some of the discussions vaguely interesting, she was in charge of the website they would eventually build, which allowed her to zone out for most of the time.

Their Ghanaian counterparts had already arranged themselves on one side of the conference table, forcing Carl and Ramya to squeeze in front of the whiteboard their annoying colleague Lynne was decorating with chicken scratch.

"Are we doing this all day?" Yawa, one of their Ghanaian colleagues, asked.

"Ha!" Ramya exclaimed.

Everyone was already bored. Lynne shot a death stare at Ramya, who quickly looked down and pretended her shoes were suddenly fascinating.

Lynne's face turned a deep red.

"Not to worry! The material I have created is engaging and should help us arrive at our decisions today. It will be most fascinating," Lynne exclaimed.

Not exactly satisfied but left with no choice, everyone settled into their seats and Lynne launched into module one of seven. Ramya surveyed the room, evaluating her exit strategies. The water cooler was behind three people and accessing it would require them to move, so she would use the one outside. The women's restroom was clear across the hallway; a trip there could kill a lot of time. She silently rehearsed a script for two other classic exit strategies—a coughing fit and a quest to find unnecessary office supplies. All told, she figured she had enough excuses to keep her out of the room for at least one module.

After an excruciatingly long day, Ramya and Carl bolted out of the building, desperate to get away from Lynne.

"Did she reply?" Carl asked once they were outside.

Ramya was already holding her phone towards the sky, praying for it to pick up a signal.

"Come on, come on…"

Finally, the signal bars appeared, and her notifications came through. Her heart skipped a beat. Juliet had indeed replied.

> **Juliet:** Let's meet tonight. When r we gonna voice verify?

"Oh my God, what do I say?" Ramya asked Carl.

"Tell her that sounds nice, and you'll call her soon. Why are you so bad at this?"

"Dating apps are not for overthinkers!"

> **Ramya:** That sounds nice. :-) I can call you in 20 mins, ok?

They jumped into the first taxi that pulled up.

"I'll pay whatever you want, just go!" Ramya commanded.

The driver smiled wide and took off in the direction of the hotel. The price was hefty, and Ramya hoped the payoff would be worthwhile. She pushed her way out of the car before it had come to a complete stop.

"Be careful if you meet up! Tell me where you go!" Carl shouted after her.

She raced up to her room and tried to dismiss the thought that this gorgeous woman was probably not the person at the other end of the messages. Right on time, she called Juliet.

"Hello?" a woman replied.

"Uh, hi."

"Hey."

"Uh, hi."

Ramya's nerd words were failing her.

"So, what did you wanna verify?" Juliet asked.

Her accent was African, though it sounded different than everyone Ramya had met in Ghana.

"That you're a real person."

Ramya faintly heard a second voice on the other end of the phone, a male voice, that sounded muffled and panicked. She could barely make out the words the voice said,

"How did this happen to you?"

Ramya's heart sank. Maybe this woman was who she said she was…and maybe she was married. Maybe this woman was speaking to Ramya in the middle of a marital dispute.

"Ok cool, so where we gonna meet? And what time?" Juliet asked.

The muffled voice continued in the background and Ramya's reservations were building with Juliet's impatience. Her friends who didn't work in international development thought she was foolish for going out on dates with strangers in foreign countries. To Ramya, continent hopping for work was her life, and dating in new countries was a normal part of that. Dating internationally had taught her never to assume anything about anyone, and she decided she couldn't potentially miss out on a hot hookup during this awful work trip. In any case, she knew how to stay safe.

"Let's meet at the downstairs bar of the Movenpick Hotel at 7 p.m."

"Ok dear, see you there."

The bar was well lit and always had patrons from around the world. She could easily escape if Juliet turned out to be shady. She texted Carl her plans in case something went wrong. He responded immediately.

Carl: Fingers crossed she's real!

Dealing with another taxi driver wasn't worth the stress and so Ramya walked over to the Movenpick Hotel. Though Ghana was one of the West African countries more tolerant towards homosexuality, its level of queer acceptance and diversity couldn't match Ramya's current home —London—and her past home, New York City. Ramya felt everyone on the street was staring at her disapprovingly, as if they knew she was on her way to a date with a woman.

She tried to focus on her surroundings. The sidewalk edges had reflective ribbons of green, yellow, and red paint that matched the Ghanaian flag and helped people see so they wouldn't fall at night. In the distance, she saw a sand-colored square archway that contrasted against a big glass government building and a modern-looking white bridge that looked like it was held up with giant chopsticks. The street was quiet at that hour, with only a few lingering mopeds, cars and bicycles circling the roundabout near the Movenpick's grand entrance.

Ramya arrived a few minutes early and scanned the bar. Seeing none of the people inside were Juliet, she sat down at an empty table and opened an issue of *The Economist* she had brought with her to appear smart and give cover for an embarrassing situation in case no one showed up.

Fifteen minutes past the hour, she had only read three paragraphs of one article and retained exactly none of the information. It was impossible to concentrate. Fortunately, Juliet texted around 7:20 p.m.:

Juliet: On my way.

Ramya did her best not to squirm at the idea that Juliet was real and single and would be interested in her.

Juliet arrived about ten minutes later, appearing in the corner of Ramya's right eye. Ramya's body temperature immediately began to rise, and she sweat like a shy teenager who had been called on to speak in class. She was so nervous. Juliet was tall in her impossibly high heels and literally turned heads as she made her way around the tables.

Ramya didn't need to look directly at Juliet to know that her style was impeccable. She had on form-fitting pleather pants and a black crop top that showed off her toned arms and smooth skin. Not a single man, woman or child in the bar failed to notice Juliet, and Ramya suddenly felt very special knowing that Juliet was there to see *her*.

"There you are," Juliet said.

Ramya took in a deep breath to steady herself, and carefully lifted her head to look into Juliet's dark brown eyes. She was relieved to see they were kind, inviting and expressive. Juliet's smile calmed Ramya and her heart rate finally came down enough to stop throbbing.

"Sexy eyes," Juliet whispered.

Her perfect lips were neatly outlined and filled in with makeup. They danced when she spoke.

"Wow, you're beautiful," Ramya said.

Juliet looked at Ramya bashfully, even though Ramya guessed Juliet constantly heard that comment.

"What are you drinking?" Juliet asked.

"It's a mojito that looks like a Long Island iced tea."

Ramya pointed at the off-putting brown lines swirling in her drink. She was pretty sure that to make the drink, the bartender had just tossed in the first five ingredients he reached.

Juliet raised her hand to call the waiter over, who practically threw the food he was holding and raced across the bar to Juliet's service, trampling over anyone who got in his way.

"Yes, uh ma'am, wow you're beautiful ma'am, uh what would you like ma'am?" the waiter stammered.

Ramya noticed Juliet didn't respond to his "you're beautiful" comment.

"I'll have the mo-jee-toe," Juliet said, trying to sound out the drink from the menu.

"One mo-jee-toe," the waiter repeated eagerly.

Ramya saw the waiter rush back to the bar. He stood there to grab Juliet's drink as soon as it was made, the other customers be damned. The bartender looked up at Juliet before immediately making the drink, showing off a level of skill Ramya hadn't thought he had. The waiter brought over to Juliet a beautiful-looking glass.

"How is that the same drink?" Ramya asked.

"What?" Juliet asked.

"Nothing, never mind. How are you?"

Having dated pretty women in the past and being a woman herself, Ramya wasn't one to gawk. That didn't stop everyone else in the bar. Ramya ignored the eyes on her back and instead focused on her date who was most definitely, most miraculously, not a catfish.

"I'm good. And you?" Juliet replied.

"I'm great! I can't believe you're a real person!"

"What were you expecting?"

"I was hoping for you of course…you're stunning compared to everyone else on Tinder."

"Yes, Ghanaian women don't dress up."

"Oh, you are not from Ghana?"

"You didn't know? I'm Nigerian. I'm visiting my friend and her husband."

"Ooh! The guy I heard on the phone was…" Ramya started.

"Ah ah, I didn't know he was home. Yes, it must have been my friend's husband," Juliet finished.

Ramya relaxed, having solved the Mystery of the Guy in the Background.

The irony of the situation was not lost on Ramya. She had turned down four separate job offers with the United Nations in Nigeria because the country criminalized homosexuality. One of her former colleagues at UNICEF had asked his Nigerian colleagues what they thought of gay people. No one would give him a direct answer, which told Ramya everything she needed to know.

Since life had stagnated in New York, she had taken a job in London. They sent her on this work trip to Ghana and she was now sitting at a bar with a beautiful Nigerian woman who she longed to kiss. The situation felt like a lopsided full circle.

Ramya and Juliet sipped their drinks slowly, soaking in enough alcohol to diffuse the awkwardness that comes with any first date but careful not to cross the line into drunk-face. They chatted about how Juliet was good at foreign languages (Ramya wasn't) and Ramya was a good artist (Juliet wasn't), despite Juliet being a fashion designer and Ramya working in international development.

"We should switch careers," Ramya joked.

"Only if we switch salaries," Juliet joked back.

"Don't worry, I don't make much," Ramya said, laughing.

Juliet didn't find that joke amusing. Ramya steered the conversation to funnier date territory.

"Can I tell you about the most bizarre person I met on a dating app?"

"Tell me," Juliet said, leaning in closer to Ramya, who felt her heart race again.

"I went out on a date with this woman in New York. We were having a great time until she told me she's not attracted to women."

Ramya saw Juliet briefly flinch when she mentioned she went on a date with a woman, and she guessed same-sex dating was new for Juliet. Thankfully, Juliet didn't ask her to speak more softly or edit what she was saying, which Ramya appreciated.

"Why did she go out with you?" Juliet asked.

"She said she wanted to honor her gay twin sister who DIED!"

Juliet sat back in her seat and burst out laughing.

"See? Bet you can't top that," Ramya teased.

"Yes, I can dear. The worst date I met online was a man who asked me to be his pet. Like, he would fly me internationally if I got on the floor and acted like a dog!"

It was Ramya's turn to burst out laughing, even though she found the thought disturbing.

"That's so sick!" they laughed-choked in unison.

With Juliet ordering, the waiter brought them great-tasting drinks. A few sips into mo-jee-toe number three, Ramya knew she was teetering on the line of being too drunk. After she had turned thirty, too much alcohol on a date always ended badly.

"I think I'm going to stop drinking now," Ramya said.

Juliet's dark brown lip curled up. She reached across the table and grabbed Ramya's hand, sending an electric shock through Ramya's body.

"I think I'm attracted to you!"

Juliet's touch gave Ramya a shot of confidence she hadn't felt in years.

"Really? Um...is it okay if...do you want to come back to my hotel?" Ramya asked.

"Of course, I would like to."

Feeling generous, Ramya paid for their drinks without asking Juliet. She brought her wobbly feet down to the ground. Not particularly gifted in the art of navigation, she realized she had no idea how to get back to the street.

"Is it this way?" Ramya muttered to herself.

"You don't know, wow," Juliet said, touching Ramya's lower back.

Juliet's touch cleared Ramya's foggy brain, and she led them in the correct direction. They walked side by side to the taxi stand by the hotel.

The driver gave them a quick scan and decided he would show them the scenic route for a higher fare. Thankfully, he was oblivious to the two women in the backseat sitting close to each other. Juliet's hand rubbed Ramya's thigh while the beaten-up car swerved in and out of the streets of Accra to Ramya's hotel. A mix of tall buildings, gated communities, and thatched roofs flashed past them, the streaks of light illuminating Juliet's face like an angel's. Though they had only known each other for a few hours, Ramya's mind conjured hundreds of scenes of them together, as though they had known each other for years.

Ramya tried to appear calm as they walked through the lobby of her hotel. Inside her room, she couldn't wait to get her clothes off. Now without the heels, Ramya saw Juliet was about her height. She scooped up Juliet and they rolled around on the bed while Ramya's lips made their way around Juliet's torso. The sense of familiarity persisted, yet there was an excitement of being with someone new. Ramya wanted both to rush to get to every curve of Juliet's body and to go slowly to appreciate how perfect this moment was.

Ramya slipped under Juliet and could tell from the responses that she was hitting the right spots.

"Yes, like that," Juliet moaned.

And so like that, Ramya kept going for nearly an hour. She thought they were only getting started when an unexpected thing happened. In the middle of one particularly luscious moan, Juliet screamed,

"I love you!"

"You what?" Ramya said, bolting up.

CHAPTER TWO

 Juliet

 February 5

 Ghana

JULIET WASN'T SURE why she suddenly declared her love for Ramya hours after they first met. All Juliet knew was what led her to meet Ramya in the first place.

Three months ago, her boyfriend Johannes had been sitting next to her on her bed in Lagos. He was sobbing uncontrollably, begging her to forgive him as though he hadn't just confessed that he was still fucking three other women, one being his Nigerian baby mama. He had gotten her pregnant again.

"It's the alcohol, baby. It makes me lose control. You know you're the only person I love," he had said.

"Alcohol doesn't give you permission to break us."

She was so tired of that excuse.

"I'll leave her for you, I promise."

His offer only reminded Juliet of what kind of person he

was: a sad, older Dutch man who relived his bad childhood by impregnating as many women as he could, to then abandon them later. Most any pretty girl in Nigeria who dated foreign men had heard some version of this story. Lagos attracted the worst of them.

"What kind of life will she have then, Johannes?"

"It doesn't matter, I want you."

"What kind of life will your children have?"

What kind of person would that make Juliet if she agreed to Johannes leaving his family? A bad person. Someone she wasn't, she decided.

Juliet sighed thinking about her situation in Nigeria. Oh *Naija*, her country. As a young child in school, she had sung beautiful songs to remember the colors of her favorite fruit, the days of the week, and multiples of seven. A few years later, she learned with a profound admiration about her country's national heroes. By adolescence, Nigeria had taught her to stand tall and proud, for she was from the greatest country in Africa! Perhaps even the world?

Later in life, she realized there was a reason why the national heroes she learned about were all men. It was the same reason why in Nigerian movies, the only women with professional jobs were rich and married to powerful husbands. It was the same reason why the traditional communities she grew up with never encouraged the girls to go to university. Long before she had the chance to travel outside, Juliet understood that Nigeria was a land of opportunity— for men. The oil riches that bubbled below the surface of her country attracted thousands of foreign—male—workers.

She thought back to the day she met Johannes. She didn't find him attractive or charming. Yet she remembered her first thought when she saw him.

"Oh, I hope he likes me!"

Like every Nigerian woman she knew, Juliet had fought to date these foreign men, many of whom were running away from their wives, because at least they had some money and came from countries where women were considered more equal. The fresher ones spoke of gender equality, but with time, they revealed their sexism. The Nigerian women she knew were so reliant on men to survive that in turn, most men, both foreign and local, used them.

Juliet had always known Johannes was no different. He would have gotten her pregnant if she had let him. She had still given the relationship a chance, for when he hadn't been lying, he had at least been kind and tried his best to take care of her financially. She cursed herself for believing their relationship would last. The wind was knocked out of her when she heard him finally admit what she had always known:

"Juliet, we can't be together."

Spontaneity is reserved for the rich, however, and while Juliet wanted to teleport to the other side of the world, it took her a full three months to get her passport, coordinate with her friend Sylvia, book the bus to Ghana, and make the bumpy and dangerous two-day journey from Lagos.

On day two of the journey, the bus almost derailed from the road. Juliet's mind flashed back to the best and worst memories of her life in the few seconds the bus did not meet the ground, a sign she mistook, that she was dying. The bus crashed down on the back tires before the front tires found their way, too. A delay of no more than ten minutes forever changed Juliet's life. She was thoroughly shaken up and more determined than ever by the time she arrived in Accra. The sharp sting from Johannes had worn off, and she swore she wouldn't entertain another bastard who was only out to waste her time. Juliet dressed up in her finest clothes her first night in Ghana, single and ready to mingle.

"My friend, make we go club for Accra!"

"Ah, my friend. I no go fit comot. I don carry belle ooo. Na four months old," Sylva had replied.

Juliet sat down on the couch with her conflicting feelings finding out that Sylvia, who was married, was overjoyed to be pregnant. Although Juliet was happy for her friend, she realized then how lonely she was herself. Seeing Sylvia and her newlywed husband act playfully around the house had stirred up a deep desire for Juliet to have that same companionship.

With no one to keep her company at the clubs and it being her first time outside of Nigeria, Juliet turned to Tinder to meet a new love or a new friend, or both. Like most Nigerian men, the Ghanaian men on dating apps took all of two messages to say something disgusting, and Juliet knew they would end up being another bastard, only with a different accent.

For as long as she could remember, she had felt sexually attracted to some women. But Nigeria hadn't been a safe place to explore her fantasies. When she went to Nigerian blogs, nearly every comment about homosexuality invoked the devil, disgust, hatred, abnormality, and sickness. Ghanaian comments weren't as harsh. Some even sounded positive.

We are all God's children, said one Ghanian tourism account.

The perfect spot for a hers and hers date night, said a restaurant review.

My best friend is gay. He is family, a man replied to an article about loyalty.

Fueled with hope, Juliet started slowly. The first time, she stared at her Tinder settings for an hour.

I am interested in:
[x] Men
[ ] Women
[ ] Non-binary
[ ] Other: _____

SAVE

She couldn't bring herself to check another box and clicked SAVE without changing anything. The second time, she clicked "Women," but only gave herself a few minutes to see the options. The third time, she forced herself to keep the "Women" box checked and exited the app.

"I'll say I just want to be friends," she told herself.

Yes, that would work. She would explain to her new female matches that she was looking for friends.

Most of the women she saw were basic looking, not interesting enough to risk contact. Then on day three of the experiment, she stumbled on Ms. Sexy Eyes, who was Indian, though looked unlike any Indian woman she had seen before. Ms. Sexy Eyes had the young and soft face, light makeup and long hair that Juliet recognized from the many Bollywood movies she had seen growing up. Ms. Sexy Eyes was also a tomboy in the way she dressed and stood. Juliet was hooked. She swiped right. Her heart nearly jumped from her chest when her phone flashed:

Congrats! You're a match!

Steadying herself, she sent Ms. Sexy Eyes, or Ramya, as she was called, a message.

From her profile, she knew Ramya was American and a lesbian, so she didn't have to pretend she wanted to only be friends. Juliet liked the way Ramya treated her online. Ramya was clear that she liked Juliet back and didn't send gross or aggressive messages. That emboldened Juliet and she didn't want to drag out the conversation. She asked Ramya what she was doing that night and was so excited when Ramya agreed to meet.

Juliet spotted Ramya as soon as she walked into the bar. The first thing she noticed was that Ramya's profile pictures weren't bogus; Ramya did actually look younger than her even though Ramya was seven years older.

"She go age well," Juliet said to herself, finding it refreshing to go on a date with someone who took care of their skin.

As nervous as she was, Juliet walked straight up to her date and said,

"Hi Ramya. It's me, Juliet. What are you reading?"

"Hi, Juliet! It's *The Economist*. I got here early and figured I'd catch up on the news while I waited."

Juliet loved that Ramya was reading an intellectual magazine instead of watching sports highlights on YouTube like her exes would have been. She wanted to be with someone who knew about the world.

Conversation flowed easily, and even though she had moments of doubt being on a date with a woman, Juliet instantly felt safe with Ramya. She and Ramya spoke about their interests; until then, she hadn't even realized that was something she could talk about on a date. Very few people had ever asked her.

"I love fashion and I love hearing different languages. I speak four," Juliet said.

"Wow, you speak four? Did you learn those from birth or are you good at languages?"

Another question she had never been asked. Juliet sat for a moment before realizing that she was, in fact, good at languages.

"I learned pidgin English and Yoruba from being a native of Lagos. I guess I taught myself Igbo by listening to my parents and I was very good at English in school."

"That's super impressive, congratulations."

She loved how Ramya leaned back at her answer. Juliet couldn't remember the last time someone had complimented her for her brain. She felt that Ramya was as interested in her mind as her body, and it felt natural to speak in detail. They talked more in two hours than she had with her boyfriends in one year.

The only negative moment Juliet felt on their date was when Ramya said she didn't make much money. That meant Ramya wouldn't be able to support her, which Juliet quickly decided was irrelevant. Ramya was a woman after all, and it's not like tonight would be the start of a relationship. In any case, when the bill arrived for their drinks, the money comment faded. Ramya immediately paid, which Juliet felt happened not because of obligation or because Ramya expected sex in return, but because Ramya was a nice person. Normally reserved on a first date, it was an easy decision for Juliet to follow Ramya back to the hotel room.

Within twelve hours of her experiment on Tinder, Juliet was in paradise in bed with Ramya. She had never been touched with such tenderness and care. For the first time, she felt like the other person was completely concentrated on her pleasure. It was exhilarating! Her body rocked towards her third orgasm of the night. Maybe it was the sustained pleasure, or maybe it was the novelty of being with a woman; whatever the reason, something inside of Juliet's heart exploded and before she could control her words, she shouted,

"I love you!"

"You what!?"

Ramya bolted upright and sat naked a few feet away, now staring at her with a shocked expression. Immediately, Juliet knew she had ruined the night.

"How can you say you love me? We barely know each other," Ramya whispered.

"How do you know it's not true?"

She knew Ramya was right. So many men had declared their love for her within hours of meeting, which always meant they were trying to trick her into doing something she saved for serious partners. Still, as ridiculous as she felt, she couldn't decide if her declaration of love was untrue. In any case, she hadn't said it to be manipulative.

Juliet reached down for her underwear to get dressed. Ramya's face told her it was time to leave. To her surprise, Ramya jumped across the bed and grabbed her arm.

"Look, I've been the first woman for other women, and…" Ramya started.

"What makes you think you were my first woman?"

Juliet didn't like Ramya's presumption. She prided herself on knowing how to move her body in bed and was insulted that Ramya hadn't noticed.

"It doesn't even matter if you are my first woman."

"You're right. It doesn't matter and I didn't mean to jump to conclusions. What I meant to say is maybe this is a new experience for you and maybe it's hard to know how you feel?"

Juliet crumpled back on the bed; Ramya had said it well. This was her first week outside of her country and her first time sleeping with a woman. Everything felt new. Her heart, which was usually reliable, was confused.

"Ramya, I'm tired ooo."

She had had an emotionally exhausting few years with everything Johannes had put her through.

"I'm tired too…ooo," Ramya said, mimicking the drawn out "ooo" Juliet as a Nigerian said to emphasize her words.

Juliet chuckled. Ramya sounded cute.

"Let's continue what we were doing and leave the words for later?" Juliet suggested.

Ramya gave her a small smile that revealed an age her face didn't. Juliet could tell Ramya needed this as much as she did. They slipped back into position before more conversation completely killed the mood. Juliet let her body relax again over Ramya. This time, she was careful to not completely shut down her mind and accidentally slip out another "I love you."

They dozed off lying next to each other, naked and fully exposed to the kind of intense air conditioning that was only in the cinema and hotel rooms. Juliet awoke in a shiver and glanced over at Ramya, who was fast asleep. It was comforting to see a soft and beautiful woman facing her, instead of the usual hard-faced man. She reached down and carefully pulled the duvet over them before falling back into a deep sleep.

The next morning, it was obvious that Ramya wanted to talk about what Juliet had said. By then, the shock of sleeping with a woman had set in. Juliet knew she couldn't confess this shock to Ramya since she had made such a show of being offended. As she pulled on her trousers, she heard Ramya rapidly speaking,

"I know my energy can be *disarming* to *straight* women who are *discovering* their *bisexuality*."

Juliet wasn't sure what those words meant individually, though she could guess the overall meaning. Even though the naïve part of Juliet was eager to spend the day with Ramya, she didn't trust herself to calmly speak while she felt so vulnerable, and Ramya seemed like a serious person who wouldn't let this go.

"Please, Ramya, abeg, it's early. I had a good time. We don't need to say anything more, ok?"

Ramya looked hurt that Juliet cut the conversation short. Juliet didn't have the energy for a long, intellectual exchange about the matter. That's not how she'd grown up. Nigerians mostly shouted when they wanted to discuss something, and she had realized during her first few days in Ghana that's not how people in other countries dealt with things.

Juliet cautiously packed up her bag so that Ramya wouldn't think she had already gotten too attached. Surprisingly, Ramya sounded alarmed.

"Maybe we can meet up again tomorrow?" Ramya asked.

"Sure, maybe."

"I mean, I really enjoyed last night…we should do it again if that's okay?"

The panic in Ramya's voice pulled at Juliet's heart. She

wasn't sure why she was using her harshest weapon—lukewarm distance—when she already knew she wanted to see Ramya again.

"Maybe, text me."

"Of course, I will!"

Juliet gathered the last of her things and walked over to the door. She hesitated a split second before reaching for the handle, halfway hoping that Ramya would ask her to stay.

"Uh…thanks for coming. Those are nice…uh, heels," Ramya stuttered stupidly.

"Ok, thanks."

Juliet's tense shoulders dropped. That wasn't even close to what she wanted to hear. She glanced down at her feet with shame.

"Sorry, I'm not great at this part," Ramya said.

"It's okay, see you."

Juliet grabbed the door handle, which felt lighter than it had a few seconds ago, and left the room, leaving Ramya without so much as a goodbye kiss.

"I'll text you!" Ramya repeated as the door closed.

The lift took an infuriatingly long time to come. Juliet walked through the hotel lobby and out the back to the taxi stand, barely noticing the beautiful pampas, vases, carpets, and chandelier decorations that had taken her breath away last night. Her head felt so heavy, like a goat had repeatedly kicked her. She rummaged through her purse for the few remaining Ghanaian cedi she had left to pay the taxi fare.

"East Legon," Juliet instructed the taxi driver.

"No problem, my sister."

He took off in the correct direction, having decided Juliet was African enough to be charged the local rate.

Juliet stared down at the shoes Ramya had complimented. The last time she saw him, Johannes had given her these heels as a nonsense gift for ruining her life. *That* was what so many of her relationships had been, how so many relationships were for Nigerian women—men fucking up and then bribing their way back with gifts.

From Ramya's body language, she knew Ramya hadn't been acting strange because she thought Juliet was a disposable toy. Ramya had been acting strange because she wanted Juliet to stay and didn't know how to ask. Awkward as they were, at the end of their hookup, Juliet had walked away with the feeling of respect. This was the first time she had left a one-night stand feeling like the other person saw her as equal.

Still, respect didn't pay the bills and Juliet was stressed that she was now more broke than before, having had to pay for an expensive taxi fare both ways, just to have sex.

"But was that *just* sex?" Juliet whispered.

She knew what it was like to let someone touch every inch of her body yet have no emotional connection. This was not that, and Juliet wasn't sure if it was because Ramya was a woman, or who she felt Ramya was as a person, or both.

The taxi driver pulled into Sylvia's compound and announced his price: twenty-five cedis.

"Na wa ooo."

Realizing she was 7 cedis short, she picked up her phone, praying she had enough credit to complete a call. Fortunately, it went through, and Sylvia answered on the first ring.

"My friend, taxi for Ghana dey expensive! Abeg, come help me pay the remaining seven cedis," Juliet said in the mix of pidgin English and Nigerian English she used with Sylvia.

Sylvia came down a few minutes later and handed the last of the fare to the driver, who looked annoyed he hadn't charged more. By the time he sped off, Juliet was exhausted.

"My friend, how your side? How you dey?" Sylvia asked Juliet.

"I dey fine ooo."

Juliet was nervous about going into detail. She hadn't told

Sylvia that she met up with Ramya to have sex; she had made it seem like they would hang out as friends. It wasn't uncommon for Nigerians to spend the night at a new friend's house and Sylvia hadn't lived in Ghana long enough to think it was strange Juliet had come back the next morning.

She followed Sylvia up the stairs and into the main sitting area of the house. Sylvia waddled over and sat down on the couch, her pregnancy belly bump somehow much larger than when Juliet had seen her yesterday.

"Am I imagining things?" Juliet said.

"Say wetin?"

"Your belleh don grow bigger since yesterday."

"My belleh dey grow every day, Juliet! That's what happens in pregnancy..." Sylvia replied.

"Na true sha. My friend, I must be tired. Make I go rest small."

"Eh, I know say you don dance tire last night with your new friend!"

"Yes ooo, we danced all night."

Juliet was grateful Sylvia filled in the words her brain wasn't finding.

She walked over to the spare room Sylvia had given her, stripped out of her clothes, threw herself onto the mattress on the floor, and tried closing her eyes. Hard as she prayed for the sleep to enter her body, there was too much on her mind.

Being sexually active was normal for Juliet and her friends in Lagos. Being financially independent was not. Some Nigerian women, especially those from poorer families, had to choose their sexual partners based on finances. Sex had thus become both a way for these women to express themselves and necessary to survive. She didn't think of this as full prostitution, but the uncomfortable truth was that she knew very few Nigerian women who could walk away from a sexual encounter without cash or some kind of gift.

Juliet was not that privileged. Her night with Ramya had been the first time she didn't ask or expect money from her sexual partner. She was feeling both empowered and confused when her phone lit up with a text.

> **Ramya:** I hope you got back to your friend's place ok? I had a wonderful time last night and would love to see you again tomorrow. Are you free?

Juliet let out a big sigh before she responded.

> **Juliet:** Yeah, 2mrw wud be good. See you at 8pm dear.

That gave her thirty-six hours to gather enough money for the taxi fare to and from Ramya's hotel. Johannes's bribery heels were in the corner of the room.

"Abeg, let me make you useful."

Standing up, she wrapped herself in a towel and walked back out to the sitting area.

"Ah ah, I thought you were resting?" Sylvia asked.

"My friend, I want to sell these."

Juliet held up the shoes, trying to find the most flattering angle to entice Sylvia.

"Juliet, I carry this big big belleh now. It's not me who will buy them."

Sylvia was referring to her pregnancy stomach. Of course, why would a pregnant woman want her five-inch heels?

"What about your friends here?"

"I come over for this side and then got pregnant. I don't have single friends in Ghana. Sorry ooo."

Sylvia patted Juliet on the shoulder as she passed by on her way to the kitchen. The light touch was meant to be comforting, but it nearly brought Juliet to tears.

"Chai! Na how I go come reach there tomorrow?"

Her phone lit up again at that exact moment with another text.

> **Ramya:** Awesome! I'm so sorry if the taxi fare was expensive. I'll pay you back for everything tomorrow. Thank you so much for meeting me here both times.

Juliet's face responded immediately. The tears pulled back, and she broke out into a huge smile. Without the weight on her shoulders, Juliet stood up straight and said,

"It's as if this woman can read my mind."

CHAPTER THREE

 Ramya

 February 6

 Ghana

WHILE PART OF Ramya was disappointed that she didn't get to spend the entire day with Juliet, she was mostly relieved. Before last night, exactly four people had ever said they loved her: one ex-girlfriend, her best friend in second grade, and her parents, and even they had only said it a few times. She hadn't been properly equipped to respond to Juliet's declaration of love and was painfully aware she had screwed up their goodbye. My awkwardness knows no bounds, Ramya thought to herself.

She texted Carl to meet her downstairs for breakfast, who replied that he was already there.

The only pair of casual clothes she had readily available were from last night, so she tossed her suitcase on the bed to get a better look at what was in the bottom. Peering down, the impression on the bed from Juliet's body caught her eye. She mentally filled in the space and felt a pang of sadness, which wasn't justified considering she felt like she had basically chased Juliet out of the room. What should have been a joyful walk down to breakfast felt like a walk of shame.

She found Carl sitting at their usual table.

"Heya, how'd it go, what happened? Oh no, was she a catfish?"

"No, worse, she was perfect."

"Um, not following you there, dear."

Ramya's heart jumped when she heard Carl say "dear." How quickly she had come to associate that word with Juliet.

"I don't know. She was exactly who she said she was, we got along great, and the sex was amazing. Then she said she loved me while we were in bed and…"

"Ah, say no more. I know how you deal with the L word. Then what happened?" Carl asked.

"You know me! I had a long explanation about how she just *thinks* she loves me. She said she wanted to drop it. We stopped talking."

"Then what happened?" Carl asked again.

"Then this morning, I thought I was being nice when I complimented her shoes. She looked devastated I said that and left. I guess we won't see each other again."

Carl rocked back and forth slightly while nodding his head, his classic movement to indicate he thought he had sage advice. He pointed his mimosa glass at Ramya.

"Do you know for sure she doesn't want to see you?" he asked.

"Yeah…I mean…I guess I'm not sure?"

Maybe Carl was sage. That was a good question.

"You can't assume anything. Maybe her reaction had nothing to do with you. Text her and invite her to come back."

Ramya quickly debated before Carl's preferred method of persuasion—berating someone into submission—started. The worst that could happen was Juliet would say no, which was what Ramya had expected a short while ago, anyway.

"Okay, I'll try."

She typed out a message and hit send before she second guessed herself. Juliet replied almost immediately.

> **Juliet:** Yeah, 2mrw wud be good. See you at 8pm dear.

Ramya read Juliet's reply to Carl.

"See? You gotta put yourself out there more, Ramya, especially after everything you've been through. You're a good girlfriend, you just suck at the dating part."

"Ha! Thanks for the...compliment?"

"Anytime. So is she from Ghana or is she visiting family?"

"No, she's actually Nigerian..."

"Oh...wow. How do you feel about that?"

Carl dropped his fork. The loud clang against his plate echoed in the nearly empty restaurant. Ramya surveyed the room before continuing. She was always surprised at how the restaurant never ran out of food even though they rarely saw kitchen staff or waiters. Today was not the day to be overheard by a sneaky homophobic hotel worker.

"I don't know. It was a hookup, right? I'm trying not to overthink things."

"What if this turns into something more than a hookup? I can tell you really like her."

Another sage point, considering Ramya had moved to London for her now ex, who hadn't asked her to come. Ramya tended to dive headfirst into her relationships. Sometimes she ended up with a concussion.

"I don't know. Let me get through date number two before I drive myself silly with hypotheticals," Ramya replied.

Carl finished eating, and they walked back to the lobby.

Ramya's thoughts were occupying too much space in her body for her to digest food.

"I am going to spend the day reading a book in bed. I can't believe they're making us stay through the weekend. I miss Christian," Carl said, referring to his boyfriend.

He gave Ramya a quick hug and got on the elevator. As she waved goodbye, Ramya suddenly became aware that the next time she'd see him, she might have transformational news—either horrible or wonderful—about her love life.

She wandered over to the pool, the pristine blue water oddly still considering it was a Saturday. Normally on the weekends, pools in these kinds of corporate hotels were overrun by foreign workers and local business owners. Ramya was grateful for a moment of quiet and collapsed into one of the chairs. Her phone didn't listen to her needs. Vibrating in her pocket, she pulled it out to see one of those stupid notifications about a photo memory.

This day 10 years ago

The screen flashed, showing her what might have been the last photo Ramya had taken with her parents. She looked the same, she realized, and couldn't quite remember if her parents did. Either way, she was pissed to see the photo.

"Damn it, I thought I got rid of you?"

As if commanded, the photo faded on her phone before completely disappearing.

"When did Apple introduce that feature? Creepy," she said to herself.

By the time she found the setting to disable the photo memory notifications, the damage was done. Ramya was thinking about her parents. She navigated to the next photo in the album and stared down. Her parents and she stood side by side and not touching, in front of her university apartment complex. It was the only time they had visited. Her roommate had taken the photo, which showed Ramya had her father's eyes and her mother's nose. Only she knew what the photo didn't reveal—that she had none of their ambition to work herself to exhaustion for as much money as a person could hoard. The distance between Ramya and her parents hadn't only been physical.

Trying to dispel the wave of negative emotions that came with the photo, she quickly scrolled to happier memories. The scenes of her at fabulous clubs and restaurants, smiling at her ex, and traveling to thirty-four countries in the past decade only partially quelled the feelings. At the age of thirty-one, she was in a weird place in life. She still looked and felt young and agile physically, but the nonstop marriage and pregnancy announcements she saw on social media from her friends and her parents' Indian community had taken a toll.

As if on cue, a notification appeared at the top of her phone, no doubt for another baby announcement. While some people opted for self-care in these moments, Ramya had a habit of torturing herself. She clicked on the notification, which sent her to prime territory for mundane family news: Facebook.

"That's…impossible," she said.

At the top of the feed was a baby announcement from Megan, one of the few friends she had in university.

"What the hell is this? Megan is dead…"

The announcement immediately disappeared.

"That's enough, I'm losing it," Ramya said, tossing her phone on the chair.

She buried her head in her hands, trying to push away more negative thoughts. When she closed her eyes, all she saw was the image with her parents. With everything that had happened to her in university, her friends were always shocked to find out how withdrawn she was from them. Ramya, on the other hand, was grateful they left her alone and never asked about her personal life. She had never directly told them she was gay and open to marrying someone of any race. They had never asked. Ramya knew she wanted to get married and if she did, she would have to come out to her parents. If they didn't accept her future wife, she had to prepare herself to permanently cut them out of her life.

"What if I fall for Juliet?" she asked herself.

Women who fell in love with each other, regardless of the country or their nationalities, tended to move fast. Considering their strong connection, Ramya knew that it wasn't ridiculous for her to seriously consider the possibility. The thought of navigating that complicated situation made Ramya's head spin.

Right when she thought she had found a moment of reprieve, the queen of bad timing popped up.

"Ramya, there you are!" Lynne cried out, interrupting Ramya's thoughts.

"Seriously?"

An expert at acting like people didn't hate her, Lynne pretended not to hear Ramya.

"Ramya, I had to completely redo the workshop analysis and I need you to show me a few sections on the native app. With my background in software eng…" Lynne started.

Ramya crumpled into an angry ball on the pool chair before unfolding herself and replying,

"We're building a web app, not a native app. You worked in data entry, not as a software engineer. And I'm not talking about work. This is my first Saturday off in a month. I need a break."

"Hmfph, well I guess you are not as committed to the work as I am, Ramya."

"You're right, I'm not as committed."

"Well, my husband did always say I was the hardest-working person he had ever met."

"What? You're married?" Ramya asked, sitting up.

She was dumbfounded that anyone could tolerate Lynne

enough to marry her.

"No, he died."

In shock, Ramya studied Lynne's face. A normal person would show a modicum of sadness or remorse. Lynne was no normal person and appeared to be proud her husband was dead, her chest puffed out and her face perfectly still. It was still awful her husband had died.

"Oh sorry, I didn't know."

"It's okay. It was a long time ago. He died in the Rwandan genocide. He was a politician."

That was a long time ago. Quickly doing the math, Ramya calculated that Lynne's husband had been dead for nearly thirty years. She never would have guessed Lynne was that old. Somehow finding out Lynne was a senior citizen made her incessant lecturing more tolerable.

"Geez, I'm so sorry. It must have been hard to be together," Ramya said.

"It was. Those were the happiest years of my life though."

She couldn't believe she was willingly engaging with Lynne, but this story was too interesting to pass up. The Rwandan genocide was one of the most studied periods in international affairs. Ramya had spent many nights in grad school reading about it in detail—how a classification system was used, how Hutu tribe militias murdered more than a half million people of the Tutsi tribe, and of course, the major role of colonialism. Lynne's story was from an important time in history.

Lynne sat back in her chair and smiled, looking close to a likeable person, for once.

"Why didn't you two get out before the war started?" Ramya asked.

"He had a mission there and I was proud to be such an important part of it. You know, I was a very prominent figure in the Rwandan government and…"

"Really? You're American."

And white, Ramya finished in her head.

Lynne cleared her throat and started over.

"HE had a mission, and it was important to the country that HE was there. I was there to support him," Lynne conceded.

"That's intense, I'm so sorry Lynne. No one deserves to die that way. Do you think you both would have moved to the States if he had survived?"

"Oh, I don't know. There was a lot of violence against Black people back then…there still is. He didn't want to come to America."

"True, the American experience is highly dependent on skin color."

Ramya sighed deeply, amazed at how quickly her feelings for Lynne had shifted. She felt sympathetic, even empathetic. Many victims of the Rwandan genocide had been shot.

A single cloud passed over, enveloping Ramya in a new sense of vulnerability. She couldn't believe she was about to ask Lynne for help, but this trip had already been so unpredictable, and she was learning to ride the waves.

"What advice do you have for an American dating an African?" Ramya asked.

"Boy, well, I give great advice and it's hard to narrow it down to one thing. I'd say be aware of their situation, especially with money."

"What do you mean?"

"The cost of dating an American is a lot for the average African."

"Oh true, what…"

"I also recommend listening to smarter, older and wiser people like me," Lynne said, cutting off Ramya.

"Ok, that's the Lynne I know."

Her annoyance at Lynne's lectures reappeared and Ramya picked herself up from the chair. The good feelings had been nice while they lasted.

"And you shouldn't pay for drinks when you go out to restaurants. Just ask for hot water, lemon and sugar to make your own…" Lynne started.

"Great, thanks for the chat. Sorry again about your husband."

"You should also work harder, Ramya. Back to what I was saying on the native app, we need to discuss three key areas…"

"WEB APP, LYNNE. I'm leaving. See you on Monday."

Ramya jogged away from the pool, now aware of what she needed to do. Lynne's persistent chatter grew fainter as the distance between them grew.

"You really should listen to me, Ramya. You're so young and…" she heard Lynne say.

She rushed back upstairs to her room and threw herself over Juliet's bed impression. As though she could talk to remnants of Juliet in the bed, Ramya knew what she had to say. Praying too much time hadn't lapsed for her to sound natural, she texted Juliet.

> **Ramya:** Awesome! I'm so sorry if the taxi fare was expensive. I'll pay you back for everything tomorrow. Thank you so much for meeting me here both times.

Juliet immediately texted her back a smiley face. On her own, Ramya never would have thought to cover Juliet's costs. She looked up at the ceiling and said,

"Mark this day as the only one I was thankful to see Lynne."

A thump on the floor above her woke Ramya up at 5 a.m. the next morning.

"Go back to sleep," she commanded her brain.

38

Terrible at following instructions, Ramya was still awake forty-five minutes later. She slammed her arms in a V-shape on either side of her body, frustrated that she couldn't cooperate with herself. Instead, she threw herself out of bed, changed and went downstairs to the gym for a long workout. It was empty when she arrived, and it felt good to run at full speed, lift heavy weights, and stretch every muscle. After a hot shower, she felt invincible.

By 2 p.m., the endorphin rush from the exercise had worn off, and Ramya felt herself swaying from exhaustion.

"I need to be on my game tonight."

If she showed up to their date tired, Ramya would certainly say something stupid to Juliet. She managed to kick off her shoes and loosen her belt before her head hit the pillow. Normally it annoyed Ramya when the hotel cleaners left the curtains in her room closed. Now, she was grateful darkness surrounded her. Within a few minutes, she dozed off.

Somewhere in her sleep, her brain turned back on without her waking up. At first, all she saw were a series of blocks that jumped on top of each other. They leapt around until they formed one of the fabric patterns on her colleague Yawa's dress. The pattern was connected to a body part, her hip, Ramya felt. Her hip…a part of Ramya's conscious knew her dream was leading her somewhere horrible.

Until now, Ramya's sleep on this work trip had mercifully been dreamless. The stress and anticipation of seeing Juliet must have messed with her, and her sleeping mind drifted away from the present. Every time she slipped into this state, she had no idea where she was headed until a subconscious dread that she had experienced hundreds of times crept over her. Every time she arrived here, she felt her current sense of self drain away. Where she was going, she wasn't professionally accomplished. She didn't have any real skills or a graduate degree. She wasn't living in London or on a work trip in Accra. She had never been in love and hadn't been in any relationships. A past she despised overwhelmed her present.

Colors pooled together in front of her and spun like a giant pinwheel. Slowly, shapes formed and whizzed past Ramya at an impossible speed. She felt herself lurch into a vortex and landed in a classroom she hadn't seen in real life in nearly nine years.

"Bonjour tout le monde...," she heard a familiar voice say.

"Noooo, not now. Why now? Why this day?" she pleaded, finally aware of what was happening.

She grabbed the desk in front of her, shaking it with a fury of injustice.

"GET ME OUT OF HERE!"

Her screaming worked, and Ramya found herself surrounded again in darkness. Her phone alarm buzzed near her head, and she realized she had woken up. Tapping the screen, she saw it was already 7:45 p.m. Juliet would be there soon. Groaning, Ramya lifted her heavy head, slapped her cheeks and did a few jumping jacks to shake off the past that had enveloped her. She stripped down and pulled out her nicest clothes, which didn't quite frame her broad shoulders and long torso the way she wanted.

"It'll have to do."

Afraid she was late, Ramya raced downstairs. After how she had behaved yesterday, she knew she'd lose Juliet's trust if she wasn't outside on time. Fortunately, Ramya caught her as she was leaving the taxi.

"Here you go," Ramya said breathless, handing the driver the fare and a tip.

"Thanks, dear," Juliet said.

Ramya doubled over, trying desperately to catch her breath. She looked up to see Juliet walking into the hotel, her long legs striding as though she were an elegant deer. The first time they met, Ramya had noticed everything about Juliet's body. This time, all she cared about was Juliet's body language. She was nervous that Juliet would act as indifferently as yesterday, which was why hookups were bad for Ramya. Few things were more upsetting than when a woman wanted her to touch them everywhere, and then walled her off from their emotions. It made Ramya feel like an object, not a person.

"How are you, Juliet?" Ramya nervously asked.

"I'm good, Ramya. How are you?"

Juliet replied with a smile and a light touch, which brought more air back into Ramya's lungs than her deep breaths. Soon, all they would be doing was touching, but that small one was the most important of the night.

"It's great to see you, thanks for coming here again."

"No problem, I wanted to see you."

They walked side by side to the elevators. Now much more at ease, Ramya was aware of her surroundings and what she was hearing. A few notes from the speaker above seeped into her brain, stirring up a funny old memory and causing her body to swerve slightly. It was a gut-jerk reaction to one of the worst guilty pleasure songs of all time. Juliet had already taken several of her long strides and was halfway across the lobby.

"What are you doing?" Juliet called out.

"I felt some rains down in Aaaafrica…" Ramya sang badly.

"What?"

Juliet looked out of the window at the dark sky and no rain.

"Sorry, I don't mean literally. It's the song," Ramya said, pointing up.

"What about it?"

"It was popular in America back in the 1980s. It's about these white guys who discover the rains and 'savages' of Africa."

Ramya used air quotes as she said the word "savages."

During her first trip to Africa, she had been caught in a particularly hard rainstorm in a remote part of Togo. Being their first time on the continent, one of her colleagues had downloaded the song "Africa". He connected his iPod to an external speaker and blasted it through the village. Ramya found herself next to six other Americans, dancing in the streets and screaming the lyrics at the top of her lungs. It was only after she returned to the States and saw the music video that she felt conflicted.

"It's one of those songs that every Westerner sings during their first trip to Africa, even though it's like really weird and racist."

By now, Juliet had walked back over to Ramya and was staring at her with a perplexed expression.

"How many times have you been to Africa?"

Juliet looked curious, and Ramya guessed Juliet wanted to know more about her life.

"I…uh, hey, do you want to get dinner before we go up?"

Ramya's heart was pounding; somehow sharing a meal felt more intimate than sex. Thankfully Juliet replied,

"Sure, that would be nice."

They sat down at a table meant for six people so they could stay as far away as possible from the bad band that was performing near the bar. Juliet cringed at the lead singer wailing into her microphone.

"Nigeria has many fancy hotels, and I don't understand why these horrible musicians are hired. No one ever enjoys the 'entertainment,'" Juliet said, returning a pair of air quotes.

"That's so true!" Ramya said, laughing.

She handed Juliet the food menu and waited a few minutes before calling the waiter over. She didn't look at the menu herself, having eaten at this restaurant seven times in the past ten days.

"I don't know what to get…" Juliet murmured.

Ramya took that as permission to order enough food for five people in the hopes that Juliet would find something she liked. She enjoyed introducing people to new foods, and hoped Juliet would notice her generosity and patience.

"Don't get fat ooo," Juliet said with a smile.

"It's fine as long as I can afford it," Ramya joked.

"We can find a man to flirt with and cover the bill," Juliet replied.

Ramya couldn't tell if she was serious.

"I am here for work. My job will cover most of the cost," Ramya replied, the frustration in her voice obvious.

Juliet shifted uncomfortably. Ramya wasn't sure whether Juliet wanted her to brag or be humble about money, so she avoided the guesswork and changed the subject.

"Aaanyway, let me know if you need help with the menu. I eat middle eastern food a lot."

"It's okay, I recognize most of the items. I dated a Lebanese guy for two years."

Ramya simultaneously perked up and deflated. She wanted to hear about Juliet's life, but she was unnerved to hear about an ex-boyfriend. What if that meant Ramya was indeed the first woman Juliet had been with? Bisexual people faced real hurdles, and even though Ramya didn't want to discriminate, she hadn't had a real relationship come out of sleeping with a bisexual woman. Every bisexual woman she had been with eventually ended up with a man, she figured because the stigma of being with a woman was too difficult for most of them to face when real genuine opposite-sex love was possible.

"How do you like Ghana so far?" Ramya asked, changing the subject again.

"I...uh...I don't know. Ghana is okay, a bit like Nigeria."

"I've never been. What's Nigeria like?"

"Nigeria, especially Lagos, where I'm from, is full of life. We have the best fashion, movies, and food. And we have a lot of rich people, so we have a lot of nice places. Nigerians are hustlers and you find them everywhere."

"Including here?"

Juliet nodded. With a background in design research, Ramya knew the best way to get someone to offer more information:

43

silence. She patiently waited through an extended pause until Juliet continued.

"Abeg, I don't want to insult my own country, but many Nigerians come to live here in Ghana. The steady lights and stuff, you know?"

"That sounds like India. A lot of rich people and no steady lights in a country usually means government corruption."

"Oh, I love Bollywood movies…they remind me of Nigerian movies but with better dancing."

Ramya was a little annoyed that was Juliet's takeaway from her point. But she was so relieved to see Juliet happy and smiling that she tried not to kill the vibe.

"Haha, yeah, I just hate how they treat women in Bollywood movies. The men are always rewarded for being abusive or not backing down when a woman says no," Ramya said.

Juliet gave her a quick nod and looked down at her shoes. Ramya squeezed her eyes shut, cursing herself. What a shitty attempt at not killing the vibe.

"You're right, Bollywood movies have really pretty clothes and dancing," Ramya added.

To her relief, Juliet looked up with a pensive expression and slowly sat back, as though carefully weighing Ramya's words.

"True, I didn't think of the movies that way. I love the fashion and colors, but you're right. The women deserve to be treated better in those movies."

"Well said. Anyway, yeah, not having steady electricity is hard. It was sporadic where I stayed in northeast Senegal," Ramya offered.

"My dear, you put as much time into your hair as I put into my makeup. How did you survive in the bush of Senegal?"

"I guess playing that song 'Africa' helped."

Juliet's entire body shook with laughter, which made Ramya incredibly happy. She wanted very badly to keep that laughter coming.

"What brought you to all of these African countries?" Juliet asked.

"International development, mostly with the United Nations."

Even though she tried her best to be humble about her career, she was proud of what she had accomplished and hoped Juliet would be impressed.

"I love makeup," Juliet replied.

"Oh. Ok. What does that have to do with…"

"I'm sorry, I don't know what this international development is."

Ramya looked around and realized that she had climbed onto a throne of arrogance. She jumped down, suddenly not caring that Juliet didn't understand what she did for a living. Juliet liked her for other reasons, which Ramya found comforting. Maybe Ramya hid too much behind her career.

"It mostly means I work with African governments and organizations to help people get the things they need, like food and healthcare."

"Wow, that's beautiful. But why don't you help people in America get those things instead of Africans?"

Juliet sat up as though she had asked an ordinary question. It hit Ramya like a steel ball to the chest.

"Wow, straight to the point!"

Ramya sighed into her drink, wishing she had gotten a mo-jee-toe. The bourbon in her cup wasn't a good choice for the stifling heat of Accra. Very few Africans questioned her so directly and Ramya had to warn herself not to become defensive. Most of her colleagues in the continent at least feigned gratefulness at her being there. Juliet was different; Juliet wasn't talking to Ramya to get a better job.

She debated how to answer the question. Faiza, Ramya's ex, had questioned Ramya's career plenty of times as voyeuristic escapism, which Ramya had always dismissed as passive aggressive.

"You grew up in London proper and were constantly surrounded by other queer brown people. Where I grew up, I literally had no one tell me it was okay to be me," Ramya had tried explaining to Faiza.

"Please, don't blame your upbringing for your orientalist viewpoints," Faiza had replied.

Ramya had long stopped trying to get Faiza to sympathize with the various identity crises she had as a gay brown kid in conservative America. Considering Juliet's background, Ramya couldn't defend herself in the same way. Maybe she shouldn't.

"At the beginning, I think I was just running away."

She was surprised at her own honesty. That was the first time she had admitted it out loud.

"I'm not a typical American or a typical Indian, and I wasn't really accepted at home by either community. When I was young, I wanted to help people in a place where people wanted my help. I guess I found an acceptance in Africa I never had anywhere else," Ramya explained.

"I'm glad my continent accepted you."

"Thanks. I'm grateful to have spent a lot of time in Africa."

"So that was why you first came to Africa. And now? What keeps you coming back?"

"And now, I actually have skills that can help African governments and organizations. But I don't think I'm here to 'save' Africans. And I don't think I'm superior to anyone."

She quickly added the second part. Faiza had been wrong; she wasn't in Africa for an orientalist escapade.

"You know, some of the foreign men I have dated just wanted to sleep with Nigerian women. Some even worked for Black men, but they still think they are better than us Africans."

"Yeah, I've seen that too."

Noble as the mission of international development could be, Ramya had heard of way too many cases of foreign male staff abusing their power with junior "local" staff, as they were called, or with community members.

"I wasn't always attracted to Black women, and I understand why now. And now that I am, I don't hyper-sexualize them."

"That's good to hear. I hope it's true."

"It is, I'm a fellow woman. I can relate on some level."

"That's true. That means something," Juliet agreed.

Their heavy conversation revealed an intriguing side of Juliet to Ramya. While it was easy to dismiss pretty people as superficial, Juliet was quick, smart and a deep thinker. She went straight to the point with her questions, and Ramya saw that Juliet called out bullshit without being cruel or dismissive. That's the kind of partner I want, Ramya thought.

"I hope we get more time after tonight to keep learning about each other," Ramya said.

"Yes ooo, Ramya. Me too."

They had the extra food packed and headed upstairs to Ramya's room. As the elevator number display crept up, Ramya felt the tension rising. She wanted so badly to grab Juliet and kiss her before they made it inside. That wasn't an option though. She knew the only thing shielding them from disaster was that the mostly male hotel staff would never imagine the two women were headed upstairs to have sex. It was one of the few situations in which being a gay woman was advantageous.

Juliet remembered which room was Ramya's and led them down the hallway. She reached into Ramya's shorts and grabbed the key that she had seen sticking out from Ramya's pocket. Ramya found the ease Juliet had with her extremely sexy. She indulged in the thought that they were here in Ghana together and staying at this hotel as a couple. Maybe they had even been married for a few years by now...

Ramya drew her breath in at the sight of Juliet's long legs gliding over to the bed. Juliet kicked off her shoes and undressed herself before Ramya had a chance to put the food in the mini fridge. Juliet's beautiful eyes caught Ramya's, beckoning her to come over.

This can't be the last time I see her, Ramya said to herself.

This time, Ramya took a few extra moments to appreciate Juliet's face. She swore she could see straight into Juliet's soul. In that moment, she felt like her pain wasn't hers to carry alone. Their minds blended, as though they were two paintbrushes converging on a canvas and would soon create a new color the world had not yet seen. She reached out and touched Juliet. The way her body melted felt spiritual. Looking into Juliet's eyes, Ramya knew she would follow Juliet to the ends of the earth. Or even Nigeria.

CHAPTER FOUR

 Juliet

 February 8

 Ghana

JULIET KNEW SHE was beautiful and had a staying power with men. She was surprised to find out she had the same power over Ramya, who sent her international contact information just minutes after they said goodbye in Ramya's hotel room.

Unsure of what to say, Juliet didn't respond. She couldn't even decide how to save Ramya's number in her phone contacts. She tried "Ramya sexy eyes," "Fine geh Ramya," and "Ramya love" before deciding those were too risky. What if someone caught her? How would she explain describing another woman like that? Not knowing Ramya's surname, she settled on "Ramya London girl." It's not like she knew another Ramya, but for someone so special, saving only a first name wasn't enough.

During their second date, Ramya had told Juliet about mental compartmentalization to cope with the stress of her job. Now back in Sylvia's house, Juliet realized she was doing the same thing. With Ramya on a plane back to London, Juliet doubted whether they'd see each other again, which already made her feel disconnected from their time together. Juliet put Ramya in a compartment in her brain.

"My friend, how you dey?" she heard Sylvia say.

Juliet looked up; it sounded like Sylvia was speaking to her from the second floor. She whirled around in her chair before finally seeing Sylvia walk through the kitchen door. Juliet nearly fell out of her chair.

"Ah ah, are you okay?" Juliet asked.

Sylvia's enormous baby bump from a few days ago was barely visible beneath her shirt. She didn't even look pregnant.

"Of course, how your side?" Sylvia replied.

"Your belleh don reduce?"

"Juliet, you never sleep since?"

Sylvia grabbed a Ghana bun and chewed nervously, the faint smell of sugar wafting from her hand. Juliet quickly threw more memories with Ramya from the past few days into the compartment, and relaxed; Sylvia was right. She had barely slept the past four days.

"Yes ooo, I haven't slept well in a few days. I must be imagining things," Juliet agreed.

Sylvia nodded and bent down to pour herself a glass of water from the cooler near the refrigerator. Juliet knew her friend well and recognized the pause Sylvia took before bringing the glass up to her lips. In secondary school, Sylvia had been their maths teacher's favorite. She was always rewarded with the coveted position of writing lesson answers on the chalkboard. How Sylvia squared her shoulders when the other students were talking instead of paying attention to her was the way she held her shoulders now. Those were Sylvia's "answer me" shoulders.

"Juliet...why haven't you slept?"

"I had too much to drink..."

"Juliet! Abeg, I know you well. You sleep like a log when you're drunk."

Panic gathered in the back of Juliet's throat. They had been friends since they were little children. She felt Sylvia's eyes searching in her brain. It wouldn't take long to find the compartment titled "Ramya London girl." Maybe that was okay. Sylvia had always been kind and loyal to her, and even had a close lesbian friend back in Lagos. If there were a friend who she could be honest with, it was Sylvia. But saying the words out loud would make it real. Juliet wasn't sure she could handle that yet.

"Juliet?"

"You can't tell anyone, abeg."

"Juliet ooo..."

"Ok ok, we slept together, me and that Ramya woman."

The words rushed out of Juliet like air out of a deflating balloon. Once the knot was loose, nothing would stay contained.

"Juliet, I knew it. It's okay."

"Really?"

"Yes nau! Bolade, my lesbian friend, she sensed you like women, too."

"Ah ah, how so?"

"Small things now. How your energy shift when a tomboy woman walks in."

Though caught off guard, Juliet couldn't argue. No one had forced her to check out the women on Tinder. She convinced herself after less than a week in Ghana. Maybe the bus almost derailing on the way to Accra finally forced her to acknowledge her longtime sexual feelings for women. The thoughts had been churning in her head, absorbing flavor like a delicious bowl of Egusi soup. Meeting Ramya had been the perfect chance to have a taste.

"Is she nice? Was it good?"

Juliet laughed; it had been one of the best experiences she

51

had ever had in bed.

"My friiiieeennddd…" Juliet replied, snapping her fingers.

"This life sha, full of surprises," Sylvia replied.

She and Sylvia burst out laughing. What a relief.

"And she's a nice person. I felt the respect."

"I'm happy for you, Juliet. Nothing better pass respect."

For as long as Juliet had known her as an unmarried woman, Sylvia had always had a fine man attached to her side. It didn't matter if they were at church, at school, in the market or even in the toilet, the best-looking man in the area would find Sylvia and ask her out. But good-looking men and heartbreak had come together, and Juliet understood why her friend eventually settled down with a man who had an unattractive face and a fine heart. Sylvia's husband adored her, and she knew the value of a partner who showed respect.

"Juliet, make you hold this woman tight. She better pass those yeye men wey you date before!"

"Abi ooo, Ramya dey different. Maybe better than those men."

"Yes now! Juliet, make I go rest small. This pregnancy no easy…"

"Wetin dey happen?…" Juliet whispered under her breath.

Sylvia's large pregnancy belly had reappeared, and she watched Sylvia carefully climb the stairs up to the main bedroom. Juliet's mind was playing tricks on her. She glanced up at the clock to see if she had time for a nap, and saw it was around the second hour of Ramya's flight back to London. Just when she worked up the nerve to send Ramya a message, her phone flashed with a reminder. A guy she had matched with on Tinder a few days before Ramya had finally gotten back to her. They had chatted briefly that morning, and he had invited her to come out to a party on the beach.

Tinder guy: U coming 2nite?

Even with the approval of her friend and the now uncompartmentalized love she was developing for Ramya, Juliet was conflicted. Ramya hadn't said they were in a relationship and Juliet was too scared to ask. What was the point of taking such a huge risk to be with Ramya? They would be long-distance, and it didn't seem like Ramya could financially support her. What if a relationship with Ramya turned into one long WhatsApp conversation that someone discovered, waiting to get Juliet in trouble?

Juliet: Ok. C u at Labadi beach

"That's it, my friend," she heard Sylvia's muffled voice say from upstairs.

"You say wetin? I thought you wanted me to date that Ramya woman?" Juliet replied.

Sylvia didn't respond. She must have fallen back asleep.

Under any other circumstance, Juliet would dress in her finest clothes for a first date. Tonight, she wanted to look plain. She put on a basic pair of jeans and flat shoes, threw on a quick coat of foundation, and hailed a motorbike to the party. Unlike the first night with Ramya, the scenery outside looked dull and boring. Ghana had lost its magic.

The motorbike pulled up close to the party, and Juliet slowly walked over to the meeting point her date had sent. He was handsome and had a nice body; Juliet would have found him attractive a week ago. Today, she started out the night with her infamous lukewarm distance, yet everyone who saw them together immediately assumed they were a couple.

"You two look so good together! Your love is so natural!"

Natural. The word echoed in Juliet's head. She and this guy looked so *natural.* This is what couples look like, Juliet thought. We are what couples look like. Too harsh on its own, Juliet

gulped down a few drinks to lubricate the thought—*natural*.
The alcohol loosened her up. Over the next few hours, she and
her date had a fun time dancing, drinking, walking through the
streets of Accra, and maybe having sex after they blacked out
from too much tequila. In her mind, Juliet thought she heard
Sylvia's approving voice throughout the date,

"That's it, my friend."

She couldn't quite remember.

Juliet rolled over in the middle of the night. Moonlight
washed against her date's face on the other side of the hotel bed.
That's when she knew. This should have been a beautiful, *natural*
moment, but Juliet knew she'd forget this guy's name within
minutes of leaving the room. This was the best her adult life
had offered her—forgettable. Except when she was with Ramya;
Ramya wasn't forgettable. Juliet would never forget the time she
had spent with Ramya.

She propped herself up on the bed and glanced at her
phone. Ramya would have landed a few hours ago. Her date was
snoring, and Juliet imagined what her future would be like if she
married him. Her parents would put enormous pressure on her
as an African woman and within a few years, she would have
two kids with this guy. She'd be confined to a life as a housewife
and her dream of going back to school would be permanently
shattered. Maybe this guy was well-connected enough to have a
good job. Or maybe he wouldn't be able to find work and support
the family. Maybe he would become an alcoholic and abuse her
and the kids. This had happened to three of her best friends from
secondary school. Everyone suffered when there weren't enough
jobs to go around.

Juliet thought back to her dinner date with Ramya a few
days ago. She loved the conversation, and she could tell that
Ramya had thought a lot about life, which was something that
Juliet also did. No one except Ramya cared.

"How wonderful would it be to have someone who stimulates

54

my mind and my..." Juliet thought.

Her date let out a half-snore, half-belch, interrupting her thought. She decided to finally message Ramya, who started typing almost immediately but took a long time to respond.

> **Ramya:** I'm riding back home now on the train. It's really nice to hear from you! How are you?

The simple reply made Juliet smile. She was so happy Ramya thought it was "really nice" to hear from her. She noticed that Ramya liked to type her messages as one long reply. Juliet was a choppier writer and would send five messages for five sentences.

> **Juliet:** Good

And then her phone shut off.

"Fuck, no!"

She had been having so many issues with her shitty battery as of late. Grabbing her clothes, she ran outside to the street only half dressed. By the time she jammed her blouse back over her head, hailed a motorcycle taxi to take her back to Sylvia's place, and plugged in her phone, Ramya was offline. Juliet sank into the mattress on the floor, frustrated at herself for letting her phone die and for letting Ramya think she didn't care. Between the distance and her complicated feelings, Juliet felt how hard it was going to be to love Ramya.

Juliet rambled through the next few days in Ghana, aware that the best part had come early. The guy she had gone on a date with had made a few attempts to contact her. Juliet was too distracted to see him again. It didn't help that her phone now died within an hour of being unplugged and that she was too broke to get a new one, which forced her to sit in Sylvia's house most hours of most days. Even then, she suspected she was still missing some of Ramya's messages.

About a week after Ramya left Ghana, Juliet got a scary text from her.

> **Ramya:** Hey, can I call you this weekend? I want to ask you something…it's important.

Nervous as she was, Juliet agreed. It felt like an eternity had passed until it was time for Ramya to call.

"Hi Ramya," Juliet answered on the first ring.

"Hey Juliet, how are you? How's Ghana?"

"It's fine …how's London?"

She expected Ramya to say she was doing great, even if she wasn't. That's what Juliet would have done—pretend everything was perfect and that the other person was missing out by not being with her. To her surprise, Ramya said the opposite.

"Eh…I'm sad to be back in London. It's cold and grey and I hate my job. And I miss you."

"Oh wow, sorry about that, dear."

Even though Ramya was vulnerable with her, she hesitated to admit she missed Ramya as well, and badly. Their phone conversation was private, and she was safe in Sylvia's house, but she had witnessed so many gay people in Nigeria get harassed by the police. It was hard to let that go and be open. Thankfully, Ramya didn't seem to notice.

"Thanks! I love how you call me 'dear,' just like my colleague Carl. He says hi, by the way. You don't know him. I told him a lot about you."

"That's nice to hear, Ramya. So, what did you want to talk about?"

Ramya took a deep breath.

"I want to know if you'd like to be exclusive, at least until we meet again in person and decide if we want to be together."

Juliet was surprised and…happy. Then reality hit. Maybe Ramya didn't realize what her question meant.

"Ramya…I'm struggling, you know? I follow Nigerian blogs and Instagram accounts, and everyone is always saying this kind of relationship is against God."

"I'd expect that. Do you know about algorithmic echo chambers?" Ramya asked.

"No, what is algoriths echo chambers?" Juliet replied, trying to pronounce the first word.

"Algorithmic echo chambers. On Instagram, everything you see is based on what you interacted with before."

"So I'm only seeing negative comments because that's what I followed before we met?"

"Yes, exactly! Social media doesn't do a good job of capturing new things you learn in person. You have to teach it. If you follow Instagram accounts that celebrate same-sex relationships, Instagram will suggest similar accounts."

Juliet's energy picked up with the idea. Ramya sent her a few accounts, and when she clicked on them, she saw hundreds of pictures of gorgeous same-sex couples and thousands of comments praising them. One showed same-sex couples living in South Africa. It was easy to imagine Ramya and her featured on those accounts. They'd make a gorgeous couple, too.

"Wow, thank you ooo! This is what I needed to see!" Juliet exclaimed.

"Of course! I'm glad I could help…so what do you think about what I asked?"

Although a few Instagram accounts wouldn't fix everything, the couples she saw did breathe hope back into her. She'd have to be honest. If Juliet exclusively committed to Ramya and Ramya didn't help her financially, she'd have no way to pay her bills and she'd end up on the street. Her family and friends didn't have money to spare. Even if she tried them, they'd ask why the men she was dating couldn't help. What would she say?

My girlfriend doesn't give me money.

"What do you think, Juliet?" Ramya asked again, her voice smaller.

"Yes, Ramya, that'd be nice to be exclusive with you. But I don't know if I can."

Ramya was silent for a few seconds before she replied.

"Oh…wow. Why don't you think you can?"

"I'm struggling," Juliet replied.

"Not just with social media?"

"No, my phone is rubbish and keeps dropping your messages. That's why I haven't been responding. And my work only pays small money. Ramya, when I am exclusive with someone, they support me financially. It's hard for most women in Nigeria to survive without the help. You're a woman and I don't think you can provide for me."

An extended silence followed. Maybe this was too much. It was too much to say this truth out loud to Ramya.

"You don't think I can financially support you because I am a woman?" Ramya asked.

"Ramya, I…"

"No, fuck that! I can support you!"

"You can? You're not just saying that because you're offended? Ramya?"

"I'm here, love. And I understand, I'll make sure you get what you need, ok? I'll even send you a new phone."

"Really?"

"Yes, of course! I promise."

The weight of a cow lifted off Juliet's chest. She could breathe properly again. Ramya sounded genuine.

"Thank you so much, Ramya. I trust you and I want to be with you. But Ramya, there's one other thing."

"Sure, what is it?"

"I need to know when I'll see you again."

"Oh yeah! I've already been thinking about that."

"Where will we go? Do you want to come to Nigeria?"

"Eventually, yes. First, I want to take you on a proper holiday. Are you ready to see the world with me?"

"I'm ready, Ramya. I'm so ready!"

CHAPTER FIVE

 Ramya

 February 8

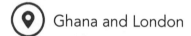 Ghana and London

RAMYA FLASHED CARL a thumbs-up from across the hotel lobby. He broke out into an exaggerated victory dance that she wished she could do herself; Carl had a freedom of expression that she envied.

"Soooo, good news?" he asked once she was within earshot.

"Yes, great news! Thank you for pushing me to message Juliet again."

"Yay! I'm glad you were smart and listened to my advice. What happened?"

"The connection was deeper, and we had another night of mind-blowing sex."

"Ok, TMI..."

"And...I don't know, she left this morning on a positive note. I gave her my number on WhatsApp to stay in touch."

The taxi arrived and they loaded their luggage into the trunk. Immediately code switching, Juliet became "he" in the conversation in case the driver was listening.

"And what does *he* think of the situation?" Carl asked.

"Well, I think *he* would like to stay in touch, but it's obviously complicated being on different continents."

"Sigh, yes. My *girl*friend and I fought a lot in the early days of being apart. That's why I moved to Geneva even though that city is boring as hell."

Ramya chuckled. As a child, she would have died out of happiness if someone had told her she could live in Switzerland. Now, she looked at Carl's living situation with pity.

"Are you going back to London looking for someone else?"

"That's the million dollar question. I don't know."

"They use pounds in London," the driver said.

Carl and Ramya laughed; they were grateful they had anticipated a nosey driver.

"Not looking forward to going back?" Carl asked.

"Would you be?"

"Of course not. I guess Fa...rzad moved out by now?"

Carl switched the female name "Faiza" to "Farzad," a male name.

"Yeah, completely moved out. We broke up a month ago and *he's* had the entire flat to *him*self to get *his* stuff out."

Ramya's last fight with Faiza had been intense. They shouted every bad quality about each other for nearly six hours. By the end, Ramya concluded they were simply terrible for each other. She was relieved but also terrified to have her own space in London.

"We're here," the taxi driver announced.

He walked around to the trunk to unload their suitcases. Ramya paused before gathering her belongings, taking a moment to absorb one last view of Ghana. Nothing about the country, not the landscape, the food, the heat, or the people had been new to her, yet she was leaving with a new perspective.

"Coming?" Carl coaxed.

"Yeah, I am. When is your flight?"

"In three hours. I wish they had routed me through London with you. When's yours?"

"In ninety minutes. I should go through security now, sorry," Ramya apologized.

"It's ok, I'll get some pasta at the restaurant. Why do so many West African airports have Italian restaurants?"

"Haha, no idea. Hope it goes down well."

"We'll know twenty minutes after I finish!"

"Ugh, gross! Have fun with your vomit pasta. Say hi to Christian for me."

"Thanks, dear. I will. Take care, ok? I'll check in next week. Have a safe flight."

After an extended hug, Ramya left Carl in the check-in area. She thankfully went through security and immigration without any incidents. The heaviness of knowing Juliet was still in Accra increased with every step towards the plane. If she hadn't been able to board as soon as she got to the gate, she would have considered not getting on at all, just like one of those cheesy romantic Bollywood movie scenes Juliet loved. She'd burst through Juliet's bedroom door with a bouquet of roses that magically appeared in her hand and sweep Juliet off her feet. They would ride off together on a horse while the villagers cheered them in the distance.

"Ma'am, please buckle your seatbelt," the flight attendant said to Ramya.

"Oh, right. Sure."

"Cabin crosscheck complete," the co-pilot announced.

The head flight attendant closed the last plane door with a definitive clunk. Surprisingly, Ramya felt calm once airborne. She and Juliet would soon officially be in different countries, and she had done what she could by giving Juliet her contact info.

All she could do now was wait and see if Juliet would reach out.

She spent her flight watching three movies that didn't require a lot of concentration and were superficial enough that she didn't feel emotional. Faiza was finishing up her Master of Arts in film, which was as pretentious as the degree sounded. It was strangely liberating to waste such an exorbitant amount of time on lame movies. Escapism wasn't always bad, Ramya decided.

The plane landed at Heathrow on time and the terminal wasn't crowded being a Tuesday morning. Ramya walked past the familiar M&S store and coffee shops, grabbed her suitcase from the baggage claim and made her way down to the Tube station. She scanned her Oyster card and arranged her bags in front of her feet with precision.

The first time she had landed in Heathrow two years ago, she cursed herself for leaving the UN to join a small NGO that wouldn't pay for a taxi ride home. Now, she knew exactly how to position herself to grab the best spot on the Tube, which was like a toy compared to the New York City subway. There were only two spots per train car suitable for stacking big suitcases. If she missed out on those, it would be an agonizing ride for her into Zone 1.

The train pulled up and Ramya pounced on the best spots like a panther. She laughed to herself as a family of six managed to back itself into two seats. The twin brothers in the family shouted at each other, causing the youngest child to cry.

"Be quiet, Jamie!" the mother hushed.

The train pulled up from underground and a rare winter London sun beamed brightly into the car, as though welcoming Ramya back. The overall calm aesthetic was ruined by the chaotic family to her right.

Feeling a buzz in her pocket, Ramya drew out her phone. She inhaled deeply—it was Juliet.

Juliet: Hey, r u back home?

"Thank God," Ramya said to herself.

The way Juliet described dating in Lagos was exactly like dating in New York. Everyone tried to play it cool and wouldn't shut up about how busy they were, which meant no one moved from a hookup to a real relationship. Ramya was so relieved to see a WhatsApp message from Juliet; she was so relieved that Juliet wanted to stay in touch.

The twin boys on the train were still screaming at each other. Ramya did her best to tune them out and formulate a good response. She needed to sound happy to hear from Juliet without going overboard. That was hard enough when speaking to someone from New York or London; Ramya had already discovered some of the cultural differences that separated her from Juliet. This would be much harder.

"Don't fuck it up," she said out loud.

The mother of the screaming boys shot her a nasty look, as though Ramya's word choice and not the woman's shouty children was the biggest problem of the train car.

Ramya: I'm on the Tube home now.
It's great to hear from you!

She paused before hitting send and decided against writing "the Tube" in case Juliet wasn't familiar with the term. She revised the message: I'm riding back home now. It's great to hear from you! Now the word "great" stuck out as too much, almost needy, so she revised again: I'm riding back home now. It's lovely to hear from you!

Ramya did another seven revisions before she realized Juliet was online and probably staring at the *typing...* prompt on her phone. She finally pressed send, not totally satisfied with the result.

Ramya: I'm riding back home now on the train. It's really nice to hear from you! How are you?
Juliet: Good

And then nothing.

Ramya checked her phone no fewer than fifty times over the next hour, heartbroken that Juliet had cut the conversation so short. Why would she bother messaging if she didn't want to talk to me? Ramya thought.

The train pulled into her stop a few minutes later, and Ramya reluctantly dragged her stuff the six blocks back to her now single-occupant flat. Her hands shook as she tried to unlock the door.

"Deep breath, you're okay," she assured herself.

Finally finding the right position, she turned the key clockwise twice, the loud thud of the deadbolt echoing in the hall. The sounds of being alone had begun.

Ramya swung open the door to…no one, and nearly nothing. Faiza had kept her word to empty out the flat of everything she had bought, leaving Ramya with only an armchair, a mattress, a few pots and pans, and a lot of mixed feelings.

The few times Ramya had started over as single had been hard, and over the next few days, she discovered that this time was no different. It was difficult to speak about herself in the singular, complete mundane daily tasks alone, and sit with her own thoughts. Much to her surprise, however, Ramya felt living without Faiza was better. The daily stress of an angry partner was gone, which gave Ramya space to imagine the future.

Ramya took off the rest of the week from work to recover from the long trip. After two days back in London, Ramya knew Juliet was a strong case of "distance makes the heart grow fonder" for her. The thought made her nervous, because Ramya put too much pressure on people who captured her attention. Every message became too meaningful, every missed call became a sign of something wrong, and every interaction influenced how Ramya pictured the rest of her life.

"It's because you're insecure," Carl had once told her.

"*Yet another reason I can't be with you,*" Faiza had once screamed.

Impatience bubbled through when Juliet didn't respond as fast as she wanted. She stared at their last conversation.

> **Ramya:** Hey, haven't heard from you in a while. What are you doing?

Two hours later

> **Juliet:** I was out. Why?

Ramya was uncomfortable with the thought of Juliet going out and having a social life, and she knew that was wrong. Juliet had the right to do whatever she wanted with whoever she wanted unless they agreed otherwise.

> **Ramya:** Just making sure you were okay. Hope the night went well!

Juliet didn't respond to those messages, Ramya guessed because she hadn't masked her distrust well enough.

Even though she was dying inside, she did her best to play it cool with Juliet. Afternoons passed by as she made elaborate dinners she didn't eat. Mornings marched forward as she drew pictures she didn't like. The neighborhood gym became her close friend, and she exhausted her building's supply of hot water with impossibly long showers. No matter what she did, no matter how productive or relaxed she tried to be, it felt like an eternity between responses from Juliet. Try as she might to shake off the feelings of neglect, Ramya took Juliet's distance personally.

Finally, Ramya's patience with WhatsApp ran out and she decided on a less than noble plan. The remaining sleeping pills, remnants from the last time she attempted this method, were still in the medicine cabinet. She grabbed and arranged them on a folding table next to her mug. Her tea was piping hot, and the sweet smell of honey wafted to her nose. She knew she should sip the tea as is, but there was no turning back. Sighing deeply, she quickly dropped the pills into the mug. The brown coating melted away from the heat, creating similar lines as the ones in her gross mo-jee-to in Ghana.

Shaking slightly, Ramya grabbed one of the armrests. To remind herself she was in control, she retraced how she got here. Her superpower had first revealed itself about a week after the most horrible day. It appeared briefly and slowly at first—like flashbacks to her childhood paired with quick glimpses into the future. With limited mobility and few friends to keep her distracted, she had plenty of time during recovery to test and eventually embrace the superpower, which she described to herself as clairvoyant dreams. The dreams showed her what it would be like if she followed her passion, ignored her parents' demands to stay in the Virginia suburbs, and accepted that she was gay. She did all those things by applying to grad school, which turned out to be the best decision of her life. The dreams, she realized, were like a supercharged substitute for intuition.

She never revealed her superpower to anyone, fearing someone would force her to see a psychiatrist, who would force her to let go of this gift. Long ago, Ramya had stopped wondering why she had the ability, and instead figured out how to use the dreams to advance her love life. In the early days of their relationship, Ramya had seen Faiza in her dreams. The images were always the same: first Faiza walking over the London Bridge, then sitting behind a computer editing a student film.

That's how Ramya knew to start looking for jobs here. Right after Faiza announced she was accepted into a graduate program in film, Ramya announced she got a job in London. Faiza had assumed Ramya was proactive, not a spy, and agreed to move in together.

"That ended in a disaster," Ramya admitted to herself.

With the angst that came from Juliet's sporadic messaging, Ramya felt like she had no other choice but to use her superpower. Her dreams would guide her on what to do, on how to get Juliet's attention again.

"Here we go," she said, taking a sip.

She settled back on the armchair, slowly ingesting the tea. When she felt her hand become slack, she slid the nearly empty mug onto the folding table and fell back. The feeling in her legs gradually disappeared, her breathing slowed to a trickle, and she felt her mind split into a near and far conscious. Having experienced these dreams before, she knew her far conscious would process what happened in the dream. Her near conscious would listen to her body if anything physically went wrong. Soon, she couldn't move. Her far conscious, however, was racing in this other world. It concentrated on Juliet's face, trying to find out what Juliet was thinking.

"Juliet, where are you?" Ramya's far conscious asked the darkness.

Darkness isn't one shade, and a familiar curtain of dread swept over Ramya before she could adjust herself, plunging her deeper into the abyss. There was only one scene that survived this far down. The classroom that she had seen in Ghana began to form and Ramya heard the same opening words,

"Bonjour tout le monde..."

She panicked, her far conscious shouting at her to wake up. Her near conscious was slow and barely active. It revved up like a car and pulled her body back before the classroom came into full view, before the coffee cup appeared on her desk. She was terrified knowing what came next.

Conscious states and body reunited, Ramya opened her eyes and shook her head. She had been expecting this dream, rather nightmare, to torment her later in the year, closer to the anniversary. Maybe it was happening now because she had to confront being alone. Or maybe she feared being alone on the anniversary.

It took Ramya a few minutes to regain control over her hands, then her torso, and finally the rest of her body. Gingerly sitting forward, Ramya let out a desperate moan. The plan wouldn't work. Her connection to Juliet wasn't strong enough to find Juliet in her dreams.

Even though Ramya didn't take any more sleeping pills the rest of the weekend, the dam had been released. Her nights were now consumed with the nightmare. The morning after her third night of fighting through, Ramya was more tired than when she arrived back from Ghana. Unfortunately, it was her first day back to work. She threw on the first outfit she could find. The shirt didn't smell great, and her clothes were a bit too casual for work.

"Like I care," she said to herself.

She felt like a zombie on her morning Tube ride. The feeling persisted on her walk from the station to the office and then as she dug around in her bag, trying to find her badge to enter the building.

"Where is it?" she shouted.

"Ramya! I see you forgot your badge. Not a great way to start your week back," John, her boss, said while walking up to the building.

"Just let me in," she whispered.

"Let's talk shop later today. I have some pointers for your wrap-up."

"Are you kidding me?" Ramya whispered, this time a little too loudly.

"Come again?"

"Nothing. I have to pee. See you later."

Ramya ducked into the downstairs toilet and did not emerge until a full minute after she heard John walking away. She hated her job. John was unqualified to tell her what to do and had a habit of giving unsolicited "pointers," the vast majority of which were unethical, illegal or contradicted research and best practices. Worse, he had no self-awareness.

"Good things come to me because of my Zen outlook on life," John always said.

Having fought way too many work battles as a gay woman of color, Ramya tried pointing out when John dismissed the struggles of other people. John never listened and she always ended up looking angry.

Finally working up the nerve to leave the toilet, Ramya went upstairs.

"Ramya! Let's meet in the conference room in an hour," John called out.

"No can do today, John. I need to synthesize my notes before I have a meaningful analysis to present."

"I can help..."

"No worries! I don't want to waste your time and mess with your chakras."

Was that how he used the word *chakras*? She struggled to keep track of misappropriated Hindu terminology.

Ramya spent the week back at work ignoring her colleagues and pretending to be engrossed in the "meaningful analysis" from her month in Uganda and Ghana. Messages from Juliet became her lifeline, and she took long breaks to sit and stare at her WhatsApp, even if she only got one or two messages per day.

On Friday afternoon, Ramya sat down at her desk following a two-hour lunch. She had recently discovered one thing that kept Juliet conversing steadily—reliving the intimate details of their two nights together—and was totally engrossed in her phone. The battery on her laptop had died three hours earlier and she hadn't bothered to plug it in.

"Hiya Ramya, how's it going?" Jeremy asked.

Ramya glanced up and gave him a quick smile. Jeremy was one of the few competent people in the office. They got along well, and he was often her voice of reason at work.

"Hey Jeremy, I'm good. You? How was your week?" she replied distractedly.

"Alright mate, just going through me slog of work. I'm looking forward to your report."

"Oh yeah, it's going really well. Lots of interesting insights."

Ramya waved her hand in the direction of her laptop, which looked as lifeless as a brick.

"I bet! But hey, whatcha doing now? You been buried deep in yer phone since you been back."

Her brown skin thankfully hid most of her blush. She thought she had done a better job of disguising her apathy. Thankfully, Jeremy was the one person in the office she felt she could be honest with.

"I...uh...damn. I met someone in Ghana. We're talking on WhatsApp."

"Oh right then! That's great for ya! Where is she now?"

Like everyone else in the organization, he had been married for a long time. Jeremy was the only colleague Ramya had told about her breakup. He was hoping she would find someone new in London to keep her there instead of returning to New York.

"Thanks, mate. She's still in Ghana. She's Nigerian and lives in Lagos," Ramya said.

"Ay, that distance is tough, mate. Me wife and I were in different cities back in the 90s. It was near impossible pre-mobile phone. One year I almost died in a car crash, and she didn't even know until two days later," Jeremy said.

"Wow, I'm sorry to hear that. Did you recover ok?"

"Aye, thanks. I don't remember waking up from the coma.

First memory after the accident was when we decided enough was enough and to move in together."

"Wow, at least some good came of it?" Ramya replied.

She hesitated to tell Jeremy about her own brush with death, finally deciding it wasn't worth derailing the conversation from the subject of Juliet.

"At least we have messaging apps now. I'm still feeling it though. I'm lucky to get one message an hour from Juliet," Ramya followed.

"Ah, don't take this the wrong way, but do ya think maybe she's not that into yer...into this relationship, I mean?"

British bluntness still took Ramya by surprise, and she hesitated. Jeremy said out loud what Ramya didn't want to admit. Maybe Juliet was slow to respond because she wasn't that into her. She cursed herself for not being able to get to Juliet in one of her clairvoyant dreams. How else was she going to find out what was happening with Juliet?

"What does she say in her messages?" Jeremy asked.

"We talk a lot about the time we had together, how it made us feel, how we wish we could relive those moments."

"That's a great sign! I don't think she would talk about yer time together if it didn't mean something to her."

"Then why do I feel like she's ignoring me?"

"Maybe the problem is she ain't clear on where you stand."

Ramya scoffed at the comment.

"Jeremy, you know lesbians are notorious for overcommitting to a relationship before we're ready, right?"

It was a mistake Ramya had made far too often. Like with Faiza...and every other girlfriend.

"I'm trying to be casual, you know? Since we're so far apart," she explained.

"Aye, ya know, it has been a long time since I was back in the dating pool. But I tell ya, in them long-distance days, being clear on the status of our relationship saved us."

Ramya nodded, suddenly overwhelmed at how much work would go into a cross-continental relationship. She would have to keep her jealousy in check this time. That required being able to trust Juliet, which required them being clear on their boundaries, which required Ramya to communicate with Juliet, not try to spy on her in a dream. Jeremy was right.

"Maybe this is more than I can handle," Ramya said, defeated.

"Or maybe not! Did I ever tell you about the luck of this office?"

"No, what do you mean? This office feels like where luck goes to die."

"Well, we're not the most advanced organization, I'll give you that. But the thing is, I've been working here for near eight years and in that time, SIX people I know have met their now spouses through work trips for us. Who knows, maybe this woman is the one?" Jeremy said.

"I guess there's only one person who can answer that for me," Ramya replied.

That night, Ramya texted Juliet and asked if they could talk. Juliet agreed and Ramya called her on Saturday afternoon. She was so nervous that she kept babbling about Carl and then almost dropped her phone in the sink.

"So, what did you want to talk about?" Juliet asked.

Be calm, dummy, Ramya said to herself. She took a deep breath and cracked her neck. The tension didn't go away.

"I want to know if you'd like to be exclusive, at least until we meet again in person and decide if we want to be together."

Amazingly, Jeremy had been right. Almost immediately after Ramya asked, Juliet revealed her complicated feelings about same-sex relationships. Ramya had indeed been the first woman

Juliet had slept with. They discussed the perils of social media algorithmic echo chambers and what Juliet could to do avoid seeing an endless stream of homophobic content on Instagram.

"What do you think?" Ramya asked again.

"Yes, Ramya, that'd be nice to be exclusive with you. But I don't know if I can."

Ramya's heart fell out of her chest. She felt so stupid for thinking Juliet would commit after meeting in person twice. When she asked why Juliet didn't think they could be together, Juliet's response shocked her.

"Ramya, when I am exclusive with someone, they support me financially. You're a woman and I don't think you can."

"You don't think I can support you because I am a woman?" Ramya asked.

Ramya's mind screamed. She recounted her every major career decision in the last decade: how she prioritized making a positive impact over making a lot of money, how she focused on Africa, how she worked so hard to dispel internalized racism. Those decisions were what had led her to Juliet, who was now saying they couldn't be together because Juliet didn't think that women could financially support other women.

Be calm, Ramya told herself.

Just like Ramya had learned to dispel internalized racism, maybe Juliet would have to learn to dispel internalized sexism. Given the fact that Juliet was so eager to dispel internalized homophobia, Ramya felt like Juliet would succeed at both. What better way to start than by Ramya showing up for Juliet in a way that Juliet felt was reserved for men? Besides, how else would Ramya get to be with Juliet?

Ramya glanced up at her degrees and certificates on the wall. She had made a damn good career in technology for international development, but she decided then it was time to use her talent in a different way and make more money.

"No, fuck that! I can support you!" Ramya finally replied.

"You can? You're not just saying that because you're offended? Ramya?"

"I'm here, love. And I understand, I'll make sure you get what you need, ok? I'll even send you a new phone."

They hung up after discussing a few more details. Ramya was more energized and felt more purposeful than she could remember.

On Monday, Ramya woke up and called the office.

"I have measle...tonsilitis, ok bye," she told John.

Clearheaded for the first time in months, she double-checked her bank balance before marching down to the Apple store on Regent Street, where she picked out the nicest iPhone and case she could find. She spent the afternoon meticulously wrapping her gift for her now girlfriend, Juliet. A colleague at another organization was thankfully going to Lagos to visit family soon, and they arranged to meet each other. Ramya rode the Tube to the outskirts of the city to hand off her precious package.

"Who is this for?" her colleague asked.

"My future," Ramya replied.

CHAPTER SIX

 Juliet

 February 15

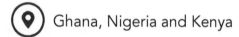 Ghana, Nigeria and Kenya

JULIET SLEPT LIKE a baby after speaking with Ramya. She awoke the next morning, unsure what to expect when she'd see Sylvia.

"It's big again," Juliet said.

"You say wetin?" Sylvia asked, waddling into the kitchen.

"Nothing. My friend, how your side?"

"E no easy, Juliet. E no easy."

Sylvia's large baby bump reappeared and this time, it stayed. Juliet spent the next few days caring for Sylvia, who was having a tough pregnancy. There was no way Sylvia could go out with Juliet and after committing to Ramya, Juliet had no desire to go to clubs or meet new friends, anyway. She decided to end her holiday in Ghana early. After a tearful goodbye, Juliet boarded the bus and found herself back in her small apartment in Lagos.

Everything at home was as she had left it, though she knew nothing inside her would ever be the same.

Ramya kept her promise to get Juliet a new phone. Instead of going to work on Monday, Ramya met her colleague, Nwakego, in London to give her the package. Juliet spoke to Nwakego over Ramya's WhatsApp.

"Hello, ma. Where should I meet you?" Juliet asked. "Banana Island. I will send Ramya the address to send to you."

"Yes, ma. Thank you, ma."

Jesus, Juliet thought. Banana Island was one of the richest parts of Lagos.

Bright and much too early on Thursday morning, Juliet pulled out her most expensive and professional outfit. No amount of clothes ironing and makeup prevented her from feeling like a little girl when she pulled up to Nwakego's beautiful mansion. It was huge.

"Oga, na the address be this?" she asked the *keke napepe* driver.

"Yes nau, na the address be this," he replied.

Juliet got out and walked down the driveway for what felt like an hour to reach the front door. A servant ushered her inside to the grand foyer, where Nwakego was sitting. She was exactly as Juliet had imagined—an older, sophisticated-looking woman. Her gown fluttered effortlessly around her as she walked, blending the light around her into a thousand tiny rainbows. This was a woman who knew she deserved space and respect, Juliet thought.

"I'll look like you one day," Juliet said as she took the package from Nwakego's hands.

"By God's grace, it will happen," Nwakego replied.

"Thank you for bringing my phone from London, ma. I am grateful."

"No problem, my child. How do you know Ramya?"

"She's a…friend, ma."

"Mmmhmm…na your good friend indeed," Nwakego said with a wink.

This woman knows, Juliet realized. It felt good to have a supporter in her home country. Nwakego gave her a light squeeze on the shoulder before leading Juliet back outside and hailing a proper taxi for her.

"Oh ma, I don't have the money…" Juliet started.

"No worry, my child. Take."

Nwakego handed Juliet much more cash than needed to go home.

"You remind me of me at your age," Nwakego said.

"How did you get out?"

"Someone took a chance on me."

"Thank you, ma. Have a nice day."

Juliet clutched the money in her hand for dear life. Only after she was safely locked inside her apartment did she fully open her palm to count the bills. After paying for the taxi ride, the total was equivalent to how much Ramya could send her for a week.

"I haven't done this before. Support someone financially," Ramya had admitted.

"I know, love. Tell me if it's too much," Juliet had offered.

"We'll make it work. We'll figure out how to make more money together."

The idea was enticing—figuring out how to build a fortune together. None of her ex-boyfriends thought that way. Juliet had always been at the mercy of their financial decisions, their careers and often, their wives in their home countries. Just two weeks into their relationship, Ramya was discussing money issues with Juliet like an equal.

"Can we afford to meet again?" Juliet had asked.

"Of course! I still want to go on a holiday with you. We can work on a budget together."

"Will you still be able to support me?"

"Yes, how about I send you $500 a month?"

"Okay Ramya, I will manage," Juliet agreed.

By now, Juliet knew that Ramya was taking a chance on her. But Ramya hadn't visited Lagos yet and didn't understand how expensive this city was. Five hundred dollars a month would barely cover Juliet's expenses. Even though she wouldn't save anything or have extra money to send to her parents, she didn't feel comfortable pushing Ramya for more. Now wasn't the time to test her new power. At least the money was enough to mostly ignore messages from Johannes and the other bastards who wanted to use her. She left the connections open though. And she certainly accepted small gifts from wealthy people like Nwakego. Spontaneous cash gifts had always been a way for the older generations to take care of younger people in Nigeria.

Surprisingly, Juliet's days didn't slow down with the small allowance. In fact, the weeks passed by quickly. Juliet's fashion styling and makeup work had dried up since she came back from Ghana, and she spent most of her time on her beautiful new iPhone exploring the places she and Ramya wanted to visit together.

Juliet had heard good things about Turkey from two Nigerian women who had gone there to work as prostitutes. The men there treated them like shit, but the women said Turkey was a beautiful country with designer brand stores in Istanbul. Maybe she could find a nice Turkish man to buy her a gift. Though she was entranced by the photos she saw online, when Juliet discovered she'd have to fly to Abuja from Lagos twice on her own to apply for the visa, she convinced Ramya to drop the idea. She imagined how the conversation would go at the consular office.

Why do you want to go to Turkey? they would ask.
For tourism.
Where will you get the money?
Um…from my friend.

What kind of friend would pay for you? Denied.

They then decided it'd be nice to go to South Africa. Ramya was convinced the best way for Juliet to apply for the visa was the official way. Even though she disagreed, Juliet dropped her application off at the collection agency and called Ramya.

"Now we wait!" Ramya happily exclaimed.

Though Ramya's faith in the application system was endearing, Juliet wasn't surprised when the rejection letter came a month later. Like Turkish people, South Africans assumed all single Nigerian women came to sell themselves.

"This is dumb and disappointing. Let's go to Kenya," Ramya said.

"Kenya? What's there in Kenya? That place is poorer than Nigeria."

"It'll be amazing, I promise you."

And in fact, once Juliet started looking up the places Ramya said they should visit, she realized how much "poor" Kenya had invested in tourism. Booking their holiday together was surreal. Nearly every day, Ramya would send Juliet another ticket or reservation with her name listed! She had never been part of something so formal, so sophisticated. Now on her way to the airport in Lagos, Juliet stared down at her notes. Two weeks in Nairobi, a three-day safari in Maasai Mara and a week on a beach resort near Mombasa. Was this real? Was this her life? Was a woman really doing this for her?

Her friend Yetunde had a foreign boyfriend who took her with him on work trips in other countries. Yetunde had prepared Juliet well for navigating her first international flight. Juliet's ticket was real, Ramya had provided evidence that the purchase wasn't fraudulent, and she had transferred US dollars to Juliet's new domiciliary bank account to show there was plenty of money to cover the trip. But that didn't stop the bag checker, ticketing agent, and customs and immigration officers from harassing Juliet for being a young female Nigerian with a nearly blank passport. She had to pull out small wads of cash to bribe her way through to the gate.

Exhausted, she settled into a booth at the Italian restaurant in the terminal. She texted Ramya.

> **Juliet:** Baby, am through

It still felt weird to call Ramya "baby", but she did it because it also felt *natural*.

> **Ramya:** Yay! That's amazing, my love!
> Great job! Are you eating? Did you
> get pasta?

Ramya's constant positive reinforcement gave Juliet much needed confidence in these new situations. She wouldn't have put herself through this, otherwise.

> **Juliet:** Yes love, I just ordered pasta,
> love. Am waiting for it, love. Can't
> wait 2 c u my love.

Over her bowl of penne pasta, Juliet's mind wandered back to the latest source of stress in preparing for this trip. Mummy had made a big scene when she accidentally revealed she would be flying to the other side of Africa. As in most situations, Mummy's first call was to a local pastor, who quickly informed them that,

"Abeg, my child, your mind is disconnected from your body in this decision. Your plane will crash into the ocean!"

Unsure what to do, Juliet had Ramya speak with Mummy.

"I understand you're concerned, but the pastor is wrong," Ramya had said.

"The pastor is a very strong man of God! He sees and knows

everything!" Mummy had replied.

"Ma'am, the flight from Lagos to Nairobi doesn't cross over the ocean," Ramya told mummy.

Mummy still insisted Juliet's plane would crash, so Juliet calmed her down by sending 10,000 Naira to the pastor. "Miraculously," the pastor's prophecy changed soon after.

"Abeg Mummy, good fortune will come," Juliet had said.

"Only if you stop wasting your time on fun. Find a man to take care of you."

The whole situation put Juliet's already strained nerves on edge.

Ramya messaged Juliet.

Ramya: You there?
Juliet: Baby, call me.

Juliet picked up on the first ring. Ramya sounded worried.

"Is everything alright? Did someone steal your stuff?" Ramya anxiously asked.

"No, love. My stuff is here. I just…I…"

"What's wrong? Are you nervous?"

"Ramya, you know the second time I went out of town to visit someone was my friend Sylvia in Ghana, where we met."

"Of course, I didn't meet Sylvia, but I remember the name."

"I never told you about the first time I visited someone."

"No, you didn't. I'm listening, Juliet. You can tell me."

Other than going to Ghana, the only other time Juliet had visited someone out of town was when she was nineteen. Her favorite club was having a party for Carnival, and Juliet met a friend there to celebrate. A handsome man caught her eye and told her she looked sexy. She was then a young woman, so the man easily impressed Juliet with a bottle of champagne, food and shisha. Over the next week, he showered her with gifts and constantly repeated a sweet line,

"I will take care of you," the man had told Juliet.

"Then he ghosted me. I didn't hear from him for a month," Juliet said to Ramya.

"That sucks. Did you see him again?" Ramya asked.

"Yeah, he reappeared. I was so relieved."

He invited Juliet to come visit him in Abuja. Not wanting him to disappear again, she eagerly accepted. The first night was great, until he wanted to have sex.

"I was still a virgin. I pretended to fall asleep."

If she hadn't, she wouldn't have heard his whispers through the French double doors that separated his bedroom and the sitting area. At first, Juliet hadn't wanted to understand what he was saying. When she finally did, it became clear how the guy had so much money. She overheard him speaking that night,

"Don't worry boss. I'll break her in tomorrow night. She'll be on the plane to Doha right after. Tell the buyers to calm down."

"Oh my God. 'Break her in.' He meant rape. He was a human trafficker," Ramya guessed.

"Yes, Ramya. He wanted to sell me as a sex slave to someone in Qatar."

Juliet had then grabbed her purse and snuck out of the window in the middle of the night. Abuja was much calmer than Lagos, and she ran a full fifteen minutes before she finally found a store that was still open. Her first call was to a politician she had once dated.

"Stay there, Juliet. I'll take care of it," the politician assured her.

Within minutes, the police showed up to the store where she was waiting, and Juliet was given a professional escort all the way back home to Lagos. She read the next day on the blogs that the guy was arrested and imprisoned.

As traumatic as that trip was, it had happened in her own country, where she could get herself out of danger.

"It's a big deal for me to come to Kenya, Ramya."

"I know, I take it very seriously. Nothing bad will happen to you, Juliet."

Juliet knew she would be powerless if something did. Trusting Ramya as much as she did was terrifying. But she decided to go because not seeing Ramya again was even worse.

Done with her pasta, she walked back over to the gate. Looking around, she saw she was one of only two African females traveling solo. The gate attendant called for some passengers to queue, and Juliet fumbled with her boarding pass. There were so many numbers typed on the paper and it was hard to mentally cross off the ones she had already used: boarding time, gate number, flight number, zone number. By the time she figured out which one she needed, she was the last in her group to board.

Her heart sank as she walked up to her window seat. The other two seats in her row were already occupied by a couple. A man sat in the middle with his giant thighs spread out wide.

"Excuse me, sir," Juliet said, trying to be polite.

She pointed to her seat. The man stared at Juliet as though he expected her to crawl over him.

"Oga shift, abeg!"

The passengers around her snapped their heads up to see who had caused the commotion, which Juliet thought was stupid. These people were trying to be high-class on this international flight, yet they were the same people who would scream themselves unconscious in the streets of Lagos. The man scoffed at her loudly before he and his girlfriend dramatically got up. Juliet stuffed her purse, carry-on and backpack under the seat, pushing her legs out to assert her space. Fuck this guy for wanting what was rightfully hers.

During the first two hours of the flight, the couple punished Juliet with their loud kissing. Juliet wasn't sure what made her angrier—the couple feeling comfortable enough to show affection in public or their disregard for her. What would she be doing if Ramya were on the plane with her? Certainly not making out like these two local people, both because Juliet thought of herself as classier and because she'd get thrown off the plane for kissing a woman.

Throughout the flight, she saw the other passengers touching the back of their seats.

"Ah ah, it's a screen," she whispered.

She tapped, not figuring out how to do anything besides turn it on. Asking the gross couple for help wasn't possible, so she put the ten songs on her phone on repeat and tried to sleep. It didn't work. When she looked up, she was surprised to see a flight attendant walking through the plane and offering every passenger food. The attendant handed Juliet a tray and glass of water. Juliet looked down at her tray, amazed that food could be packaged like this.

"Hey, look at this bush girl!"

The gross girlfriend was pointing at Juliet, who struggled to open one of the packages.

"See how she dey chop!"

Juliet felt her body radiate with humiliation. How could this haggard-looking woman and her fat, sickening boyfriend be making fun of *her*? Her clothes and makeup were on point, she knew she was beautiful, yet she had never felt so dumb. Even when she had accidentally screamed that she loved Ramya in bed, she was able to take control of the situation. Already, she felt like this trip was smarter than her.

The main dish on her tray was so bland that she winced, suddenly craving her Nigerian food. She wished the airline had served beef suya instead. Though the food tasted like cardboard, wasting it was an unbearable thought. She would never be irresponsible enough to throw out anything safe to eat.

She subtly glanced around her tight space and saw her phone light up. The last message Ramya had sent her before she had put her phone on airplane mode briefly flashed. It suddenly occurred to Juliet that she wasn't that hungry. She stuffed the remaining packaged food on her tray into her bag.

"Madam, respect yourself, I don chop a big plate of pasta wey better pass this rubbish food!" Juliet screamed at the woman.

Making it known she had eaten something better before they had taken off shifted the power dynamic and thankfully, the couple left her alone for the remainder of the flight.

Three hours later, Juliet found herself in a long line in a crowded, hot room in the Nairobi airport. Ramya had explained to her that she would need to fill out a form and show the eVisa Ramya had emailed her.

"Next! Welcome to Kenya, dear! Why are you here?" said the immigration agent.

"Hello madam, I am here for tourism. My friend is waiting for me outside."

"No problem, my dear! Pay me 50 USD and I will let you through."

Juliet panicked and looked around the room. She saw the other single female passenger from her flight handing another agent money and decided she should do the same. She pulled out a $100 bill, part of the money Ramya had sent her, and gave it to the agent.

"Very good! Welcome to Kenya!" the agent screamed again, waving Juliet through.

From the other time she had flown, she knew how to get her suitcases from the carousel. As she lifted the second one onto a luggage cart, her heart was beating heavily with excitement. Just a few more minutes until she could hug Ramya again. She was so proud of herself for making it through an international flight alone that she looked up at the man standing to her right, half expecting he would congratulate her. He quickly glanced up before walking to the exit, and Juliet knew she was meant to appreciate this achievement on her own.

Outside, it only took Juliet a few minutes to spot Ramya,

who had positioned herself far away from the other Indians waiting near the terminal. As soon as Ramya saw her, Juliet ran in Ramya's direction, not stopping until they were hugging each other tightly. Ramya smelled so good, and her hair tickled the side of Juliet's face. She could feel their breasts touching, which was still a new and arousing feeling.

"Oh my God, baby! I missed you so much! I can't believe it has been two months since we saw each other!" Juliet exclaimed.

Ramya stepped back and the smile on her face faded.

"Baby, are you okay?" Juliet asked.

"Sorry ma'am? Are you talking to me?"

The confused expression on Ramya's face was very convincing. Juliet wasn't sure what was happening.

"Ah ah, wetin dey happen? Did you hurt your head?"

Ramya continued to stand there looking confused, her expression like that of a lost child Juliet once had to rescue at the Balogun local market. Juliet would never forget the tiny human standing alone and crying in the middle of countless rows of merchants. It had been heartbreaking.

"It's me, Juliet! From GHANA!? Helloooo!?"

"Ghana? What do you mean Ghana? I've never been to Africa," Ramya replied.

CHAPTER SEVEN

 Ramya

 April 1

 Kenya

THE EXPRESSION OF the woman standing across from her told Ramya that she had said something terribly wrong. Face transfixed as if frozen, the woman's eyes were bulging so far out that Ramya was afraid they would pop out of the sockets. Had Ramya electrocuted the women mid-sentence and then pressed the pause button on the world?

Finally, the woman broke her stare and practically shouted,

"Hello! Ramya, what's up with you!? Why are you acting like you don't know who I am!?"

The truth was that Ramya was having a hard time placing where she was and who she was facing. Somehow through the half-formed present, Ramya recalled that these episodes had first started about nine years ago. They were at first frequent and involved minor things, like what she had for lunch, which apartment in the building was hers, or what she was supposed to do tomorrow. Over time, the episodes had become less frequent, and the breadth of missing information had grown. She recalled that during a work trip three years ago, she forgot mid-flight where she was going. Faiza had blown up at her last year when she not only forgot their anniversary but forgot they were in a relationship.

Now, Ramya was standing in front of a woman who was insisting they knew each other. This was the first time Ramya had forgotten an entire human being.

"Abeg, Ramya. This is fucked up. Stop pretending you don't know me!"

Discreetly, Ramya surveyed the scene, desperate for clues. The weather was slightly warm and not humid. She saw the cars were driving on the left side of the road. In the distance, there was a mountain range. A lot of people were speaking in English in an accent she couldn't place. She stole a quick glance in the direction of the woman, and saw a sign that said "Terminal 3."

"Okay, I'm at an airport," Ramya said.

"Jesus, where else would you be? Let's go now!"

The woman was staring daggers in her direction. Ramya tried looking away; the anger was distracting. She glanced at the hands of a group of people walking in her direction. Most of them were carrying passport books that said, "Republic of Kenya." It was only then that she saw a sign in the distance that said: Nairobi—10 km.

"What am I doing in Africa?"

"Abeg, what is this rubbish, Ramya? Let's get out of here, I'm tired."

The woman's tone had shifted from confused to concerned to angry to defeated very quickly. Ramya knew the window to fix this mess was closing.

"Ramya, please. I can't go through this, not here. Please stop, my love."

"Come on, you can do it. Find it!" Ramya encouraged herself.

With each episode, there was a trigger that brought her memory back. One time it had been taking a bite of food. Another time it had been rubbing her head. A third time, it had been listening to music. Ramya ran her hands over her body, jumped up and down, and waved her arms, praying she would figure out how to refill her mind with the lost memories. Nothing worked. Juliet was looking at her like she was a feral cat.

"Just kidding!" Ramya exclaimed, trying to buy herself more time.

"Ah ah! Why would you pretend not to know me after I flew here to see *you*?"

"Do I live here?" Ramya asked herself under her breath.

"That was so scary, Ramya. Why would you do that?"

"Just a joke…my love," Ramya said, copying the "my love" the woman had said before.

The woman began walking away from the terminal, before stopping to glance back at Ramya, who was following aimlessly.

"Baby, is it this way?" the woman asked, pointing ahead.

Ramya's hand lightly grazed the woman's and an image of them sitting at a bar flashed through her mind. The woman reached out again and gently touched Ramya's shoulder. A picture of them together in a hotel room materialized.

"It's your touch!" Ramya exclaimed.

"You like it, huh?" the woman replied.

Ramya grabbed the woman and held her in a tight embrace. A flood of memories fell from the sky and landed in her brain, mixing in with the memories she had retained. She remembered meeting Juliet in Ghana, calling each other for countless hours, crying over a rejected South African visa, and celebrating when they booked their tickets to…here, to Kenya. As she held Juliet, she remembered she had been to Africa many times for work, though this was the first to spend time with someone she loved.

Now she remembered that coming to Kenya was already a big deal for Juliet, who had just told her about that traumatic trip to Abuja. The gravity of the episode finally hit Ramya, and she realized how scared Juliet must have been.

"Juliet, I'm so sorry for that insensitive joke. I love you and I'm so happy you're here."

"That was fucked up. But thank you for apologizing."

While she wanted desperately to tell Juliet what really happened, she decided it was safer to pretend she was a jerk who had made a horrible joke. It had been two long months since she touched this woman and of course she had an episode today. Sometimes she thought her mind was sabotaging its own happiness.

Juliet's tense body relaxed in Ramya's arms and the two women held each other for an amount of time that was certainly socially unacceptable where they were. Ramya didn't care, ignoring the judgmental stares from the people around them who couldn't handle two women of different races showing affection in public. She had spent much of her life convinced that she didn't deserve feeling loved. Juliet had spent a lot of time on the phone reassuring her that she did. Ramya didn't want to waste their time together appeasing strangers.

Juliet was the first to pull away and whispered,

"Come, my love, let's get back to your flat."

"Our flat."

Trying to make up for the rocky start, Ramya grabbed as many of Juliet's bags as she could carry and led them to the car park where their driver was waiting. A tiny man, he came running out of the corner of Ramya's left eye as soon as he spotted them.

"Attentive driver," Juliet remarked.

"All for you, love."

The driver neatly arranged Juliet's suitcases in the trunk of the SUV, and Ramya climbed into the backseat next to Juliet.

Ramya prayed the worst-timed episode in history wouldn't destroy this holiday she had so carefully planned.

"Sorry about that stupid joke. That was so insensitive of me. I don't know what I was thinking."

"No wahala, love."

From their conversations, Ramya knew that meant "no problem."

She grabbed the sweater Juliet had brought with her for the plane and strategically placed it in between them. Her hand slipped underneath, and she signaled for Juliet to do the same. This was the first time she had come to Africa for a holiday, and she wasn't sure how careful she needed to be with showing affection. Too much, and they'd be unsafe. Too little, and Juliet would think she didn't care or that their relationship constantly put them in danger.

The tiny driver was surprisingly strong and carried all of Juliet's bags in one trip. Ramya tipped him generously and practically pushed him out the door. As soon as she was sure they were alone, she galloped over to Juliet and gave her the biggest, sloppiest kiss she could. Ramya smiled back at Juliet's laugh and reached up. She felt Juliet's faint pink lipstick smeared all over her face.

"I want it all over me, baby!"

"Let's take this to the bedroom," Juliet whispered into Ramya's ear.

Her voice was so seductive.

Two months apart had only heightened their passion and the sex was better than Ramya had imagined. Like in Ghana, she took her time to appreciate every curve of Juliet's body. Unlike in Ghana, however, she was equally excited for what came after—to simply lay in bed with Juliet. They cuddled close, stroking each other's bodies and chatting about Juliet's flight. Juliet told Ramya about the rude couple next to her, panicking in front of the immigration agent and accidentally repaying for the visa, and how happy she was to leave West Africa for the first time.

A warmth grew inside her as Ramya listened to Juliet, the woman she had fallen in love with over long WhatsApp calls and thousands of messages. She glanced up at the clock and saw that she and Juliet had been reunited for all of four hours. That was enough time to know she had made the right decision. Being with Juliet was the right decision.

The first two weeks went by fast. Ramya finally understood Juliet's favorite expression—"full of life"—when they were together. She knew if she had spent these same two weeks alone, she wouldn't have had even a fraction of the laughs, the learning, or the appreciation. With Juliet, time was truly something special to enjoy.

They went to a sanctuary on the outskirts of Nairobi to feed giraffes, where Juliet spent an hour joking with the staff about how the animals have black tongues.

"Are you sure they were born this way? Did they eat paint?"

"No ma'am, no paint," the staff assured.

"How about oil? I'm Nigerian, you know. We have oil. These must be Nigerian giraffes."

Ramya was amazed at how Juliet's charm opened the world in front of them. Juliet's banter led to the sanctuary staff giving them a private tour of the facility and a detailed giraffe anatomy lesson.

"Wow, we were there for five hours. Last time I came here, I barely stayed for thirty minutes."

"Our money must complete, Ramya!"

Juliet was fixated on getting their money's worth, which was good since Ramya's bank balance was depleting quickly.

Later that week, they went to one of the best restaurants

in Kenya to eat sushi made from fish straight out of the Indian ocean. Ramya sat there amused as Juliet tried to convince the chef to cook the fish before serving the sushi rolls.

"Raw fish is good for sharks, not humans," she explained.

From most anyone else, the comment might have come off as insulting. Instead, the chef sent a free bottle of wine and one of the most delicious desserts Ramya had ever tasted.

"Wow! I've never got anything for free at this restaurant before."

"Ramya, love…our money must complete."

Later that week, they hiked on a scenic nature trail through the mountains.

"Okay sha, I admit, exercise isn't just for tomboys. This feels good ooo!" Juliet said.

"Race you to the top of the hill!"

On the way up, Ramya's terrible sense of direction almost led them off a cliff. Thankfully Juliet led them back to the proper trail and down to safety.

Yesterday, they had gone to a new outdoor mall, where the staff at the Mac makeup store were in awe of how good "friends" they were. Juliet even gave the makeup artists a few pointers and the night manager half-jokingly asked her to come work for them.

"Maybe, but I think Nigeria is where I will make my money," Juliet replied.

Ramya tried pushing that thought away.

Of all the things to discover about their new relationship, Ramya was most surprised that she enjoyed the mundane things with Juliet. With her exes, she had felt her time was well spent only while doing a nonstop barrage of activities. The parts that Ramya enjoyed the most with Juliet were trips to the grocery store, picking out a toothbrush at the pharmacy, cooking, and watching TV. That level of intimacy was what Ramya needed most, and it gave them time to just talk.

Ramya learned that Juliet had grown up in a conservative and religious household, and that the church had dictated every aspect of their lives.

"Mummy took the word of the Bible over the word of her children."

"I'm so sorry. It must have been hard to be close to her."

"Abi ooo. Ramya, my kids will not fear me like I feared Mummy."

"What about your father? Are you close to him?"

"He was the best father in the world. His advice got me through some difficult times."

"Was?"

"Yes, Ramya. He's alive in body, but not in mind."

Juliet's parents had been young adults during one of Nigeria's golden economic ages. When Juliet's religious mother saw her teenage children weren't faring as well as she had, she blamed them, not the situation.

"She said we were suffering because we didn't have enough faith in God."

"And your father?"

"He understood how hard it was for us as youths in Nigeria."

When she was seventeen, Juliet's father had an accident and couldn't work anymore. Eventually, the money her parents had saved ran out and Juliet's mother turned to her children for support. By then, Juliet had been living on her own for years.

"It was too late for me to go home. Too much had happened. I send what money I can."

"That's a lot of responsibility on you."

"It is, Ramya. It's a lot of responsibility on me."

Ramya wondered if that indirectly meant that was a lot of responsibility on her.

In a way she had never spoken about before, Ramya told Juliet that she considered herself Hindu.

"It was like, the one thing I carry from my parents," Ramya explained.

"What do you like about Hinduism?"

"My parents love the rituals. I find strength in the philosophies, mantras, and lessons."

"Do you go to temple?"

"Sometimes. Most Indian communities make me uncomfortable. Would you come with me?"

"Of course! Would you come with me to church?"

"If you want me to, yes. I'm glad we would support each other."

Ramya loved that she found someone open to queerness *and* religion. Most of her exes had denounced all religions because they felt entrapped by the institutions. Without a community supporting her, Ramya had learned a long time ago to pray in solitude behind a computer.

She glanced over at Juliet, who was sitting on another part of the sectional couch. It was nearly 6 p.m. and they hadn't even left the flat today, having decided it was a relax day. Juliet's obnoxiously loud ringtone went off and she leaned over to look at the screen before picking it up.

"My sister, how far?" Juliet answered.

They launched into a discussion in Yoruba, one of Juliet's native languages. Though not especially gifted in anything other than English, Ramya loved conversations in other languages. Through the mix of Yoruba and English, Ramya listened intently to Juliet's conversation to search for her name, which did not appear. She knew Juliet had to keep their relationship quiet, but it was still disappointing.

"How is she?" Ramya asked Juliet after she hung up.

"She's fine ooo, working hard."

"Alright, if I remember correctly, you speak to your siblings in Yoruba, authority figures and colleagues in English, people on the street in Lagos in pidgin English, and your parents in Igbo?"

"Good memory! Now if only you could remember the Yoruba words I taught you..."

"Baby steps! At least I'm getting some of the pidgin English, na wa!"

Juliet burst out laughing.

"Your accent is so cute. What about you? Do you speak to your parents in Telugu?"

"Not really."

Though Ramya's parents were both native Telugu speakers, they had insisted on only speaking to her in English.

"They thought speaking English perfectly was incompatible with speaking Telugu."

"Why?"

"I think they were ashamed."

Her parents were American doctors in English. They were the children of poor farmers in Telugu. In their eyes, anything Ramya learned in the West was superior to what they learned in the East.

"That's why I can speak French but can't even put together a full sentence in Telugu."

"But you said they're traditional?"

"They are, and they still haven't forgiven me for not being their perfect Indian child."

"So they wanted you to be a good Indian girl, but not to be prideful of their language?"

"Strange, isn't it?" Ramya replied.

"Yes ooo! My children must know my languages. And yours?"

Ramya paused, debating whether to answer as though her children would be Juliet's children.

"I don't know...English of course, maybe French. I'd love if my parents taught them Telugu. And of course, whatever languages my partner speaks...Yoruba, for example."

"Haha, very funny."

Ramya retreated, trying to cover up her embarrassment.

"I'm just kidding, Juliet."

"Oh really? That's too bad. Our kids should speak Yoruba."

CHAPTER EIGHT

 Juliet

 April 15

 Kenya

"ARE YOU SURE? You don't want me to come?" Ramya asked.

"No, not this time. I should go alone."

Juliet adjusted her hat and skirt and checked herself in the mirror one last time. She debated changing into more drab clothes to match the Kenyan women she had seen on the street. Two weeks in the country had made it obvious to her why Nigerian clothing was the envy of Africa. Nothing could beat Nigeria's colors, patterns, and boldness.

"My nyash go show me as Nigerian," Juliet muttered to herself.

Even if she dressed in all gray clothes, her big butt was a giveaway she wasn't from Kenya. She'd have to blend in by staying quiet. Her bright yellow, orange and black outfit would do the talking for her.

Kenyan men were generally calmer than what she was used to, and she enjoyed the relative peace on her walk over. There were some characteristics of the street that reminded her of home, but the bright green grass that lined the sidewalks, the mountains in the distance, and cool temperature outside were reminders that she was far away. Ramya had done that for her, and she was grateful to see a new part of the world.

The Catholic Church was just a few streets away. In her adulthood, there hadn't been many times that she turned to the church for comfort, yet something had told her to memorize the route from the flat the day after she arrived. Today, she woke up to an irritated Ramya and decided she needed some outside guidance.

Like everything in Kenya except for the landscape, the church was more toned down than what she was used to in Nigeria. Church to her was an explosion of colors, light, and singing. The Kenyans in the pews mostly stayed quiet as the priest delivered his sermon. She waited for the last person to leave before she walked up to the confessional booth. The inside was hot and musty, and she prayed the time inside would be worth the discomfort.

"Bless you, my child."

"Forgive me, Father, for it has been…five years since my last confession."

"You're here now, that's what matters. What is your confession?"

"I am Nigerian. I came to Kenya to visit a…friend. I feel guilty that I can't always trust her."

"When did your friend lose your trust?"

"When she came to greet me at the airport. I had told her I was scared to come here, and she pretended she didn't know me. It was like she was mocking me."

They were about two weeks into their holiday, and Ramya had mostly been the sweet, kind, and loving person Juliet had fallen in love with. But lately, Ramya seemed vexed. Every time they came close to an argument, Juliet pulled back, remembering the sick joke Ramya had played on her at the airport. How could she argue with someone she couldn't trust? Church confessional was a way to get free advice from someone who wasn't biased towards either of them.

"We must forgive those around us," the priest said.

Juliet sighed. This was the nonsense non-advice she hated from confessional. That didn't help her decide what to do next.

"Yes, Father. But how can I forgive her?" Juliet asked.

"You must evaluate what she means to you. Do not hold onto darkness when she will pass from your life quickly."

"I hope she doesn't, she's my..."

"Yes, friend. But she is not your helper," the priest replied.

"How do you know that, Father?"

"It is the word of God, child."

Juliet didn't squeeze her eyes shut in time to prevent the tears from rolling down her face.

The last time she had come to church was four years ago, when she had been seeking shelter from her worst ex-boyfriend. Within six months of being together, she felt like he had ruined her life. The last time she caught him cheating, they got into an explosive fight, and he nearly hit her. Not knowing where to go, she wandered the streets before finding herself on a pew inside the biggest Catholic church in Lagos. As her rage subsided, she gathered herself, stood up, and lit three candles. The flames danced before her; she willed them to burn through her body and cleanse her soul.

"Let me find my helper. Help me leave this suffering." she had whispered, over and over.

"My friend is not my helper, Father?" Juliet asked.

"No, my child. She is not."

"Are you certain?"

"God does not lie."

Juliet made it outside before she broke down. She had fallen in love so quickly that it was overwhelming to think Ramya was not her helper. How could such a profound connection dissolve into nothing? What did the priest see? Did Ramya have a darkness inside that Juliet had only glimpsed at the airport? Maybe Ramya would soon turn sinister; women could also be evil.

"Ma'am, why are you crying?" a man from the church asked.

"It's fine, sir. I'm fine," Juliet stammered.

"You are not fine. Take this."

The man handed her a handkerchief, which Juliet used to wipe the tears and snot off her face. She tried handing it back to the man.

"Please, keep it. I have plenty."

"Thank you, sir."

"It's emotional coming here, eh?"

"Yes, it is."

"You should come more often. Church guidance is key to a good life," the man said.

"Maybe I will come again. When is the next sermon?" Juliet asked.

"Tomorrow morning. We will discuss the importance of traditional women in society. Our earth will fall into the pits of hell, otherwise. Come, you'll like it."

"EH? Who is delivering it?"

"Same father as today," the man replied.

Suddenly feeling stronger, Juliet picked herself up. Without so much as a second glance, she walked away. The man beckoned her to come back.

"Where are you going? The kingdom of heaven awaits!"

How quickly she forgot. The same priest she had just spoken to would lecture everyone tomorrow about how the earth would crumble if women do not cook and clean for their husbands. Most of the church thought independent women, not the people who oppressed others, were the cause of global suffering.

"Abeg, who is that man to say if Ramya is my helper?" Juliet said to herself.

Still as confused as before, but now clear that church was not going to decide her relationship with Ramya, Juliet walked back to their apartment. The streets were more alive than when she left, and she stopped a few times to take in the scenery and buy a mango from a woman on the side of the road.

"Hey, how did it go?" Ramya asked once Juliet was inside.

"Ok, love. How are you?"

"I missed you."

Juliet sat down next to Ramya on the couch and closed her eyes as Ramya lightly massaged her back. This tenderness was so sweet. She wished every moment were like this.

"So what's the plan for tomorrow?" Juliet asked.

Ramya sighed and Juliet knew the tenderness had disappeared. She braced herself for a mean response and wasn't sure if she would serve one back.

"Nothing has changed, Juliet. The van will be here around 6 a.m. We'll reach the safari campsite around noon."

"Na wa oo, why did you book something so early?"

"I told you it was the only option. I asked you ten times before I made the reservation."

"Geez, calm down, Ramya. It shouldn't be a problem for me to ask you again."

"Listen the first time and I wouldn't have to repeat myself. Sorry, I'm sorry," Ramya followed.

"I appreciate everything you've done for this holiday, Ramya. Let me go make dinner so we can go to bed early," Juliet said.

"I'll come and help you."

"No, it's my turn to cook. I'll talk to you soon, ok?"

Juliet walked into the kitchen before Ramya could argue. Exasperated, she flung open the fridge and tossed random vegetables onto the counter. She picked up a knife that was much too big and took a deep breath to steady herself before she started chopping. The last thing she needed was to accidentally hurt herself.

Welcome to Kenya! Come with ten fingers, leave with nine, she thought.

Not even an hour later, Juliet looked over at Ramya, who had walked into the kitchen and was staring at her too intensely for comfort. She had always been very good at reading people's energy, but it didn't take an empath to know Ramya's had been erratic the last few days. One minute, they were happily talking about languages and the next, Ramya looked like there was so much pressure built up inside her that she would explode.

"Are you okay?" Juliet asked.

"Yeah, stress from finding a new job. Juliet?"

"Yes?"

"You look beautiful."

"Thank you for your compliment."

She genuinely appreciated Ramya's words, considering she wasn't wearing makeup or a wig. Ramya was only the second partner she had allowed to see her natural hair and naked face. Not once had Ramya made her feel insecure about being her complete self, which had been a blessing.

"I'm going to take a nap," Ramya said.

"Sure, go rest. Let me finish dinner for us, ok?"

Juliet watched Ramya walk back to the bedroom. Ramya carried herself like a man, which combined with her long hair and feminine hips, aroused Juliet in ways she couldn't quite describe.

Apart from Ramya's sinister joke at the airport and the sour mood lately, their holiday had been beautiful overall. Juliet loved introducing Ramya to her favorite Nigerian musicians and laughed every time Ramya pretended to know the lyrics of her favorite song, "Easy Jeje" by Reekado Banks. Ramya had come alive and shed insecurities in these past two weeks, and Juliet knew she was the reason why. It was gratifying.

But recently, if Juliet left Ramya alone for even a few minutes, Ramya would return to her with a dark cloud hanging overhead. Yesterday, Juliet went to go shower. When she came back to the bedroom, she found Ramya curled up in a ball and clutching her head. It took Juliet thirty minutes of coaxing to get Ramya to stop. She prayed whatever Ramya was dealing with would resolve before they left for the safari in Maasai Mara tomorrow.

Off to the side, Juliet saw her phone screen light up. It was Sylvia. Years on the streets had taught Juliet to be careful about what she told friends and family. Apart from Sylvia and Mummy, everyone had found out through social media that she had come to Kenya. That's why her sister had called her earlier that week. Sylvia checked in on her every day to make sure she was safe.

"My friend! How you dey nau?" Sylvia asked.

"My paddy! I dey cook. How your side?"

"Eeeeh, so you dey cook like say you dey for Nigeria?"

Juliet wasn't sure if Sylvia was implying anything. She wanted to correct it regardless.

"My friend, e no be like that! Ramya cooks a lot and wey well. It's my turn," Juliet said.

"E good say she sabi cook."

In every relationship Juliet had had, a significant amount of her time would be spent in the kitchen or tidying up after her boyfriend. With Ramya, they split everything—the cleaning, the grocery shopping and arranging things in the apartment. Juliet wanted Sylvia to know that she felt like an equal in this relationship.

Sylvia quickly switched the conversation to her new favorite topic – her cheating husband. In the eight months they had been married, he had already picked up at least three prostitutes. How quickly their sweet love had turned sour.

"My husband no gree wear condom," Sylvia explained.

She tried to make it sound casual though Juliet knew this was serious. Contracting HIV and other STDs was a big concern among Nigerian women. Everyone knew someone whose life had been destroyed by unsafe sex. Yet no matter how common the problem, nothing could convince many Nigerian men that wearing a condom was necessary.

Like a typical Nigerian, Sylvia had the television blaring in the background as she and Juliet spoke. The newscaster's and Sylvia's voices drowned each other out, and Juliet was having trouble hearing. She turned off the stove and stayed as quiet as possible, still only getting part of what Sylvia was saying.

"Over to the news in the Americas…"

"My husband dey useless, Juliet…"

"Tomorrow marks the anniversary…"

"But wetin I go do?"

"Shooting. Virginia is a state in…"

"Na wa! The matter don tire me…"

"Thirty-two people died."

Juliet's ears perked when she heard "Virginia." She remembered that's where Ramya grew up. Juliet had tried Googling the word to see how it was spelled before Ramya finally wrote it down for her. V-I-R-G-I-N-I-A. Now Virginia was on the news and Juliet wanted to hear why.

"My friend, abeg, make I video call you," Juliet said.

By the time Sylvia accepted the video call and held her phone up to the TV so that Juliet could see clearly, the newscaster had finished out the segment.

"Now back to our headquarters in London."

Juliet read the closed captions out loud, which were delayed by a minute.

"Shooting in Virginia. Thirty-two dead," Juliet read.

"Ah ah, these Americans like guns too much!" Sylvia added.

Other than its music and films, everyone in Nigeria knew one fact about America: its obsession with guns.

"Americans dey CRAZE for guns! Ramya, she dey craze like that?"

"What kind of stupid question is that? Abeg, of course Ramya no get gun!"

The commotion woke Ramya from her nap, who had stumbled back into the kitchen and was staring at Juliet, her arm dangling awkwardly by her hip.

"My friend, make I call you later, you hear?" Juliet said, hanging up on Sylvia.

"Who were you talking to? Did I hear you say something about guns?" Ramya asked.

"Sylvia was watching the news while we were talking. They said something about a shooting in Virginia. Jesus, you Americans like to shoot each other!"

"I didn't hear anyone else on the phone. What did you see about the shooting?"

"Why are you Americans so crazy? Does everyone in America have a gun?"

At first, Juliet didn't notice Ramya's meek voice and expected Ramya to do what she normally did—go into a long explanation about the politics and history of what happened. Instead, Ramya started shaking violently and turned so pale that Juliet thought she could see Ramya's heart pumping.

"Are you ok!?" Juliet asked.

"I can't deal…no…I…" Ramya stammered.

Without another word, Ramya spun around and rushed out of the kitchen. Juliet didn't even have time to put her phone down before she heard the apartment door slam shut. Ramya's heavy footsteps on the stairs leading to the ground floor quickly faded. She was gone.

CHAPTER NINE

 Ramya

 April 15

 Kenya

JULIET STOOD UP to go make dinner. Ramya wanted to run straight after Juliet but knew that she had been losing herself lately. It was obvious that Juliet needed some time apart that didn't end dramatically, like Ramya's near meltdown yesterday while Juliet was showering. So instead, Ramya sat completely still and concentrated on the faint sound of Juliet chopping vegetables. She was afraid that if she moved too much, the sound would disappear, and she would lose her bearings without the knowledge that Juliet was in the next room.

Usually, Ramya was quite good at functioning independently…except this time of the year. She grabbed her phone and opened the calendar app, sighing heavily at the dot that marked their impending trip to Maasai Mara. She had tried a thousand different arrangements to avoid their holiday landing over this week, but Juliet had committed to being her girlfriend on the condition they'd see each other again soon. A combination of spiking ticket prices and Ramya finally quitting her job in London meant their window had been narrow.

"Maybe we could travel on my birthday?" Juliet had sweetly asked Ramya during their planning.

"Of course! When is it?"

"April 23rd, love."

"Where do you want to spend your holiday? In a big city, at the beach, or on a safari?"

"Oh, a nice beach! Is that possible?"

The only way to accommodate Juliet's birthday wish and Ramya's budget and fulfill Ramya's dream of going on a safari was to go to Maasai Mara tomorrow, the anniversary of the most horrible day of Ramya's life. Ramya addressed her anxiety by telling herself that enough years had passed and that she could handle the timing. Now Ramya wasn't sure. Her mind kept going somewhere dark in the moments she was apart from Juliet.

The smell of dinner wafted from the kitchen and Ramya decided enough time had passed to join Juliet. She walked over, trying her best to disguise her negative thoughts since Juliet was always able to pick up on her energy.

"Are you okay?" Juliet asked.

"Yeah, stress from finding a new job. Juliet?" Ramya said.

"Yes?"

"You look beautiful."

"Thank you for your compliment."

The pot on the stove began to bubble over, and Ramya and Juliet lunged in its direction at the same time, bumping into each other. A loud "bleeergh!" erupted, and a thick wave of sauce exploded over the stove.

"Na wa ooo, this pot is very angry!" Juliet exclaimed.

Ramya glanced over and gave her a smile that Juliet must have known was strained.

"Hey, give me a kiss," Juliet said, as if sensing Ramya needed the boost.

They shared a quick peck before Ramya turned down the stove heat, grabbed a wad of paper towels and carefully wiped off the sauce.

"You look so beautiful," Ramya repeated.

"Beautiful ke? With my housewife look?"

"Housewife look, fashion model look, professional look, you always look beautiful, Juliet."

Juliet inched away, which told Ramya to give her more space.

"I'm going to take a nap," Ramya said.

"Sure, go rest. Let me finish dinner for us, ok?"

Ramya walked to the bedroom and collapsed in bed exhausted, as though she had just run a marathon while writing about the meaning of life. This time of the year was overwhelming.

She drifted asleep before she could arrange herself in a comfortable position, her arm smooshed underneath her body. Almost immediately, her consciousness separated into two parts and her body floated back to the most horrible day. The coffee on her dream-self breath was strong, and she felt herself yawning. Her desk was off to the left side of the classroom, near the door. To her right, she saw her classmates settling into their desks as her professor greeted everyone. The presence of those around felt light, even though her far conscious was unnerved knowing what would come next.

"Get up and leave!" she tried shouting.

No present awareness could change the past. Her mouth was stuck in the same yawn as it had been nine years ago. Everyone around her was doing the same things as nine years ago. Her classmate Paul sighed loudly. Her friend Megan continued unpacking her bag. A few people in the front of the classroom took notes as the professor explained today's lesson,

"*Il faut aller…*" the professor said.

"Please, no," Ramya's far conscious pleaded.

"Take me back to Juliet. Find the bus," she commanded herself.

There was a flash of light in Ramya's mind. The classroom faded out and she was thrown into a seat on a bus next to Juliet, who was singing loudly to her music. She had been confused the first time her mind had transported her here, but after hearing about Juliet's journey, Ramya now knew this was the bus Juliet had taken to get to Ghana.

"Abeg, madam, reduce your volume!" another passenger shouted at Juliet.

Juliet turned and gave him the middle finger.

"Prostitute," the passenger said.

"Hungry, smelly man! Go take a shower!" Juliet shouted back.

Ramya turned to face the passenger, who sank back in his seat looking embarrassed. Ramya's far conscious remembered Juliet explaining that one of the worst insults to a Nigerian is to say they smell.

It's like how you Americans feel when someone calls you fat, Juliet had explained.

"Juliet!" Ramya tried calling out.

She knew Juliet couldn't hear her and wouldn't respond. Already, Juliet had returned to the music on her phone. Ramya peered over to see the messages on the screen. A few were from Sylvia, the friend Juliet had stayed with in Ghana. Juliet typed out a quick reply and then went to a message from someone she had named "Johannes Dutch guy" in her phone. Juliet deleted the message before Ramya could see what it said, then sat back and sighed. Ramya's far conscious tried to relax beside Juliet.

"Oga driver, how much longer?" another passenger shouted.

The driver ignored the passenger.

"Oga driver! How much longer?" Juliet repeated for him.

The other passenger flashed her a thumbs-up as a thanks.

The driver rolled his eyes before replying,

"Impatient people! We're almost there."

Juliet's face broke out into a big smile. Ramya smiled back at her, even though Juliet couldn't see her.

"I'm going to meet you soon, baby," Ramya said.

"Ah ah! Driver, careful!" Juliet exclaimed.

The bus had bumped violently, and Juliet had grabbed straight through Ramya's dream body onto the empty seat.

"Calm yourself, passengers! There was a tree branch on the road," the driver explained.

"Stupid man ran over a tree," Juliet whispered.

"Don't worry, baby. The next few minutes will be scary, but you will be ok," Ramya's far conscious tried explaining.

The bus started rattling again, alarming some of the passengers.

"Stop and check what is happening!" one of them shouted.

"We have a schedule!" the driver shouted back.

"I'm sorry you went through this!" Ramya's far conscious said.

Suddenly, Ramya's near conscious perked up. It rallied her body and Ramya heard Juliet shouting outside of her dream state. She knew it was time to return to reality. The shouting continued and Ramya heard that Juliet was on the phone. Listening intently, Ramya heard Juliet say "Sylvia" a few times, though she couldn't hear another voice on the other end of the call.

"Maybe Juliet finally listened to me and is using headphones," Ramya reasoned.

"Shooting in Virginia. Thirty-two dead," Juliet said from the kitchen.

"What?!"

Ramya leapt out of the bed. Her right arm had fallen asleep under the weight of her body, and she jumped up before the feeling came back. Positioning her arm at her hip for support, she bolted into the kitchen and stared at Juliet, who had just hung up the phone.

"Who were you talking to? Did I hear you say something about guns?" Ramya asked.

"Sylvia was watching the news while we were talking. They said something about a shooting in Virginia. Jesus, you Americans like to shoot each other!"

"I didn't hear anyone else on the phone. What did you see about the shooting?"

"Why are you Americans so crazy? Does everyone in America have a gun?"

Ramya felt her body convulse, like someone had drilled a hole and was draining out her life. She was losing control—first her breath, then her sight, then her ability to stand.

"Are you ok!?" Juliet screamed.

"I can't deal...no...I...AAAHHH!!"

She tried screaming to reorient herself. All that did was make Ramya feel like her head was going to explode. Juliet's words slowed down and slurred into a deep, distorted voice, before morphing into sound waves that crashed into Ramya's chest. Juliet collapsed into a pinwheel of color that spun rapidly.

"What is happening? Who were you talking to?" Ramya screamed.

Ramya knew if she stayed inside any longer, she would throw up or faint. Without thinking, she summoned her last ounce of strength, and ran out of the front door and into the darkness. She didn't stop until her lungs prevented her from going further, which was a few feet outside of a coffee shop. The cool night air calmed her down. Reaching into her pocket, Ramya felt a wad of Kenyan shillings.

"I can't keep lying to Juliet. I'm losing myself. I'm losing her," Ramya said to herself.

As quickly as it appeared, the panic disappeared. Ramya

stepped inside of the coffee shop, determined to collect her thoughts.

CHAPTER TEN

 Juliet

 April 15

 Kenya

JULIET DIDN'T REACT quickly enough to catch Ramya, who had completely disappeared into the night by the time Juliet ran outside. She came back inside to an empty apartment and reality set in: Ramya had abandoned her. She was living her worst nightmare. This was exactly what Juliet had feared would happen if she came to Kenya.

"Fuck, Ramya, please come back."

They had discussed all kinds of embarrassing, private, and vulnerable ideas.

"What did I say? Why did she react this way?" Juliet asked out loud.

When no one responded through the silence, Juliet tried messaging Ramya's phone.

Juliet: Baby come back. I'm sorry.
Let's talk, love.

After she sent the fifth message, she heard a buzz through the quiet flat. She walked over to the bedroom and saw Ramya had left her phone on the nightstand. Juliet tapped the screen and Ramya's phone lit up with her messages. The word "unread" grew, before jumping off the screen and taking over the room.

"She'll come back, she's not like that."

Her rationality calmed her down long enough to serve herself a plate of food. She even prepared another plate for when Ramya came back.

"It'll be soon. She'll come back soon."

Juliet got three bites down her throat before she realized she was wrong. The food became tasteless after that. She dragged herself to the couch. Still with no way to contact Ramya, Juliet fell into a distressed sleep around midnight.

Ramya was still gone when Juliet awoke, sending her back into a tailspin of panic. She felt dizzy when she tried to raise herself from the couch. Every movement sent a sharp stabbing pain down her spine. Hunger was catching her stomach, but she was too nauseous to eat anything. They had three weeks left in Kenya together, and she had no idea how to get herself to the safari or to the beach or if she would be allowed to stay in their rental flat until it was time to fly home. She doubted her debit card would work here, so she couldn't buy enough food to survive. Worst of all, she had no idea if Ramya would come back or if she'd want to see Juliet again. She tried typing a message to her siblings.

Juliet: Hey sis…hey bro…

She gave up before hitting "send." No one in her family had

money to send her or would know how to change her flight back home.

"How could I even leave without seeing her again?"

Juliet briefly considered going to the police, but the thought of walking into a station in a foreign country was terrifying. In Nigeria, the police wouldn't do anything without a bribe and Juliet guessed it would be the same here. That made her feel better about deciding to wait in the flat and…just wait.

For days, Juliet had asked Ramya to repeat the details for their safari in the hopes Ramya would say they could leave later. By then, Juliet knew they had missed their van. She spent a restless day ambling around the flat and checked the window for Ramya so often that the neighbors must have thought she was spying on them.

She thought about calling someone in her family to pass the time, before deciding that even she, a reliable secret keeper, could not stay silent about what was happening. She rocked her body back and forth on the couch for hours. Confusion turned into anger; anger turned back into confusion; confusion turned into exhaustion, and she fell back asleep after being awake for fewer than eight hours.

Ramya didn't reappear until 7 a.m. the next morning. Even though her first reaction was relief, Juliet skipped straight to outrage.

"WHERE THE FUCK DID YOU GO!"

"I'm sorry, I just needed to step out for a bit."

"A BIT!? YOU WERE GONE FOR MORE THAN A DAY!"

"What are you talking about? I was gone for maybe an hour. I went to the coffee shop near the main intersection."

What kind of fucking senseless person was Ramya? First, she pretended to not know who Juliet was, then she acted like a moody bitch, then she abandoned Juliet. Now Ramya stood facing her, trying to look bashful and innocent, claiming to have

117

stepped out for "a bit."

"You were gone for more than a day!"

Juliet stormed over to the couch and grabbed her phone.

"SEE?" she screamed, shoving it at Ramya.

Ramya tapped on the screen, revealing the date—15 April. Juliet looked outside at the dark sky and almost fainted. She checked her phone again. It still said 15 April.

"That's a mistake. A few minutes ago, it was the morning of April 17th," Juliet insisted.

By now, Ramya had fetched her phone from the bedroom.

"They both say the same thing, Juliet. It's April 15th."

"What the fuck is going on?"

"Did you fall asleep while I was gone? Sometimes you fall asleep when you're stressed."

Ramya's face softened.

"You were probably dreaming. I'm sorry I left without saying anything. I had already been dreading telling you about tomorrow. And then…" Ramya's voice trailed off.

"Shit! Yes, I guess that must be it. I was dreaming."

That seemed like a ridiculous explanation, but Juliet didn't have a better one. She took a few breaths to calm her nerves and walked back over to the couch. The room was spinning, and she propped her feet up for stability. Years of being broke had made her sharply aware of where she was, who she was with, and how much time had passed in a situation. Ever since Ghana, she felt that sharpness fading. Maybe she was getting complacent dating Ramya, who despite their issues, she trusted more than anyone else in the world.

"Wait, what do you mean, tell me about tomorrow?"

Juliet sat up with a jolt, suddenly remembering what Ramya had said. The room was dark, and Juliet had to squint to see Ramya was undressing. Maybe this woman was unhinged and thought this would be a good time to have sex. Ramya stayed far back after she had drawn down her jeans, though. She was

118

pointing to her hip. Juliet carefully made her way over in case Ramya tried to run again. She ran her hands over the area Ramya was pointing to, which had a deep scar Juliet had noticed a few days ago when they took a bath together.

"He didn't hit an artery, thank God, or I would have bled out within a few minutes. But it did hit the bone and blew out a big chunk of flesh. There was enough blood that I was able to play dead. Everyone else died immediately and he thought he had gotten me too, so I survived," Ramya said.

The weight of Ramya's words crushed Juliet, pushing out the air from her lungs. Ramya's scar opened up before Juliet's eyes like a small screen, replaying the scene Ramya had just described.

"You were there? He shot you?" Juliet whispered.

Tears were streaming down Ramya's face. Juliet grabbed Ramya, who sobbed into her shirt like tidal waves.

"I'm sorry I didn't tell you sooner. It has been nine years and I thought I'd be strong enough to handle being here."

"Baby, it's okay, I'm here. Let it out, I've got you, my love."

Ramya kept crying uncontrollably. Juliet held her for what seemed like a second, for what seemed like a year. She felt like Ramya was crumbling in her arms and she tried to hold the pieces together. Somehow, she kept Ramya intact.

CHAPTER ELEVEN

 Ramya

 April 15

 Kenya

THE DOUCHEBAGS HAD gotten the last blueberry muffin.

"Sorry ma'am, do you want a maple pecan instead?" the cashier had asked her.

"I'm allergic to tree nuts," Ramya had angrily replied.

Nine years ago, April 16th had started out like any annoying morning on campus. Ramya had arrived at her French class pissed off that the small coffee shop on the ground floor had run out of blueberry muffins, no doubt due to the group of douchebag frat boys who had swarmed in just before Ramya had arrived.

She already despised guys like that: guys who didn't have to try to fit in or who never had to consider their place in the world; guys whose lives were easy and fun and respected not because they worked hard or were good people, but because they were born in a certain body. Guys who belittled others whose lives were not as simple. How dare they take the last blueberry muffin.

Ramya's undergrad university was conservative, judgmental, and homogeneous. She hated it there because they hated who she was. By her second semester, she had already dismissed the idea that she would find her place among the crowd. She knew she was a deep thinker. And she knew she was gay. The two did not go well together in that environment.

She was grateful she was smart and tried to convince her parents her academic career would not suffer if she studied abroad or spent a semester working in a city. They angrily responded that laziness had no place in their daughter's life. When she asked if she could transfer to a more progressive school in an urban area, they admonished her for wanting to waste their money.

"Ask us again and we will stop paying for your tuition altogether," they screamed before slamming the phone on her.

At least they're paying, she had reasoned, and told herself to carry on.

Paid tuition did not help her escape the constant harassment on campus or the loneliness the harassment caused her. During the time she was forced to live in that confining environment, Ramya spent most of her nights alone and sad.

By her final year of university, she had discovered a small saving grace—a student group she ran, which brought together a nice set of relatively progressive people who wanted to fight the injustices of the world. Some of the student group members were in her advanced French class her last semester, and she enjoyed their morning routine of chatting over coffee and a blueberry muffin before their professor started the day's lessons. It was one of the few times on campus she didn't feel miserable.

Still cursing the douchebags for ruining her blueberry muffin ritual, Ramya was only half paying attention to her professor that morning. The shooter burst through the door just a few minutes after class began. Ramya's professor didn't stand a chance.

"*Il faut aller...*" her professor had said, seconds before she was gunned down.

Not being familiar with the sound of a gunshot, Ramya wasn't sure what was happening until she saw her friend Megan collapse to the ground, a chunk of her brain missing. There was so much blood. In every shade and in every corner, within minutes, there was so much blood.

If he hadn't been standing in the middle of her classroom with an AR-15 cradled in his hands, Ramya might have mistaken the shooter as one of the guys the douchebags bullied for being too pale, too short, too thin, or too whatever. In another life, Ramya and this guy might have bonded over surviving harassment. In this life, this guy was a shooter and Ramya had to survive him. His white shirt was soaked in blood, sweat and dirt by the time Ramya realized she was injured. The mask he had used to cover his face slipped down. Ramya saw he was grinning. Her one good look at him before she hit the floor told her he loved the sight of what he had done.

Nothing had prepared Ramya for this moment, yet she knew her one way of making it out of this university she hated and finding the life she wanted was to play dead. By now, the blood covered most of the classroom floor in a thick coat, and it was impossible to move without creating ripples. Ramya laid on her stomach under her desk with her breath drawn in, staring at Megan's lifeless body.

Thankfully, the shooter didn't kick Ramya in the face like he kicked her classmate Stephen, who spent his final moments alive clutching his broken nose. Thankfully, he didn't shoot her at point-blank range like he shot Stephen. The shooter left an eternity after he came in, which was probably five or six minutes. By the time the paramedics swept the classroom to check for survivors, Ramya lay among seventeen dead bodies. There were fifteen more in the shooter's wake.

Ramya was the only survivor in her French class.

CHAPTER TWELVE

 Juliet

 April 16

 Kenya

GOING ON A safari seemed stupid to Juliet now. Her life had just shattered and pretending to care about animals was tiring. She peeked out of the corner of her eye from the bed and saw Ramya arranging her clothes in a suitcase.

"Are we still going?" Juliet asked.

"Of course, why wouldn't we?"

Juliet sighed and dragged herself to her feet. The clock in the corner of the bedroom said 5:47 a.m. Even though her brain had experienced more than a day of fear, somehow fewer than ten hours had passed. How could that possibly be explained by a bad dream? What was happening to her? What was happening to Ramya?

Juliet grabbed Ramya's waist—the same spot where Ramya had been shot—as she passed by. She felt Ramya shudder under her touch in a way that she knew wasn't bad. They had stayed up late last night talking about Ramya's "most horrible day."

It wasn't just the thought of Ramya coming so close to death that shook Juliet; it was that Ramya felt guilty about surviving.

"Why do I deserve to be here?" Ramya had asked, right before she fell asleep in Juliet's arms.

Even with everything Juliet had been through in her life, she had never once questioned her right to live or be happy. It was sad that Ramya didn't feel the same way.

They walked outside in the final moments of the sunrise. Juliet drew a sharp breath in, feeling the cold Nairobi morning air. This was the coolest outside temperature that Juliet had ever experienced, and it activated her brain.

"The van will pick us up here and take us straight to the safari campsite," Ramya said robotically.

Juliet glanced over, examining the clothes Ramya had picked out for the occasion and the stiffness of Ramya's body beneath. She wondered how America could provide Ramya with so much—good clothes, a good education, good food, constant electricity—yet make her feel guilty about *surviving* a shooting? What kind of country was that? What kind of people allowed that? Juliet shook her head in disbelief, grateful to be Nigerian.

Out of the corner of her eye, Juliet saw the van a few streets away. She looked over at Ramya, who stood completely motionless until the van pulled into their compound driveway. The driver was huge and had a booming voice.

"Ramya and Juliet?"

Ramya nodded and the driver looked surprised.

"What is it, oga? Why the look?" Juliet whispered to herself.

The driver shrugged his giant shoulders and tossed their heavy bags into the trunk as though they were as light as pillows. He got back into the driver's seat and Juliet saw the tires compress beneath his weight.

"Where do you want to sit?" Ramya asked Juliet, uttering

her first words in nearly twenty minutes.

"Baby, I love you."

Ramya managed a small smile. Juliet surveyed the empty van, grabbed Ramya's hand, and led them to the back.

"It will be bumpy, but private."

Ramya nodded in response, clearly grateful for the space. Juliet sat close to Ramya on the bench seat, ignoring the stares of the driver who was fixated on the two women.

"I hope we will have peace in this van," Juliet said.

Before leaving the city, they picked up three more couples in two different hotels. Juliet examined the others. She was the only African passenger.

Oga giant was surprised to see an African sister, she said to herself.

She glanced down at the tickets Ramya had printed off in London. This was one of the cheapest safaris they had found, yet one ticket was still equivalent to two months of wages at her old restaurant hostess job. African tourism was not meant for most Africans.

They drove for a few hours and mostly sat in silence, tuning out the other passengers who chatted happily in front of them. Ramya had barely said anything since they boarded the van.

"Are you okay, baby?" Juliet asked.

"I always wonder where Megan, Stephen, all of my classmates who died would have been now," Ramya whispered.

Juliet didn't know how to respond except to squeeze Ramya's hand. She had also known people who died too young, and some of those people had died in violent and sudden ways. But there was something especially cruel about the way Ramya's classmates had died that Juliet couldn't quite describe. Maybe it was them dying as a group or dying in a place where they were supposed to be safe. Or maybe it was the media attention. If America could let everyone in the world know about those deaths, why couldn't America prevent those young people from dying in the first place?

"There's no way to know, Ramya. You only have to know that you're a good person and you deserve to be here, ok?"

Ramya gasped, trying to push down air that had got caught in her throat. She was fighting back tears.

"Thank you, I needed to hear that."

"Oh baby, you deserve all the happiness in the world. Come here."

Juliet held Ramya against her chest, her heart breaking. Though she had dated many foreigners before, this was the first time she had felt truly sympathetic for one. Every foreigner she had been with had grown up with far more privileges than she had. Happiness and cruelty were everywhere, she recognized.

Ramya's silent sobs into Juliet's chest continued until they stopped for lunch.

"Passengers, you have an hour for sightseeing and to eat," the driver said.

"Are you ready?" Juliet gently asked.

"Yeah, time to face the day."

They gathered their backpacks and followed the rest of the passengers to the front of the van. Juliet kept her hand on Ramya's lower back for support.

The driver had positioned himself right next to the door and handed each passenger a food voucher as they got down. The other passengers grabbed the voucher easily from his hand, but he held on to Juliet's for a few extra seconds.

"Hello, my sister," the driver whispered in her ear.

Juliet scoffed and elbowed him away from her. She didn't need this shit on an already stressful day. Ramya still looked pale from last night and Juliet decided not to say anything.

"African tourism is not for most Africans," Juliet said out loud with anger.

Not able to control her urge to touch Ramya, Juliet grabbed Ramya's hand as they walked down to the grassy valley. Ramya didn't resist. The driver's eyes seared through her skin, and Juliet was happy to realize she didn't care.

On the way down the hill to the dining area, a giant valley came into sight.

"Wow!" Juliet exclaimed.

In front of her was the largest and deepest field of green she had ever seen. Every centimeter was a slightly different color. One area looked blue-green, another looked dark green, and all throughout were patches of light green and yellow plants. The valley was so big that it looked like the entire city of Lagos could fit inside. Even with the light fog, Juliet couldn't remember ever being able to see so far in the distance. Lagos was usually too polluted.

Ramya had already fallen into Juliet's picture routine and was waiting for Juliet to strike her first pose. Staring out into the valley, however, Juliet wanted something different.

"Come here, love," Juliet said.

She drew their bodies close and gently kissed Ramya, holding the camera in front. They held themselves still as the camera clicked. Juliet turned her phone screen around and saw the picture was exactly what she wanted. The sunlight behind them blurred out their faces to create a silhouette in front of the massive valley. Juliet was overcome with emotion thinking about how nine years ago, Ramya lay alone against a sea of red. She was comforted to know that at least today, Ramya was with her against a sea of green.

CHAPTER THIRTEEN

 Ramya

 April 16

 Kenya

NO TWO ANNIVERSARIES of the most horrible day were the same. Some years, Ramya felt strong and secure in the world, as though she had come to terms with what had happened and could move on from the trauma. She spent those anniversaries discovering something new and celebrating those who perished. On year three, she had spent the day with Carl wandering through the smallest streets of Paris before hosting a vigil for the victims. By year six, she had discovered her love of cycling and went on a 32-mile bike ride through New York City, completing one mile in honor of each of the lives lost.

Other years, Ramya felt as though her world would implode. During year five, she barred herself from all forms of social media for a month. The online tributes to the victims were too jarring, for they always focused on how the victims had been so happy and deeply appreciative of their lives. In the years leading up to the most horrible day, Ramya, on the other hand, had thought many times about how much better it would be, how much more appreciated she would be, if she had died young.

"I can't describe the immense guilt I have for surviving," she had told Juliet last night.

"Is that why you ran away from me? Because you feel guilty?"

"Maybe."

No, it wasn't. Ramya knew that Juliet's tone and word choice had set her off. It was too much to hear someone she loved talk about what happened with such insensitivity.

Her career had taken her to nearly every continent in the last decade. Irrespective of the language, the people, or the politics of where she was, a conversation about gun violence in America would usually come up within a few days. Literally no one in the world, especially communities living in active violent conflicts, understood America's obsession with guns.

"Why would a country that isn't at war let its civilians carry wartime weapons?" a Syrian colleague asked her on a work trip in Sri Lanka.

Political corruption? Lobbyists? Ignorance? She couldn't justify a situation she never agreed with and that nearly killed her. What words could she say when the grotesque images depicting mass shootings in America—scenes fit for a thrasher movie—were her story?

On the rare occasions she admitted what she had experienced, she mostly felt dehumanized. Everyone had an opinion about her most horrible day. Sometimes she felt like the only reason people listened to her story was so they would have their own.

I met this woman who almost died in a mass shooting. I was so traumatized hearing what happened, they could boast to their friends.

As the years passed and shootings in America became a more common occurrence, she became a statistic. The only thing worse than her story being a unique center of attention was her story being ordinary. There was no defending what happened, not to her or to any other shooting victim, no matter how many. But when people spoke about gun violence the way Juliet had, in terms of Americans being careless, it triggered Ramya. The world she had grown up in wasn't made for people who looked or identified like her. Life had already been a constant battle to stay safe. How much more responsibility could she take for her own security?

Exhausted from last night, exhausted from the situation, exhausted from life, Ramya raised her heavy head and stared into the massive green valley in front of her. She squinted her eyes to push out the sadness, and the endless stretch of flora and animals pulsated in front of her.

"Baby, are you ok?" Juliet asked, squeezing her hand.

"I'm sorry about what happened at the airport," Ramya replied.

"It's ok…we have different senses of humor…"

"No…I…Juliet, what happened wasn't voluntary."

"You mean you couldn't control it?"

"Yes. I couldn't control it. Something has been wrong with me for a long time. I forget things. I'm sorry I didn't tell you."

Juliet nodded her head with the same gravity Ramya felt.

"It's ok, love. We'll get through it," Juliet replied.

Tightly holding Juliet's hand, Ramya felt their hearts race and synchronize with the beat of the animal kingdom in front of them. Like her parents' homeland, this continent had absorbed so much pain brought over from abroad. Although Ramya hadn't meant to let her burden escape here, she was relieved to have the help. She was relieved Juliet wanted to help. In nine years, the load had gotten too heavy to carry alone.

While overlooking the breathtaking Kenyan landscape, Ramya understood that while overwhelming, this was the anniversary that something had fundamentally shifted. Ramya now knew she wasn't going through the motions of living to avoid squandering her second chance at life. This would be the year that she was truly grateful to be alive. Year nine would be when she finally understood what it meant to survive: it meant being with Juliet.

CHAPTER FOURTEEN

 Juliet

 April 17

 Kenya

JULIET SET HER alarm for 4:30 a.m. the next morning, determined to wake up in time to do her five-star makeup. The half-broken and dirty mirror in the gross bathroom of their tent didn't deter her; many times, she had made do with far less. Her foundation layer alone took ten squats to pick up the various tubes and brushes. By the end of her routine, her legs were on fire and her face looked even hotter. There was no way she'd let this occasion go without looking her absolute best. She wanted to record every moment for her Instagram followers. Other than the clubs of Lagos, she hadn't had much to show them.

She tried to push aside the sadness of yesterday and concentrate on the exciting day ahead of them. Back in Nairobi, Ramya had shown Juliet some of the animals they might see on the safari, none of which she had seen in person. Long ago, most of the animals that had once roamed her part of Africa had left for cooler, greener, safer areas. Today would open her eyes to so many different things—that's what she loved the most about being with Ramya.

"Wow! You look amazing!" Ramya exclaimed, drowsily rising from the bed.

In some ways, Juliet felt as though they had been together forever because it felt so *natural*. When Ramya complimented her, Juliet knew the relationship was still fresh, for the words washed over her like a wave of warm water. Ramya was looking at her like she was the only thing in the world that mattered, even though the past few days had been hell.

"Now that's love," Juliet replied.

"You say wetin?" Ramya asked in pidgin English.

"Hey, you're learning! Nothing, my love. How are you?"

"I feel at peace. Maybe for the first time since it happened," Ramya replied.

Now *that* was love. She knew that Ramya had spent a long time tormented by what happened, when what Ramya really needed was the love and support to move forward. Juliet felt both empowered and nervous with that responsibility. Fortunately, all they needed to focus on today was the safari.

"Are you ready?" Ramya asked.

"Yes ooo! Let's be adventurous!"

"Yes ooo! But first, can we get food?"

"Make we go chop, my love," Juliet agreed.

Their faces fell as they stepped into the meal tent. Breakfast at the campsite was a mix of stale bread, old cheese and orange juice. Ramya took one look before she turned around and walked out.

"I'll wait for you outside," she told Juliet.

Juliet drank three glasses of juice, deciding none of the food was worth the calories. She hesitated before walking away empty-handed, however, and stuffed some bread in a plastic bag for the road. Ramya had brought a container full of snacks for their six hours on safari and Juliet wanted to contribute in the little ways that she could. The bread would have to do.

Ramya climbed into the van first and was halfway down the length of it before Juliet entered. The driver still made faces at her every time she boarded. She had no doubt that goat was trying to make her feel inferior to him because he felt inferior to the other passengers. Ramya still hadn't noticed.

"I go swear for you oo, oga," Juliet hate-whispered at the driver.

The driver settled into his seat, started the car, and grabbed the mic to explain where they were going. Within minutes after departing, they were back in the thick bush. Juliet assumed they were in a remote corner of the wildlife preserve, but they slowed down to follow a long line of other vans headed in the same direction.

"Eeeh, what is this safari traffic jam?" Juliet exclaimed.

Ramya and the other passengers chuckled. Juliet was proud of herself for making these people laugh. Although she was closer to Ramya in skin tone, she knew Ramya was closer in culture to them. This little victory meant something.

Their van's first stop overlooked a much smaller valley than yesterday's. The ground was covered in a layer of neon green grass that reminded Juliet of a fabric she had bought from her friend a few months ago. Having lived in Lagos her entire life, only then did it occur to her that her favorite patterns were inspired by nature. Everywhere Juliet's eyes went, there were animals grazing, insects buzzing, and plants dancing.

"What lucky passengers you are! There's a rhino!" the driver shouted and pointed.

He opened the sunroof of the van so they could stand and take pictures. A rush of cold air ran over Juliet's naked arms, and she realized she had forgotten to cover her body as well as she had her face. She looked around and saw she was the only one without a jacket. Ramya noticed as well and reached into her backpack.

"Here, my love. I brought you an extra hoodie."

"Thanks, baby. Look at you, always thinking of me."

They stood up together, bodies pressed tightly, to take photos. Juliet had always considered herself a good photographer until that moment, when she discovered she had no idea how to take anything other than herself. She gave up after several tries. None of her photos captured the rhino's majestic beauty. Instead, it looked like a light grey blob.

"Abeg, let's move on!" she complained.

Ramya grabbed her hand, calming her. She watched Ramya turn her phone vertically, position the rhino in the bottom half, hold her arms tightly to her side and tap her finger on the screen to focus the lens. Juliet was surprised at how well these small adjustments worked. The picture Ramya took looked great, which encouraged Juliet to try again. She steadied her breath and arms, waited for the rhino to turn around, and snapped her own perfect photo.

"Oh wow, it's beautiful!"

Ramya's beaming smile was the next thing Juliet captured.

Juliet discovered a newfound love for animals that day. She felt nervous as a chunky baby elephant lost its footing and almost fell down a hill. A lion emerged from its early morning meal and cuddled with its partner; their companionship made Juliet so happy. Rhinos walked with an authority that Juliet hoped to achieve in her career. Giraffes and deer galloped with a gentle grace. Zebras always moved as though they were late for an appointment. Juliet was in awe of each animal's personality and vibrancy.

They stopped for lunch at a different campsite. Long lines of tourist groups passed the buffet tables to scoop dehydrated noodles, a thick soup of beef and vegetables, and overcooked rice onto their plates. The food looked disgusting to Juliet, but she filled her plate to maximum capacity, her stomach grumbling from skipping breakfast.

"Ramya love, why aren't you eating?"

"Everything looks gross."

Ramya shuffled through her backpack for the snacks she had brought. Juliet watched as Ramya placed granola bars, small tomatoes, and ham and cheese on the table.

"I wish I had something to make a sandwich," Ramya said.

Juliet's ears perked up at the words, and she proudly presented the bread from this morning.

"Here you are, my love."

"Perfect, thanks! You saved me."

She silently congratulated herself for anticipating Ramya's need.

They finished their meals and headed back to the van, a familiar dread overtaking Juliet as they got closer. She would need to deal with the driver today, she decided. This man should not ruin her holiday. When they were a few steps away, she saw the driver was squatting down, his massive shoulders covering nearly a fifth of the van.

"Passengers, we're very sorry. There will be a small delay. A back tire is deflated, and we need to wait for the mechanic to come," he announced.

"What do we do now?" one of the Polish passengers asked.

"You may go into town to visit the local merchants or head this way to see a waterfall."

The driver pointed the passengers in the two directions and told them to be back in an hour.

"What do you want to do?" Ramya asked Juliet.

"We just saw a waterfall in Nairobi…"

"Ok cool, let's go to town."

Just a few streets into their walk, Juliet realized she had made a mistake. She had hoped the "town" would be meant for tourists and sell cute souvenirs like the "I ♥ Maasai Mara" t-shirt the loud Spanish woman in their van had bought yesterday. To her disappointment, the town looked more like a small village near where her parents had grown up. Other than a few women selling meat and vegetables on the road, there wasn't much to buy or to see. In fact, the village looked mostly abandoned. Juliet turned to go back to the van.

"Ramya, are you coming?"

"Hey, check this out!"

Halfway down an abandoned street, she saw Ramya staring and pointing to a beaten-up sign above a shanty building. Never having been to Kenya before, Juliet didn't have expert knowledge about the area, yet she knew something was off. How could a village within walking distance of a major tourist site be empty like this?

"Ramya, let's go back. I don't think it's safe here," Juliet called out.

"We're fine! I've been to remote parts of Africa like this."

"Ramya…"

"The sign says SPIRITUAL READINGS. In all capital letters."

"Be careful, love."

The sign was waving dangerously on rusted hinges, ready to fall on anyone who stood below. Ramya's head was too close.

"Spiritual? Does it mean like fortune tellers?" Ramya pressed.

"Ramya, let's go."

"No, let's give it a try."

Juliet was surprised at Ramya's sudden desire to know about the future. She had spent the last three days bringing Ramya back from the past. In any case, Juliet recognized these "spiritual readings" for what they were: a scam. Too many people in her parents' village declared themselves a "spiritual advisor." The most successful one duped so many people for so much money that he was able to buy a new Range Rover.

"I mean…we don't have time to see the waterfall now. Why

not?" Ramya followed.

"But do you think it's a good idea? With what happened the last few days?"

"I'm ok, Juliet. It'll just be for fun, I promise."

Juliet hesitated to reveal her last attempt at spirituality; she decided that Ramya didn't need to hear about the priest who said God said they weren't meant to be together. After three weeks together in person, she recognized Ramya's impatient body language. She didn't have long to convince Ramya this was a bad idea before Ramya went off and did it anyway.

"Ramya, love, let's go back. I don't think this is good for you."

"Juliet, please?" Ramya pleaded.

"My love, this isn't a good idea…"

"It'll be fun. Please?"

Juliet sighed. Ramya looked excited and energized for the first time since they got to Maasai Mara. She felt terrible that Ramya's dream safari was being ruined by the shooting anniversary. Had she known, she never would have suggested they celebrate her birthday at the beach. Sensing this scammer SPIRITUAL ADVISOR would go horribly wrong, she agreed, nonetheless. She couldn't disappoint Ramya.

"Ok, love. We can try if you want," Juliet conceded, walking over.

"Yes! Thank you!"

"Hello? Anyone there?" Ramya asked, peering into the shanty building.

"You may enter," a raspy voice replied.

They slowly stepped inside; the energy of the shanty building immediately unnerved Juliet, as though it was scanning her body looking for flaws. Mummy was both devoted to the Catholic Church and believed fiercely in local spiritual advisors. The unsettling feeling searing through Juliet made her hesitate. Was there a chance Mummy's faith in spiritual advisors wasn't nonsense? What if this person did possess a deeper power? Or worse, what if Ramya believed a scam?

"What do you want?" the voice asked.

"I...uh. Can you do a reading for us?" Ramya asked, her voice shaking.

Juliet saw a fragile-looking woman emerge from behind a curtain; she looked exactly as Juliet had guessed. The woman wore dozens of rosaries, four layers of fabric, and had powder-drawn symbols all over her face and arms. Her thinning white hair was pulled tightly into a bun at the back of her head, stretching her wrinkled face at the hairline. The woman carried incense sticks, a stack of cards, and a notepad that was almost full. If she had higher cheekbones, lighter skin and thicker wrists, this old lady could have been Juliet's late grandmother. Juliet wasn't fooled by the look. She was on guard.

"Scammer," Juliet whispered.

"What?" Ramya asked.

"She's a scammer."

"Twenty thousand shillings, pay now."

"What?" Juliet shouted.

That was more than what it cost to buy a week of food in Nairobi. Before Juliet could stop her, Ramya whipped out the money.

"Here."

"What do you endeavor to know?" the woman asked.

"I guess...what does the future hold?"

"Specifically?"

"Does my future involve..." Ramya trailed off.

"Me," Juliet finished.

Ramya had just paid a small fortune to a scam artist. Juliet had no patience if this woman was homophobic. Whatever nonsense the woman said to Ramya, Juliet would have to make it sound positive later. That's how she had navigated years of manipulative "spiritual predictions," like when Mummy's local priest "predicted" her plane to Nairobi would crash into the ocean.

"Dates of birth?"

The woman handed Ramya a piece of paper, motioning for Ramya to write them down. Juliet briefly broke away from her anger when she saw that Ramya had already memorized hers.

"Aw, baby."

"I'll never forget, love."

The woman nodded and began chanting in Swahili. She then lit five incense sticks, filling the shanty building with a thick brown smoke that made Juliet cough. Her final ritual step was to pick up a stack of cards and throw them in the air, shouting,

"Reveal yourself!"

To Juliet's horror, Ramya was enchanted.

"You don't believe her, do you?"

"Let her do her thing. I want to know if we're going to be together forever."

"And you'll believe her if she says we won't?"

"REVEAL YOURSELF!"

A clap of thunder shook the shanty building, suddenly clearing the brown smoke. The woman had arranged her rosaries in a pattern on the table and was leaning over them as though reading a newspaper.

"What does it say?" Ramya eagerly asked.

"Patience, child."

Juliet sighed and glanced at Ramya's watch. They had to be back to the van in ten minutes.

"Please rush," Juliet said.

"Patience, child."

The woman stood still for the next five minutes, while Juliet and Ramya shifted uncomfortably on their feet. There was nowhere to sit or rest their eyes.

"I am ready," the woman finally said.

"Quick now!" Juliet shouted.

"I cannot provide the requested information."

"What the fuck does that mean?" Ramya said, finally angry.

"You have asked if you will be in each other's futures."

"Yes, and?"

"I cannot answer this question because you have not been in each other's past."

Juliet burst out laughing, clapping her hands loudly.

"Heeeey, 419er!" Juliet exclaimed, calling the woman a scammer.

"It is not a scam, my child. Your connection is not natural. You have not been a real force in each other's past, and therefore you cannot be in each other's future."

"Jeeeesus! Come on, Ramya!"

Not wanting to hear another line of bullshit, Juliet dragged Ramya out of the building before the woman screwed more with her already fragile girlfriend. She was so pissed!

"What the fuck was that?" Ramya exclaimed.

"A scam artist, Ramya! I told you."

"Shit, I'm sorry. I don't know what came over me. I just wanted to know about our future together."

Juliet stopped walking and looked back. Ramya was so sweet and so stupid. How could she think a scam spiritual advisor in the bush of Kenya would encourage their relationship? It was *unnatural*, after all.

"Ramya, you don't need a fake prophecy to tell you if we're meant to be together."

She felt hypocritical saying the words, considering she had visited a church wanting to know the same thing just a few days ago.

"What do you feel?" she asked Ramya.

"Optimistic."

"Good! Me too. That's all we need, right?"

"It is, you're right."

Convinced she had finally got her point through to Ramya,

they raced back to the van and as usual, were the last people to board.

"African girl, you are late again. I will leave you next time," the driver said.

"Hey, don't speak to my girlfriend that way! I'll report you to the safari travel company," Ramya shouted.

The other passengers nervously shifted in their seats until finally one British guy said,

"Leave her alone, man. So disrespectful."

"Yeah, that's disrespectful," the other passengers agreed.

Juliet was surprised, then irritated that Ramya had "rescued" her instead of letting her deal with the driver her way. At least the spiritual advisor scammer had woken Ramya up to what Juliet had been dealing with for two days. If only the European passengers would come to her defense if she were the one to shout. They returned to their seats; the tension was still thick.

"Ramya, you should have let me deal with that on my own. I'm a grown-ass woman."

"You're right, I'm sorry. I couldn't believe how he spoke to you."

"He has been like that since we started the journey."

"Really? I didn't notice. I have been out of it. Sorry, Juliet."

"No wahala, love. Let's talk before making decisions for each other, ok?"

"Ok, love. That's fair."

Juliet glanced up and smiled at the driver who looked disappointed he hadn't caused Ramya and her to fight. Still recovering from the embarrassment, he tried to steady his voice,

"Dear passengers, we have a longer drive now. We'll be on the road for about two hours."

They pulled back out onto the main road. The changes in the scenery had slowed down a lot, and Juliet was tired from the scam, smoke, and shady driver. She pulled out her phone from her bag and saw Ramya had already fallen asleep on the other half of the long bench seat. No matter how hard she tried to concentrate on Instagram videos, she was distracted by Ramya sleep-talking. The loud van engine and uneven roads drowned out Ramya's voice to everyone except Juliet. If the other passengers had heard, Ramya's words would sound random, maybe even cute.

"No blueberry muffin? Hi Megan. Bonjour tout le monde..."

Juliet knew something sinister was stirring in Ramya's mind. Ramya was having another nightmare about the shooting. Though Juliet had only found out about it a few days ago, she already felt as though she knew every detail of the scene.

"Sometimes my body drifts through the building hallways. Sometimes I can feel my messenger bag slapping against my back as I walk to class. Sometimes I feel joy seeing Megan smile at me when I walk in. But every time, I feel the spot in my hip where he shot me. I can still feel the unbearable pain," Ramya had described.

Reaching out to wake Ramya up, a bump in the road caused Juliet to miss touching Ramya's body. With those extra seconds, she hesitated; she was surprised Ramya said new words,

"Victim number thirteen is male, early twenties, blond hair, wearing a pink polo shirt. He's unresponsive and not breathing, over! Victim number fourteen is female, early twenties, blonde hair, wearing a green dress. She's unresponsive and not breathing, over! Victim number fifteen is female, early twenties, brown hair, wearing a blue shirt. She's..."

Juliet realized that Ramya was repeating the words of the paramedics who had saved her.

"Any survivors!?" Ramya continued.

"They're all dead, George! These kids...they're dead."

A horrifying image of Ramya seeing the scene through the eyes of the paramedics popped into Juliet's mind. Ramya would see herself on the blood-soaked floor, unsure if she was dead. Juliet had heard enough. She leaned over and gently shook Ramya awake.

CHAPTER FIFTEEN

 Ramya

 April 20

 Kenya

"OH MY GOD, I'm exhausted," Ramya said.

She tossed their suitcases in the corner of the sitting area and collapsed onto the couch. Despite how overwhelming their last night in Nairobi had been, a holiday rental flat had never felt more like home.

"Make I thank God for hot showers oo," Juliet said.

"Abi ooo. I don't think I could have handled another cold one in that tent."

"Ah ah, you're sounding more and more Nigerian."

Ramya chuckled. "Abi ooo" had rolled right off her tongue. It sounded so much better than her American "I agree." She wondered what other expressions she had picked up from Juliet, and what she would in the months to come. Her speech would be halfway Nigerian before setting foot in the country.

Juliet turned on a few lights to brighten the apartment against the setting sun. Her footsteps still brought comfort to Ramya, who listened as Juliet walked over to the kitchen and poured them glasses of water.

"Here, love."

"Thanks, is this bribery for you to shower first?"

"Yes now, did it work?"

"Of course, enjoy! I'll go right after you."

She watched Juliet walk to the bedroom and heard the bathroom door close shortly after. Unlike four days ago, an instant feeling of panic did not sweep through her body at the thought of Juliet stepping away. Ramya scanned the room, half expecting to see a sign congratulating her for surviving anniversary number nine.

"Not how I thought my first safari would go," Ramya said to herself.

Faint sounds of Juliet singing in the shower reached Ramya, giving her a slight boost of energy. She wandered into the kitchen to get a snack, and found they were out of food. They only had two days back in Nairobi before it was time for them to travel again; it wasn't worth going to the grocery store and food delivery services there only took cash. She walked over to her backpack to check how much she had left. Five thousand shillings thanks to her idiotic purchase of the year.

Although she had spent enough time in sub-Saharan Africa to know the difference between actual spiritual figures and scam artists, something had pulled Ramya to the "SPIRITUAL ADVISOR," something she couldn't explain. Maybe she really was looking for answers. Maybe she was desperate to know if Juliet felt as strongly about her as she did for Juliet. Maybe if she were back home in London or New York, she would have taken Juliet out on a romantic date to set the mood and asked in the right moment. Maybe in the nature of southwest Kenya, paying a spiritual advisor was the only way she could think to find out.

Whatever the case, the spiritual advisor/scammer had dredged up something deep inside of Ramya's mind. While she slept in the van, her states of consciousness had remained united…and useless. Without her usual near conscious to talk to her body, she slipped so far into her recurring nightmare that a new memory surfaced of the paramedics announcing her classmates were unresponsive…and dead. In any other situation, that would have shaken her. Having Juliet by her side when she woke up had brought her clarity.

One reason she loved Africa was because so much of its land was unlike anywhere else on earth; Ramya felt like she was unlike any other person on earth. Yet Ramya had defaulted to seeking out girlfriends with similar levels of education or professional experience, characteristics that were at best, irrelevant. The most horrible day had set Ramya apart from most of those people. None of her exes had been through anything that difficult. Juliet was different. Juliet had had a difficult life and had somehow emerged stronger. Ramya didn't need a partner who lectured her to stay positive when faced with adversity. Ramya needed someone who had lived through adversity themselves and stayed positive. She needed someone who could empathize with her emotional baggage. She needed someone like Juliet.

"Hey love, I'm done."

A thick trail of steam followed Juliet from the bathroom, threatening to close Ramya's already tired eyes. She barely managed to follow the steam back to the bathroom and clean off her tired body. Juliet was curled up in bed by the time Ramya emerged.

"How was your shower?" Juliet asked.

"Fantabulous!"

"Nice one! Come here."

She jumped into bed with Juliet, and they snuggled in each other's arms. Decompressing before sleeping was needed.

"I learned a lot about myself this week," Ramya said.

"Me too, love. What's on your mind?" Juliet replied.

Ramya smiled. The first time she had asked Juliet that question, Juliet had gotten upset, accusing Ramya of not trusting her. Apparently, that wasn't a common question in Juliet's Nigerian culture.

"Why would you ask me that?" Juliet had screamed.

"To know you better," Ramya had replied.

Only recently had Juliet believed her. Now that was one of their most common questions for each other.

"You...and us. I feel like we're perfect for each other," Ramya replied.

"You do?"

"You don't?"

The hesitation in Juliet's voice caught Ramya off guard, and she sat up so quickly that she knocked over the ticking clock behind her.

"Abeg, Ramya. I'm tired, let's talk tomorrow."

"No! Tell me, you don't think we're perfect together?"

"Haba, I didn't say that. This relationship is wonderful. But we have a lot to figure out."

"So? Which couple doesn't?"

"Why do you think we're perfect, Ramya?" Juliet asked.

"Because of what we've lived through! Just look at what our minds do to us! We have real things to overcome. Now we can do it together..." Ramya's voice trailed off.

Among her various crises, Ramya remembered that they hadn't spoken about the time lapse Juliet had experienced in the hour Ramya went to the coffee shop alone. She was quite sure neither of them believed Juliet simply had a nightmare. During their phone calls before coming to Kenya, Juliet had told Ramya about her years of "living on the streets," when she was basically homeless. Ramya suspected that Juliet's lapses in time were a psychological reaction to the trauma she had faced, just like

Ramya's nightmares and memory loss.

"You thought I left you for more than a day. Maybe because of your life on the streets?"

"Stop, Ramya."

"I admire you for everything you have faced…"

"Ramya, stop."

"I'm just saying, the trauma…"

"STOP! You don't need to bring that up."

"It's not a bad thing! I admire you for everything you have survived."

"What else do you admire about me?"

Ramya hesitated a split second too long. Juliet sprang up from the bed.

"You mention my past a lot."

"Of course, our collective trauma bonds us."

"We need more than trauma to unite us, Ramya. I need to be respected for more than my struggles."

"Wow…I…that's not what I meant."

She did truly admire Juliet for her struggles. What Juliet knew about life couldn't be taught in a classroom, a conference or a boardroom. Because of her experiences, Juliet was wiser than anyone Ramya had ever previously dated. But if Ramya was more than her trauma, so was Juliet.

"I admire your wisdom, your intelligence, your sense of humor, so many things," Ramya finally answered.

"Are you sure you're not just saying that to resolve this fight? You are educated and have a successful career. What do I have?"

"You'll have the same one day."

"How? How will I get those, Ramya?"

Juliet raised her hands and motioned for Ramya to stop talking; Ramya finally did. Now the steam radiated from Juliet, who silently crawled back into bed and fell asleep quickly, her shallow breaths drowning out the lingering noises on the street. Ramya leaned back against the headboard, her mind reeling at the idea that she was just using Juliet to work through her past. She sat in the dark room, concentrating hard on her feelings. Yes, their struggles bonded them with a profound empathy. But it was who Juliet was as a person that inspired Ramya to be better and stronger herself. That was not something to take for granted.

"Or abuse," Ramya whispered to herself.

Suddenly wide awake and aware of what to do, Ramya walked back to the sitting area and pulled out her laptop. The first thing she did was check her bank accounts, in which she saw the alarmingly small balances. Their time in Kenya had wiped out most of her savings, which made her feel both clever and stupid. She would not be considering what she was without this holiday, and this holiday might hinder what she was considering.

"I should have enough," she convinced herself.

Her next stops online were a series of websites, blogs, and documents. Seven hours later, she was still researching. The clatter from her keyboard caught the attention of Juliet, who wandered in after peeing.

"What are you doing awake?"

"I found a few options."

"Options for what?"

"For you, for school."

She motioned for Juliet to sit next to her, verbally recapping the long list of notes she had written. There were three universities in Lagos that had adult learner programs.

"This one has a few branches throughout the country."

"Wow, that branch is close to my apartment. When can I enroll?"

"When are you ready?"

Thanking her career for her computer skills, Ramya sat with Juliet, and they filled out the paperwork and paid the tuition online. They went over the last steps Juliet needed to complete her enrollment in person at the school.

"How will I do my assignments? On my phone?" Juliet asked.

"Let's buy you the perfect laptop."

Together, they ordered it and scheduled the date Juliet would pick it up after she got back to Nigeria. By the end of the day, Ramya was down to her last two thousand dollars. She couldn't be happier.

CHAPTER SIXTEEN

 Juliet

 April 22

 Kenya

"NA WA! What is this rubbish?" Juliet shouted.

The driver in front of them banged on the car boot a few times while jiggling the key in the slot. Juliet heard a loud click, and the boot finally sprang open.

"Let me help you with these," the driver said.

Although Juliet approved of how he loaded in their suitcases, no amount of care could prevent the pile of dirt in the back from swirling up like a tiny tornado.

"Is this the only available car?" Juliet asked.

"Yes, sorry ma'am."

"I didn't book this! I got the 'friendly, African luxury transport car,'" Ramya exclaimed.

"Um...ma'am, this *is* the friendly, African luxury transport car," the driver replied.

"Abeg, let's just go," Juliet pleaded.

The Mombasa airport had a dangerous energy and Juliet was eager to leave, even if that meant suffering with this dirty car. Ramya climbed into the backseat and Juliet followed, immediately collapsing into Ramya's lap. The driver started the engine, which coughed like it had pneumonia.

"Please abeg, turn up the air," she said.

Her normally dry face was drenched in sweat. She was used to the grey Lagosian sky, not this boiling direct sun of Mombasa. Ramya muttered something about how the temperature was above 100°F that day, which Juliet took to mean it was hot. This temperature nonsense still didn't make sense to her.

"Sorry ma'am, the air con is all the way up. It's not working so well."

Juliet felt faint from the heat, so Ramya pulled down the windows as far as she could without risking them getting robbed.

"What kind of suffer is this?" Juliet whined.

"Sorry for the inconvenience, ma'am. This is Africa, you know. This car is the authentic African experience!" the driver said.

"Oga, WHAT? I am NIGERIAN. Authentic Africa does not mean poor."

From Ramya's lap, Juliet looked up at the driver, who briefly met her eye. Something about his expression made her think he was about to agree with what she said. He stayed quiet instead. Satisfied that she still had won the argument, Juliet turned her attention to what she saw out the window.

"This place isn't as pretty as Maasai Mara."

"Yeah, humans destroy everything. One of the prettiest coastlines in the world is a half-kilometer to the right," Ramya replied.

"And all we see is a brown dirt road lined with dull grass," Juliet finished.

Heat radiated from Ramya's lap, which Juliet knew was because of the "temperature" outside...and anger. A glance at

Ramya's bank balance while they bought Juliet's laptop had told her Ramya was nearly broke. Seeing this suffer car for the steep price must have been agonizing. Juliet prayed their hotel wouldn't be a third scam of their Kenyan trip.

The bumpy ride and loud air blowing through the windows didn't make for good conversation, which gave Juliet time to reflect on their last fight. Her frustration at Ramya had reached new levels that night. She was so disappointed that the reason Ramya thought they were meant to be together was primarily trauma. As she slept it off, Sylvia's voice appeared in her head, echoing what she thought,

"How did this happen!? She doesn't deserve this!"

She was therefore surprised when she woke up the next morning and discovered Ramya had been researching schools for her. In fact, she remembered why she wanted to be with Ramya in the first place. What bonded them wasn't just the sex or the physical attraction or a similar level of past trauma. No one else she had dated would have walked away from their argument and decided to invest in her education. And therefore, no amount of heat or broke-ness would keep Juliet away from Ramya now. She dug her head into Ramya's leg and felt more empowered than ever before.

Juliet dozed off until she heard the driver,

"We're here, ma'ams."

He carried their bags to the front atrium of their hotel, which Ramya had found online.

"This place caters to rich people on yoga retreats," Ramya whispered.

As if summoned, a middle-aged white man dressed in linen and too many wooden beads came outside and greeted them.

"Welcome, I am the owner. You may call me guru Michael."

"Uh…I'm just going to call you Michael. Guru has a real meaning in my religion," Ramya snapped.

Juliet wished she knew more about Hinduism so she could

join Ramya in tormenting this yeye man. Michael swallowed nervously.

"Very well, please sit so I can explain how our resort works."

"Oga, explain what? We pay you to stay here. Finish," Juliet replied.

"Please, just…argh! Just sit!" Michael shouted.

Juliet and Ramya stood impatiently. Michael spent the next fifteen minutes babbling about the "special energy of the resort," which Juliet figured out meant they only served vegetarian food.

"The granola we make at the hotel is famous. You can purchase extra bags for 8,000 shillings."

"Abeg, do you put gold in the granola?" Juliet replied.

Chuckling, Ramya turned her head and pointed to the main building. Relieved, Juliet saw the hotel description was accurate. Every room in the hotel was in a partially covered giant treehouse. The main office was made from a beautiful stone and pieces of stained glass. She hoped their room would be as pretty.

"Can we go up now?" Juliet asked impatiently.

Michael sighed, finally understanding they were not his typical guests.

"Maurice, come," Michael said in a commanding voice.

A man appeared dressed in a uniform that looked like it was designed for primary school children.

"Why is that man dressed like a two-years-old baby?" Juliet asked.

"Have a good stay," Michael said coolly, then left.

"Ow!" Maurice exclaimed.

Juliet and Ramya whirled around to look at Maurice, who had dropped a bag and was cupping his foot.

"Where are your shoes?" Juliet asked.

"To preserve the energy of the resort, Michael is the only staff member allowed to wear shoes."

"How many times did Michael make you rehearse that line?" Ramya asked.

"Please ma'am, let me take your bags upstairs."

Juliet grimaced as Maurice lugged her heavy suitcase; the four flights of concrete stairs must have been torture on his feet.

"Here's a tip," Ramya said, handing him 1000 shillings.

"To preserve the energy of the resort, staff are not allowed to…"

"Just take the damn tip, Maurice. I'll lie to 'guru' Michael if he asks."

"Thank you, ma'am! Enjoy your stay."

Maurice limped out of the room. Two of his toes on his right foot were swelling.

"Baby, stop tipping so much if you are broke," Juliet complained.

"He deserves the money. I'll figure out how to make more."

"Ah ah, he does though. Michael is creepy! At least this place is beautiful."

Even with the bizarre start, there was no doubt the hotel was stunning. Their suite was a giant circular room with the beds—they had to book a double to make it look like they were friends—sitting in the middle. A wraparound balcony allowed them to see breathtaking views of an endless green forest on one side and the Indian Ocean on the other. The bathroom had a massive stone shower and ceramic tub.

"Um, ma'ams, your dinner is here."

Maurice knocked lightly on their door and Juliet walked over to let him in. On the way over, she glanced down at the bed and saw there was a piece of paper sticking out of her purse, which she grabbed and held.

"Thanks, Maurice. You can come in."

Still barefoot, Maurice carefully navigated around her already sprawled-out clothes and placed the heavy dinnerware on their dining table.

"Here's another tip, thanks," Juliet offered.

Ramya's tipping habit was rubbing off on her. Maurice didn't protest this time and quietly shut the door behind him.

"Ugh, this food needs salt. What's that, baby?" Ramya asked.

"A message our driver slipped in my bag," Juliet replied, examining the note.

"What does it say?"

"You're right, Africa ≠ poor. Call me if you need a good car. +254 (0) 359 66639. Oh my God, call him, abeg. I can't sit in that sweat machine again."

Ramya grabbed her phone, dialed the number and put it on speaker so they could both hear. The driver picked up on the second ring.

"Hello, is this the driver from earlier today?" Ramya asked.

"Yes, hello! My name is Joseph. Sorry about that car, ma'ams. Michael makes us bring the rubbish ones to pick up his guests and to say they are authentically African."

"I knew it! That is a bad man," Juliet shouted.

"He is and he won't change. People tolerate him because it's hard to get jobs this far away from Mombasa."

Juliet sighed hearing Joseph explain Michael's family background. Colonialism was still present, this time showing itself as baby uniforms and bare feet.

"So ma'ams, can I help you with a nicer car?"

"Yes! In fact…hold on…" Ramya started.

"Juliet, can I talk to Joseph alone?"

She smiled and nodded, knowing that Ramya needed to finish planning something special. The unsalted food sat on their dining table, which Juliet picked at with a fork. Juliet was more interested in Ramya's whispering, which the open air hotel carried to her ears.

"Could I hire you for the day? Tomorrow is my…uh… friend's birthday."

Juliet couldn't stop giggling through the phone call. Ramya finally hung up and walked over to her.

"What do you have planned?" she asked.

"Guess!" Ramya replied.

"You know what, it doesn't matter."

"Are you sure? You were so excited last week."

"Ramya, I'm going to school. Anything else you give me is a bonus."

Juliet did something rare the next morning—she woke up before Ramya. The sounds of the crashing Indian Ocean waves washed over her, and she took in a deep breath of the salty air that wafted through their open room. At the horizon, she saw the sun was also slowly dragging itself out of bed, first covering the water, then the beach, and then their clean white sheets and her body in a bright rainbow.

"This is perfect."

She poked Ramya, whose head flopped lazily. Today was one of those mornings when Ramya slept so deeply that her body looked lifeless. Ramya's nightmares had vanished over the last few days, telling Juliet that Ramya was truthful about being at peace. Energized and with nowhere to go alone, Juliet walked over to their bags and studied them intently.

"Should I look? Where is it?"

Ramya had claimed to be an excellent gift giver but had also been very sneaky about what the gift was and where it was hidden. Juliet quietly flipped through Ramya's neatly organized clothes, papers, and shoes. Thirty minutes of searching didn't turn up anything, and Juliet admitted Ramya's hiding skills were too good to break. It didn't matter to Juliet. She was honest when she said any gift felt like a bonus. Soon, she'd be enrolled in university; nothing else mattered.

She wandered back to the bed and saw her unplugged phone on a side table.

"Chai, I didn't charge my phone! Not today, abeg!"

Ramya had plugged in her phone overnight and its charger was easier to grab than Juliet's, which was buried at the bottom of her suitcase. She plugged her phone in before noticing the photo memory notification on Ramya's:

This day 10 years ago

Normally Juliet wouldn't go through someone else's phone, but Ramya had given her the passcode and permission last week.

"I have nothing to hide. Besides, it's a good idea in case of emergencies," Ramya had said.

Not so much because of an emergency, but rather a burning curiosity, Juliet swiped on the notification and entered the passcode. Ramya's phone sprung to life and Juliet clicked on the photo app. She gasped. Nothing in the photos themselves were alarming, but Juliet looked between Ramya sleeping on the bed and Ramya in the photos no fewer than thirty times. Her wise, mature, brilliant Ramya carried herself like a thirty-one-year-old woman, yet she looked exactly the same as ten years ago.

"How is that possible?" Juliet asked.

"Hmm?" Ramya stirred.

"Shit!"

Juliet quickly turned off the phone and tossed it back on Ramya's side table.

"Hmm?...wetin dey happen?" Juliet said, pretending to wake up.

"Morning, is everything...Juliet...HAPPY BIRTHDAY!"

Ramya opened her big eyes even wider and wrapped Juliet in a big hug. Juliet giggled as Ramya kissed her entire body and worked over to Juliet's stomach. Any doubts about Ramya quickly disappeared and Juliet guided her lower, turning the kissing session into delicious morning sex.

"Ooooh, that was gooood," Juliet moaned.

"Honored to be at your birthday service, my love."

"I'm so happy we're here together."

"I wouldn't have missed this for anything, Juliet."

"Thank you for making this work. I know it was hard. So, what's the plan?"

Ramya called Joseph and confirmed they would meet him in an hour. Juliet hopped up, determined to both look fly and to not waste too much time getting ready. She pulled out the outfit she had long planned—a beautiful matching jumper set she had made herself. The material was a geometric pattern of yellow, red, green, gold and black squares, triangles, and stripes. Complete with her nicest wig, a new pair of sunglasses, and fancy slippers Ramya had brought her from London, she looked like a million-dollar baby.

"We need to be quick leaving the hotel grounds," Ramya warned.

Joseph was bringing them a nice car that goat Michael hadn't authorized, as though Michael controlled the entire town. Juliet's slippers thumped clumsily behind a jogging Ramya, who rounded the corner outside of the main compound. A hundred meters away, Juliet saw a fine-looking Range Rover SUV waiting for them.

"Morning, happy birthday!" Joseph greeted her.

"Thank you! Now *this* is the car I need for my birthday!"

"Abi ooo!" Ramya agreed.

Juliet burst out laughing. Ramya's transformation into a Nigerian was so funny.

They climbed into the car and drove toward the beach town near the hotel. There were few things and fewer people to see on the way. All Juliet could pick out was the occasional small hotel or walking path marked "Beach this way." Juliet thought back to her childhood, when her parents were building their new house in a far corner of Lagos. She remembered how expensive it was to carry the building materials to the construction site.

"Joseph, when did Michael's family arrive in Kenya?" Juliet asked.

"Ah…well, Michael's grandfather came to Kenya from Italy."

"When did his family build the hotel?"

"Michael's grandfather got investors for a stained-glass business that did well. His father used that money to build the hotel, which Michael inherited. The family still supplies stained glass to hotels in East Africa."

"So, Michael's white European grandfather accessed money Black Kenyans couldn't?"

"Yes, you're right."

"Ehya, and Michael treats Black Kenyans like that," Juliet finished.

Ramya grabbed her hand and gave it a squeeze. Juliet turned back to stare out of the window. The people walking on the street blurred into one streak of color. She imagined how many more white men like Michael were staring down at them from their mansions tucked away in the bush.

Not knowing anything about the matter, Juliet tuned out Ramya and Joseph as they discussed Kenyan politics. She was glad to have a few minutes to let her thoughts fly free. She was seeing a different side of Africa on this holiday, one reserved for rich non-Africans. As much as the lifestyle suited her, it had been hard seeing people who looked like her line up obediently and serve people who looked like Michael.

"Is this what rich places in Africa look like?" Juliet accidentally said out loud.

"You okay?" Ramya responded.

"Yes ooo, my love. This reflection something no be easy."

"I know, it's hard sometimes to process so many new thoughts. Hey, we're here."

"Joseph, would you like to join us?" Juliet offered.

"Yeah, you should come."

"Oh, no thank you! I'll be right next door. Enjoy your meal."

Ramya led them down to a building painted in bright yellow, which was a Kenyan-owned Italian bakery. The signs inside were painted in a mix of Italian and Swahili words that Juliet recognized. She pieced together their meanings and translated for Ramya.

"I really am good at languages."

"Yes, you are. I'm jealous."

"Good morning, are you Juliet and Ramya?" the waitress asked.

"Yes, that's us."

The waitress wished Juliet a happy birthday and returned a few minutes later with an elegant tray of pastries, tea and coffee.

"I figured this is better than the tasteless oats they'd serve us at the hotel," Ramya said.

"Are you sure you can afford this, Ramya?" Juliet gently asked.

"Of course, love. I think that new contract will work out."

"I'm sorry it's not what you want, love."

"It's okay, my dream job is out there somewhere. Besides, today is about you!" Ramya exclaimed.

Juliet didn't need to be convinced. She was confident in Ramya and the food was excellent. The restaurant had selected a beautiful arrangement of buttery, soft, crunchy, fruity, creamy, and for Juliet, nutty pastries. She felt her stomach bulging over her pants, but she didn't care. This holiday with Ramya had taught her how luxurious food could be and she wanted to eat everything.

"What are you most looking forward to in your new year of life?" Ramya asked.

"More time with you. And school! Thank you again, Ramya."

"You're welcome. I believe in you. What do you think you want to study?"

"Maybe psychology. I want to know why people think the way they do."

Juliet had been thinking nonstop about her new life as a student. For a decade, she had prayed one of her boyfriends would hear her pleas and pay for her to go to school. Every one of them had made it seem like the tuition was too expensive, the enrollment was too complicated, and the time she'd spend in class would be too strenuous on their relationship. She and Ramya had nearly completed her enrollment in fewer than four days and while in Kenya. Those bastards had been lying. And soon she would be a student. How terrifying and how amazing, all at once.

"Anything for the road?" Ramya asked.

"Nawa for you oo. I will tear my trousers if I eat more. Let's go love, abeg."

They settled back in the car and Joseph drove them to a remote location that Juliet could tell wasn't for foreigners.

"Authentic Africa," Juliet joked.

Joseph got out of the car and motioned for them to follow. He spoke to the fishermen in Swahili before turning to explain.

"They will rent their boat and crew for a few hours. They'll take us to the ocean and back to shore."

The fishermen inspected Juliet before tossing her a dirty life vest.

"You'll need it," he said.

"Eww, I can't wear this."

"Well, I guess I'll send you pictures of the beautiful fish then," Ramya teased.

Juliet reluctantly put it on, and she was soon thankful she had. The water was choppy the first few hundred meters as they sailed against the waves. Eventually the water calmed down and their boat rocked gently. The deep blue ocean surrounded them in all directions. Juliet wouldn't have known which way was back to shore.

"Look," Ramya said, pointing down.

The bottom of the boat had two glass pane openings through

which Juliet saw an incredible variety of fish. They came in every size, color, and shape and swam at different speeds. It was like the water equivalent of the animals on safari. She recognized a few species from the local markets in Lagos, but most of the life beneath her was new.

The fishermen said something to Joseph, who translated for them,

"They don't come out here often. It's one of the last protected areas of the east African coastline. The fish that escaped come here."

Juliet grabbed Ramya's hand and they carefully walked over to the far end of the boat. Although she had grown up near the ocean, the coastline of Lagos was a never-ending line of oil rigs, commercial vessels and speedboats. Out here, the ocean was left to the animals.

"Thank you for letting us visit your sanctuary," she said.

They made their way back to the shore and as always, Ramya gave the fishermen a big tip.

"My baby, always generous."

"It's the best reason to live above one's means."

"Don't drive yourself into the ground lifting others, Ramya."

"What if it's the only way to lift myself?"

"Abeg, enough philosophy talk! What's next, love?"

Joseph drove them back to the hotel, again stopping well outside of the entrance. Juliet wanted to feel like a queen on her birthday and almost asked Joseph to take them through the hotel entrance in their fine, fine car. She knew she'd be risking his job though and agreed to walk instead. Michael didn't deserve more of her energy, not today.

"Ah ah, what is this?" Juliet asked, once inside their hotel room.

"They're masseuses, for us."

"I've never had a massage before."

"I know, I'm terrible at giving them and you need this. Let

yourself melt under her hands," Ramya said.

The masseuse was a friendly woman and Juliet found it easy to listen to Ramya's advice. As the woman's hands dug deep into her, she felt years of stress dispel with every breath she exhaled. The masseuse worked through knots in her shoulders and Juliet thought back to the years of grueling work that she, her parents and her siblings had endured to save for her family's house. Long days at school, long afternoons at Daddy's construction site, and long nights at Mummy's restaurant had damaged their bodies.

Feeling the masseuse's hands on her calves, Juliet thought back to the chronic stress of her years on the streets. As the masseuse rubbed her temples and head, she tried to forget the toxic boyfriends who had killed her confidence, questioned her intelligence, and used her for sex. The masseuse asked Juliet to turn over and covered her nearly naked body with a towel. Juliet shuddered as the woman dug into her feet, and her mind flashed to endless nights dancing at clubs, hoping to pick up a rich man who would spray her plenty money. Nearing the end of the massage, the women carefully rubbed Juliet's face. She felt the judgment of being in a same-sex relationship slowly flutter until it flaked apart.

"We're done madam, thank you," the masseuse whispered.

A few tears ran down Juliet's face.

"Please madam, it's okay, let it out," the woman said.

"It's just drainage," Juliet pretended.

"Massages are for more than physical restoration," Ramya replied, looking at Juliet.

"Abi ooo, that was the spirituality I needed."

Juliet laid on the massage board for a full minute before pushing herself up to get dressed, amazed at how much tension had accumulated in her lifetime. One massage couldn't get rid of all the bad energy, but it was a good start.

Ramya over-tipped the two masseuses. This time, Juliet couldn't argue. They were worth every shilling. She and Ramya chilled together for an hour before Joseph called Ramya.

"When you're ready, get dressed so we can go to our next place," Ramya said.

Juliet couldn't believe there was more planned. After sneaking back out to their paradise car, Joseph drove them to their next stop—a private outdoor bar overlooking the sunset. The waiter walked over and asked for their order.

"One sunset breeze and…" Ramya started.

"And one mo-jee-to, of course," Juliet finished.

The waiter brought their drinks over. Juliet's was served in a tall, elegant glass. Ramya's was fun and sloppy inside a shorter cup.

"The glasses match us," Ramya said.

"Abeg, maybe in your head. We are both elegant."

"And sloppy."

"Of course, we're human," Juliet replied.

"Cheers, my love. Happy birthday."

Their glasses clinked satisfyingly, and Juliet let the cool mint flavor of her mo-jee-to coat her mouth. It was almost as good as the mojitos in Ghana.

"Thank you for everything, Ramya."

"You're so welcome. What's on your mind?"

"A lot, this. Why can't Nigeria do this—invest money in our own country and create a tourism industry to employ young people? Show the world our beautiful country?"

"Yeah, it's…"

"And if we do have tourism, it shouldn't just be white people who get to create the businesses. Ah, this journey with you, Ramya…I swear, it has opened my eyes to many things."

Juliet now understood why Ramya was so obsessed with traveling and working in other countries. She had learned so much about her own country by experiencing Kenya. Most of her last birthday she had spent locked inside her small self-contained apartment, broke and mad at the world for treating her like a puppet. If someone had told her then that she'd spend her next birthday watching the sunset on the other side of Africa, she would have smacked them for lying. Being here, seeing how different life could be made her hungry to see more…to understand more of the world.

They finished their drinks and walked back to the car. Joseph chatted with them excitedly about their next destination, a seafood restaurant and crab farm out in the middle of the water. They drove deep into the forest and pulled up to a stone driveway.

"Careful getting out, sometimes one of the crabs escapes," Joseph warned.

The restaurant operated without electricity, and so they turned on their phone flashlights to guide them. Slowly, Juliet led them along the walking path to a small outdoor restaurant entrance near the shoreline. They were pointed down another narrow walkway, like a small wooden pier, that would lead them to the dining area. Juliet angled her phone down and saw millions of crabs scurrying just a few feet below them, their claws grasping at the bottom of the poles that held up the walkway.

The walk lasted a full ten minutes and with each step, the noise on the land faded and the crabs scurrying over each other grew louder. Ramya breathed a sigh of relief after their feet were securely inside the restaurant. Juliet wished they could keep walking. She thought the sound was soothing.

"Hello, we have a reservation," Ramya said to the host.

"Are you joining the Mehta party?" the host asked.

Even in the moonlight, Juliet saw Ramya's face flush with embarrassment.

"No, just the two of us."

"Very well, here you are."

"Why are you so distant from Indians here?" Juliet asked after they were seated.

She thought back to the airport, before Ramya's memory

loss, and how Ramya had positioned herself as far away from the other Indians as possible.

"It's a combination of things."

"And it's my birthday," Juliet teased.

She knew it was a sensitive subject, but she expected Ramya to offer her more today.

"Ha, got me. I guess I never fit in with Indians back home because I was gay and interested in more than just our own culture. A lot of Indian communities in Africa are even more insular."

"Do you have a lot of Indian friends in New York and London?"

"No, but the few I do have are open-minded.

"Would you mix with the Indians living in Nigeria?"

She wasn't sure why she suddenly wanted to know. Maybe because they would be leaving Kenya in less than a week and hadn't decided when they would next see each other. Ramya looked surprised at the question.

"It depends on the individual people, of course, but no, probably not as a community."

"What do you think our life would be like in Nigeria? Would you move to Nigeria?"

"Honestly, I don't know. I turned down a few jobs there because of the homophobia."

"Would you be willing to try for some time?"

"Would you be willing to have me?"

"Of course, baby. Tell me when, ok?" Juliet said.

They held each other's hands tightly under the table. The moonlight reflected off Ramya's soft face, illuminating her like a ghost, like she had looked that awful day in Nairobi. This time, Juliet wasn't scared at this strange view of Ramya. Only a month had passed in Kenya, but Juliet felt like she was the moonlight itself, penetrating through Ramya's skin and seeing into her soul.

The waiter emerged from the maze of walkways and Juliet

was relieved to see he had nice shoes on. He placed their huge order of fresh crab, vegetables, cheddar biscuits and wine in front of them. Without electricity, other than the moon, the only light they had was a single candle. Juliet had a wonderful time showing Ramya—who she had thought knew everything about food—how to crack open the shell and suck out the meat. Ramya mostly stuck to the biscuits and wine.

Finally, back at the hotel for the night, Maurice delivered a surprise cake and a bottle of champagne to the room. Halfway into her slice, Ramya got up and walked over to her backpack. Juliet realized she had completely forgotten about her gift; it had been such a beautiful day. She pretended she didn't know what was happening as Ramya rummaged in the front pocket and drew out a black envelope.

"What is that?" Juliet asked.

"Thank you for your patience, my love. I wanted to give this to you at the end of the day. I hope you like your gift."

Ramya set down the envelope beside her. Juliet carefully looked inside and saw a flat object wrapped in gold paper.

"What is it?" she asked.

"I put together a book about our relationship. This page is a list of our favorite musicians. This page contains the little phrases we say to each other that no one else understands."

"Where did you get this information?"

"I went through all of our WhatsApp and iMessage conversations, and some parts are from memory."

Juliet was stunned and amazed at how much time and effort Ramya had put into the gift. It showed how closely she paid attention to their conversations and how important Juliet's words were to her.

"What do you think?" Ramya asked nervously.

"Ramya, this is the best gift I have ever gotten."

CHAPTER SEVENTEEN

 Ramya

 May 23

 New York City

RAMYA SURVEYED THE storage unit. However well-organized, her worldly possessions were on the ground in what could only be described as a tin box. She couldn't escape feeling like she was homeless.

"Should I leave these behind?" Ramya asked.

"What? I can't hear you. The echo is next level," Carl replied.

"Should I leave these behind!?"

Ramya held her phone over a pile of clothes for Carl to see. She saw him squint into his camera lens, trying to get a better look at the contents of her life.

"Why would you need thick winter jeans?"

"No, not those...ugh, forget it. This isn't working."

"Yeah, no shit. Besides, I didn't call you to stare at your old clothes, Ramya. I called to catch up."

"Sorry, I know. How are you?"

While Carl rambled about his persistent hatred of Geneva and how Lynne had somehow become even more annoying, Ramya continued separating her possessions into piles. She had an irrational aversion to checking in a third suitcase and was determined to make every inch of her two bags count.

"It's like, Lynne, shut up! No one cares about your damn stamp collection," Carl moaned.

"Do you think I should bring a suit?"

"What? Ramya, this is important! Lynne is still driving those of us who didn't quit the project nuts. And yeah, you should probably bring at least one suit."

"Thanks. Does Lynne ever mention her husband?"

"What? No, that horrible woman is not married."

"I meant her…never mind. How's Christian?"

"He's good! He says hi. We're flying soon."

Ramya shuddered. Carl's pilot father had been taking him flying since he was a child. As a grand gesture to convince Carl to move to Geneva, his boyfriend Christian had gotten his pilot's license.

"How long has Christian been flying? I can't remember," Ramya asked.

"Ugh, how many times do I need to remind you. It was when…wait. I forgot."

"Ha! Probably not worth risking your life then. We almost died once, after all."

"Wow, look at you joking about that! Someone is feeling good."

It was true; Ramya felt less strained talking about the shooting. Carl had always been relatively nonchalant about his near-death experience, the circumstance of which Ramya was also having a hard time remembering. In any case, the pictures Carl posted on social media of flying around the Swiss Alps were always gorgeous, but Ramya was terrified every time the two of them went up.

"Those tiny planes are so dangerous. I wish you would stop going."

"Ramya, this is literally the only thing I look forward to here."

"What time are you leaving?"

"I have a few minutes. Soooo tell me, how was your sexy holiday with your sexy woman?"

"Ugh, gag. It was amazing...overall."

"Overall?"

Her shoulders slumping, Ramya dropped the suits in her arms and sat down in a chair to properly face Carl on the phone. She told him about the anniversary of the most horrible day, the episode she had at the airport, and Juliet's time lapse when Ramya ran out the door and to the café.

"Those parts were awful. We need to talk about what happened eventually."

"Wow, yeah. Maybe you two should see a therapist? Would Juliet go?"

"I think so. Her psychology classes have already opened her eyes."

"Oh dear, Christian is calling me to go get ready. Catch up later? You'll almost be in the same time zone as us soon!"

"No worries, I'll call you a few days after I land."

Carl hung up and Ramya sat unmoved, staring at herself in the reflection of her phone. A monumental task sat before her, and she heaved herself out of the chair to get back to work.

UNICEF had reached out while Juliet and she were still in Kenya and asked her to rejoin the organization. At first, Ramya wanted to decline the position, until she read the job description and realized she could do everything remotely. It took some convincing, but they eventually agreed she didn't have to come into the office.

Rather than spend her new influx of cash on an apartment in New York, she decided to move to Lagos to be with Juliet. In her mind the move was temporary, which made packing even more annoying. She wasn't sure what to bring and so now here she was, trying to sort through a large storage container that held every object she had accumulated in adulthood.

Her phone rattled and Ramya bent down to see why. Juliet had messaged.

> **Juliet:** My love, my professor said my comments in class today were brilliant!

Ramya smiled and responded.

> **Ramya:** Congrats! NOW do you believe me when I say I admire your intelligence?

Juliet's confidence had grown substantially being back in school. Ramya knew she had made the right choice to spend her precious little money on Juliet's tuition and laptop. New York would feel empty without Juliet, so Ramya had gladly used her first UNICEF paycheck to pay for Juliet's new, spacious, modern apartment. She was meant to be in Lagos with Juliet. And she was meant to have air conditioning there.

Finally satisfied with the piles of stuff, Ramya opened her suitcase as far as she could in the remaining floor space. In Kenya, she had watched in horror as Juliet overstuffed every bag she owned, breaking the zipper one out of three times. Ramya had always been a meticulous packer and silently congratulated herself when she fit the last bits of her clothing in and the suitcases closed easily.

The late spring sun beat down on her outside of the storage unit facility. Cars blared their horns at each other as they inched their way off the Queensboro bridge. The side to Manhattan, fortunately, was nearly bare and Ramya waved down a taxi quickly. She would be staying at her friend Deepa's place for the week leading up to her flight.

"Where are you headed?" the taxi driver asked.

"East Village. 17 Avenue C, thanks."

Ramya stared out the car window at the glistening skyscrapers and bridge. She had lived in New York for a total of seven years; its views never got old. Her taxi turned onto FDR Drive, and she winked at the UN Secretariat building as it passed by. She chuckled remembering Juliet's blank expression in Ghana when she first mentioned working at the UN. How important she had felt being associated with the institution. How insignificant it seemed now. All that mattered was that she could provide a decent life for Juliet.

"Is it this one?" the driver asked.

"Oh wow, we're here already. Yep, that's the one, thanks."

She put the taxi charge on her card and over-tipped the driver in cash. US dollars wouldn't be as useful in Lagos. Better to get rid of them.

The taxi sped off and her eyes drifted to the top floor of Deepa's nondescript building. Ramya sighed. Deepa was one of Ramya's close Indian childhood friends, partly because Deepa didn't flaunt her family's money like so many other Indians did. Being spoiled was a rite of passage. In that moment, Ramya wished Deepa had taken *a little* advantage of the money and at least moved into a building with an elevator.

After struggling up the stairs, Ramya sat down at Deepa's small kitchen table with a cold glass of water. A bead of sweat dripped into the cup, causing the water to ripple and reflect Ramya's young face over and over. Even though she was constantly amazed at how well she was aging, the past few years had given her a tired look. For the longest time, Ramya thought it was due to work. After meeting Juliet, Ramya realized it was due to loneliness. Now she looked better than ever.

Ramya wandered into Deepa's bedroom and smiled at a childhood Polaroid of the two of them. Deepa had scrawled a little message—"Miss you, friend"—on the white strip at the top. They had shared a strong bond in the years they lived in the same town, even though neither of them had known back then what they had in common.

When she was eleven, Ramya's family moved to Virginia and Ramya cried herself to sleep the whole week. She couldn't forgive her parents for ripping her away from the one person who understood her. Ramya's parents promised they would take her to visit Deepa. Even as a child, she knew they were lying to shut her up. Her parents rarely sat with her for a meal in between their call schedules as doctors. They would never take the time to drive her to another state.

Unlike her parents, Deepa's mom had always been supportive of her interests, which instilled a confidence in Deepa that few Indians—gay or straight—had. *I landed here and immediately embraced my masculine side. My mom always encouraged me to be proud of who I am*, Deepa had written in a Facebook post.

That drove a lot of women, especially the feminine women, wild with attraction. Deepa never had trouble dating and had found her wife Audrey when she was in her mid-twenties.

Meanwhile, Ramya was struggling just to be seen. When she first moved to New York, she had been ecstatic to reunite with her childhood friend and rekindle their connection. Ramya had reached out to Deepa countless times to hang out, but she would reply rarely and randomly, and only with mass Facebook or email invites to group events. Even the invite to stay in Deepa's apartment this week had come through a group email. Ramya's love life was similarly disastrous in New York. Her most successful relationship had been with Faiza, who would have left her if Ramya had not used her clairvoyant dreams to figure out Faiza's next move.

Instead of concentrating on friendships or romantic interests,

Ramya had gotten lost in her career in international development—traveling to far corners of Africa, Asia, Europe, and South America—in some quest to make the lives of people she barely knew or understood better. She wasn't sure if she believed in the mission of her work anymore. She was 100% sure, however, that she was meant to have the career she did, for it was the reason she had met Juliet and the reason she had the cultural competency to make their relationship work.

For years, she had been scared to go to Nigeria due to its extreme laws on homosexuality. But she trusted Juliet more than anyone in the world. She trusted Juliet would keep her safe. Ramya looked out of Deepa and Audrey's bedroom window, which faced due east, towards Lagos. Come what may in Nigeria, Ramya was looking forward to being with her soulmate. She was ready.

Deepa and Audrey were out of town the first five days Ramya spent in their apartment. She used the time to clean up her life in America by consolidating bank accounts, meeting with colleagues in the office, double checking she had closed out her old gym memberships and buying the last supplies she needed for Nigeria.

Her five days of racing around finishing life admin stuff paid off, and by day six, she woke up ready to hang out with her old friend. Deepa and Audrey came back around 10 a.m. that day, of course while Ramya was in the bathroom. She heard them barge through the front door in the middle of a debate.

"Mais non, Deepa! C'est pas comme ça alors!" Audrey said.

"Mais si, Audrey! La dernière fois, t'as dit le même chose, mais c'est vrai!" Deepa replied.

"Shit!" Ramya exclaimed.

Ramya had dropped her contact lens in the sink and was

having trouble finding it. Deepa and Audrey continued their disagreement. Through the bathroom door, Ramya used her mediocre French skills to deduce they were debating whether New York City taxi drivers were allowed to keep their cars at home overnight.

"There you are!"

She finally found the contact lens in the corner of the sink. Frantically swirling it in her remaining contact solution, she jammed it back in her eye and dabbed off the excess moisture, so it didn't look like she had been crying. Excited to see her friend, she ran back out to the main sitting area.

"*Salut les filles!*" she shouted.

Deepa and Audrey were nowhere to be found. In a corner of the apartment, Ramya saw they had tossed their stuff on the ground, haphazardly covering Ramya's neatly packed suitcases. She ran to the kitchen window and saw they were already halfway down the block.

"What the hell! How did I miss them?"

Over the weekend, they somehow completely missed each other several more times, despite Ramya coming to the various group events Deepa and Audrey had planned at the local biergarten, the Tenement Museum and Tompkins Square Park. Either Ramya showed up too early or there were too many people at the event, and she couldn't catch Deepa's attention. At night, Ramya would either come back while Deepa and Audrey were asleep, or they would return while she was.

While Ramya was disappointed that she didn't get a chance to tell her friend about her wonderful new girlfriend, over the years, she had become accustomed to feeling isolated from Deepa. Her last day in town, she scribbled a thank you note for letting her stay and attached it to the fridge using one of the tacky magnets Deepa had collected from her cross-country driving trip with Audrey.

I'll send you a fridge magnet from Lagos, she wrote.

On Monday morning, there was no one around to help her with her suitcases. Ramya balanced each one at the staircase landing and gently slid them to the bottom. The dirt they collected was a fair trade-off for not getting sweaty before her flight.

Two hours later, Ramya stood in front of her gate at JFK airport. She didn't have enough time to go to a lounge, but she did have enough time to visit her favorite airport bar for a beer. Her non-international development friends thought it was hilarious that she flew enough to have a favorite airport bar.

"How is that one?" a guy at the table next to her asked.

"It's a pretty basic IPA, but it hits the spot before a long flight."

"You're a stronger person than me. One beer that size and I'd probably pass out on my flight! Where are you headed?"

Ramya paused, unsure whether to engage. Single men at airport bars were either lonely or chatty, sometimes both, and often creepy. She surveyed him and decided his demeanor was innocent enough.

"Lagos," Ramya replied.

"Portugal?"

"No, Nigeria."

"Do you work for the UN or something?"

"Yeah, I do actually, but that's not why I'm going...my partner is from there."

"Oh wow! That's cool. I hope you called your parents and said bye."

What a weird thing to say. Seeing Ramya's face, he quickly added,

"My daughter is twenty and I couldn't imagine her flying that far alone. Not like she cares about what I think..."

"Gotcha, I don't talk to my parents that much either. We've grown apart over the years."

"Yeah, ha. Kids are hard. My daughter woke up one day,

dyed her hair green and told me to fuck off because I didn't acknowledge her inner spirit."

Ramya shook her head. She could never imagine speaking to her parents that way. Indian parents would not tolerate such words; they'd rather cut their kids off. Dyeing her hair, however, was relatable.

"I also had a hair phase my senior year of college. When I tried to bleach it, it came out this awful gray-brown color. And my favorite shirt was a neon blue. I looked like a walking upside down cupcake," Ramya said.

"That's hilarious. Maybe I'll try telling my daughter she looks like pistachio baklava."

"Haha, that will definitely repair your relationship."

"Well, I gotta go catch my flight. Thanks for the laugh. And…hey, call your parents before you leave, ok?" the guy said.

Ramya gave him a thumbs-up in agreement, not wanting to lie with words. She had thought about her parents recently. After the most horrible day, both of her parents had taken off a whole month to stay at home with her, which was a Herculean task considering their workloads. Strange as it was, that was one of the happiest periods of her life. It was one of the few times she could remember them together as a family.

Predictably, right after Ramya started walking, her father went back to the hospital a few times a week. Her mother did the same after Ramya could make it up the stairs by herself. As her parents' normal schedules resumed, Ramya found herself sitting alone in her childhood house, which was a repeat of her actual childhood.

Ramya didn't tell her parents when she applied to grad school. They didn't tell her when they found out and called the school to pay for her tuition and a nearby apartment. She didn't ask them to visit her in the city and they never offered to come. She decided to spend the holidays in New York while they went back to India. After her first year in grad school, she didn't tell them she'd be spending three months in Senegal to do field research as part of an internship with the UN. After graduation, she didn't tell them when her office in Senegal reached out and asked her to come back as a full-time staffer. Then they didn't mention when they sold their house to split their time between Florida and India. Then she didn't mention when she moved back to New York or got the job in London. And so the cycle went, until Ramya and her parents effectively became strangers.

Before the guy at the airport, she ignored everyone who told her to call her parents. Inexplicably, five minutes before she boarded her flight, she picked up her phone and dialed their home number. The answering machine clicked on after three rings, and the prerecorded voicemail from the telecom company began,

"You have reached the voicemail box of the Durgas. Please leave your message after the tone."

Ramya took a deep breath and stuttered,

"Hey uh uh…Mom…and uh Dad, I uh, it's me, Ramya. Um…I guess I never told you that I'm gay. I met someone four months ago and I think I'm going to marry her. She's from Nigeria. That's in Africa. I'm moving there today. Ok, bye."

Ramya hung up and walked onto the plane.

CHAPTER EIGHTEEN

 Juliet

 April 29

 Nigeria

AN INTIMIDATING BUILDING stared down at Juliet. She craned her neck, allowing her eyes to slowly absorb the façade. A life-long Lagosian, she was amazed there was still a corner of the city that overwhelmed her.

"Madam, wetin dey happen?" a man said to her.

He passed by and motioned for her to get out of the way. She had been standing at the door for nearly twenty minutes, scared to take the next step. The stack of papers in her hand felt like they weighed 1000 kilos.

Her phone lit up with a message from Ramya.

"Morning love, did you go already? I know you'll do great!"

As it had on her way to Kenya, seeing Ramya's words of encouragement gave Juliet the momentum she needed to move forward, and she carefully stepped inside. Like everything in her relationship with Ramya, this school matter was going very fast.

She replayed how exactly she had gotten here, as though she were afraid this was a dream.

No, this wasn't a dream. Juliet was here, in the hallway of her new university. Following the other students, she laid out her belongings on the conveyer belt to pass through the metal detector.

"Excuse me, sir. Where is the admissions office?" she asked the security guard.

"Over there," he said, waving casually.

A thick, harsh-looking woman was inside the office, and she stared at Juliet before she had even stepped inside. Juliet sighed. Unlike in films, in real life, Nigerian women were expected to be smart *or* beautiful, not both. While she had purposely dressed down for the occasion, she was still stylish and pretty enough that the woman immediately looked at her with distrust.

"Miss, what do you want?"

"Please madam, I am here to finalize my admission."

"Have you completed the enrollment online, paid the school fees, brought your original transcripts, and obtained the affidavits?"

"Yes madam, I have the required papers here."

She handed her precious stack of papers to the woman, who sifted through and looked surprised to see everything was in order. The woman did a second pass, and Juliet knew what was coming.

"Ah ah, I see you have completed the wrong form. You have #4818. We need #4819. Come back later when you have finished the requirements."

The woman shoved the papers back at Juliet, whose heart raced so intensely that it pulled her a few steps forward. She felt her normally dry hands pool with sweat. What the hell was she going to do now?

Her phone flashed again with another message from Ramya.

"Wait please, let me call my friend who helped me with the forms."

Ramya picked up on the first ring.

"Ramya dear, please speak to the woman at the admissions office."

The woman reluctantly took her phone and repeated the problem. Juliet heard Ramya on the other end,

"The registration page lists form 4818 since Lagos is the main campus. The form you are talking about is only for campuses outside of Lagos."

The woman looked angry at being corrected, but Juliet knew she had no choice but to let her finish enrolling. She muttered something to Ramya and practically threw the phone back at Juliet.

"Your friend is not correct in the matter, but I will allow an exception this time."

Juliet was in awe at how Ramya's American accent and choice of words commanded the respect of every person they met. She didn't think it was fair her Nigerian accent disadvantaged her, but she was glad Ramya's authority at least benefitted her.

"Here," the woman said gruffly, shoving a piece of paper into Juliet's hands.

Juliet glanced down and saw five combinations of letters and numbers.

"Register for these courses upstairs. The professors will contact you directly. Do not come to me with questions about course material."

The woman waved her hand for Juliet to get out. Juliet didn't need to be told twice. Outside in the hallway, she stopped to catch her breath before she went upstairs. Her mind flashed back to a series of her education misfortunes. Since childhood, her father had said he believed in her intelligence.

"I'll make sure you go to the best university in this Nigeria," he had told her.

She had grown up believing him, believing that a university education was her destiny. The dark and rainy day her father sat her down and explained he had no money still seared in her mind. Her life fell apart in that moment.

Then she remembered how four years later, she finally managed to enroll herself at a university in a neighboring state, only to find out the admission had been a scam. A year's worth of wages disappeared with her crushed dreams. Years later, when she did gain a real admission, her money ran out and she couldn't complete the payment for the semester tuition. The university administrators demanded sex from her instead of trying to get her a scholarship. She had to drop out halfway into her first three courses. Until now, higher education had been synonymous with fear and humiliation.

The top sheet of paper the woman had handed her said "ADMISSION COMPLETE" in big red letters. Suddenly, the bad memories of the past weren't paralyzing her. She felt strong looking ahead to a brighter future and went upstairs to register for classes.

When Juliet was in secondary school and deciding on which university she wanted to attend, she had a dream that she later realized was quite common—to change the corruption in the Nigerian government by becoming a stealthy, yet honest politician. The years since had beaten back her ignorance and this time, she decided against a political science major, what she thought she would study when she was sixteen-years-old.

Instead, Juliet chose psychology, which turned out to be a great way to process her life events. Juliet fell right back into school and was able to relate what she learned in her classes with her real experience. She learned that childhood trauma affects people in adulthood, that the human brain develops fully around the age of twenty-five, and that development is slower in boys.

"Na wa, those small men I dated were actually big boys," she said.

Her young boyfriends may have been men in appearance, but they were boys in their minds.

Her favorite class was sociology, which was guest lectured by a Brazilian woman who was conducting field research on Afro-Brazilians and the Yoruba villages from which they descended. Every time Juliet walked into her class, she remembered how much she had learned and how her thirst for knowledge had expanded. Last night, she had used Ramya's Netflix account to watch a documentary about the Afro-Brazilians her professor was researching. Two months ago, she would have watched *The Real Housewives*.

"Welcome class!" Professor Silva said.

Juliet loved her thick Portuguese accent.

"Today we are studying sociological imagination. So…what it is, class?"

Professor Silva often inverted her word order. The less mature people in Juliet's class would snicker in response. Juliet thought her professor's way of speaking was charming.

Juliet raised her hand and Professor Silva called on her.

"Yes, my star student, what it is, sociological imagination?"

"It means that some of our life outcomes are not because of us as individuals. It's because of where we grew up. The systems may not be fair."

"Yes! Brava, my star. Do you have an example?"

"Nigeria does not treat women fairly. The reason my female friends don't have jobs is because of sexism. Tell me, how is that their individual fault?"

While some of the male students in the class shifted uncomfortably, Juliet felt the women collectively lean forward to listen more intently, and she grew stronger as they looked at her with admiration. She had just called out a common problem most Nigerians didn't want to acknowledge.

"And what must we do with this, sociological imagination?" Professor Silva asked.

"We must work hard as individuals, forgive ourselves when a problem is out of our control, and fight to change the system," Juliet replied.

"Amen, my sister," her classmate called out.

Professor Silva waved her over at the end of class.

"Juliet, you understand sociological imagination so well. How that is?"

"Experience. I had always thought it was my fault I couldn't elevate my life. When I read about sociological imagination, I understood a lot is determined by society."

They chatted for a few more minutes before Juliet excused herself to walk over to her developmental psych class. She sent Ramya a message on the way over, explaining what had happened. Ramya wrote back immediately,

> **Ramya:** Congrats! NOW do you
> believe me when I say I admire your
> intelligence?

Juliet smiled down at her phone, grateful for the life she and Ramya were creating for each other.

Juliet arranged her school papers on the table and told the waiter to bring her a mo-jee-toe. She was well into her second one before Chiamaka, her eldest sister, showed up.

"Ah ah, you're an hour late."

"Last hour, this hour, what's the difference? I'm here now. How you dey?"

The words printed on Juliet's psychology assignment were shaking. She slammed her eyes shut, nauseous at the thought that she would soon tell Chiamaka her secret. Her body shook and her breath became quick and shallow, as though she were treading water in the ocean. To the side, Juliet saw Chiamaka lean over and shake her shoulder.

"Hello! Are you there!?" Chiamaka shouted.

Juliet looked up and saw Chiamaka staring at her intensely. In fact, half of the restaurant was peering in their direction.

"Na wa, you called me here so I will watch you sleep?"

Juliet glanced at her phone and saw they had been sitting together at the table for half an hour.

"How did time go so fast?"

"Juliet, abeg, why am I here?"

"I'm with a woman."

"Yes ooo, we are sitting here together as two women that we are."

"No, I mean I…my friend nau!"

Why weren't the words coming to her? Why was Sylvia's voice stuck in her head again?

"Who be that? What friend?" Chiamaka asked.

"Ramya nau, my *friend*…no be only friend something. We are *together*."

"Ah ah, are you serious? That Indian woman? Heeeey na wa!"

Chiamaka's big hand clapped the table a few times, sending the cutlery and the remnants of Juliet's second moo-jee-to flying into the air. She caught the cup before it flipped over and destroyed her psychology notes.

"It's not a bad thing…" Juliet started.

"Abeg, there are many lesbians in this Lagos!" Chiamaka shouted.

Juliet sank in her chair praying no one around them heard her loud sister. She cursed herself for inviting Chiamaka out to a public place to deliver the news. Chiamaka was better off at home.

"It's great you told me! Now I know I won the bet," Chiamaka followed.

"What bet?"

"With my roommates now. You posted so many pictures of that woman in Kenya. I knew you were *with* her. They didn't believe me, so I bet them 15k Naira."

"I'm glad you are okay with us being together. It's very stupid of my sister to win money on my life though."

"Abeeeeeg, Nigeria no easy now. I go make money anyhow, so long as I don't steal it."

"Do you think anyone else in our family knows about Ramya?" Juliet asked.

"I don't think so. No one else is on Instagram...why?" Chiamaka asked.

"I thought about telling others..."

Chiamaka burst out in a sinister laughter, slapping her hands against her thighs. At least Juliet's drink was spared from the earthquake this time.

"My sister, our family will not accept this. Let's keep it a secret for now, ok? You don break up with Johannes?"

"Yes ooo. We no go see each other in months. I broke up with the yeye man after I came back from Kenya."

"So, what is it about this woman that make you go away from men?"

Juliet didn't react, as that's how she would have described her own situation six months ago. Why would a fine girl like her, who could get any man she wanted, be with a woman? Many Nigerians thought lesbians were damaged and needed a good man to become straight. She was ashamed she had thought some version of that rubbish.

"No be like that nau. I still like men. But I also like her."

Juliet chose her words carefully. Her sexual attraction to Ramya was undeniable, just like her attraction to men. She had read on blogs that meant she was probably bisexual or pansexual, and the loooong words Ramya had said their first morning together in Ghana made more sense.

188

"I like her body. And she dey very nice to me and she respect me pass my previous relationships."

"Waiter, bring me two of those!" Chiamaka shouted, pointing at Juliet's drink.

"Chiamaka, listen nau!"

"I'm listening nau! What if she runs away like those yeye men?"

"Our relationship is strong sha…"

Juliet didn't know how to describe the bond Ramya and she were forming. They were making each other better people, which wasn't something that had happened in her previous relationships. Her personal growth had always been on her own. Now she was growing with someone else.

"Yes ooo, stick with her if she go make you to travel," Chiamaka said.

"E gree more than travel."

"Money?"

"Ramya helped me enroll in school."

"Juliet, please, take me picture."

Chiamaka held out her phone for Juliet to snap photos with her drink, and Juliet patiently waited as Chiamaka touched up her full-face makeup that made her look older. Her sister arranged herself to look like a sophisticated businesswoman, her youthful face no longer a prize they had once pined after. Chiamaka posed to the left, to the right, with the drink in front, off to the side, looking pouty, looking happy, looking sexy, looking…

"Enough! So, what do you think? Of me and Ramya."

"If you like the sex, there is no problem for me."

"Jesus! What do you think of the relationship? Not the sex."

"Juliet, it's fine for me! E good say she get respect for you. Just don't tell Mummy. You know her. She go tell one useless pastor, who will advise her that the devil has possessed you."

"Do you really think everyone in the family will react so badly?"

"My sister, I don't know, honestly. You know Lagos is not the same city as when Mummy and Daddy arrived."

It was true. Lagos was the tale of two cities. Her parents were from one side, and Chiamaka and Juliet had settled on the other.

"So why are you telling me about your relationship now?" Chiamaka asked.

"Ramya go come here soon. I go like make you meet her, my sister. It's important she knows someone in the family."

"Of course! I would love that, Juliet."

"Good, we can meet next week."

"Sure, sis. Juliet, one important question for you."

"Yes?"

"You're buying these drinks, abi?"

Juliet burst out laughing and nodded. Now she remembered why she had asked Chiamaka out to a public place. A conversation over alcohol always went down easier with her sister. Chiamaka ordered another round for them.

"Wetin be dat?" Chiamaka asked, pointing to Juliet's notes.

"I don enter school now, remember? These are my term papers."

"Eeeeh! School ke! You were always the smartest child of the family. Daddy wouldn't believe it was a school holiday until you said so. He thought we were lying."

"I know, I loved school too much to skip class."

"Ehya, Juliet, I am sorry you couldn't go to university back then," Chiamaka said, snapping her fingers behind her head.

Juliet blew bubbles into her drink, afraid she would cry if she spoke. The memories were still so painful.

"When he died ooo…" Chiamaka's voice trailed off.

"Yes, I know…" Juliet's voice trailed off too.

When Eze, her eldest brother died, a part of Juliet's father's soul died as well. Juliet knew that's why her father had his work accident. He never fully recovered and neither did his business.

190

Their neighbors said the family was cursed. All Juliet knew was she missed her brother, her father was in pain and very quickly, there was no money for her to go to university.

"Better times ahead, abi?" Chiamaka said.

"Yes, my sister," Juliet said and clinked her glass against Chiamaka's.

Juliet hugged Chiamaka tightly before they parted ways. Her sister had a strong personality, and they hadn't always gotten along. Out on the street, Juliet watched Chiamaka weave through the foot traffic and flag down a taxi. It meant everything to have someone from her world accept her love for Ramya.

She also splurged on a proper taxi home and lost herself staring at the skyline of Lagos. Shanty houses using old gas-powered generators peppered the left side of the bridge, while new, giant glass and steel buildings dominated the right side. Lagos had become two cities. One was the traditional part her parents knew and loved. The other was cosmopolitan, had a thriving entertainment industry, and was a more tolerant place for gay people. Sitting in the middle was Juliet, her taxi driver fighting through traffic to get her back home.

Ramya called as Juliet stepped through her apartment door.

"Hey baby...how'd...your sister?"

The WhatsApp connection was spotty. Ramya was at the airport and Juliet only heard every other word.

"Good ooo! She said she accepts us and wants to meet."

"That's...I'm so...going...easier...sister now...I...met... guy and...parents and..."

"My love, the connection is bad. I can't hear you. Let's talk tomorrow when you arrive here, ok?"

"Sure...love...much. Bye."

"Bye, love."

She walked over to her bedroom window and took in the sounds. Her street was being reborn. Three construction sites buzzed on her block alone, their workers racing back and forth to reface old mansions into self-contained apartments. Most of the mega-wealthy of Nigeria had permanently immigrated abroad, and these vacant houses were remnants of a world they would never return to. Young people who could piece together the rent would soon move in, just as she had done a few weeks before. A new Nigeria was unfolding on her block, and it was complicated, messy and beautiful.

"Hey Juliet, you're back! How was it?" her neighbor, Isatou, called up from the compound driveway.

"Hi, Isatou. It was good."

"Make your waiting, I'll come."

Isatou's family had moved from The Gambia when she was thirteen and her pidgin English was rough. Isatou joked she was half-Nigerian, half-African.

In her first month in the new compound, Juliet had sat outside on the building stairs talking to Ramya. Even though she had had her own place before, after years of living with fifteen roommates, it was hard to break her old habit and have every phone conversation inside. One night, Isatou heard her speaking, and they got to chatting. Isatou was a lesbian, and it was her advice for Juliet to tell at least one family member she could trust about Ramya.

"My friend, hiding your relationship from some people dey possible. But e go hard for you if you to hide it from everyone you love," Isatou had said.

Isatou appeared at Juliet's front door a few minutes later. Juliet let her inside and they sat down on the couch; Isatou was practically jumping with anticipation.

"How did it go? Was she okay with it?" Isatou asked.

"It went well ooo, my friend. My sister was accepting."

"Ah, that's wonderful news, to have a family member on your side!"

"It feels so good to have her support, but what happens next?"

"Juliet, the support of my eldest brother kept me going for years. It takes time."

'It takes time, be patient' had been Juliet's way of operating for eight years. She had spent so many days lying in bed, waiting for something to happen. Being proactive and poor were incompatible for women in Nigeria. Now things were finally moving.

"I want to get to the finish line of the matter," Juliet said.

"There is no finish line here, Juliet. There are only steps forward."

However wise, Isatou's words weren't what Juliet needed in that moment. She put together a big takeaway plate of rice for Isatou, thanked her for coming and gently showed her out of the apartment.

Juliet's bed bounced lightly when she threw herself on top. A photo she had pulled from her family album slid toward her. She saw seven smiling people in the ornate clothes Mummy had made. Everything had been so perfect then. The traditional side of Lagos had served them well. Their family devotion to the local Catholic church and traditional communities had helped her father establish a thriving construction business. She and her family members had happy social lives that revolved around other church members.

She lost faith in those community pillars after her brother died. Despite her family's longstanding devotion, the community said they couldn't support her father's business in his absence. Left with no other choice, he was forced back to work too soon. A normally quick man, the grief of a dead child had weighed him down. He didn't see the metal beam fall from the crane until it was too late, until it smashed into his skull.

The community that had demanded so much from her family didn't come to their rescue after the accident, when her father lost his mobility and his mind declined. He lost his business within the year. At first, Juliet held faith that her dreams would still come true. She prayed her community would uplift her. But she finally realized that growing up, when the community praised men and insulted women, they were serious. Those were their actual beliefs.

As they had done for countless intellectually inferior boys, the community did not band together to send her to university. Her father had been the only person who saw her education as a worthy cause. Once he couldn't provide for her, Juliet had no other options. The traditional community hadn't been there for Juliet when she needed it most. So, years ago, Juliet had left that version of Nigeria.

Though she had never looked back, it wasn't until recently that she finally knew which way was forward. Forward started with picking up Ramya from the airport.

CHAPTER NINETEEN

 Ramya

 June 1

 Nigeria

"I'M SORRY, DO I know you?" Juliet said coyly to Ramya.

"I deserve that. I love you. How are you?"

Ramya wanted to grab Juliet and plant a giant kiss on her lips but settled for a quick hug and peck on her cheek. She looked up at Nigeria for the first time, searching for signs the country did not want her gayness there.

Instead, she saw normal airport stuff—a businessman running to catch a last-minute flight, families emphatically reuniting, unsanctioned porters trying to trick tourists into using their services, tired children asking their parents if they could go to sleep, and mountains of bags. So many bags.

Earlier in her career, she had imagined her first trip to the country a hundred different ways, each time landing in Abuja and searching for her UN driver to take her to an impersonal hotel. Now here she was in Lagos, looking at her soulmate and about to go to their new home. Life was funny.

"Where's the taxi?"

"On the other side of the airport. For safety measures," Juliet said, the last part sarcastically.

"Seriously? You would think with all these police people…"

"Careful, love. Don't mention these oga police people too loudly."

Despite branding itself an international city, the airport of Lagos was not equipped for such a status. A recent string of suicide bombs in the far north of Nigeria had spooked the local government in the south, and they now demanded that all passengers walk half a mile to hail a taxi or meet their driver. Ramya thought back to the weeks after the shooting, when her hip was healing, and she couldn't walk. She had no clue what a person in a wheelchair would do here and thanked God she had made a full physical recovery. The jury was still out on her mental health.

They walked together, wheeling Ramya's suitcases in the stifling heat. Lagos had two seasons: hot and wet and hot and dry. She had landed right in the middle of the former. Sinister rainclouds hovered above them and Ramya knew from experience that the impending rain wouldn't cool anything down. Sweat soaked her shirt and the humidity caused her hair to balloon to twice its resting size by the time they found the taxi Juliet had hired.

"Wow, this heat is oppressive," Ramya said, fanning herself in vain.

"Na wa, my broom," Juliet muttered, patting Ramya's hair down.

The driver took one look at Ramya and put the air conditioning on full blast. Enjoying Juliet's strokes on her broom head, Ramya looked out of the car. The international airport terminal was connected to the main highway by a single narrow paved road, which was another airport feature hardly worthy of

Lagos, Africa's biggest city. They made it all of three hundred meters before hitting their first traffic jam.

"The government was supposed to redo the road, but a politician stole the money and escaped abroad," Juliet explained.

"I hope he suffers through this airport like the rest of us. Is there a place to eat close by? The plane food was awful."

"I got you food, dear. Here."

Juliet handed Ramya a plastic bag with the words *Chicken Republic* written in red font across the side. It looked like the Nigerian equivalent of KFC.

"What is this?"

"Our national dish, jollof rice! Ours is the best."

Ramya knew better than to argue. Every West African country had some version of jollof rice, and every country claimed theirs was the best. She knew Juliet would ask her to leave Nigeria if she admitted she liked Senegal's version of jollof rice more. Such blasphemy would not be tolerated.

"Nigeria has the best jollof rice in Africa!" the taxi driver exclaimed.

"Of course, it does," Ramya dutifully agreed.

Juliet nodded approvingly.

As Ramya opened the bag, a wonderful aroma of spices wafted out and into her nose. It was a divine smell and unlike anything Ramya would ever see at KFC. She sank her teeth into a juicy piece of chicken and shoved a spoon of rice into her mouth.

"Oh my God, this is SO good! I'm going to get fat!"

Juliet and the driver burst out laughing, satisfied that Ramya recognized the superiority of Nigerian food.

Being a child of a family that rarely ate together, Ramya had to force herself as an adult to eat at an acceptable pace.

"Screw that!"

She inhaled the entire meal, barely stopping to breathe.

"This is the fast-food version, you getting me? I thought

it would be good for an American. I'm happy you enjoyed it," Juliet said.

"That was one of the best things I have ever eaten. New Yorkers would buy this by the bucket. We should totally franchise a Chicken Republic there."

"We should?"

The spices of the food bubbled up through Ramya's throat when she realized what she had blurted out. She let out a belch that smelled like jollof seasoning and embarrassment. Her body temperature rose, and she frantically tried to dry off her sweaty palms.

"Is the A/C working? I was just joking. But yeah, you should come to New York with me eventually, you know?"

"Yeah, visiting New York could be cool."

"Yeah…visiting…cool. Is it okay if I take a nap?"

"Sure, love. Lie on me," Juliet replied.

Ramya laid down in Juliet's lap and discreetly grabbed Juliet's leg out of sight of the driver. By now, she had discovered her love language with Juliet was touch. Feeling Juliet on her body often reassured her more than any words they exchanged. After a few minutes of Juliet rubbing her back, she knew Juliet's hesitation to come to New York wasn't uncertainty in their relationship. Words, however, would be required for Ramya to know exactly why. They were right at the beginning of their new chapter together, and Ramya prayed Juliet would eventually tell her what she was thinking.

It took nearly two hours for them to get to the Lekki Phase 1 area of Lagos. Juliet's apartment was located off a bridge that connected a gentrified area with a vast traditional-looking part of the city. Ramya tried her best to remember the turns to get there from the bridge, but soon gave in to her horrible sense of direction.

"I guess you'll have to come with me everywhere for a while."

"No wahala, I'm here. I won't abandon you."

"I didn't aban…never mind. Is this the place?"

"Yes, you're welcome!"

They pulled into a gated complex that contained a tall glass building and several smaller structures set in a semicircle. If Ramya blocked out the background, she might have mistaken the complex for something in New York. This was modern Africa and Ramya was excited to live in it. Together, they wheeled Ramya's suitcases into the lobby and caught the first elevator upstairs.

"Thank you for the welcome! I love your place!"

"You mean you love *our* place."

"Yes! I love *our* place."

Ramya dropped her suitcases and surveyed her new home. Juliet's style came through in the decorations and Ramya immediately felt the warmth. The bedroom was painted a soft cream color and Juliet had hired a carpenter to custom-build an impossibly tall lavender shelf and mirror. Ready-to-assemble furniture was rare in Nigeria. A bright red couch was in the middle of the sitting area, which popped against the black and white-striped walls. Ramya was grateful to see a modern kitchen. Her favorite thing to do in foreign countries was go to the grocery store, and she imagined the many meals they would cook together here.

"This place looks like it's out of a music video, it's beautiful."

"Yes ooo, I wanted a calm and relaxing vibe in the bedroom, and upbeat energy coming out of the sitting area."

"You did a great job. I feel both."

The part of the decorations that Ramya loved the most was next to the mounted TV. She walked closer to see the details of a photo of them together in Kenya. Ramya examined the dark and lush greenery behind their silhouettes, grateful for the memory and saddened by what the day had commemorated.

"I hope it's okay I chose a picture from the most horrible day anniversary," Juliet asked.

"Of course, it's okay. And it's okay to call it the shooting. Besides, this is a beautiful photo. My face has never been a part of anyone's décor."

"Oh, baby. Come here. Your heart is a part of me, so your face must be part of this apartment."

They held each other on the couch for a few minutes, until Ramya realized the smell coming from her clothes wasn't from her Chicken Republic meal.

"I should shower."

"Sure dear, let me show you the bathroom."

Juliet explained to Ramya how to turn on the water heater and left her to clean up. Ordinarily, unpacking her toiletries after a long trip was a mundane task, but Ramya was uplifted each time she opened a bag and pulled out a full-size container. It meant she would be here for a long time. Africa was home again, Nigeria, precisely.

After a long shower of oscillating hot and cold water, Ramya found Juliet sitting on the bed. Unlike in Kenya, they didn't rush straight to having sex. Ramya instead curled up in Juliet's arms, breathing in the perfume on her chest.

"Baby, are you ok? Are you tired?" Juliet asked.

"I'm so happy to be here. This feels like home."

"Me too, love. Thanks for coming to Nigeria."

"Juliet?"

"Yes, Ramya?"

"I have to ask you something."

Juliet looked scared as Ramya stood up from the bed and peered down at her feet, unsure if she should keep going. She had just landed, after all. But so much had happened in Kenya that she knew they could only address in person. A WhatsApp conversation wouldn't have been sufficient for this heavy conversation. And who was to say something wouldn't happen tomorrow? What if they couldn't risk talking about this later?

"What do you think of us going to a therapist? We haven't

discussed so many things that happened in Kenya."

"I don't know, Ramya. We can't reveal we are a couple to a therapist here in Nigeria."

"I can find someone to call in the States."

"Will they understand my culture? Will they understand my point of view?"

"How about someone in a third country? Maybe South Africa?"

Juliet sighed loudly and buried her face in her hands, evaporating Ramya's little confidence in the situation. Maybe she was pushing too hard too soon.

"Ramya, you just landed. Why are you so impatient? Why did you bring this up now?"

"My memory loss…your time lapses…I can't control my episodes and I don't think you can control yours, either. We live together now. What if it happens again? What if that breaks us?"

From Juliet's body language, slumping against the wall and shrugging, Ramya saw she was gaining ground. Sometimes impatience was justified.

"What do you think?" Ramya pressed.

"I don't know what happened. One minute it was Sunday, the next it was Friday. I don't know why thirty-six hours for me was only one for you."

"And I don't know why I completely forgot who you are. Or why I couldn't hear Sylvia on the phone. Or why I wanted to visit that scam spiritual advisor. Are we going crazy?"

"Ramya, I've never felt saner. Are we releasing the crazy?" Juliet replied.

"Wow, I never thought of that."

Maybe Juliet was right, and the episodes weren't a sign that something was wrong. Could this be Ramya's mind letting down its guard? She thought back. When she had forgotten that she was in a relationship with Faiza, they had been having the best night of their lives at a close friend's birthday party. When she forgot her plane's destination, thanks to in-flight WiFi, she had just found out she got a promotion. Whether it happened while she was still or in motion, the episodes had indeed occurred when she was happy, not when she was upset.

"But your time lapse happened when you were scared," Ramya said to Juliet.

"Yes, and you were about to do something important when you lost your memory."

"Our minds are picking inconvenient moments."

"But they are not putting us in danger. Maybe these episodes are not something to fear," Juliet said.

"We wouldn't know that when it's happening to us though."

"Ramya, love, I guess that means we need to rely on each other."

Juliet kissed her on the cheek and went to the bathroom to get ready for bed. Ramya knew there was more to discuss, but now was not the time. Juliet was not ready. She fell asleep to the comforting thought that they were in this together.

"No no, grab the cord here, not there!" Juliet screamed.

"Aaaaargh! I did it! Oh shit, no. Let me – aaaargh!"

The blaring noise of fifteen small generators drowned out Juliet's voice. Ramya did her best to lip-read, but Juliet spoke in pidgin English when she was frustrated, and Ramya couldn't decipher the instructions without hearing. She looked around her and sighed, amazed that their costly rent and impressive-looking glass building didn't come with steady twenty-four-hour electricity. There were a few daytime hours they would have to manage their own generator here on the fifth floor landing. Unfortunately, those were also Ramya's prime working hours, and she couldn't be without power.

"How did I manage this in Senegal?" Ramya screamed.

"What?"

"I said how did I manage this in Senegal?"

"What!?"

"Oh, I guess someone did this for me on the UN compound."

"What!? Hello?"

Juliet stepped away to take a phone call and Ramya officially gave up. The starter cord of the generator snapped back inside, as though taunting Ramya and her failed pulls. She called over the security guard who had been staring in her direction with a bemused expression.

"Can I pay you to do this for us?" she asked him.

"Of course, ma."

They worked out a daily price and exchanged phone numbers. Ramya handed him the first week's worth of wages. He casually walked over to the generator, and with a frustrating nonchalance, threw back the cord in one easy swoop. The generator kicked on and Ramya rolled her eyes.

"I wasn't made for manual labor."

"Ramya, let's go inside," Juliet shouted.

"Who was that?" Ramya asked, once inside.

"It was my sister, Chiamaka. She said she's free next week for lunch."

"Are we both going?"

"Do you want to?"

"Of course!"

Ramya knew Juliet's parents and two of her siblings were in Lagos. She had been wondering if Juliet would introduce her to any of the family.

"Do you think she'll like me?" Ramya asked.

"Of course, I wouldn't have you meet if I didn't."

"What do you think she'll think of me?"

"That you're a very serious person. My exes were fun, but immature."

"Better to have a partner who is fun and takes life seriously."

"Abi ooo."

They had been referring to each other as "partners" in conversation lately. Where the line between "girlfriend" and "partner" was drawn, Ramya did not know, though she did know crossing the line was important. "Partner" had a nice ring to it. Not as much as "fiancé" or "wife," though.

Juliet left to get a mango from the kitchen. Ramya walked over to their big bedroom windows to stare down at the lagoon that faced the apartment. One of the few things Ramya had in common with her father was that looking at big bodies of water put them in a reflective mood. Meeting a family member of her *partner* was a seminal moment she had not yet experienced, and she thought about how far she had come since her first visit to Africa nearly a decade ago. This continent was where she had done so much for the first time—from working a professional job to now meeting her partner's family.

"Maybe one day I will learn how to turn on a generator."

She grabbed her phone from her pocket and dialed her American number, then hit "0" as her own voicemail played.

"You have no new messages. To hear your saved messages, press 1."

Sigh.

"Still nothing?" Juliet asked, walking back in.

"Nothing. They're not going to respond, are they?"

"Are they out of town? Maybe they haven't heard it?"

Ramya tossed her phone on the bed, exasperated. Though the message she had left her parents wasn't articulate or well thought out, it was a hard thing for her to do after so many years of no contact. The least they could do was acknowledge receipt.

"Should I try them again?" Ramya asked.

"And say what? Here is another message for you to ignore?"

"What do you think of meeting them one day?"

Juliet stopped biting her mango and sighed.

"Ramya, a young Nigerian woman like me won't get a tourist

204

visa to the States."

The thought hadn't occurred to Ramya. Where could Juliet meet her parents? The only places they went were the States, India, and an occasional extended layover in between, usually in Europe. The racist immigration systems wouldn't let Juliet in as a tourist since she was a young Nigerian citizen with no other permanent residence.

"Well, we could get engaged and move to New York!"

"Please, don't joke about that, Ramya."

Ramya wasn't joking. That was a separate loaded conversation for another day. She knew Juliet was thinking about what their future together held, as well. Growing up gay, Ramya had had decades to think about committing to another woman. Juliet had had all of six months to get her mind around the idea. Ramya had to be patient.

"Can I have some?" Ramya asked, walking back over to Juliet and her mango.

Juliet cut a piece and gently dropped it into Ramya's mouth.

"Mangoes remind me of my childhood," Ramya said.

"Oh really? You don't talk about your childhood much… except about how lonely it was."

"The rare weekend my mother wasn't on call at the hospital, we would go to the Indian grocery store, bring home a bag of mangos, and spend that evening cutting them and making mango chutney as a family."

"Aw, that's a beautiful memory. Thank you for telling me."

There was a rumbling in the distance, faint at first. A storm cloud opened, dumping buckets of water on the lagoon below. The spontaneous rainstorms of Lagos were both impressive and terrifying. The distant skyline disappeared, as their visibility was reduced to fifty feet beyond the complex.

"Baby, I spent a lot of my life feeling alone. I don't feel like that when I'm with you," Ramya said.

"I know, Ramya. I'm glad you feel that way."

"I don't know what the future holds for us, but I do know that eventually, I want the world out there and your world here to meet."

Juliet grabbed her hand and squeezed. The rain outside graduated to thunder and lightning. Juliet's voice was barely audible over the storm.

"You go eat the last piece of mango, abi?" Juliet asked.

CHAPTER TWENTY

 Juliet

 June 8

 Nigeria

HABITUALLY LATE, JULIET made sure she and Ramya got to the restaurant early. Before Chiamaka arrived, she went to the toilet three times to make sure her wig, makeup and clothes were perfect. She didn't want her sister to think that she looked like a mess. Being with a woman didn't mean Juliet had stopped trying to look nice, quite the opposite.

"Are you ok?" Ramya asked when she got back from her final trip.

"I'm fine, love. Please don't act like mumu."

"What? No, I'll be on my best behavior."

"Not you, her."

Juliet nodded at the door, where Chiamaka had just entered. The eldest, Chiamaka was also the tallest sibling of their family; she had to bend down to give Ramya a hug. Sometimes, Juliet thought Chiamaka looked like a giant child.

Learning her lesson from last time, Juliet had picked 3 p.m. on a Tuesday at the Hard Rock Café as their meeting place. The restaurant was nearly empty, and Chiamaka had the entire left side of the main dining hall to scream inappropriately without an audience.

"Nice to meet you, my sister's lover!" Chiamaka shouted.

"Nice to meet you too, my…lover's sister," Ramya whispered.

Juliet saw Ramya glance around to make sure Chiamaka hadn't given away their position as partners.

"Don't worry, no one will hear her," Juliet whispered.

"Ah ah, lovers' secrets nau!" Chiamaka exclaimed.

"Hey, what would you like to order? I'm paying," Ramya said.

Free food got Chiamaka to focus like few other things, and she threw her large frame into a chair and inspected the menu with an unusual patience. Ramya gave Juliet a silly smile and whispered,

"See? I'm fun."

In the background, Juliet heard Chiamaka sounding out each menu item. Juliet inhaled deeply and tried to concentrate on the good of the moment. Looking up, she discovered she was, in fact, happy to be there. Two of the most important women in her life were sitting next to each other.

Chiamaka placed her order of a mixed drink, a soda, two appetizers and an entrée.

"I'll get my dessert later."

"Please, get anything you want. It's fine," Ramya assured.

"Good, she's not cheap!"

"No, she takes care of me."

"I know, your skin is glowing. You almost look younger than me," Chiamaka teased.

"Thanks, sis. I no dey bleach my skin anymore," Juliet replied.

A few months ago, Juliet had stopped putting her body through the hell of bleaching creams. Her exes would have complained that made her darker. Ramya only cared about Juliet being healthy and not getting skin cancer.

"You have been here in Nigeria for a week now, abi?" Chiamaka asked Ramya.

"Yes, almost. It has been wonderful! Lots of things to do."

"Ah ah, really? I guess there are things to do if you have mooooney ooo."

"Abi? And if you don't spend it carelessly," Juliet agreed.

The money her exes hadn't sent home had been spent on alcohol at the clubs. Juliet had thought that was the only thing to do in Lagos until Ramya arrived. Instead, they spent their free time at the cinema, a nice bowling alley, fancy restaurants, the gym, a spa, beach cabanas, and a game hall. Juliet had never done so much in her own city.

"Juliet told me you have your own business. Congrats, that must be a lot of work," Ramya said to Chiamaka.

"Yes! My friend, you are right. The hustle no easy, but business dey grow small small."

"What do you do?"

"I sell luxury items."

Juliet knew this meant Chiamaka sold any foreign items that she could find—clothes, phones, jewelry, bags and once, a crate of Red Bull.

"Hey Ramya, you should bring me stuffs from America!"

"She no go send you stuffs from America, abeg!" Juliet interrupted.

"Then YOU go send me things from America, abeg!"

"I no dey go America!"

How dare Chiamaka suggest she would go to the States? She had been avoiding the topic with Ramya for reasons that were slowly becoming clear to her. It wasn't fair to get Ramya's hopes up.

"Hey there, how about we sit and enjoy this lovely food?" Ramya nervously suggested.

Juliet felt Ramya's warm hand press against hers and she took another deep breath to calm down. Chiamaka knew exactly which buttons to press to piss off Juliet. Why couldn't Ifeoma, her calmer sister, be the one accepting of gay people?

"You go bring me nice things when you come back from America," Chiamaka repeated.

"Chiamaka, why you dey behave like this? I never said I will go to America."

"Juliet, you talk about Ramya morning, noon and night. You know women marry women in America, abi? So, you're telling me, hmm, you will not follow Ramya to America one day?"

"We don't know what the future has for us," Juliet responded.

"Do you want to marry my sister?" Chiamaka asked Ramya.

"I…uh…geez…I mean…"

"Ah ah! That's a yes! Well GOOD. Because my sister was a tough person before you. And I heard you were too sensitive before you met her, abi?" Chiamaka asked.

"Yeah, I guess so," Ramya admitted.

Juliet couldn't argue. At the beginning of their relationship, Ramya made fun of herself so much that Juliet thought she was depressed. If Juliet tried to playfully joke back with Ramya, she would accuse Juliet of being mean and they would fight. Finally, Juliet had to sit Ramya down and explain that was manipulative behavior, perhaps even why Ramya's exes broke up with her.

Thank you for explaining that to me. I didn't have anyone to date until I was twenty-three. I guess I'm still making basic mistakes, Ramya had said.

"See? You people fit each other," Chiamaka said, sitting back in victory.

Chiamaka barked at the waiter to bring her another drink. He was so startled at her booming voice that he nearly dropped his tray of food. Ramya was also caught off guard at the noise, and Juliet looked at her to make sure she was okay. Her partner looked exhausted yet still managed to give her another silly smile.

"I love you," Ramya mouthed.

"I love you, too," she mouthed back.

"Juliet, take me picture," Chiamaka said.

Grabbing Chiamaka's phone, Juliet leaned back and observed her sister through the camera lens. She took an endless stream of pictures of Chiamaka and her food.

"Let me see," Chiamaka commanded.

"Here, take."

"Na wa, my scar go show."

"Scar?" Ramya asked.

"Yes now, from when I rose from the dead!" Chiamaka exclaimed.

Juliet sank in her chair. She had forgotten to tell Chiamaka to avoid the death talk, one of her sister's favorite subjects. Chiamaka's near-death experience had been one of the scariest days of Juliet's life.

"What happened?" Ramya asked.

"A bogus television ooo! I plugged in that nonsense thing and BOOM!" Chiamaka said.

A local merchant had convinced a younger Chiamaka that he was selling discounted televisions. Desperate for entertainment in their boring neighborhood, Chiamaka saved money for a month, bought the biggest television from the merchant, and came back to their parents' house to plug in her prize.

"That television exploded and electrocuted me!" Chiamaka explained.

"Oh my God, were you ok?" Ramya asked.

"Yes ooo, I passed out and this my sister here found me soon after. But look at me now, haha!" Chiamaka replied.

"Did you perform CPR? Or did you call the ambulance?" Ramya asked, turning to Juliet.

"I…forgot," Juliet replied.

Years had passed since Chiamaka nearly died. Juliet couldn't quite remember what had happened in the minutes after she found Chiamaka. What mattered was that her loud sister was okay and accepted Ramya as her partner. What mattered was that Ramya and she would be okay too.

"How are you feeling? We don't need to talk about this," Juliet offered Ramya.

"No, it's fine. I'm feeling strong, thanks," Ramya replied.

"Eh, why wouldn't you be fine? Cramps?" Chiamaka offered.

Ramya and Juliet burst out laughing. Juliet was grateful they could now find humor in the situation.

"I almost died too," Ramya explained.

"Me too," Juliet said.

"Ah, so we are three strong women," Chiamaka said.

"Abi ooo!" Ramya and Juliet said in unison.

Juliet sat back and listened as Ramya and Chiamaka explained their near-death stories to each other. While these were sad stories to tell, Juliet smiled hearing them talk. Many of the struggles Juliet had faced, Chiamaka had too. Yet, a free meal was enough to satisfy her sister. Juliet had always wanted more. Now she had a partner who appreciated her struggles, wanted to elevate her, and journey through this wicked and fantastic world together. What else was she looking for in this life?

"Yes! I knew it!" Juliet screamed.

"What happened?" Ramya asked.

"I'm at the top of all of my classes!"

Juliet threw her term papers in the air, pretending they were Naira bills raining down on her. One day, she would throw actual Naira in the air, Naira she had earned.

"Congratulations, let's celebrate! Want to go out? You

pick the place."

"Thanks, love! Let's get messy!"

"A mud bath?"

"No, worse. Let's go to Bunker."

Bunker was her favorite restaurant and bar because it was always hopping, and it had the best pizza in Lagos. Only at Bunker could she do shots of tequila and still not get wasted. Her nights out with Ramya at Lagos's poshest restaurants were romantic, but she had worked hard this semester and wanted to cut loose tonight.

Clubs in Lagos were some of the nicest in the world, and Juliet started getting ready four hours before they left. No matter how grown or how educated she would be one day, Juliet knew she would always love her long going-out ritual. There was something divine about picking out her clothes, designing her makeup look, styling her wig, lacing up her sexy heels, and admiring her final look. She turned herself into a walking piece of art.

"You could be a spy with your dramatic transformations," Ramya said.

"Maybe in my next life. Hey, are you coming?"

"Oh yeah, I was taking a nap. When are we going?"

"In ten minutes, na wa!"

"Ok, no problem. I'll get dressed."

They were ready to go at the same time.

"I hate my body. I hate what I am wearing," Ramya complained.

"Baby, you look sexy. Maybe try switching it up next time?"

Ramya did look sexy to Juliet, even though she wore the same thing on their nights out—a tight black t-shirt, jeans, and stylish flat black oxford shoes. It was the same outfit Ramya had on in her Tinder profile picture. She also always wore the same style of makeup, no matter if they were going out to party or if Ramya was getting ready for a work video call. Juliet's creativity came through her appearance; Ramya's came through her words.

Clubs weren't great for words though. As soon as they entered the crowded space, Juliet grabbed Ramya's hand and led them to a corner that only regular customers knew existed. She sat them down at a table covered in a camouflage cloth to dodge the men who were hovering around like vultures. She wanted Ramya to feel comfortable while being close enough to the dancefloor so that she felt energized.

"Are you ok?" Juliet mouthed to Ramya over the thumping speakers.

"I'm fine! This is your night, let's have fun."

Juliet was about to suggest they get their first round of tequila and pizza, when a sound even louder than the speaker filled her ears.

"My SIIIIISTER!" a booming voice screamed.

Ramya jumped up, startled. Juliet whirled around to see Chiamaka; she had no idea she'd be here.

"Juliet! What are you doing here? I thought you were on international travel to Kenya!" Chiamaka continued.

Juliet rolled her eyes. They had seen each other several times since Juliet had gotten back from Kenya. This was Chiamaka's unsubtle way of announcing to everyone in the club that she was related to someone who traveled internationally.

"Sorry love," Juliet mouthed to Ramya.

"It's fine," Ramya mouthed back.

"Do you want to join us, Chiamaka?" Ramya offered.

"Are you sure?"

"Yes, come sit. We have enough room."

Ay, this woman was too sweet, Juliet thought. She appreciated how hard Ramya was working to give her a good night. Juliet was excited to spend the night out with both her partner and her sister.

"I thought you people didn't like clubs, you get me?" Chiamaka said.

"We're celebrating!" Ramya exclaimed.

"Celebrating what?"

"My school marks. I got the highest in my courses this semester," Juliet said.

"That's wonderful news, my sister! We need to toast to your success," Chiamaka replied.

"Let me get us a round of drinks," Ramya offered.

"I'll go with you, love," Juliet said.

"No, sit! Have fun with Chiamaka. I'll be right back."

Juliet didn't need to be told twice. She and Chiamaka immediately got up and danced like madwomen. Blessed with a big *nyash*, a big butt, Juliet twerked to the beat of the music. They pulled out their phones and posted each other's best moves for the world to see. Knowing Ramya was a few feet away in this her favorite club gave Juliet such an indescribable sense of joy that she lost track of time.

"Where are our drinks nau?" Chiamaka shouted.

"I don't know ooo."

The music had swept Juliet's mind away, and only when Chiamaka asked did Juliet count how much time had passed. Ramya had been gone for six full songs, at least thirty minutes. Juliet glanced at the main bar, which wasn't crowded. Most people at Bunker chose to get bottle service at their table.

"Do you see her?" Juliet asked Chiamaka.

Chiamaka stretched to elongate her already tall frame.

"Yes nau! There she is, standing and talking to that Dutch guy."

"What Dutch guy?" Juliet asked.

"Your Dutch guy nau. What was his name? Gogannes?"

"Johannes! He's here!?"

Panic immediately set in. Juliet grabbed her purse and ran to the bar. By the look on Ramya's face, she knew she was too late.

"Johannes, leave her alone!"

"Juliet! I was just telling your tomboy friend here how we

used to fuck," Johannes said, pointing at Ramya.

"What the fuck are you doing here?" Juliet replied.

"Celebrating life, like everyone else. Where have you been? You haven't responded to my messages in two months."

"Two months?" Ramya asked.

Horrified, Juliet stood still as the same pale, transparent look she had seen in Kenya spread over Ramya's body. Johannes didn't react, and neither did Chiamaka, who had finally joined them. Juliet knew then that only she could see what was happening to Ramya's body.

"You were still talking two months ago?" Ramya asked again, getting paler.

"No, love, it's not like that!" Juliet pleaded.

"It's not like what?" Johannes asked.

"Fuck off, Johannes. I'm taken. I'm in love."

"With who? With this girl? Ha!"

The insult was too much for Ramya to absorb, and Juliet watched in shock as her loving partner ran out of the club.

"No, it's not safe!" Juliet screamed.

She and Chiamaka bolted after Ramya, who easily outran them in flat shoes. By the time Chiamaka and Juliet rounded the corner from the bar, Ramya had disappeared.

"Maybe she went to the hotel?"

Chiamaka pointed to the glistening Radisson Blu in the distance. They took off in its direction, Juliet aware of how dangerous it was for any of them to be outside on the road at this time of night.

As they ran, the people around Juliet slowed down to a crawl and the distance between her and the hotel multiplied. The Radisson Blu sign that had just been clearly visible shrank to a thumbnail and then to a speck, until it completely disappeared. Soon, she couldn't see the building or her sister.

"Ramya! Chiamaka! RAMYA! CHIAMAKA!"

The people on the street didn't notice Juliet was in crisis and she screamed into a void of silence. Their faces began to stretch until they were painted so thin that they too were invisible. The street around her crumbled beneath her feet.

"RAAAMYAAAA!" she screamed again.

"It's okay, my daughter."

"Daddy?"

A face she hadn't seen outside in a decade looked at her. Her father's hand was outstretched, as if to help her float back down to earth. Unsure at first, she grabbed him and held on, feeling a strength that had long left his body.

"What are you doing here, Daddy?"

"I saw my daughter was in trouble, so I came."

He looked at her and laughed softly, as though the explanation were that simple. She looked at her hands, expecting to see their seventeen-year-old version. How else could she explain how her father stood before her, tall and proud, still indestructible?

"You were the top student this semester. Congratulations, my daughter."

"Daddy, what are you doing here? Am I dreaming?"

"Ramya will be back soon. She just needs a minute. Let's wait here together until she's ready."

"You know Ramya? Do you like her?"

"Yes, she is a good person. Let's wait for her, shall we?"

Her father led her to the sidewalk, repelling people out of his path as he walked. He waved his hand and a bench appeared.

"Juliet, here, you sit."

She looked up at his strong face and suddenly felt calm. Was she dreaming? Was she hallucinating? For now, she didn't care and was content to feel his arms wrap around her.

"Let's wait for Ramya, Juliet," he repeated.

"Do you approve of her, Daddy? Do you approve of us?"

"Let's wait here, my child."

CHAPTER TWENTY-ONE

 Ramya

 June 15

 Nigeria

RAMYA LOVED TO go to clubs. Lesbian clubs, that was. Though the energy at Bunker was distinctly predatorial, Ramya sucked in her discomfort for the sake of Juliet's celebratory night out. She appreciated how Juliet compromised on their position once inside by picking a table that would allow Ramya to remain unnoticed if she so chose. Once Chiamaka appeared, the vibe was too good for Ramya to hide, however, and she gladly offered to get them a round of drinks. Because most people in this club got table service, she was able to order right away. As she waited for her drinks, an old white guy approached her.

"Hi, my name is Johannes," the guy said to her in a thick Dutch accent.

"I'm not interested," Ramya replied.

"How do you know Juliet?"

"What?"

Glancing to her side at this Johannes guy, Ramya quickly understood this was one of Juliet's exes. Johannes had a hungry, angry look as he peered around Ramya and stared in Juliet's direction. Ramya had been in Johannes's position once, and she knew how livid she had been then, too. It was best not to engage.

"My drinks are here. I'm leaving. Have a good night," Ramya said.

"No no no, wait. How do you know Juliet?" Johannes insisted, grabbing Ramya's arm.

"Gross, don't touch me, old man!"

"How do you know Juliet!? She was the best fuck I've ever had," Johannes shouted.

"Fuck off! Don't you dare talk about Juliet that way."

Ramya was so pissed. She didn't care she was nearly a foot shorter than Johannes or that she had never physically been in a fight. A rage took over her and she lined her body up to kick him in the nuts and make him apologize. Before she could lift her leg, she heard Juliet's voice in the background. Juliet screamed at Johannes to leave Ramya alone, which calmed her; Juliet was defending her, not this asshole. Only when Johannes replied to Juliet did Ramya realize why Juliet was so desperate to get him away.

"You haven't responded to my messages in two months," Johannes said to Juliet.

"Two months?" Ramya asked.

Ramya felt the color drain from her body. She had been committed to Juliet for nearly four months. Juliet had put so many conditions and stipulations on her to be exclusive. EXCLUSIVE.

"You were still talking two months ago?" Ramya asked again.

Johannes continued to argue with Juliet until he reached a predictable conclusion.

"You're with who? With this girl? Ha!" Johannes said.

Ramya had heard enough. She had been skeptical of dating bisexual women for this very reason. Even if they had been committed, most of their ex-boyfriends felt emasculated when they found out the new love interest was a woman. Some ex-boyfriends would hurl insults at Ramya like she was a punching bag, not a human. Johannes was one of those assholes.

Without a second thought, Ramya stormed out of the club. Grateful she always wore flat shoes, it was easy for Ramya to outrun a screaming Juliet and Chiamaka behind her. Being a woman, however, she was frightened to be outside, alone and in the dark in Nigeria. As she ran at full speed, she surveyed her surroundings, and spotted the massive sign for a Radisson Blu hotel not too far away.

Though the cost was hefty, Ramya decided to spend the last of this month's paycheck on a room for the night. She needed to regroup and figure out what to do. By the time Chiamaka pounded on the door, Ramya had already taken off her shoes and was lying on her hotel room bed.

"Ramya, it's me, Chiamaka, your lover's sister! Abeg nau, open the door."

Ramya felt conflicted. She knew it was her privilege as an American that had allowed her to walk into one of the nicest hotels in Lagos looking like a sweaty mess and still book an unreserved room. She also knew Chiamaka would continue to scream "lover's sister" until security hauled her away. She reluctantly opened the door.

"Come in. Where's Juliet?" Ramya asked, peering down the hallway.

"My sister is so slow. I had to leave her. She's probably in the lobby."

Chiamaka walked inside and threw her bag on the table as though she were in her own room.

"Make yourself comfortable," Ramya muttered sarcastically.

"Thank you ooo."

After checking herself out in the mirror, Chiamaka walked over to the minibar and helped herself to a Coke, then removed and tossed her wig on the bed. If Ramya hadn't been so pissed, she would have found it amusing how similar Chiamaka's mannerisms were to Juliet's.

"Ramya, dear, why are you so upset? Why does it matter if Juliet stopped talking to Johannes two months ago?"

"Are you serious? Juliet LIED. She agreed to be exclusive with me way before that. She waited too long to break off contact."

"My sister is not a LIAR! Take that back!"

"Really? 'Cause it sounds like she lied."

"Well, she didn't cheat!"

"Okay, so she did lie?" Ramya pressed.

Chiamaka sighed.

"Ramya, did you hear me at the Hard Rock? Juliet talks about you morning, noon and night...she's in love with you."

Ramya melted at those words, and she sat back down on the bed. Chiamaka came over and rested one of her large hands on Ramya's shoulder.

"Ramya, asking a Nigerian woman to be exclusive no be the same as asking an Americana."

"I told her I would take care of her."

"You have done well for Juliet. She managed those first few months with what you gave, but I saw it wasn't easy for her in the beginning."

Ramya felt ashamed. She earned £50,000 a year in London. British salaries sucked, and until she had met Juliet, it hadn't mattered. In her world, the bills were split evenly between lesbian girlfriends. Ramya felt like she had really stepped up financially for Juliet.

"I thought she had enough to live."

"She tried. But she had to save some of the money in case you left her. And our parents? It's up to us, their children, to take care of them."

"What changed? Why did she finally stop talking to that Johannes guy?"

"You invested in her, she saw that."

"Her tuition?"

Chiamaka nodded. The amount of responsibility Juliet had in her life was enormous; Ramya had spent their first few months together frivolously spending money instead of truly honoring her commitment. Still, Juliet had not pressured or cheated on or broken up with her.

"She gave me time to grow up."

"Mmhmm. So go. Don't sit in this hotel room alone and lose her."

Ramya nodded. She watched as Chiamaka grabbed three more drinks from the minibar before excusing herself from the room.

"Well, that's not going to help with the bills," Ramya muttered.

After thoroughly searching, Ramya concluded Juliet was nowhere in the hotel lobby. The calls to Juliet's phone weren't going through and Ramya didn't have a key to the apartment. Under any other circumstance, Ramya would not have been reckless enough to wander outside alone at night in a foreign city, but love made people dumb and desperate. She retraced her steps back to Club Bunker. Miraculously, her horrible sense of direction did not betray her, and she found Juliet about halfway there. Juliet was mumbling and sitting on a cardboard box, hugging herself like it were freezing outside,

"Ok Daddy, let's wait. Let's wait," Juliet kept repeating.

Ramya guessed this one of Juliet's time lapse episodes had come with hallucinations. She knew Juliet's father was at home on the other side of Lagos.

"I'm here," Ramya said, grabbing Juliet's waist.

Juliet snapped back to reality and turned to face Ramya.

"Baby, I'm sorry."

"I know, let's go talk in the hotel."

Ramya grabbed Juliet's hand, not caring if anyone stared at them for the mild display of affection. Not being able to love her girlfriend in public was already tiring. It had only been two weeks.

Back at the hotel, Juliet poured her heart out to Ramya.

"My love, sometimes I had to have multiple boyfriends. I hated it, but I did it to survive."

"I never judged you for your past. But I told you I wanted to be exclusive."

"What if you changed your mind about being with me?"

"I...you're right. I might have. But why did you lie? Why not be honest?"

"Ramya...you're such a good person. You were insecure. I didn't cheat, Johannes and I barely spoke, and I couldn't lose you, so I lied. I promise, it was harmless."

Ramya held back tears; she believed Juliet. She believed Juliet wouldn't do anything to hurt her. If Juliet hadn't cut off communication with Johannes, it wasn't for nefarious reasons. She knew it was time to ask a question she had been afraid for Juliet to answer.

"Is this relationship too much for you, Juliet?"

"No, Ramya. It's not. Not anymore."

The ruined celebratory night was the catalyst Ramya needed. She knew their relationship was at an inflection point. If she wanted to make it work with Juliet, it was time to make more money. Her job was no longer just for her; it was also for someone else's future. She couldn't keep pushing off a career change she had long considered.

"And submit," she said to herself.

Emails went out to twelve companies, leading to three interviews that month.

She really could not picture her future without Juliet. Despite her best effort, she also could not picture her future in Lagos. Ramya found the city to be unmanageable being so expensive and crowded. Lagos was not as tolerant of gay people as Juliet pretended or as much as Ramya needed. Juliet wasn't interested in moving elsewhere in the country. That meant Ramya had to convince her to leave Nigeria if they wanted a future together.

Ramya decided that to bring up the subject, it would have to be during an enjoyable occasion.

"Date night?" Ramya suggested.

"Yes! Where? Nothing too expensive though."

"Bowling and dinner? Chinese at that fancy restaurant with the basic prices?"

"Perfect, I'll get ready."

Being a weekday, the restaurant was nearly empty when they arrived. The waiter led them to the front and seated them at one of the tables that overlooked the ocean. Juliet looked stunning as she sat down. The sun reflected through the floor-to-ceiling windows and cast a beautiful glow over her perfectly contoured face.

"Can you order me the sesame chicken? I'm going to the toilet," Ramya said.

"Sure, love. Hurry back."

By the time she made it to the bathroom stall, Ramya had sweated out everything she needed to pee, even with the air conditioning blasting throughout the restaurant. Her nerves were on hyperdrive. She accidentally brought down the toilet seat with so much force that the banging noise startled the person next to her.

"Take am easy nau!"

"Sorry!"

Sitting on the seat, she buried her face in her hands. Juliet had done her eye makeup for their special night out, which Ramya saw she had smudged. She probably looked like a raccoon by now. Her eyes shut so tightly that she saw streaks of light beneath her eyelids. Music wafted through from the restaurant and Ramya heard the angelic voice of one of Juliet's favorite singers, Simi.

"I…I…I…want to be your weakness, baby…"

It was a beautiful song and the lyrics calmed her down. Now more relaxed, she asked her mind to flash back to several of her perfect memories of them together: holding each other and talking late into the night, having sex in multiple beautiful hotel rooms, meeting Chiamaka, enrolling Juliet in school. Beyond any one memory, however, was the kindness, compassion, and care they had for each other. They had the same life goals and they treated people with the same respect; they were meant to be together.

Vibrations from her own voice combined with Simi's, which slowed her heart rate down to a resting pace. She concentrated on starting her breath in her mouth and feeling it travel down to her feet. Slowly, her meditation worked, and she drifted into a trance. As though she were in one of her clairvoyant dreams, her mind detached from her body. It was peaceful, floating above, like unencumbered consciousness.

"Your weakness, babyyyyy…" Simi's voice concluded.

Floating, Ramya did not know the lyrics of the next song, and she nearly lost her concentration. Around the third verse, a woman opened the bathroom door and said,

"Ramya? Baby, are you in here? Are you ok?"

Ramya's floating mind slammed back into the swaying body beneath. When she reopened her eyes, she had no idea where she was…and after a second, she discovered she had no idea *who* she was. Her body felt like her own, yet she didn't possess any memories. The hand outstretched was hers, yet she had no recollection of what the hand had touched.

The woman continued to call out,

"Ramya, are you here? Baby, what's happening?"

She knew no one else was in the bathroom and decided to face the person on the other side, a woman she did not know. Carefully unlocking the bathroom stall, she took a few steps forward.

"Ramya, what are you doing? Are you sick? Baby, come here, let me help you wash your hands."

The woman waved her hand under the sink and water spurted out. She gently grabbed Ramya's hands, lathered them with soap, and wiped them with a paper towel.

"Come, let's go sit down."

Something told her to obey this woman, who led her back through a huge restaurant with tables set for parties of twelve, gilded goblets, and elegant chandeliers. From the confident way the woman walked and the waiters who smiled at them, she guessed they had been here before. They sat down near the front, close to windows that overlooked the ocean and a setting sun. When she looked at the view, the word that popped into her head was gorgeous. She couldn't recall where else was "gorgeous" though.

Had she seen the view before? Had she seen the ocean before? How did she know those words without knowing what they were? Had she travelled to the ocean with her parents as a child? But who were her parents and what kind of child was she? Did they miss her? Were they on their way to join this woman and her? Each second that passed and every object she saw brought a hundred questions. She had no idea how to start answering them.

"Ramya, are you having another episode?" the woman asked.

"I…I'm not sure who…"

"I wonder what you forgot this time. I guess you wouldn't know?"

"This place is gorgeous. Is home too?"

"Yes, home is beautiful too because it's with you. I love you."

Suddenly, she wasn't she anymore. She was Ramya. Memories flooded back, snapping into their rightful places, creating pictures in her brain and feelings in her heart.

"I love you too," Ramya said.

"I love you so much, Ramya," Juliet repeated.

The woman's name was Juliet. She was Ramya and she loved Juliet. Juliet was in front of her, and she and Juliet had made this time for each other because Ramya needed to ask her something very important.

"Baby, it's okay. I remember now," Ramya said.

"Are you sure? You still look pale, my love."

"I remember now, I'm sure. Thank you for finding me. Juliet, I want to spend the rest of my life with you. What do you think about getting married?"

"Yes, Ramya. I think I would like that."

CHAPTER TWENTY-TWO

 Juliet

 June 23

 Nigeria

TO KNOW IF she would say yes to a marriage proposal, there was only one place in the world Juliet needed to take Ramya. It took her three attempts to correctly dial the number, she was so anxious. Mummy picked up on the eighth or ninth ring.

"Hello?"

"Mummy, it's Juliet."

"Who?"

"JULIET, Mummy!"

"Ah, Juliet! How are you nau? How's your body?"

"I'm fine, Mummy. How are you? How is daddy?"

"E no easy, Juliet."

"I know, Mummy…I want to come visit. And I will bring a friend with me."

"Who be that?"

"A friend, Mummy. She is American and is a very nice

person. It's only to say hello."

Through the static of the bad connection, Juliet heard Mummy breathing deeply on the phone. Mummy's deteriorating hearing didn't mean she was deaf to the meaning of words.

"Na same Kenya friend?"

"Yes, Mummy. The same friend who went with me to Kenya."

"Your friend wants to see our Nigerian life, abi?"

Juliet knew how suspicious this sounded. The only people who stopped by her parents' house didn't come because things were going well. Her parents' misfortune had long become a scene for the neighborhood to pity.

"She's a very nice person. It's only to say hello."

"Hmm...you should come see Daddy. Okay Juliet, you and your friend fit come on Saturday."

"Thank you, mummy. I'll see you and Daddy soon."

She hung up the phone. Ramya was on her way back from the gym and the construction on their street had recently stopped, giving Juliet a rare moment to sit in silence with her thoughts. After her brother Eze died, her parents stopped hosting weekly church gatherings at the house. They stopped having people over altogether. This visit would be a lot for Mummy, who in her declining health, spent all her time taking care of Daddy and repairing the house's problems from its dated construction. Juliet wouldn't bring Ramya to the house if it weren't important.

"I'm back, baby. How are you?" Ramya called out.

"Hi love, I'm fine. I spoke to my mother."

"Oh? Everything ok? You don't talk to her often."

"They're fine. Hey love...I want us to go to their house on Saturday."

"Really? I didn't think you wanted us to meet."

"I know, but I'll take you there as a curious friend, okay? Not as my partner."

"Yeah, that makes sense. We should bring a huge bucket of

Chicken Republic!"

"Oh lord! Your happy place."

That was Ramya, always thinking about the food. It was a good idea though. She knew her mom would still cook, but their contribution would take away some pressure. And she needed Ramya to be happy that day.

For most of her adult life, Juliet hadn't been much of a planner because there hadn't been much that she could control. Now that the possibilities were endless, Juliet would often find herself thinking ahead to the next five steps. She tried anticipating how the visit would go, but people changed so much when they were at the beginning and near the end of their lives. No visits back to the family house had been the same because her parents were always different people.

The tension of the upcoming visit did not slow down time and instead, the rest of the week flew by. Suddenly it was Friday night, and they were preparing for the visit tomorrow.

"What about this?" Ramya asked.

"Love, please just wear a skirt or a dress."

"I want to feel like *me.*"

"You can't feel like you in a skirt? Where my parents live is very traditional."

"I know, but I think this works."

Ramya twirled around and frowned at herself in the mirror. She wore a long Nigerian shirt over jean shorts. It looked weird, and Ramya's lack of confidence didn't help.

"Here, let me fix this," Juliet offered.

"I want to wear this one."

"Ramya, please. You must look more feminine tomorrow."

"It's itchy!" Ramya complained.

Juliet felt like she was negotiating with a child.

"Why are you being so difficult? I'm already nervous about you meeting them!"

"And I'm not? This is my first time meeting any partner's parents!"

Juliet let out a guttural scream and threw the skirt in her hand on the bed. Then she cried. Not a few tears, not a slightly sad cry. She cried a full-on ugly cry. The kind she saw the women on *The Real Housewives* cry when they found out their husbands were cheating with the office secretary.

"Hey hey, Juliet. It's okay, come here."

"No (sob)…go away…(sob)…"

"Why is it so important I wear a skirt? You know I have worked in the most conservative parts of Africa and wore pants," Ramya said.

"I…(sob)…know…(sob)…"

"Then what's wrong? Is this about more than a skirt?"

Juliet hadn't told Ramya what she saw during her time lapse the night they went to Bunker. This was between her and Daddy, and to find out what happened, she needed everything to go perfectly tomorrow.

"Are you afraid your parents won't accept me if I don't wear a skirt?" Ramya asked.

"This is very stressful for me, Ramya. Please."

"Okay, okay. If it means that much to you, I'll do it."

"Thanks (sob), love."

Even with the skirt drama resolved, Juliet couldn't sleep that night. She spent seven hours staring at the ceiling and listening to Ramya's light snores. Saturday morning arrived before Juliet was fully ready. They left the house early, timing their departure so they would arrive at the Chicken Republic nearest to Juliet's family house right as it opened.

Juliet's normal way of getting to her family house, the bus, was unsafe for a foreigner like Ramya. The first two Uber drivers she booked left after hearing they'd have to go all the way to Surulere, a neighborhood in mainland Lagos. Ramya offered to hire the third driver for the day.

"Where in Surulere?" the driver asked.

"Bode Thomas Street," Juliet replied.

"20k Naira for the day," the driver said.

Juliet felt guilty about the price considering her last conversation about finances with Ramya.

"Baby, it's okay. It's to see your family. What better use of money is there?" Ramya reasoned.

As they inched their way through traffic to the other side of Lagos, the nerves in Juliet's stomach turned into a nasty nausea. When they reached Surulere, she tried concentrating on how Bode Thomas Street had changed. The middle-class neighborhood was full of apartment complexes, single family houses, shops, and schools, and every block had become more developed since Juliet had last visited. Her heart sank seeing the vibrant neighborhood's contrast to her family house, which looked even more neglected than she remembered. Her stomach churned even harder. By the time they pulled up to the house, she thought she would throw up. Fresh air helped a little, and Ramya and she grabbed the gifts they had brought—palm oil, rice, biscuits, meat and bread, and the bucket of Chicken Republic—from the car boot.

"I'll wait there," the Uber driver said.

They watched him pull over to a quiet section of the street, roll down the windows, lower his seat and close his eyes.

"Okay, it's time," Juliet whispered.

Juliet walked to the front door, stepping over the weeds that had grown through the cracks of the front outdoor stairs. Mummy opened the door before she knocked, and Juliet gingerly pushed Ramya forward. Ramya and Mummy weren't sure how to greet each other and made awkward eye contact before Ramya presented the gifts.

"Thank you, my dear," Mummy said.

A flood of emotions hit Juliet as she entered the house. Specks of paint flaked off the walls. The carpet that had once been expertly stretched over the floors was now bunching at the corners. The television that had electrocuted Chiamaka was still bracketed to the wall, even though she knew it had never been fixed. Juliet set the gifts down in the kitchen, where she saw one of Mummy's old recipes for a spicy Sunday chicken taped to the wall, the paper yellow and crinkled. Black soot, remnants from the kerosene cooker, colored the white ceiling. In the corner, Juliet saw an old gas stove that Mummy hadn't refilled in years.

Back in the main sitting area, Mummy motioned for them to sit. She and Ramya arranged the folding chairs that mummy gave them. Juliet guessed the couch still had a broken leg. The bunched-up carpet made the floor slightly uneven, and Juliet's chair lightly rocked back and forth every time she reached for her glass of water.

Juliet was terrified to imagine what was going through Ramya's mind. Rich Ramya, whose doctor parents had paid for her education in cash and who owned two fine houses in two countries. Would Ramya recognize the money and effort that had once gone into this house? Would the house's current condition make Ramya question why Juliet was with her? Would Ramya find Mummy strange and quiet instead of understanding how hard mummy had to work to take care of Daddy? Juliet's anxiety must have been obvious, for Ramya leaned over and whispered,

"It's okay, remember what I told you?"

Her nerves calmed down quickly as she recalled what Ramya had said in the car ride over.

"I've spent a lot of time speaking to West African women your mom's age."

That international development business that Ramya spoke about on their first date, Ramya's professional life, became clear to Juliet that afternoon. Ramya smiled wide, leaned forward to show her attention, complimented Mummy's traditional headdress and asked about Mummy's old restaurant. They chatted about Nigerian dishes, most of which Juliet knew

233

Ramya disliked, but pretended to love for Mummy's sake. Soon, Mummy was comfortable with Ramya, maybe too comfortable. Mummy brought out an old family album, and sat with Ramya at the dining table, the two of them happily shouting about the childhood photos of Juliet.

"She no like suffer, even back then! Look at her angry expression! She was not meant for a place like this," Mummy exclaimed.

Mummy pointed to a family portrait that was taken when Juliet was seven, the same photo Juliet had been staring at on her bed. The rest of her family had lined up obediently and smiled for the camera. Juliet was scowling.

"Everyone was happy, it was a special occasion. But my daughter, she just dey complain ALL DAY! 'I need air con, Mummy, I need air con to look pretty.' We no get air con in this part of Lagos back then. But my daughter, she no like suffer!"

"Some things never change! She still no like suffer," Ramya agreed, laughing.

"I'm going to see Daddy," Juliet said.

"Go, go," Mummy said, waving her away.

Juliet walked to the bedroom quietly and softly knocked on the door, trying not to startle her father.

"Daddy?"

"Hmm?" he said, with a smile and his eyes closed.

He was curled up on one corner of the bed, his hands tucked underneath his head like a little baby. She was so happy to see him. They had been very close during her childhood. While mummy had worked long hours at her restaurant, it had been Daddy who helped Juliet get ready for school, cooked dinner, and washed Juliet's clothes. That was radical for a Nigerian man of his generation.

"Hi Daddy, it's me, Juliet. I saw you the other day."

"Hmm? Juliet? Who be dat?"

"Daddy, it's me, Juliet. I said I…"

"He no fit understand, Juliet. His dementia don progress," Mummy said, coming up from behind.

Juliet walked over to the other side of the bed so she could see him clearly. The wrinkles were more pronounced in his thinning face and his once thick head of black hair now only held a few small patches of white. He glanced up at her. His eyes were as soft as ever. And blank. She knew he had no idea who she was.

"Him don be like this for long time?" Juliet asked Mummy.

"Three months since he last recognized anyone, including me."

She reached out to adjust his pillow; a single tear hit the fabric. The daddy she had seen outside of Bunker wasn't here in this body.

"Um…Juliet. Are you okay? Can I get you anything?" Ramya called out from the hallway.

"Ramya, come. This is a family moment," Mummy said.

Ramya slowly came up to Juliet's side and without thinking, Juliet grabbed her hand. Ramya tried to pull away. When Juliet glanced up, she saw Mummy looked happy. She held on.

"Daddy?" Juliet whispered.

"Hmm?"

Ramya came. I waited and she came, just like you said she would, Juliet said silently.

They sat around her father, watching him sleep. Birds chirped outside of the window and sunlight flooded the normally dark house. Juliet looked over and saw Ramya smiling softly at Daddy. She knew then how she would answer if Ramya asked to marry her.

"Shall we go home?" Juliet asked.

Ramya nodded. They both hugged Mummy on the way out. Juliet burst into tears during the car ride home.

"Juliet, why are you crying? Are you ok!? Did I do something wrong?" Ramya asked.

She turned to face Ramya, another ugly stream of tears pouring down her face. She could care less about looking pretty.

"Juliet, why are you crying? Please, tell me what's happening," Ramya repeated.

"I never brought any of my boyfriends to the family house. When I moved out, I swore I never would."

"Why not? I had a great time. It was an honor."

"Because we lost everything, Ramya. Because I was ashamed, and I couldn't handle it if my partner judged me. But you...you don't judge. You were just grateful to be there."

CHAPTER TWENTY-THREE

 Ramya

 June 30

 Nigeria and South Africa

ALTHOUGH RAMYA AND Juliet had established that they were not something to fear, their episodes still made Ramya nervous. The one at the restaurant had really shaken her. How could she be anyone's wife if she suddenly couldn't remember who either of them was? How would she protect Juliet? How would she protect their future kids, or even herself?

She consulted a half-dozen websites that all listed the same most likely cause:

stress. Stress. STRESS. STRESS!

It wasn't as though Ramya had previously ignored her episodes of memory loss. Shortly after the first one nine years ago, she had visited a series of doctors for extensive testing. There weren't tumors in her brain or evidence of aneurisms. There was no medical explanation other than PTSD. The doctors had advised her to find better methods to cope with her STRESS, as though it were her responsibility to successfully navigate the world as a victim of a mass shooting.

Now staring at the endless list of medical websites, she saw the same advice regurgitated. Consistent exercise, adequate rest and healthy eating weren't enough anymore.

"We need to make a change," Ramya said.

"What do you want to do?" Juliet asked.

"I know you don't want us to spend money, but…"

"It's okay. You're making more now with that side job. And this would be to invest in us, abi?"

"Yeah, it would be an investment in our future."

Nigeria wasn't giving them what they needed—to hold hands and kiss in the street, to go an entire day without fighting with the generator, and to talk to a professional about the tricks their minds were playing on them. They decided to try South Africa again and this time, Ramya agreed for Juliet to use her connections to help her get the visa. It worked. Ramya cashed in five years' worth of credit card points to buy their plane tickets and an Airbnb gift card.

They had so much fun planning their trip, slowly drinking coffee at a shop that let them hang out all day without ordering food. Ramya searched online and found them discounted tourist attraction tickets. When they took a break from planning, they would talk about the future and what it would mean to get married. Ramya was so relieved Juliet was enthusiastic about the idea. Their Airbnb in Cape Town overlooked Table Mountain, and Ramya decided that's where she would propose.

Finally, their travel day came. STRESSful as the Lagos airport was, Ramya enjoyed the fact that this time, she was traveling with Juliet, not just waiting for her on the other side. She followed closely behind Juliet as they walked down the runway to the plane.

"I'm right behind you, go ahead," Ramya said.

"Stop pushing!" Juliet exclaimed.

"That's not me. Ma'am, stop pushing!" Ramya said sharply to the woman behind her.

The other passengers were impatient, moving as though the last people to board would be forced to stand. After fighting through the crowd, they found their seats.

"You take the window," Ramya said.

"Thanks love, I also need your shoulder."

Juliet laid her head on Ramya. It felt so good having Juliet beside her. She had come to associate planes with the countdown of their time together or the countdown of their time apart. This plane was not a countdown. It was just a part of their day.

Soon, Juliet was snoring softly. Trying not to wake her, Ramya carefully lifted her bag up with her feet and used her right hand to feel around the middle pocket. The jewelry box was tucked deep inside and had thankfully gone undetected by airport security. She was determined to surprise Juliet. Finding the perfect piece on a budget had been difficult in Nigeria, so Ramya got a placeholder from Juliet's favorite seller. The bright pink stone had a lovely gradient on the outer edges, and the gold was a decent quality. Ramya wanted to get Juliet something more luxurious later when she could afford it. Maybe she would buy a ring in India if her parents ever responded.

"You'll do for now. We have time," Ramya whispered.

Juliet shifted to her other side, propping her head against the plane window. Ramya used her newly free arm to touch her screen. The in-flight entertainment window came on, and Ramya navigated to the information section. They had only been onboard for forty-five minutes; there was still another six hours to go until they reached Johannesburg.

As the time passed, Ramya occasionally checked to see which country they were over. This was the first time she had been on a cross-African flight with her partner. She couldn't stop imagining what would be the punishment if their plane made an emergency landing and they were arrested for being in a same-sex relationship. They departed from Nigeria, which gave fourteen-year prison sentences unless you had bribe money. If they were rerouted to Mauritania, they'd be sentenced to death. In DR Congo, they'd probably get off with a verbal warning. Only in South Africa would their relationship be legal and recognized. Whether it would be celebrated was another thing.

They landed in Johannesburg in the middle of the night and hurried through the airport to their connecting flight to Cape Town. The South Africans were quickly ushered through immigration and customs. Ramya made sure Juliet went first in case they tried to detain her. Juliet hesitated when it was her turn at the immigration window.

"What are you doing here, miss?" Ramya heard the agent ask Juliet.

"I…uh…am here to see my partner," Juliet replied.

Good answer, Ramya thought. Technically, it wasn't a lie and it sounded more concrete than "tourism." The immigration agent stared at Juliet's visa for a disconcerting amount of time before asking her to step aside. He called up Ramya, who put on her best understated smile before approaching. She knew from her many visits around the world that immigration agents were like French people: they thought anyone smiling too enthusiastically was either naïve or a criminal.

"What brings you here, miss?" the immigration agent asked.

"I am with my girlfriend here to tour Cape Town," Ramya said, pointing to Juliet.

"And what do you do for work?"

Ramya was surprised at the second question. She usually got a grunt and a nod before being waved through.

"I work for the United Nations."

"You work for the UN in South Africa? Where is your attestation letter?"

"No, I work for the UN in New York. I am here on holiday with my girlfriend."

She waved her UN ID badge in front of the agent, who took one look and stamped her passport.

"You're welcome," he muttered, waving them through.

Ramya didn't leave anything else to chance and slipped her badge over her neck to be on full display. She hated grandstanding UN staff who ran around Africa and acted as though they owned the continent, while simultaneously denouncing colonialism.

"I feel like an asshole," she muttered.

"You look like an asshole," Juliet agreed.

They smiled at each other and walked over to the baggage carousel, then booked an Uber to their Airbnb. Their host was a nice Afrikaner who had a nearly indecipherable accent.

"Enjoy your stay. See you in a month to get the keys," Ramya thought he said.

Juliet managed to post a video of their apartment on Instagram before her head hit the pillow. While Juliet was fast asleep, Ramya quietly arranged their bags in the bigger of the two bedrooms, trying desperately to ignore the piece of jewelry in her backpack. The temptation was overpowering. Before she was aware of what she was doing, she had created a display around the ring on a side table in the corner of the sitting room.

"I can't believe I'm doing this," she whispered.

By then, the exhaustion of missing an entire night of sleep charged in her direction, slamming into her like a bull. She sat down on the couch nearby, feeling warm and fuzzy about the question she would soon ask Juliet. The last thing she saw before her eyes shut was the glint of the red rose petals that she had secretly packed.

Since the recurring nightmare had vanished, her conscious had stopped splitting into near and far. Her body was safe while she explored the depths of her mind, which drifted to past anniversaries of the shooting. She saw the candles she had bought and the signs she and Carl had drawn for the anniversary she spent in Paris. The writing on the signs looked a bit juvenile,

Ramya saw in her dream, with a mix of calligraphy and block letters in every color that came in the pack of Sharpies. What a bad combination of styles for her, a decent artist. It was as if someone else drew the sign.

"Why were Carl and I visiting Paris in the first place?" her mind asked.

She couldn't recall. Carl's outstretched hand lit the candles before turning into an outline. Then she was in New York on her bike. Her pedometer was steadily turning as she pedaled.

"One mile down, I dedicate this to Stephen. Two miles down, I dedicate this to Megan. Three miles down, I dedicate this to Eboné. Twenty-nine miles down, I dedicate this to…"

Ramya forgot the last few names. There were too many victims to keep track.

Her mind finally brought her to the most recent shooting anniversary and with it, to Juliet. They were back near the massive field of green on the way to Maasai Mara, holding each other. Juliet made her feel so safe and secure, and that memory meant Juliet would be there to protect her in future anniversaries.

What would the next anniversaries bring? her sleeping mind wondered. As if answering her question, she flashed to a scene of Juliet standing next to a newspaper dated April 16th. Juliet looked different though, almost like she had when they first met. Her hair was the same style Ramya had seen on her in Ghana, she was bleaching her skin again, and her clothes fit snugly over a thinner body. Was this the past or the future? How could this be the past if Juliet knew about the anniversary? How could this be the future if Juliet looked like she did in the past?

"My love, where are you? I brought flowers," Juliet said in Ramya's dream.

"Thanks baby, I'm right here," Ramya tried to respond.

Ramya was confused at what she saw next. Juliet tightly gripped the bouquet, which she set down on the floor. One flower at a time, Juliet carefully ripped off their petals, which she dropped in handfuls in front of a picture. Ramya couldn't make out the face in the photo, but the motions Juliet did were distinct. They were commonly done in a Hindu prayer—usually for funerals.

"Will Mom or Dad die by the next anniversary?" Ramya asked into the void.

Juliet's voice appeared in the distance, waking Ramya up.

CHAPTER TWENTY-FOUR

 Juliet

 July 20

 South Africa

EXHAUSTED WHEN THEY arrived at the Airbnb, Juliet still managed to record every centimeter for her now growing Instagram fanbase before she passed out.

"THIS is the five-star kitchen appliances! Maaaan, check out the heated shower floors! And my God, that VIEW!"

The apartment looked straight out of a storybook, yet it was cheaper to rent than her apartment in Lagos. As her head hit the feather pillow that was covered in luxurious bedsheets, she felt like a new life was upon her.

Five hours later, Juliet was startled awake by a loud bang outside.

"Ramya!"

Juliet panicked, seeing an unfamiliar bed that was empty on the other side. Having only woken up in a few cities in her life, the glistening mountains outside of the window were even more alarming. Her mind flashed back to Kenya. Afraid that she was once again abandoned, Juliet ran down the hall to the sitting area. Ramya was passed out on the couch; her neck was awkwardly positioned to the side and a big clump of hair covered her forehead. She looked lifeless except for her slowly rising chest.

"RAMYA!"

"What!? My love! What happened!?"

"Wake up!"

Ramya snapped awake, blinking furiously to block out the blinding sunlight that flooded the room. Juliet rushed into Ramya's arms, knowing Ramya would hold her the way she wanted.

"What happened?" Ramya asked again.

"I got scared that you left."

"Oh, my love. No, I'm here for you. Hey, do you notice anything about the room?"

"Yes ooo, it's beautiful."

Juliet inspected the décor. Her style included lots of bright pinks and reds and dark blacks, though the white furniture on white carpeting on white walls was stunning. Everything about this place looked sophisticated. Maybe it was time she upgraded.

"I want a room like this one day," Juliet said.

"Maybe we can have it together?"

"Hmm, yes. I'm not sure where to get these fine, fine things in Nigeria though."

"There are other places to live."

"Ramya, I'm not moving to New York."

"Oh my God, will you look left?"

Finally, Juliet saw what Ramya had been nodding at— flowers. Ramya swelled her chest with air, lifted Juliet up, and slowly guided the two of them over to an end table. The arrangement caused blood to rush to Juliet's head. She nearly passed out as Ramya dropped to one knee.

"Juliet, I love you die," Ramya started.

It was Ramya's favorite expression; one Juliet had taught her meant "I'll love you until death."

"Nothing is simple about our relationship, except our love. I love you," Ramya continued.

"I love you, too."

"I will take care of you. I will love you how you want to be loved."

"I know, baby."

"And we can decide together where we will love. Maybe here, South Africa. Will you marry me?"

Juliet's breath quickened. For so long, she had prayed that if she stayed in Lagos and fought hard, she would be absorbed into the city's wealthy elite. Now looking down at the gentle face in front of her crystalized reality. Never would she have expected her partner to be a woman. Ramya wasn't the person she had envisioned in this moment, and it wasn't a straightforward answer as a Nigerian woman. But it was the right answer for Juliet.

"Na wa, of course I will."

Cape Town was the most gay-friendly city Juliet had ever been to, and their week was filled with celebrating their engagement. Their first night, the DJ at a lesbian club made an announcement in front of everyone. The clapping rang in Juliet's ears until the next day, and she knew the prideful feeling that came with it would last forever.

The next afternoon, the owner of a local restaurant gave them their entire meal – two entrees, a dessert and four drinks – for free. Their third night, Ramya bought Juliet the prettiest scarf and kissed her in the middle of the street, which caught the attention of a local news channel that filmed them as part of a segment on interracial love. They had become one of those beautiful same-sex couples Juliet admired on Instagram.

"It could be like this all of the time, you know?" Ramya said.

"It is beautiful here," Juliet agreed.

"We should look at apartments."

"Maybe. We'll see."

Juliet looked up at the glistening lights that outlined the V&A Waterfront. She had learned a lot about South Africa since they had arrived, and she knew these beautiful spots had been built on top of a lot of misery. As a tourist, it was easy to get lost in the majestic beauty of Western Cape and ignore the decades of apartheid that caused most of South Africa's streets to be so dangerous. She saw it all the time with the foreign workers who came to Lagos to party, and she knew everything would be different if they moved here.

"There she is," Ramya said.

Ramya threw her arms in the air and shouted,

"Sarah! Over here!"

Sarah, Ramya's friend from a previous visit to Cape Town, jogged over to hug Ramya. If Sarah's wife Beth hadn't followed closely behind, Juliet might have been jealous. It was a new feeling, being jealous of someone's relationship with Ramya. To date, Juliet hadn't met any of Ramya's exes or friends. Ramya hadn't met any of Juliet's friends. Sylvia never responded whenever Juliet called to introduce Ramya.

"Congratulations you two!" Sarah exclaimed.

Her thick accent was hard for Juliet to understand. These Afrikaners sounded more like Johannes speaking Dutch than English.

"Thank you!" Ramya replied.

"Didn't think you had it in you, my friend."

"What can I say? I had to find the right person."

Sarah's face twitched slightly. Juliet recalled how Ramya thought Sarah had a crush on her. Ramya had turned down

Sarah because they were too similar.

"I need someone who is full of life. Someone like you," Ramya had said.

Ramya grabbed Juliet's hand and they followed Sarah and Beth down to the other end of the Waterfront. A giant Ferris wheel full of people rotated above them, reflecting off the water and making it look like it was coated in diamonds.

"We're going to see so many more beautiful things together," Ramya whispered to Juliet.

"Abi ooo, we'll see the world together."

"How's South Africa treating you?" Sarah asked Ramya.

Juliet decided she had no reason to be worried. She dropped Ramya's hand and mouthed,

"It's okay, go."

Looking back at the Ferris wheel of sparkling people, Juliet slowed down and scanned the entrance, hoping it wouldn't close before they finished dinner.

"Do you want to go up?" Beth asked.

"Won't we miss our dinner reservation?"

"Eh, it's okay. The food at the Waterfont isn't great. Our table will be available later."

"You two should go. We can hold your places," Sarah suggested.

Juliet hesitated; she didn't need anything going wrong on this holiday. The idea of leaving Ramya alone with Sarah tested her confidence in their relationship.

"Baby, are you uncomfortable? I'll go with you on the Ferris wheel," Ramya said.

"Nothing will happen with you and Sarah, right?"

"Ah ah, are you jealous? It's not easy being with a hot, in-demand woman."

"Shut up, just go."

She pushed a laughing Ramya away, annoyed she had exposed her doubts. How useless of her to question their relationship after Ramya had forgiven her for Johannes.

"Come on, it's this way," Beth said, pointing ahead.

They walked toward the ticket booth. Juliet became aware this was her first time stepping away from Ramya in South Africa, who had become like a crutch in foreign countries. Surprisingly, Juliet found her footing quickly and felt more legitimate as an international traveler as their distance grew.

"Congratulations on your engagement," Beth said.

"Thank you! How long have you and Sarah been married?"

"Three years. Will you two remain in Nigeria?"

Beth's energy was calming, and Juliet immediately liked her. She sensed Beth was also full of life and could be trusted with real answers.

"I want to, but Nigeria won't allow our marriage."

"Wow, that's hard if you must give up your country for a person. Where will you live?"

"I know Ramya wants to go back to New York."

"New York! What a dream!"

Juliet sighed. That's what everyone said when they found out that's where Ramya called home.

"Just two?" the Ferris wheel attendant asked.

"Yes, here," Juliet said, handing him the money for both tickets.

"I can pay you back," Beth said.

"No, it's fine. Thanks for the company."

The attendant showed them into their pod and shut the door. A few minutes of loading other passengers later, and they were finally lifted to the top. The view wasn't as impressive from up above; the night sky had settled, and they mostly saw darkness.

"You don't want to go to New York?" Beth guessed.

Out of the corner of her eye, Juliet glanced at Beth's face. South Africans were every shade of skin color, yet they divided each other up into many race categories that Juliet did not understand as a Nigerian. She decided Beth was similar enough to her to understand her predicament.

"Americans kill Black people a lot."

"I know, we see it on the news here."

"What if they kill me?"

"Ramya is Indian. Does she understand?"

"She does. She suggested we move here, to South Africa."

Beth fell quiet. Juliet peered down. They were far from the ground, and Juliet knew from the strong silence that there was something Beth needed to explain, something Juliet would not see about South Africa from up here.

"South Africa is dangerous. You should move to New York," Beth said.

"Americans kill…"

"Yes, yes, I know. But targeted violence is not a uniquely American thing, Juliet."

Juliet felt her body go rigid at the thought of immigrating to the States. She had seen videos of so many Black people in America getting killed by the police or another angry white person. Few of those killers went to prison, and Juliet felt there was nothing to stop them. Even if she weren't killed, what would happen if she were hurt or imprisoned? What if Ramya had a memory loss episode and couldn't help? Her family wouldn't get a visa to come save her. Then what would she do?

But Beth was right. The reason Juliet was scared to settle in America was the same reason Ramya was scared to settle in Nigeria. Woman, queer, Black, Indian—Juliet and Ramya were part of groups that were targeted for violence in both countries. Would moving to South Africa fix that? Would moving somewhere else? Maybe not. Juliet didn't know.

"I've been through a lot," Beth said.

"Me too. I know we just met each other…will you tell me what happened?"

Outside of their pod, the dark ocean looked nearly invisible.

"I lost my father when I was a teenager."

Her story started out much like that of Juliet, who closed her eyes, sensing it would soon turn more sinister.

"He was a tough man. Part of me was relieved when he died because it meant I could live freely as a lesbian," Beth continued.

Beth told Juliet about how liberating it was at first, sneaking out to the queer bars of Cape Town, getting drunk, sleeping with women.

"I didn't care about what rumors got back to my township. My father was gone; I didn't think it mattered."

Like every city, Cape Town had many sides. Beth told her how the rich white areas, the parts where the queer bars were and the only parts Juliet and Ramya had experienced, felt like central London. Half the population was queer; it was normal and accepted.

"My township is on the other side of Cape Town. Once the neighbors found out what I was doing...my father was gone, and there was no one to fight away the criminals. That's how they think, anyway."

The townships were socially conservative, and with the man of the house dead, Beth had become vulnerable without knowing.

"One night, these guys broke into our house," Beth said.

"How many?" Juliet asked.

"Four. And they...they..."

"Raped you?"

"Yes. I've been on depression meds since. It destroyed me."

Juliet sat back in her seat in horror. A similar crime had happened to one of her friends, who eventually turned to drugs to cope with the pain. Attending her friend's funeral was one of the hardest things Juliet had ever done. She never let go of the anger.

"Did the men go to jail?" Juliet asked.

"The bastards went away for a month. They're back on the street now."

"Nowhere feels safe to protect me in all my identities," Juliet said.

"And nowhere will be. New York City is at least much safer than where we are from."

"It's safer than where Ramya is from," Juliet added.

"Take advantage of that."

"You're right."

They walked back to the restaurant in mostly silence, their steps in sync. Juliet was relieved to find Ramya looking bored alone with Sarah. Beth had been right; the food was a little better than terrible, and they barely spent an hour eating. After dinner, Sarah offered to give them a ride back to their apartment. Once in the car, she suggested,

"Hey! Let us drive you to our favorite gay bar in South Africa!"

"Oh…I don't know. We've had a long night," Juliet started.

"Yes!" Ramya shouted.

Even though Juliet wasn't in the mood, Ramya was so excited that she couldn't argue. They drove for thirty minutes across Cape Town to a nearly deserted part of the city. If Ramya hadn't been by her side with two friends sitting in the front seat, Juliet would have been scared. Sarah rounded the corner and Juliet saw faint lights in the distance. As they pulled up, she saw a dusty old building decorated with cheap Christmas lights.

"There it is! THIS is the BEST gay bar in South Africa!" Sarah exclaimed.

Sarah and Beth were excited to be there and went ahead of Juliet and Ramya. Juliet walked slowly, forcing Ramya to hang back.

"How was the Ferris wheel? You've been quiet since." Ramya asked.

"Intense, my love. Beth told me something awful."

"Oh, no. What happened?"

"It's a lot, Ramya. It's better if I tell you about it tomorrow."

Dragging the heavy story on her shoulders, Juliet was the last to reach the bar. Before she could suggest they just sit outside and take it easy, Ramya stepped inside.

Despite the outside looking rundown, the music, lighting and dance floor inside were great, and Juliet felt guilty as she loosened up.

"Hey girls! Want a shot?" a guy asked Juliet and Ramya.

"Only if you pour it in front of us," Juliet replied.

"Oooh, being wise, this Nigerian," the guy replied.

He motioned at the bartender, who poured eight shots and handed them out like candy. Juliet and Ramya hadn't been drinking much lately and had to sip theirs.

"You two are so beautiful together. I'm from Namibia and we never see mixed-race couples in my country," the guy said.

Juliet looked around the room and saw many combinations of couples. Unlike many of the mixed-race couples at home, these pairs seemed like each other's firsts, not each other's affairs. His compliment replenished some of Juliet's drained energy.

"Come love, let's dance," she said to Ramya.

Moving their bodies to the music, Juliet looked over at the guy, who was dressed like everyone else in the club—he was average looking. In the few queer clubs she had been to so far, everyone was dressed to perfection. Juliet knew from experience they did that to reaffirm their fierceness or to outshine an enemy. Seeing the loosely fitted jeans, oversized hoodies, and plain t-shirts on these patrons meant being in a queer space was a normal event. Being queer was normal.

Two drinks later, they realized that Sarah and Beth were nowhere to be found and they were too far out to get an Uber back to the apartment.

"We're looking for our friends, have you seen them?" Ramya asked the guy.

"What are their names?"

"Sarah and Beth. Do you know them?"

His face fell from happy to somber.

"The only Sarah and Beth I know are outside on the patio."

"That was a weird response," Ramya said after he left.

"Abi ooo, very weird."

They decided to split up and look.

"I'll check the toilet stalls," Ramya shouted to Juliet over the music.

"Okay, I'll look outside."

She set her empty drink glass down and pushed her way to the exit. A blast of cool air hit her face and she took a moment to come down from the alcohol. Walking down the huge patio, she saw a small group of people huddled together with lighters. She decided the guy must have made the face because Beth and Sarah smoked.

Nearing the group, she walked past the fake plants and a big, hand-painted sign. Beth and Sarah were nowhere to be found. Fortunately, her phone vibrated with a text.

Ramya: Found them! We're near the karaoke machine.

Feeling chilly, she hurried back inside, not stopping long enough to get a good look at the sign. The fake plants covered some of its text:

Rest easy, our girls, Sarah and Be(covered)
5 September 20(covered)

CHAPTER TWENTY-FIVE

 Ramya

 August 1

 South Africa

Dr. Pillay took in a deep breath and blew a typhoon of air out over the microphone, causing it to screech like a banshee.

"Ow!" Ramya shouted.

"Sorry, sometimes this thing gets dusty," Dr. Pillay said.

"No wahala, it wasn't that loud," Juliet said.

Ramya rolled her eyes. Only a Lagosian wouldn't think that was loud.

She looked around, trying to search for clues it was the right choice to drag Juliet here. Dr. Pillay had a nondescript office. Only a few photos of her kids, one potted plant, a desk and a gray sectional couch decorated the space. This was the best psychiatrist Ramya had found online, not being part of South Africa's national health plan.

"So, you are here today to discuss 'episodes' you're having? Is that correct?"

"Yes. My memory loss episodes are becoming more extreme. And Juliet has had time lapses."

"Are you stressed?"

"Yes, but…"

"Well, don't be stressed! Case closed. Pay at the desk up front."

"Say wetin?" Juliet shouted.

"Just joking! I think we can try hypnotherapy for you both. Let's see what we can uncover, yaw?"

"Ramya goes first," Juliet suggested.

"So long as you go after!" Ramya exclaimed.

It had been Ramya who insisted they come, so she couldn't argue. Dr. Pillay asked Juliet to step outside during Ramya's session, which Ramya felt was unnecessary. The doctor then instructed Ramya to remove her shoes, lie down on the couch, and count backwards from twenty. Ramya went slowly.

"Ramya, I want you to think back to when you were in university."

"The day of the shooting?"

"Let's say the day before. How would you describe yourself back then?"

"Depressed. Lonely."

"Good, now think back to your last episode. How would you describe yourself?"

"Happy. Committed. Physically safe."

"Hmm."

"What?" Ramya asked, bolting up.

Dr. Pillay waved her hand, motioning for Ramya to lie back down.

"Nothing, we just started. Usually, I can narrow in quickly on a negative change of state, a stressor. You seem happier now than back then, which is unusual for your symptoms."

Ramya sat back up. She felt dumb for admitting this after dragging them to a psychiatrist. The stress she had been feeling in Nigeria had reduced greatly and she hadn't lost her memory once, not even in a minor way, since coming to South Africa. She and Juliet barely fought, no doubt because they could express themselves as a couple in Cape Town. Juliet had finally agreed to move with her to New York. They were okay on money, and she had an interview for a big new job coming up. Her bizarre dream before proposing to Juliet was still on her mind though.

She glanced back over at the photos of Dr. Pillay's children playing at the beach. They looked so happy and comfortable. Ramya couldn't recall a similar feeling from her childhood.

"Can we talk about my parents?" Ramya asked.

"Sure, whatever you want."

"I think I have basically lied to Juliet, to my friends and to myself for a long time."

"Ok, do you want to elaborate?"

"I've told people I'm not close to my parents, that we don't talk often."

"And that's a lie? In what way?"

"It's not that we talk rarely. Like…I haven't had a conversation with them in nine years. We don't talk at all."

"That's a long time. Why do you think that happened?"

Something had shifted between Ramya and her parents in the months after the shooting, but not in the way the other survivors described. Instead of growing closer, they split further apart. Ramya was only now coming to terms with this as she thought about what it would mean to settle down with Juliet and eventually have kids.

"My parents went from dictating everything about my life, to letting me do whatever I wanted."

"Why do you think they shifted so dramatically?"

"I think they felt guilty because they made me go to the university I attended. And I almost died because of it."

"Why do you think they don't talk to you now?"

"I think they hate who I became."

Nearly two months had passed since Ramya left her parents a voicemail. She had checked religiously every day for a response, but there was nothing. No return voicemail, no email, no social media messages, no texts, nothing. Their lack of communication wasn't unusual.

"Was that the only time you tried reaching out to them?" Dr. Pillay asked.

"No, I've tried before. My mom used to occasionally email me. That stopped a few years after the shooting."

"You've been calling it the shooting, not your most horrible day."

"That's what it was. It was a shooting. I almost died in a shooting. My parents let me become who I am after I almost died, and now they hate who I am."

The door burst open, and Juliet came running into Ramya's arms and said,

"Oh, love! I'm so sorry! I don't know if your parents hate you, but we're going to start our own family and we're going to love each other for the great people we are!"

"Juliet, you should wait…" Dr. Pillay started.

"No! My wife needs me," Juliet said.

"Wife! God, that sounds nice. Soon enough," Ramya said.

"Well, you made a great breakthrough in fifteen minutes. Congrats, that's not easy. Should we talk about you, Juliet, with the rest of our time?" Dr. Pillay asked.

"Abeg, not alone. I need Ramya here."

Although Ramya thought Juliet would handle the session on her own just fine, she figured at 3000 Rand per session, they might as well get group therapy out of the leftover time.

"Well, that's not conventional, but I suppose we can try," Dr. Pillay agreed.

"I'm here ooo. Fix my brain," Juliet joked.

"Come on love, take this seriously," Ramya urged.

Juliet shot a battalion of daggers with her eyes at Ramya, who wished she could erase the last fifteen seconds.

"Jesus! Why did you bring me here, Ramya? To scold me like a child?" Juliet started.

"No, sorry! I'm obviously worried about your episodes too," Ramya replied.

"What about Juliet's episodes are concerning to you?" Dr. Pillay asked.

"I mean…we're getting married, and we agreed to move to New York. What if Juliet has an episode there? What if I'm out of town or sick and can't help her?"

Dr. Pillay was rapidly writing notes. Ramya couldn't tell if they were real or a way to appear professional. Juliet shook her head, whether in response to the potentially fake notes or to Ramya's comment, she didn't know.

"So, I finally agreed to move to New York and now you are not sure you want me there? This is a huge risk for me too! Abeg Ramya, you are tiring!" Juliet exclaimed.

"When do you have these episodes?" Dr. Pillay asked.

"I don't know. When I am stressed."

"Stressed about what?"

"Stressed when we fight. When Ramya goes away…" Juliet's voice trailed.

"I'm right here, love. I have been since we met," Ramya offered.

Juliet smiled and moved closer to her on the couch. Ramya reached out with her hand as a peace offering. She hadn't come here to fight.

"We've had a few nights when I wasn't sure," Juliet said.

"Juliet, what do you need to feel assured Ramya will remain by your side?" Dr. Pillay asked.

"I don't know."

"Ramya, are you willing to commit to Juliet without knowing?"

"I don't know."

Dr. Pillay set down her notebook and rubbed her eyes behind her glasses.

"I was robbed at gunpoint a few years ago," Dr. Pillay said.

"Oh wow, I'm sorry that happened," Ramya replied.

"Thank you. I had horrible insomnia for a year after."

"How did you get rid of it?" Juliet asked.

"I knew my insomnia was driven by fear, and I knew rejoining the world instead of hiding would relieve my insomnia. But I didn't know if I went out that I would be safe."

Ramya sighed. She understood Dr. Pillay's point. The decision rested with her.

"I don't get it…" Juliet said.

Ramya turned to face Juliet, choosing her words carefully.

"My love, I think Dr. Pillay is saying that I must commit to you fully or your fear of losing me will cause more time lapse episodes. But I won't know if your episodes will stop until after I commit," Ramya explained.

"Exactly!" Dr. Pillay exclaimed.

"So, you do commit to us? We are still getting married, and I will still move to New York?" Juliet asked.

"Juliet, I commit, you have my word."

"Now *that* is a breakthrough," Dr. Pillay said, smiling.

Dr. Pillay instructed them to pay on their way out and to call back for another appointment whenever they needed help. Ramya and Juliet walked outside to the crisp morning air and stood at the edge of a steep parking lot that looked down into an empty street.

"How do you feel?" Ramya asked.

"Good, are you satisfied?" Juliet asked.

"Yeah, I think so. I'm glad I finally admitted how my parents have ignored me since the shooting."

"Oh, my love. You are a strong woman."

"Thanks, baby. And I'm glad we decided what to do next."

Juliet didn't respond, instead standing uncharacteristically still and quiet.

"What are you thinking?" Ramya asked.

"We decided the same thing we already decided before. I'm glad you got what you needed though."

Juliet was right. They had ultimately come to the same conclusion. The reasoning of the decision, however, was clearer to Ramya. She had taken so many risks professionally that she had been far less sure of. Why not commit to a new life with Juliet, someone she loved and deeply trusted?

Ramya leaned her head against Juliet's neck. She was so tired, and it was too early.

"I promise I will never drag us to a psychiatrist's office at 8 a.m. again."

"Good, otherwise I don't think this marriage thing will work."

"Haha, I don't blame you. Look, there she is."

A little blue Volkswagen pulled up. Sarah rolled down her window and said,

"Morning, early risers. Come on."

"The backseat is mine," Juliet said, climbing in.

"Thank you so much for taking us, Sarah. Sorry Beth had to work today," Ramya said.

"No worries! As a lifelong Cape Townian, I couldn't let you escape South Africa for a *third* time without seeing Stellenbosch. Is she asleep?"

Ramya pulled away her seatbelt and turned to face the backseat. Juliet was sprawled out and her chest was slowly rising. They had been in the car for less than a minute.

"Yeah, she's gone," Ramya said with a chuckle.

"I don't blame her," Sarah said.

Ramya nodded and turned to face the scenery outside. A few kilometers outside of Cape Town, the mountain range that lined the city was already receding to flat fields. The gentle rolling was peaceful, and Ramya tried her best not to fall asleep as well.

A light came on in the car dashboard.

"We need to stop and get petrol soon," Sarah said.

"Let me know how much I owe you."

"It'll be around 1200 Rand."

Ramya grabbed her bag and dug around. She pulled out the money and set it in the cupholder.

"There you go."

"Thanks…hey, if you don't mind me asking, where are you getting the money for all of your adventures?"

"I know it's surprising. You've always seen me broke."

They pulled into the petrol station and Sarah got out to fill the tank. The station was desolate so early on a Sunday morning, and Ramya wished Sarah would get back in the car while the tank filled up. She had heard of people being robbed while waiting.

"Thank God," Ramya said as Sarah reentered.

"Here's your change, rich woman."

"Keep it. To answer your question, I've doubled my income in the last year."

"Juliet must be a good luck charm."

"It's more than that. She makes me happy, and it shows. People want to work with me now. I used to just get the interview. Now I get the job."

"Wow, that's great. Are you staying at the UN?"

"I'm trying to get out. I've got a big interview coming up. What about you? How are things with Beth?"

Shocked only began to describe how Ramya felt when Juliet told her what had happened to Beth. Juliet's decision to move to New York came suddenly, and Ramya knew it was in response to what Beth had endured. While she was heartbroken that Juliet's decision was based on where Juliet was least likely to be killed, raped or beaten, she understood the logic.

"I'm so sorry about what happened to Beth. It's awful," Ramya added.

"Yaw, thanks. I love Beth with all my heart. Understandably, she has a lot of bad days. She has been on suicide watch for five years."

"Has she been able to get help?"

"We try our best. The government doesn't pay for much."

"I know the feeling. America doesn't pay for PTSD treatment, either."

"Sorry, Ramya. You went through something traumatic, too."

Ramya leaned back and concentrated on not crying. The pain inflicted on her body, Beth's body, Juliet's body, was inexcusable, yet common.

"I used to say that I was lucky to not have experienced sexual assault. Isn't that fucked up? To say I'm 'lucky' to not have gone through such trauma," Ramya said.

"It is. It's fucked up."

"Then I almost bled to death in a shooting, and I stopped describing trauma that way. Referring to trauma as 'unlucky' allows society to deflect its responsibility."

"There's no excuse. Societies don't need to be built that way," Sarah said.

"Exactly."

The wild fields gave way to well-manicured estates, and Ramya knew they were close. Experiencing Stellenbosch had been another big item on her Africa tourist list, and she steadied her breathing. Violent crimes committed to her body had already sucked away so much of her energy, and Ramya was determined not to let them ruin another day.

Signs for Stellenbosch appeared, and they arrived at their first of three vineyards a few minutes later. A château sat at the end of a long gravel driveway, facing an enormous field that stretched all the way to the horizon. Ramya felt like they had stepped back to the Victorian era, which was fitting considering they were the only non-white people there.

"Shall we?" Sarah asked.

"Yes, let's hope we have a great time. We should be so lucky," Ramya replied.

Ramya gently shook Juliet awake, and the three of them

walked inside. As their designated driver, Sarah stuck to drinking juice for the day. Lightweights Ramya and Juliet had all of four glasses of wine before they were wasted. All three of them feasted on an endless supply of charcuterie boards and small plates.

Characteristically her charming self, Juliet kept the customers at all three vineyards spectacularly entertained. Together, the three of them made fun of the uptight nature of the establishments, while also appreciating those who sacrificed to create the industry in South Africa. Ramya laughed, cried, learned, ate, drank, stumbled, and felt so many wonderful things that day.

Back in Cape Town, Sarah pulled up to their apartment and thanked them for the outing.

"I had a wonderful time."

"So did we. Come to New York and visit future us."

"Come back to Cape Town and revisit the past."

Hands interlocked, Ramya and Juliet used their other arms to wave Sarah off into the sunset.

CHAPTER
TWENTY-SIX

 Juliet

 August 23

 South Africa and Nigeria

OUR MONEY MUST complete, Juliet thought to herself.

"Let's go explore this corner!" she cried out.

"Go ahead, I'm coming," Ramya shouted back.

Juliet turned back to face Ramya, who was fighting with her hair in the wind. Ramya's hands were full holding the umbrella and water bottle she insisted on bringing. After a long battle, Ramya wiggled her head, finally getting her thick hair to flow behind her in one direction, which she gathered and tied in a ponytail with one of the hairbands she always wore, but rarely used.

"Na wa, I'm so jealous of your wavy hair," Juliet shouted.

"Is that seriously what you got out of seeing me struggle?"

"Yes now, with great hair privilege comes great responsibility."

"Can we go to the café now?" Ramya pleaded.

"Ramya, our money must complete."

"Pleaaaaase?"

Juliet gave in, even though this place—Table Mountain— was fascinating. Like in Kenya, Juliet was amazed at how many landscape changes there were in such a small area. Each section was no more than ten paces. Behind them were large grey stones that formed a path to the far south of the mountain. To her left was a thick forest. A thousand meters below were yachts parked in the calm harbor. She felt like they were on another planet.

Inside the café, they each grabbed a small bottle of rosé and a wine glass and sat down in two seats overlooking the north side of the mountain.

"Cheers, baby. Congratulations. I'm going to miss you though," Juliet said.

"Thanks, love. It'll only be for a few weeks. And if this works, we'll live our new life like queens."

A few weeks felt like an eternity to Juliet. Ramya would be flying to San Francisco for a final round job interview, and Juliet was sad she couldn't go too. She felt senseless for rejecting the idea of moving to New York with Ramya for so long. Imagine her wife flying to America or Europe and Juliet not being able to come because she couldn't get a visa. Getting residency in America wasn't just about moving; it was about being able to access the other side of the world.

"Why are they asking you to interview in San Francisco if you will work from New York?" Juliet asked.

"They said they don't normally have people fly out to their headquarters. They were so interested in my idea that they wanted to meet me in person."

These people were smart, Juliet thought. Ramya had a vision of the world worth exploring.

"Are you ready for classes?" Ramya asked.

"Yes ooo, I'm ready for more knowledge to enter my brain. Classes start in two weeks."

"Can you believe your semester after might be at an

American university in New York?"

A fly buzzed near Juliet's wine glass. She smacked it down with a serviette and her hands, and wondered if American flies were as annoying.

"I overheard some of your conversation with Sarah in the car, the part about society describing trauma as unlucky," Juliet said.

"It reminded you of your friend who was gang raped in Nigeria?" Ramya guessed.

"Yes. She died from a drug overdose a year later. Me not being gang raped...that's how I described it too. 'Lucky.'"

"I'm so sorry, Juliet. It's horrible we were taught to think that way."

"I agree. So, is that really where you want us to move, Ramya? To an America that describes the shooting as unlucky?"

"I don't have access to a better place, Juliet. At least America will help you get an education and find a good job."

After speaking to Beth, Juliet realized that was one aspect of America that made her feel secure. Gaining a world class education, a real job and real money wouldn't solve everything.

"But that will help protect me," Juliet said.

"Yes, exactly. And New York is very different from the rest of the country. Guns are highly regulated, and our marriage will be respected."

The world had been and would continue to be cruel to many African women. An education, a job and money would allow Juliet to rise above much of that adversity and become truly resilient. It would mean her future children would have stability, not experience the cruelty of the streets like she had. America with Ramya could offer her those things.

"Okay, love. I'm ready to start the K1 fiancé visa application," Juliet said.

"I love you, Juliet. Let's find us a lawyer," Ramya replied.

Their time in South Africa came to an end, and like in Kenya, Juliet felt as though she grew years in the span of a month.

"Travel is good ooo," she repeated to herself.

These self-discoveries could only happen outside of her home country. A lifetime with Ramya, Juliet knew, and she would be the most introspective person on earth.

Gutted as she was to fly back to Nigeria alone, Juliet knew it was for a greater purpose. Through tears, she and Ramya said goodbye at the Johannesburg airport; Ramya would fly from there to New York to San Francisco. Juliet dreamt about the day she could join Ramya in both cities.

Now a seasoned international traveler, Juliet didn't have trouble getting herself back to Nigeria. The gates, the papers, the food and the entertainment were easy for her to navigate. She even advised a young man who looked lost on his own.

Back in Lagos, Juliet spent her last weeks before classes restarted with Chiamaka and her parents. The visit to the family house with Ramya had eased a decade of resentment. Empowered with a bright future, Juliet was able to see her parents' situation with less anger. They had survived the Biafran War and moved west to Lagos to make a better life for their family. For twenty years, they painstakingly saved the money to buy the land and build a house. There was nothing left over in case of emergencies. Backup plans were for more privileged people. Juliet knew her parents had done the best they could. It was up to her to carry the progress forward.

Before leaving South Africa, as a couple, she and Ramya had agreed to financially provide for her family. They decided on a manageable amount to send Mummy every month. As a bonus, Juliet bought her parents a new generator, a couch and a new television for the sitting area.

"Daddy, who be dat?" Juliet asked.

"He's a funny man!" Daddy exclaimed.

"Juliet, take me photo," Chiamaka said.

She took Chiamaka's phone and turned it to snap a selfie with everyone. Her parents were resting on the new couch while they watched Daddy's favorite television series. This time, Juliet smiled in the photo.

Juliet spent the night in the family house. Early the next morning, she walked to the main junction and found a taxi willing to take her to Lekki Phase I. The reception near the family house had been spotty last night, and Juliet panicked when she finally got a signal.

"Jesus! Fourteen missed calls!"

She dialed Ramya back immediately, who picked up on the first ring.

"Ramya, baby, what's wrong? What happened?"

"Where were you, Juliet? I tried calling so many times."

"I'm sorry love, I spent the night at my parents' house. Are you ok?"

Ramya's breathing intensified and Juliet thought she heard Ramya's teeth clatter.

"Ramya, I'm sorry I missed you last night. I'm here now," Juliet reassured.

"I really needed you…"

Juliet sighed. She couldn't wait until they lived together permanently and could reach each other when they wanted.

"I'm sorry. Tell me, Ramya," Juliet coaxed.

"It's okay, you were with your family. I got an email from my mother," Ramya replied, her voice steadier.

"Oh my God! What did she say?"

"She said she and my dad are going to be in Dubai on January 4th, my birthday."

"Okay…and?"

"And they want me to come. Should I? Do you want to come with me?"

Juliet struggled to collect her thoughts without delaying her response so long that she sounded distracted. Although it had just started, her healing journey with her own parents had already been powerful and cathartic. Of course, she wanted the same for Ramya. The protective partner in her was skeptical.

"Did your mother mention the voicemail you left them?" Juliet asked.

"No, she didn't."

"Did she acknowledge me?"

"No. My mother asked how I was doing, told me about their plans and said it would be nice if I came. That's it."

"Am I even invited?"

"Would your parents have invited me if they knew we were a couple?" Ramya asked.

The optimistic side of Juliet wanted to say yes. The realistic side of Juliet wasn't sure. Parents had a funny way of denying obvious characteristics about their children.

"Hold on, love, I'm coming," Juliet replied.

"Okay, baby."

Her taxi pulled into her compound, and she handed the driver the fare and a nice tip. Ramya would be proud. Juliet ran upstairs to her apartment and positioned herself well on the couch before continuing. This conversation required her entire concentration.

"I'm back, love. Can I ask why you want to see your parents after they ignored you for nine years?"

"I need closure. If this hangs over me, I'm afraid it will affect our relationship. Besides, you plan to leave your family behind to immigrate to the States. Might be nice to have a family here," Ramya explained.

Ramya made sense. Even though Juliet had come to terms with them being alone together in America, they both came from family-oriented cultures, and Juliet knew living in isolation would be hard long-term.

"I agree, Ramya. And you know I've always wanted to go to Dubai. If I come with you, it must be for the right reasons, not because I'm being selfish."

"I know, I appreciate that. But honestly, Juliet, I don't think I can do this without you."

"Okay, you visited my parents for me, so I will do it for you," Juliet agreed.

"Thank you! I'm glad we're doing this together. I guess you'll need another visa?"

"That part I have covered. Don't worry. I love you. Talk soon?"

"Sounds good, I'm going to sleep. Love you," Ramya said, hanging up the phone.

Juliet tossed her phone on the couch and sat back, allowing the surprising situation to set in. Over the course of their relationship, Juliet had come to terms with the fact that none of Ramya's family wanted to be involved in their lives, and she was okay with that. Now she was faced with the reality that she would have to appease her in-laws. Her educated, rich, Indian in-laws. What would they think of her?

She pushed her concerns out of her mind and turned back to her phone. Ramya would never forgive her if she missed this Dubai trip, and she didn't want to waste time preparing.

A year ago, after a horrible fight with Johannes, Juliet had stormed out of his apartment and ended up at a new club. It was there she met a strange guy named Chike, who wore a three-piece suit, a bowler hat and a monocle, among the sea of men in loose jeans and button-down shirts. Juliet thought Chike was funny, and she was the only woman in the club who gave him ears. That turned out to be a blessing, for Chike was an up-and-coming musician and had gone to Dubai to film his latest music video.

She opened WhatsApp and messaged Chike:

Juliet: My friend, abeg send me your
Dubai visa contact.
Chike: Juliet, my sister! No wahala, I
go send am.

Chike put her in contact with a guy living in Abuja, who knew the right person to help her get an Emirate visa. It arrived by courier just a week after she sent in her passport.

"I'm glad you already got it! It's all part of their marketing scheme," Ramya said over the phone.

So long as it wasn't a scam or illegal, Juliet didn't care. Every Nigerian, herself included, was entranced by the many high-end Nigerian films shot in Dubai. In the most recent film, the lead actress started her day by sipping cocktails next to a crystal-clear pool. Then she got a massage in an opulent spa, ate lunch inside the Burj Khalifa, shopped for a new bag at Chanel, took a bath in a tub bigger than Juliet's kitchen, wore a couture dress, ate dinner prepared by her private chef, and took her limousine to a VIP lounge, where she met her celebrity husband. The actress was the envy of all Nigerians.

"What was the plot of the film?" Ramya asked.

"Who cares?" Juliet replied.

Juliet couldn't wait to create her own intoxicating Emirate dreams. In any case, fantasizing relieved her anxiety about meeting Ramya's parents.

CHAPTER TWENTY-SEVEN

 Ramya

 August 30

 San Francisco

EVERYONE ON HER last flight looked the same. All two hundred passengers—men, women, and nonbinary people—had slight variations of an Away carry-on suitcase, a black hoodie with a tech company logo, oversized noise-canceling headphones, and slip-on shoes. This is what the pinnacle of professional success looks like in San Francisco, Ramya thought. She had missed the memo and sat in a bright red graphic t-shirt and khaki linen pants. Thank God she'd be living in New York.

The Uber to her hotel came quickly, and she showered while rehearsing her pitch. Lunch was a bland salad and water. Carbs or anything else that made her bloat were to be avoided until after the interview. While she seriously doubted the company cared about the shape of her stomach, Ramya refused to go to the office feeling rounded.

"Welcome! Please sign in," the receptionist told her.

Expecting to see a sheet of paper, Ramya laughed when she saw the sign-in information was collected on a shiny, expensive iPad. She only needed to type the first letter of her name before it recognized who she was. The name badge that the receptionist handed her looked impressive.

"I think I'll keep this," Ramya said.

"We actually need it back before you leave."

"Well, hopefully I'll get a permanent one soon enough."

A few minutes early, Ramya took her time walking over to the conference room the receptionist had pointed out. The office was in a refurbished warehouse, with high vaulted ceilings, exposed wood beams, a coffee shop and an overall industrial feel.

"So douchey," Ramya said.

Never had she worked for an American company or expected to go into the tech industry, considering it notoriously anti-diverse. Seeing the salary ranges, however, had prompted her to do more research. She was surprised to see the number of initiatives the tech industry, this company particularly, had taken to become more inclusive, global, and open to addressing real societal issues. She wrote to a few companies whose products she had used, and three wrote back. One was serious; this one.

There were five people waiting in the conference room when Ramya arrived. She recognized one of the women as her hopefully new boss, an upbeat woman named Amara who Ramya guessed was half-Ethiopian. Having another person of color in the room calmed her.

"Welcome, Ramya! Hope you had a good flight?" a guy who introduced himself as Jonas asked.

"Thank you! My flights were good."

"Oh right, you were coming from Africa?" Jonas replied.

This is not the UN, Ramya was reminded. As if the décor and location of the office didn't make that clear, a colleague referring to "Africa" as a single location certainly did.

"Uh yes, I was with my fiancé in South Africa. But she's Nigerian."

Ramya hesitated, afraid of their reaction to the word "she."

"That's great! I'm glad you were spending time with her," Amara said.

"Yes, thanks. I miss her already."

"Aw, that's lovely. So, Ramya, we were intrigued by your proposal to create a new team. Can you tell us about that vision?" Amara asked.

"Of course. I spent almost a decade building digital tech tools for international development programs, and most of the software developers I've met use your products."

They spent the next hour discussing Ramya's vision for a new team that would work with the UN and major INGOs to strengthen, amplify and support digital tools that served a social good. Even though it wasn't an entirely new concept, the approach and Ramya's network would push the industry boundaries.

"Imagine this team making a real impact in global poverty reduction, food security, public health, criminal justice reform, you name it," Ramya said.

"Reducing gun violence. That's an issue I'd like this team to address," Amara said.

"Me too, I'd like to address that issue, too," Ramya agreed.

By the end of the interview, Ramya felt the conversation couldn't have gone better. The staff who spoke to her knew nothing about her fields of expertise, yet they were open and willing to learn. Over the years, Ramya had discovered that was the most important part.

"Ramya, thank you for coming here, all the way from Africa. This was great. We'll let you know our decision within a week," Jonas said.

"I look forward to hearing back."

"See you soon," she said to the receptionist, handing her

the visitor's badge.

Instead of going out and celebrating, Ramya headed straight back to the hotel and ordered dinner to her room. She had something far more important to do than grabbing drinks at a bar.

Three hours later, Ramya studied her spreadsheet. She was going cross-eyed staring at the detailed notes she had written. The third row was bolded and that still seemed like the right choice.

Though an expert in a niche field of technology, Ramya sucked at filling out online forms and didn't trust herself with Juliet's American K1 visa paperwork. She was grateful at the influx of extra cash her growing side consulting business was bringing, and the possibility of an even larger salary coming her way soon. She could comfortably afford to hire a lawyer.

"I think we should go with Xavier. But wait, what did you think of Katherine?" she asked.

"Baby, anyone!" Juliet said over the phone.

Juliet's voice was groggy. With the big time difference between San Francisco and Lagos, Ramya had worked late into the night while Juliet had risen before dawn. Ramya rubbed her face, rehashing the conversations with the five lawyers who had done a pro bono call with them while they were in South Africa.

"I want this to be *our* decision!"

"Baby, I trust you. I know you'll make the right choice for us."

Sucking in as much air as her lungs could hold, Ramya let out several ounces of exasperation. Juliet had perfected the art of complimenting Ramya when Juliet didn't want to do something. Which lawyer they retained was a serious choice, and Ramya preferred not to hold the entire responsibility. But they had waited so long already; it was time to decide.

"Fine, Xavier it is," Ramya said.

"Great, love. Tell him," Juliet sleepily replied.

Xavier answered right away, saying he was eager to take their case.

> Wonderful, let's speak again tomorrow morning,

Ramya replied to his email.

From what Xavier said, their case was straightforward given Ramya's income, neither she nor Juliet having been previously married, neither having kids, and them having spent a lot of time together in person. Ramya still had a gnawing feeling in her stomach that Juliet's visa would get denied. Growing up in conservative Virginia, most everyone around her thought that lesbian relationships weren't real and should be scrutinized. As an adult, she had dismissed that as ignorant people having a silly idea. But what if the foreign affairs officer who decided their application had silly ideas?

"Baby, can I go back to bed now?" Juliet asked.

"Of course, love. I'll call you later."

The top right corner of Ramya's computer screen flickered briefly before the clock reset: Tue 00:00. She had been awake for nearly thirty-six hours. With the most pressing tasks done, she finally felt like she had earned the right to sleep and closed her laptop.

Intending to rest for a few hours, Ramya slept until almost 2 p.m. She checked her phone and saw Juliet had sent her a text message.

> **Juliet:** I think you're sleeping, love. I'm going to the family house now. Love you!
> **Ramya:** Sorry I missed you, baby! I was so tired. Have a good time with your parents.

The message didn't go through and neither did Ramya's calls. With no way to speak to Juliet, Ramya ordered in more food and turned her attention back to the fun part of the visa paperwork—gathering the evidence to prove their relationship was real.

Formatting anything on her screen to look orderly and pretty was satisfying, and it was even more indulgent when the subject was her own life. Ramya stared at the trove of their pictures on her computer, smiling at the lovely memories they had created together.

She decided on the format of the captions and dates for each photo and set up a template in her favorite prototyping software. From what Xavier said on the phone, she knew to start with photos of them together with family and friends. Chiamaka, Sarah, Beth, Juliet's parents, Juliet and she soon decorated the first page. She made sure to show they were in different outfits, in different locations, and together at different times of the day.

BING!

A notification reserved for important emails popped up on her computer as she was working on the second page of photos.

"Maybe it's Carl? I think he's back from Spain," she said to herself.

Her eyes were fuzzy from the grid lines, and she decided to take a break from her formatting escapade. She opened her email and nearly fell out of her chair—the message was from her mother, who had never replied to her voicemail.

Ramya shook as she clumsily moved her mouse to the email. Afraid of what she might find on the other side, she waited a full minute before clicking on the message. She reread her mother's words several times:

Hello Ramya,

It's Mom. I'm sorry I haven't written
in a long time…I used to write to
you more often. I'm not sure why I
stopped. Forgive me. Your father and
I are spending most of our time in
India now. We're stopping in Dubai
on the way to Florida after the New
Year. We'll fly in on the 2nd and will
be there for your birthday. We would
like to host a small celebration for you
in the Burj Khalifa. Please join us. I will
send you the details.

Love,
Mom

Tears poured down Ramya's face before she knew she was crying. The surge of emotions knowing her mother wanted to know about her life was too great to handle in silence. She called Juliet repeatedly, fourteen times in total. Juliet didn't call back until well into Ramya's night.

"Ramya, baby, what's wrong? What happened?"

"Where were you, Juliet? I tried calling so many times."

"I'm sorry love, I spent the night at my parents' house. Are you ok?"

Ramya's body shook as she read the email out loud. At first, Juliet was skeptical about the situation.

"Can I ask why you want to see your parents after they ignored you for nine years?" Juliet asked.

She explained how she needed closure and how it might lead to Juliet having more than only Ramya to count on as family in America.

"Okay, you visited my parents for me, so I will do it for you," Juliet agreed.

Juliet had the right contact to get the Emirate visa, and Ramya trusted her to get it done. They hung up the phone and Ramya navigated to a picture of the Burj Khalifa on her computer. The impressive building had been unveiled to the public the same day as her birthday. She had always wanted to go, and her parents never had the time to take her. The location of this birthday celebration was as significant as the celebration itself. Ramya was both ecstatic and terrified to reply to her mother.

Hello Mom,

It's really nice to hear from you! I left you and Dad a voicemail about three months ago. Maybe you were already in India and didn't get the message? I hope you two are enjoying your time there. Tell everyone I said hi.

Mom, I need to tell you something . . . I'm gay. I always knew. Maybe you did too? Remember Deepa, my friend in Maryland? That's why she and I were close. She's gay too. She found her wife when she was young. It took me longer to find someone. In fact, we're engaged. Her name is Juliet. I want you and Dad to meet her, so she'll come with me to Dubai. We'll see you on my birthday.

Thanks for celebrating me, I'm excited!

Love,
Ramya

CHAPTER TWENTY-EIGHT

 Juliet

 September 22

 Nigeria

"WHAT'S THE TRACKING number again?" the woman asked.

"X805842094," Juliet said for the third time.

"Madam, we no get record for that in our system."

"X! 805842094," Juliet shouted.

"One moment. Okay, I dey come."

The woman returned with a package that looked like it had been through hell. The cardboard lining was soaked through with water, and Juliet feared the documents inside were damaged. She opened the package and screamed when she saw she was right.

"Abeg, wetin dey happen! Half of my papers don spoil!"

"We go offer the sender a partial refund," the woman casually replied.

"Do that, you idiots," Juliet screamed.

Juliet waited until she was home call Ramya.

"Did you get the package?" Ramya eagerly asked.

"Baby, they ruined it! Half of the papers were soaking wet!"

"How!? I put them in plastic covers!"

"Two of the covers ripped. I'm so sorry. What should I do?"

"FUUUCK! I don't have time to resend anything. You'll have to go print them."

"Sorry, baby. The income statements and your tax returns were damaged. Send me those, ok love? I'll go tonight."

"Of course, those are the most sensitive documents. Okay, I'll send you everything now. Bye."

Ramya hung up the phone before Juliet could say goodbye. Juliet didn't try calling back, knowing how frustrating these past few weeks had been for Ramya. What should have been a quick visit back to the States had already dragged out to three weeks. The company that had flown Ramya to San Francisco was "still deliberating" whether to bring her in for another interview. Then Xavier, their immigration lawyer, made a mistake filing the K1 visa paperwork, which forced Juliet to take a much earlier interview appointment than they had planned. That forced Ramya to express mail the documents Juliet needed to Nigeria, costing a small fortune. Now half of those papers had arrived damaged. Juliet's interview was tomorrow, and Ramya couldn't be there. Juliet's nerves calmed slightly when she saw a WhatsApp message from Ramya.

> **Ramya:** Sorry, baby. I know it's not your fault. I'm just frustrated.
> **Juliet:** I know, love. It's okay.
> **Ramya:** Sent you the stuff. Let me know if you need help. Please be careful with my SSN.

Juliet checked her email and sighed. The list of documents

she had to take to the American Embassy was endless, and Ramya had done a beautiful job organizing everything for her in that package. Now she stared at the seventeen individual PDFs she would need to print at the local cybercafé, all of which contained Ramya's "SSN," which Ramya had told her stood for "social security number."

"If a fraudster gets my SSN, they can steal my identity, take my money, and I won't be able to take care of you," Ramya had explained.

That one number, the SSN, is why Ramya had spent so much money to send the original documents from the States instead of emailing Juliet everything.

Ramya was scared the American Embassy would reject Juliet's visa because of homophobia, a smaller income than she had hoped, and general paranoia. Xavier had prepared Juliet well and assured them everything would be fine. After he made the mistake with their paperwork, Juliet had her doubts.

Whether the stress or anticipation, something was causing the voices in Juliet's head to reappear. Sylvia's was the stronger one, constantly telling her,

"You go get better, Juliet. You go get strong, my friend."

Juliet prayed her friend was okay and the voices weren't a sign of something serious. She tried calling Sylvia to figure out what was happening, but Sylvia hadn't picked up her call or replied to her messages in months. Juliet hadn't had time to chase her down.

The voices persisted faintly in Juliet's head all the way to the cybercafé, which was crowded as usual. Little boys would steal pocket money from their parents, then run straight here to watch porn. The owners didn't care, so long as they profited.

"I need a fast computer with printer access," she told the attendant.

"One thousand Naira an hour. Pay now. You can use number five," he replied.

Juliet handed him the money and sat down in between two teenagers watching disturbing sex videos. She logged into her email and waited for the documents Ramya had sent to download to the computer. It took her a full three minutes to open and print each one off. What a waste of time. She should be resting for tomorrow.

Ramya called her right as she left the cybercafé.

"Hey love, I got them printed. Yay!" Juliet cheered.

"That's good. Sorry I snapped earlier. Did you delete the files from the computer?"

"No vex, love. No, I didn't. Why?"

"What!? Juliet, you gotta go back and delete everything! Otherwise, anyone who can access the computer can get my SSN."

"It's okay, Ramya. They delete everything off the computers at the end of each day."

"Are you kidding me? That's in six hours! Go back, Juliet! NOW! Don't be so fucking lazy."

Juliet didn't argue, even with Ramya's disrespectful words. They had come this far in their journey, and she wasn't about to let one bad day ruin everything. By the time she got back to the cybercafé, the voices in her head were screaming and she could barely concentrate. Worse, her computer was occupied by a young man.

"Oga abeg, make I delete my documents."

"Sister, I don pay for the time already. You go sit there," the young man said, pointing to computer #6.

"Abeg shift! The documents are on this computer. I go pay you for the time."

"Ah ah, what is so important you delete?"

"My girlfriend don send me…" Juliet stopped.

It was too late. The guy laughed and pointed.

"Ah ah! Your GIRLFRIEND? Where is she? We go do a threesome, abi? Then you can have this computer."

"FUCK OFF!" Juliet screamed.

She raised her hand to give the guy a hot slap.

"Hey! No no no no no! You get out!" the attendant screamed at them, running over.

"FUCK YOU! I need to..." Juliet started.

Surprisingly strong for his small frame, the attendant dragged Juliet and the young man out by the arm. He shoved them onto the street, shouting at them to go away.

"You get out! Stupid people!"

"FUCK YOU BOTH!" Juliet screamed at the top of her lungs.

She thanked God for her loud voice in that moment. The young man was frightened by her force and ran away before she could confront him again.

"Mad woman," he muttered as he ran.

The voices in Juliet's brain were still getting louder. Their dull buzz had grown into shouting in a megaphone. She clutched her head and felt her body rocking back and forth uncontrollably, desperate to block out the noise.

You dey strong, Juliet. E go get better with time, Sylvia kept repeating.

How did this happen to her? The man's voice asked.

"What is this!? Leave me alone!" Juliet shouted.

And then, suddenly, she was back on the bus to Accra. The familiar stench that had come from tired, dirty passengers who hadn't showered all day filled her nose. She looked out the window and saw they had just crossed the Togolese/Ghanaian border. The soldiers who had stamped her passport were disappearing in the distance, waving the next bus forward.

"Juliet, hi baby."

Juliet whipped around, shocked to see Ramya sitting next to her.

"Ramya? What are you doing here?"

"Sometimes I have these dreams. This is the first time I

could talk to you here though."

"Am I dreaming too?"

"I don't know. Should we listen to music together?"

"That'd be nice."

Ramya reached over to grab one of her ear buds. Juliet scrolled through her playlist, finally selecting a song by Simi.

"Do you want to lean on me?" Ramya asked.

Juliet smiled and nodded, setting her heavy head down on Ramya's shoulder. The warmth of Ramya's body soothed Juliet, and they sang along to the sweet words of the song,

"I, I, I want to be, your weakness baby."

Hours passed, and together, they watched the changing scenery as the bus rolled closer to Accra. It was so beautiful experiencing this with Ramya. Only when she saw a familiar junction did Juliet realize what would soon happen.

"Ramya, I think we're going to derail from the road."

"It's okay, my love. So long as we're together, we can face anything."

"Ramya, we need to get off this bus!"

"It's okay, Juliet. You're strong. You'll be fine," her father said.

"Daddy?"

Juliet turned to face the seat next to her and saw that she was no longer resting against Ramya; she was resting against her father.

"Daddy, what are you doing here? I just saw you at home."

"Juliet, we both know only my body is at home. My mind has been traveling for a long time," he said, snapping his fingers.

"Then how come I can see you here, Daddy?"

"My child, it's time we leave this bus. Will you follow me?"

"Yes, Daddy, I dey come."

Daddy grabbed Juliet's hand and led her to the front of the bus. With a slight motion, the doors opened, and they carefully walked down the stairs to the ground, as though they hadn't just been traveling at eighty kilometers an hour. Shaken but safe,

Juliet stared down for a few seconds to regain her composure. Daddy was gone by the time she looked up.

"Your phone dey ring," someone said to Juliet as he walked by.

Juliet reached into her purse and drew out her phone. Five minutes had passed since she left the cybercafé, which was a few feet in front of her.

"Hello? Ramya?"

"Hey baby, I'm really sorry I shouted at you earlier. You didn't deserve that. I was a jerk."

"It's okay, love. I know you're stressed out. I am too."

"Did you get everything? Delete everything?"

"Yes, love. I got everything. And I deleted the files," Juliet lied.

"Thank you, I love you. I can't wait to spend our lives together. Good luck tomorrow."

"Thanks, dear. I'll call you after."

Juliet hung up without saying goodbye. She was tired of saying goodbye. It was time to say hello to a new life ahead.

Today is the most important day of my life, Juliet thought. She woke up in the middle of the night, turned on the bedroom light and for the hundredth time, checked she had her belongings in order. After her time lapse last night, she couldn't be too sure. Evidence? Check. Passport? Check. Documents? Check. Bag? Check. Clot...

"Turn off the light, Juliet, abeg!" Chiamaka shouted.

"Sorry sis, time don reach. Make I go get ready."

She and Xavier had thoroughly prepared for this day, covering every aspect of her and Ramya's relationship, including where they planned to get married, what Ramya did for a living, and what Juliet would do after she immigrated to New York. He was confident the K1 visa would work in Juliet's favor.

"Your relationship is real. It doesn't matter that you're a same-sex couple," he had said.

If only Ramya would listen. Ramya's constant worrying that Juliet would get a homophobic consular officer did little more than make an already nervous Juliet more worried. Despite the harsh words last night, Juliet missed Ramya like mad. Yet, she was grateful Ramya was far away today. This visa was about their relationship, but the interview was all on Juliet. The last thing she needed was a paranoid Ramya casting doubts.

"Sis, time to get up. Sorry nau," Juliet gently said to Chiamaka.

"Jesus! This relationship of yours no dey easy sha. Juliet, you go bring me stuffs from America."

"Anything you say, sis. Anything you want."

Phones weren't allowed in the US Embassy, so Chiamaka would have to stand close by outside for the several hours Juliet would be busy. Juliet knew how to dress for every occasion, and she was proud of her simple suit, blouse and professional makeup. Admiring herself in the mirror, she thought about how she would carry this look for her first job in America. Chiamaka, on the other hand, dragged herself out of bed and put on joggers, slippers and an oversized t-shirt.

"I look homeless," Chiamaka muttered.

"You look perfect."

Remnants of the rainy season trickled down on them, and Juliet was grateful she had picked up from Ramya the habit of carrying an umbrella. The remnants became heavier, and rain beat down on their car; Juliet prayed this wasn't an omen. The Uber driver got them right up to the outermost entrance of the US Embassy, and she and Chiamaka walked up to the security guard together. He looked at her paper and instructed her to proceed through the main gates. Chiamaka would have to wait before the barriers in the rain.

288

"Sorry, sis. I go bring you plenty things from America."

"You better do," Chiamaka replied.

Now an expert at traveling, Juliet handled the US Embassy security easily. She pulled out her IDs, forms and documents without hesitation, and praised herself as the other applicants with her same appointment time stumbled.

The inside of the US Embassy was even nicer than the already beautiful exterior. The carpets were a deep regal blue, the floors a polished marble, and everywhere Juliet looked, she saw the golden American eagle symbol. She walked slowly through the hallway, admiring the portraits that hung on the walls. Like Nigeria, there were no female US Presidents, but Juliet was at least a little inspired by the many pictured women who held other important positions.

"Secretary of State—Hillary Clinton," she read out loud.

A man directed her to a waiting room, and she took a seat with two dozen other US immigrant hopefuls. None of them had the thick folder of evidence Juliet carried, and most of them looked totally terrified. Juliet felt calm, then nervous again. Was she missing something?

"Which visa are you here for?" she asked the closest woman.

"K3. My husband don dey America for a year. You?"

"K1 visa. My...fiancé dey America too."

She didn't mention her fiancé was a woman. Who knew where these people were from?

One by one, the applicants were called forward to one of the desks in the open arena. Juliet looked at each applicant and consular officer, amazed that she was witnessing one of the most critical moments of these strangers' lives. This was what they had all been counting on for days, months, maybe even years. How strange Juliet ended up with them now in this room.

From their expressions, Juliet could tell nearly every one had been successful. Though they were strangers, she was so happy for her fellow Nigerians and felt a sense of community.

"Congratulations!" they wished each other.

As the seats emptied, Juliet scooted closer to the front, and heard when one woman was told to come back on Thursday.

"Bring that form and we'll get you sorted. See you soon," the consular officer said.

"Ok sir, thank you sir, see you."

"Juliet?"

"Yes, that's me."

A friendly-looking man with pale skin and a brown beard smiled at her. She felt like she could trust him.

"So, we have a VIP room set up for you," he said.

"Really?"

"Haha, something like that. Right this way."

She followed him to the back section of the open arena, which was demarcated by a thick curtain and rope.

"It's not soundproofed, but no one will be able to hear us so far back. I know you're applying for a K1 visa, and your petitioner is a woman?"

Juliet's heart raced. Ramya had been right. This consular officer was going to throw out their application because they were a same-sex couple.

"Juliet? Are you okay? Don't be nervous. We have this back area as a precaution. It was requested by your lawyer."

"Oh! I thought you were going to dismiss my application."

"No! Oh, I'm sorry. I should have clarified that at the beginning. We just want to make sure same-sex applicants can speak freely."

"Na wa, my fiancé has messed with my head. Yes, my love, Ramya, is a woman."

"Perfect, and you two honestly have some of the best formatted evidence I have ever seen," he said, pointing to her files.

"Yes, that's my Ramya."

She chatted with Ryan, the consular officer. They covered

the basic questions Xavier had predicted. Juliet told Ryan about their plans to marry in Central Park, how Ramya worked at the UN and was hopefully starting a better paid job in the tech industry soon, and how Juliet planned to continue university after her papers came through.

"Well, you seem very smart. You should consider applying to Columbia University. I went there," Ryan said.

"Thank you, Ryan. I will look at the application."

"Wonderful. Well, you're all set. The visa will be issued today or tomorrow. It should arrive by courier no later than Tuesday."

"Okay, Ryan. Wait…so I got the visa!?"

"Yes, you got the visa! You can fly to the States right after you get your passport back."

Juliet burst into tears and buried her face in her hands. Ryan had probably seen that reaction many times and knew exactly what to do. He gave her a tissue, gently patted her on the shoulder and after she had composed herself, helped her back to the main sitting area. Juliet collapsed into one of the chairs before she regained enough strength to stand up. The interview had been fifteen minutes, but the preparation had taken her entire life.

"Congratulations!" the remaining applicants called out.

"Thank you ooo!"

Chiamaka was in the same spot as when Juliet went inside. The rain had let up, and Chiamaka had bribed one of the security guards to loan her his chair.

"My sister, how far about the visa? How did it go?" Chiamaka said, jumping up.

"My sister, I go bring you stuffs from America!"

"Eeeeyyyyy! My siiiiiiister!"

"Abeg, hand me my phone."

Ramya picked up right away.

"Are you out? How are you? Did you get the visa? Do you know?"

"Baby, we got it. We got the visa!"

"AAAAAAHHHHH!"

That was the happiest moment of Juliet's life. She and Ramya had already accomplished a lot together, and Juliet was so, so, so proud of herself that she did her part to make sure their journey would continue. She was immigrating to America. And she deserved it.

CHAPTER TWENTY-NINE

 Ramya

 October 10

 New York City

"WELL, YOU KNOW what they say. Good things happen slowly, and great things happen all at once," Carl said.

"What?"

"Ugh, Ramya! Pay attention to me! I'm having an introspective moment and I need an audience."

"What?"

"OH MY GOD."

Carl slammed Ramya's laptop shut and tapped his pen rapidly on the table.

"Hey! What are you doing?" Ramya shouted.

"Ramya! I was talking to you."

"I didn't hear you. I have a million things to do."

In the past two weeks, Ramya's life had come together after three weeks of feeling like it was falling apart. Ramya cursed herself for picking Xavier the lawyer, whose first move was to incorrectly select the date of Juliet's visa interview appointment. When Ramya found out that she couldn't fly back to Nigeria in time, she nearly had a panic attack. Somewhere in that chaos, Ramya expedited her documents to Lagos, half of which had been ruined in transit. Ramya had nearly ruined their relationship in response. She was so ashamed of how she spoke to Juliet the night before the interview, apologizing no fewer than a hundred times.

"I'm surprised Juliet didn't break up with me. I would have deserved it," Ramya told Carl.

Fortunately, as Xavier predicted, Juliet's K1 visa application had been immediately approved. Juliet called her at 5 a.m. and told her their effort was successful. Ramya burst into tears when she heard the news. It was a full circle moment for Ramya. She had started her journey with Juliet while at the US Embassy in Ghana, and Juliet had found out they could be together permanently at the US Embassy in Nigeria.

"We're getting married, this is real," Ramya had shouted.

"Ramya, I'm so ready to be your wife!" Juliet had responded.

Miraculously, the next day, the company that had asked Ramya to interview in San Francisco finally reached out and told her she got the job. She had stayed in San Francisco to complete her new job onboarding before flying here, to New York, to look for an apartment. Carl happened to be in town for work.

"And now we're drinking coffee," he said.

"And now I go to this listing."

"Ugh, fine. I guess I'll be the supportive friend or whatever."

She booked them an Uber to the first apartment, which was on the west side of Harlem. The brownstone building was slightly rundown, but the apartment was well within budget and took up the entire top floor. To Ramya, it was perfect.

"Ew, look at this kitchen," Carl said.

"Baby, I agree with Carl. This is so ugly!" Juliet cried out over the phone.

"Thank you! Ramya, it's two against one. Next!"

Ramya wasn't quite sure when she had introduced Juliet to Carl, let alone when Carl became an equal third opinion. She knew better than to argue. This was the beginning of a new era and she probably needed to make some lifestyle adjustments. Unfortunately, the next three listings she booked were worse.

Defeated at the day's prospects, she and Carl walked back to her hotel room. The longer the apartment hunt took, the less time she would have to prepare for Juliet's arrival.

"Where the hell have you been looking?" Carl asked.

"Streeteasy, Craigslist."

"CRAIGSLIST? Do you want to get murdered?"

"Where should I be looking!?"

"Honey, dear. What's your starting salary?"

She told him the number and he fell off the bed. Both were used to sacrificing their own financial well-being for the sake of trying to do good in the world. Somehow Ramya had created a job that didn't pit one against the other.

"Uh, no more of this cheap shit. We need to find you a real place," Carl said.

He grabbed her computer and created an account on a website she had never heard of.

"I found out from a rich ex-boyfriend that all the luxury buildings in New York are on a different website."

"There's a bad joke about housing segregation in there."

"Here, I booked you four listings for tomorrow," Carl replied.

They woke up bright and early and headed to Chelsea to look at the first apartment. The street, of course, was amazing, but the apartment was "for babies" as Juliet described it. The entire floorplan was the size of a closet. The second place was in Tribeca and had a great vibe, though Ramya wanted to Craigslist murder Carl when she saw the prices at the closest grocery store.

"Eight dollars for an apple? I don't need each one individually wrapped."

The third apartment was in the Upper West Side. Ramya burst out laughing as they pulled up to the entrance.

"Carl, this place has a driveway. A DRIVEWAY in Manhattan. There's no way I can afford this."

"Don't despair, it's in our budget."

"You mean *my* budget?"

"Oh, honey, no. I mean the budget Juliet and I agreed on last night," Carl replied.

Before she could protest, the real estate agent met them out front. He handed Ramya a folder with her name on it, which further proved to Ramya she couldn't afford this place.

"It's on the 21st floor, this way," the agent said.

They rode upstairs and although Ramya wanted to hate it, she loved everything about the building, which was a block away from Central Park and had a bike room. The interior halls were painted a lovely shade of blue, with matching carpets, vinyl walls, and soft-lit chandeliers.

Ramya gasped when she saw the apartment and its incredible view. The open plan kitchen faced floor-to-ceiling windows that overlooked three avenues, the Hudson River and New Jersey. She could see half the length of Manhattan. It was a proper two-bedroom; they could use one as a dedicated office since Ramya would be working from home.

"The sunsets are gorgeous, the pool in the building is lovely, and the washer and dryer in your pantry are new," the real estate agent said.

"Washer and dryer in-unit! Jesus, Ramya, you have to take this," Carl shouted.

Ramya was already calling Juliet.

"Baby, this place is amazing, look. A washer and dryer in-unit means we've made it!" Ramya exclaimed.

"Oh my God! Baaaaby! That place is a dream! Please take it!"

"And it's walking distance from Columbia," the agent said.

Ramya applied for the apartment before they left. The application was approved within minutes.

CHAPTER THIRTY

 Juliet

 November 5

 Nigeria

"MY LOVE, I'M so glad to be back," Ramya said.

Juliet held her wife-to-be tightly, breathing in unison. A visit away that was supposed to be for two weeks had turned into more than two months, and there had been scary moments when Juliet thought Ramya would never set foot again in Nigeria.

"I was scared we'd lose each other, Ramya."

"I know, baby, I'm sorry. Thank God everything worked out."

It had worked out so well—the gorgeous apartment that Carl had found was theirs! They signed the lease the same day Ramya called to show it to her. In between classes since then, Juliet had picked out their major pieces of furniture, which Ramya had delivered and assembled. Juliet couldn't wait to set foot in her new home in her new country and put the final touches on it.

A version of the sophisticated room she had seen in South

Africa would soon be hers in New York.

"When do you want to fly to the States?" Ramya asked a few days later.

"Tomorrow?"

"I wish. According to your visa, the last day you can arrive is March 26th. You'll get back to Nigeria from Dubai on January 7th."

"Ok, January 8th, then."

"Let's say the 20th? Gives you a few weeks to pack," Ramya suggested.

"Fine, love. The sooner, the better."

"Booked! The countdown begins!"

Juliet literally shook with excitement. There were only seven weeks to go until the holidays, and she knew the time would pass quickly with Ramya working remotely and her finishing up classes for the semester. Ramya had agreed to start her new job right away on the condition they allow her to work from Nigeria and then take an extended holiday for Christmas, New Year's and her birthday. By mid-December, Juliet found out that she again got perfect marks in her courses and could rest well after many nights of balancing school and life.

Finally, the holiday season came and for the first time in months, they were able to breathe without the expectation to go anywhere or do anything. They spent hours and hours lounging on Juliet's couch and watching TV, going to the Spar store to pick out Christmas decorations they were too lazy to hang, and dreaming up romantic date nights they would have next year. The kinds of things Ramya described a person could do in New York were beyond what Juliet understood, and she couldn't wait to experience everything together.

Even with Ramya's now big salary, the several plane tickets to Lagos, Dubai and New York added up. They gave each other non-material things for Christmas. Juliet massaged Ramya from head to toe. Ramya put together another book, this time of New

York recommendations suited to Juliet's interests.

"What is Mood?" Juliet asked, looking through the book.

"It's one of the largest fabric stores in the world. Celebrity designers shop there."

"I can't wait to go."

"I can't wait to take you."

Juliet knew that so many things she was doing would be for the last time in Nigeria, at least for a while. An era of her life was closing, and while she couldn't be more excited, a part of her was sad. She spent extra time at the local market, with her parents, and at her favorite club, absorbing what it meant to leave these places behind. A new version of herself would soon emerge, and even if these places stayed the same, her relationship to them would forever change. That was something to both commiserate and celebrate.

Instead of a wild night out, they chose to spend a quiet New Year's Eve at their favorite Chinese restaurant with Chiamaka and Isatou, who were two people who had been critical to them surviving as a couple. They spent hours laughing and toasting each other. Chiamaka even presented Juliet with a gift.

"This is a list of stuffs wey you go bring from America."

"Abi sis, I'm on it."

As they approached midnight, Ramya invited the waiters to sit with them for a drink. The corks came out of the champagne bottles with a satisfying pop, and suddenly, it was the year that Juliet would immigrate to America. It was the year that she would marry the love of her life. It was the year that she could look back and know that she had made it.

CHAPTER
THIRTY-ONE

 Ramya

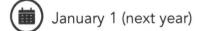 January 1 (next year)

 Nigeria

"MAYBE I'LL COVER the date? Or stuff my passport?" Ramya muttered to herself.

"What are you saying?"

"Nothing, just practicing."

A month after she had first arrived in Lagos, Ramya and Juliet had spent a particularly hot and sticky afternoon waiting under a tent by a police station. Her two-year multiple entry visa allowed her to be in Nigeria for a month at a time, but she had read online that she needed to go to a police station and apply for an extension to stay longer.

That cost her $300 and a bad case of heatstroke. She didn't bother with another extension. Now leaving Nigeria for the second time past her expiration date, she prayed holding her passport in a strategic way plus a wad of cash would get her through immigration.

"Next!" the immigration officer screamed.

Ramya looked around the normally crowded room and saw she was already at the front of the line. The airport was nearly empty. Nigerians don't fly on New Year's Day, Ramya mentally noted for future visits. She put on her calmest face and presented her passport.

"It's my birthday," the immigration officer muttered.

"What?"

"It's my birthday," the officer muttered again, motioning with her head at Ramya's passport.

"Oh, I...uh...is that code for...uh...happy birthday? I didn't bring a gift."

The officer pouted and then shrugged.

"Okay, go."

"Really?"

Ramya shrugged back, surprised the officer didn't press harder for a "birthday gift," aka bribe. The sluggishness of the rest of the airport staff persisted, and fortunately, Ramya easily made it through immigration.

"That's the last time I apply for a Nigerian extension," she said to herself.

Now a baller, Ramya had pridefully applied for an expensive credit card that gave them both lounge access. She didn't quite know how to scan them in, but Juliet had practiced with enough YouTube videos to save her from embarrassment. Juliet whipped out the digital pass on her phone and got them through.

"Welcome, Juliet!" said the lounge attendant.

"Thank you!" Juliet replied.

At their table, Ramya crammed the wad of bribe cash into Juliet's backpack and pointed,

"This is for packing expenses."

"I guess that will do," Juliet replied.

They had time to eat a small breakfast and grab a not-$8 apple before their flight boarding announcement.

"Egyptian Air flight 56 to Cairo is now boarding," they heard over the speaker.

With half-vacant flights, their trip to Dubai was mostly uneventful. Having the entire row to themselves, they cuddled close and tried their best to start the same movie at the same time so they could watch in unison. Ramya fell asleep halfway through.

Emirate immigration was handled by automatic kiosks and one guy watching a soccer match on his phone. They were both through in five minutes. The four suitcases Juliet had insisted on bringing barely fit onto the luggage cart, and Ramya ended up wheeling two to their hotel shuttle. Exhausted, they spent a peaceful night with their heads buried deep in the hotel pillows. The next morning, they rode over to the Airbnb Ramya had booked, which was half the price, twice the space and had more amenities than the hotel.

"Hey hey, *this* is where I am meant to be!" Juliet exclaimed when she saw their view.

Up until Dubai, Ramya had had concerns about Juliet immigrating to New York. Lagos was a massive city, but the packed and continuous skyline, diversity and intricate public transportation system made New York a different world.

Seeing Juliet in Dubai, Ramya's concerns quickly faded. Juliet loved the architecture of the buildings, riding the metro, the fancy stores in the modern malls, and their contrast to old town Dubai, where she negotiated the price of *everything* down to the bare minimum.

Juliet thrived in Dubai. Ramya knew she would in New York as well.

As they had done in Kenya and South Africa, they saw the hell out of Dubai. Way too expensive to have chill days doing nothing, Ramya reverted to her old habits and crammed in as many activities as she could. In thirty-six hours, they had gone to the Aquarium, Miracle Garden, and three malls. After her birthday with her parents tomorrow, she had planned a boat tour, dinner in the Marina, a visit to the Palms hotel and riding the Observation Wheel.

"Abeg! I need to sit down! We've been out all day!" Juliet cried out.

"No! We need to go to the other side of the mall for the Burj lightshow!"

"Ramya, we're watching it here. Waiter!"

Juliet took a seat at the table in front of her. As always, the waiter noticed Juliet's beauty and trampled over the other customers to rush to her side.

"Yes madam, what would you like madam?"

"A mo-jee-toe."

Ramya had long stopped trying to correct her pronunciation.

"Make that two mo-jee-toes, please," Ramya said.

"How do you feel about tomorrow?" Juliet asked.

"I feel good!"

"You're lying."

"Yes, yes I am," Ramya admitted.

Sometime during today's twelve-hour excursion, Ramya realized another reason she had packed their days was to keep her mind distracted. She was so nervous about tomorrow. Her mother had copied her into the mass email about the party. Even from her distant parents, she thought it was weird to not get any individual correspondence about her own birthday.

"Are you excited to meet them?" Ramya asked.

"I don't know…I mean, you haven't made them sound like warm people."

"I didn't want to give you a false picture."

"Show is starting," Juliet said, pointing up.

The spot Juliet picked was nicer than the one Ramya had

planned, with the perfect vantage point to view the entire Burj Khalifa. Its exterior was made up of more than a million LED pixels on which the hourly light show was displayed. Slow at first, with only a small bottom section illuminated, the tallest building in the world was soon covered in streaks of brilliant neon colors. Ramya had to physically move her neck to take in everything.

The light show morphed into stunning scenery of Dubai, animals in East Africa, and mountain ranges throughout the world.

"It's telling our story!" Juliet exclaimed.

Juliet leaned forward and kissed Ramya on the cheek.

"Thank you for bringing me here," Juliet said.

"Thank you for choosing me."

Whatever happened tomorrow with her parents, Ramya's journey with Juliet was just getting started. Nothing mattered so long as they had each other.

CHAPTER THIRTY-TWO

 Juliet

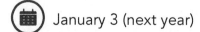 January 3 (next year)

 Dubai

JULIET TAPPED ON her phone calendar, which displayed "3 January."

Though she had deleted Tinder long ago, Juliet still remembered the date of her first message with Ramya—5 February. In nearly a year of knowing and loving her, Juliet had never imagined what a nervous wreck a usually calm and collected Ramya would become with the two of them meeting Ramya's parents tomorrow. For that reason, Juliet put up with Ramya's ridiculous Dubai touring schedule. While their trip had not been the lavish time she had imagined from the Nigerian films, Juliet knew she was not a useless actress with no real-world responsibility. She had a fiancé to take care of.

Juliet cranked up the hot water in the shower and relaxed her muscles under its strong pressure. Her feet felt like they would fall off from the many kilometers of walking they had done the past two days. Their schedule had been packed so tightly that Juliet hadn't even had a chance to pick up Ramya's birthday gift. Instead, she had to sneak away to the toilet and beg the shop to deliver the gift to their building lobby. Exhausted as she was, Juliet needed to stay up long enough to sneak it inside the apartment.

She grabbed a luxurious towel from the heated rack and rubbed it all over her face and body.

"Ooooh, this is the life," Juliet moaned.

The towel was somehow soft and strong at the same time, which Ramya said was because the building staff had put it in a machine dryer. Suddenly hanging clothes outside on a line seemed very local to Juliet, and she dreamt about how she would soon move to New York, where they had a dryer inside of their apartment.

She glanced at the clock on the bedroom wall and saw it was nearly 11:30 p.m.

"You coming to bed?" Ramya asked.

"Sure love, I need to call Chiamaka and then I'll come."

Juliet grabbed her clothes to get dressed in the sitting area, and quietly closed the bedroom door behind her. Ramya's soft snores escaped through the cracks just a few minutes later, and Juliet soon heard Ramya sleep-talking the same nightmare as every night for the last week. She guessed the nightmare had reemerged with Ramya's stress.

"Victim number fifteen is female, early twenties, brown hair, wearing a blue shirt. She's unresponsive and not breathing, over!"

Throwing on her clothes, Juliet decided to step out onto the narrow balcony of the apartment before calling Chiamaka. There was barely enough room for one person to stand and Juliet couldn't turn around without scraping her elbows to close the screen door behind her. Up on the fifty-fourth floor, strong gusts of wind sailed into the room and battered against the furniture.

She glanced down and, as it had yesterday, dizziness nearly

caused her to pass out. In Nigeria, she was used to intermittent electricity that only illuminated a few big buildings most nights. Here in Dubai, the lights from the ground and the buildings reflected off each other into the sky. There were more colors painted at night than during the day.

Being this high up, the speeding cars below turned into long streaks of light. The ground was a never-ending crisscross of bridges, tunnels, highways and ramps, which looked like they were breathing as one. This floor was the highest she had ever stayed on. It was breathtaking to look across the street and see hundreds of buildings that dwarfed her where she stood. There was still higher yet to climb in Dubai. There was still higher yet to climb in the world.

Juliet knew most people would feel insignificant standing in the middle of this concrete jungle, but she had never felt more important. Dubai was the playground of Nigerian celebrities, and she could now count herself among the privileged few who enjoyed this city as a tourist. Several women who had once lived with her were later trafficked into Dubai. One of her friends eventually made it home alive and told her that some of the others had been beaten, tortured, raped and even murdered. Juliet guessed the same was happening down below her.

She was grateful to have found a way to go from suffering on the streets of Lagos to here, the fifty-fourth floor of Dubai. In that moment, Juliet realized money wasn't her only motivator, and she wanted to go to law school and dedicate her career in America to helping those women who were still in need. There was no higher calling, figuratively speaking, that she could imagine.

A gust of wind blew her back against the screen, and she shuddered at the cool air.

"This na the time to get Ramya's gift," Juliet said to herself.

She threw on a wig and a hat before putting on her slippers. Ramya had dragged them out of the apartment early that morning and Juliet timed that without stops, the lift would take her down to the lobby in twenty-four seconds. Fifty-four floors in twenty-four seconds!

The luxury building had residents from every continent and of every color. Juliet smiled, thinking about how Ramya said New York City was even more diverse. The only way to tell who a resident was and who was a staff member was by the quality of clothes and the confidence of the person. Juliet had always carried herself with a poise that was uncharacteristic of her background. The concierge smiled at her and handed her the package, no questions asked.

Although her eyes were drooping by the time she got back upstairs, she forced herself to stay awake a little longer. She had promised Chiamaka she'd call to show her Ramya's gift, and thankfully she picked up right away.

"Let me see it!"

Juliet held up her phone over the box and slowly turned its contents for Chiamaka to inspect.

"What do you think?"

"She's going to love it! This is exactly what she needs."

Juliet told Chiamaka goodnight and carried the box into the bedroom. Ramya was fast asleep, and she was still struggling with her nightmare. Juliet reached out, put her hand on Ramya's hip and whispered,

"I love you."

Ramya stopped moving and Juliet fell into a peaceful sleep beside her.

CHAPTER THIRTY-THREE

 Ramya

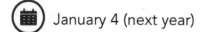 January 4 (next year)

 Dubai

"HAPPY BIRTHDAY!" Juliet shouted.

"Thank you, my love. Being with you is the best present ever."

"Ok good, because I didn't get you anything."

"What?"

"Kidding, got yah!"

Juliet handed Ramya a big box, which Ramya tore open to reveal a suit.

"I had it custom-made here. It's for the party tonight."

The coat and the pants were made from a soft silk, with an intricate floral pattern in dark blue, red and yellow sewn in. It reminded Ramya of the Japanese blossoms they had seen at the Miracle Garden yesterday. Juliet explained that the lining of the jacket was the softest cotton on the market, guaranteed not to irritate Ramya's sensitive skin.

"Don't forget these," Juliet said.

She pulled out a fine pair of loafers to complete Ramya's look.

Ramya tried on everything and smiled at herself in the mirror. The outfit was a perfect combination of her feminine and masculine styles. For the first time ever, Ramya looked at her physical self with admiration.

"This is exactly how I want to express myself," Ramya said.

"I know, my love. I might not always have the right words, but I do know how to feel comfortable in my own skin. I want you to feel that way too."

"Thank you, it's perfect."

Carefully putting the clothes away for tonight, Ramya turned to Juliet with a small request.

"Will you come with me for one more outing before we meet my parents?"

"Ramya, I'm so tired, but ok. It's your birthday. Where do you want to go?"

"It'll be worth it, I promise. I need to do this with you today."

They rode the bullet elevator down to the lobby and set their bags down on their usual bench. Ramya booked an Uber, which in this fancy city was a Porsche SUV. Ramya climbed into the backseat next to Juliet and relaxed, staring at the scenery. As they drove through the streets of Dubai, Ramya watched an endless number of skyscrapers rush past them. Large sections of desert or concrete separated the buildings, which to her made Dubai look like a giant hairbrush with prongs of life and troughs of nothing. Combing through a side street, without warning, the driver took a sharp left into a more traditional part of the city. He pulled up to one of the two entrances Ramya recognized from her many searches online.

"The best ones are at the far end," the driver said.

"The best ones what?" Juliet asked.

"Come on, let me show you," Ramya replied.

Juliet shook with excitement as they approached the entrance.

"Oh my God, I think I know where we are!"

"Welcome to the gold souk!"

Having grown up knowing only Indian and American jewelry, Ramya was dazzled by the designs displayed in each of the storefront windows. Twists went with mounds went with leaves went with patterns went with striking jewels and gold of every type. She saw the architecture, fashion and diversity of the Middle East reflected in the jewelry of Dubai.

Ramya guided them to a store tucked in a corner, one of the more discreet places in the market. She had found out about this shop in a blog post on queer travel. Like Juliet must have done for her suit, she had called ahead and worked with the owner for weeks to create the perfect order.

"This one, really?" Juliet said.

"Yes, this one. Trust me."

Ramya led them through the door.

"Welcome, are you Ramya?" the shop owner asked.

"I am. Are you Ahmed?"

"I am and I have your order, give me a minute."

He went to the back and returned with ornate red boxes.

"Have a look."

Juliet carefully opened both to reveal matching rings—hers was taller and more traditional, and Ramya's was a feminine take on a male wedding band.

"Look at this," Ramya told Juliet.

She raised the two rings to be at eye level. Juliet gasped. When looking directly at the diamonds and under an overhead light, Ramya and Juliet saw the Pride flag colors refracted.

"It's a one-of-a-kind cut, meant to represent something you know how to see, but can't openly display to others," Ahmed explained.

"Oh Ramya, this is so beautiful!" Juliet exclaimed.

Juliet jumped into Ramya's arms, then withdrew.

"Don't worry, you're safe in here," Ahmed assured them.

Ramya wrapped Juliet in a hug and gave her a kiss, a privilege not normally allowed same-sex couples in this country. She removed the ring from the box and slid it onto Juliet's finger. It fit perfectly, just like Ramya's suit.

"You two know each other really well," Ahmed said.

"We do. We were made for each other," Ramya replied.

Dressed in her best and nervous as hell, Ramya took a deep breath before stepping through the door of the restaurant. Juliet followed closely behind her, periodically touching Ramya's lower back as she had on their first date in Ghana. Despite the awe-inspiring, intimidating façade of the Burj Khalifa, the restaurant inside was surprisingly inviting. Soft lights cascaded across the cream-colored walls, which made Ramya feel like she was wrapped snugly in her bedsheets. Counter upon counter of buffet food lined the area near the hostess.

A sign read: "Ramya's Birthday Party"

And pointed them to a private back room. Ramya was relieved that this event wasn't a hoax.

"Oh my God!" Ramya exclaimed upon entering.

She saw her parents had blown up an old photo of her that had been taken a few months before her university graduation. A flower garland wrapped the photo, which had been placed in the center of an elegant slate gray table. The smoke from two incense sticks trickled up to the ceiling, casting a beautiful sepia glow over her face.

"It's gorgeous," Ramya and Juliet agreed.

Ramya eagerly looked around the room for her parents. She spotted her father in the corner and grabbed Juliet's hand to race over.

"Hi Dad, thank you for my party! This is Juliet!"

She was too slow; another guest intercepted Ramya's father's attention first. He was soon immersed in conversation and didn't look up to see his daughter. Ramya twirled around the room, finally locating her mother. As usual, she was too busy with the decorations to acknowledge anyone's presence.

"Can't she stop arranging those flowers long enough to greet us?" Juliet asked.

To most people, her parents being so distracted would have been odd considering Ramya was the guest of honor. Growing up, Ramya's parents had scolded her on countless occasions for wanting too much attention. She regressed to the same excuses that got her through childhood.

"It's fine, they're so busy! Let's just wait our turn, ok?" Ramya pleaded.

Juliet sighed before nodding in agreement and squeezing Ramya's hand.

"Happy birthday, baby."

Guests milled about with cocktails and small finger foods. No one noticed Ramya was there, which didn't surprise her since she didn't recognize a single person. Having no one to mingle with, they made their way to the back tables and the food. That was always Ramya's favorite part of a party, anyway.

"Wow, look at this spread," Ramya remarked.

"Ramya, what is this?"

Ramya was impressed at the range of foods available, with options for vegetarians, vegans, carnivores, and picky eaters. Her parents must have spent a fortune on this catering. Juliet, on the other hand, noticed something Ramya had overlooked, and Ramya saw Juliet seemed concerned.

"Why are most of the dishes covered in almonds and walnuts? You're allergic."

"Wow, I missed that. I guess they forgot."

"Oh baby, I'm so sorry."

314

Having Juliet by her side to bring her to reality, Ramya was beginning to agree that this party was much less about her than it was about her parents. Somehow, they were celebrating while neglecting her. The same sadness she had felt as young Ramya stripped away what should have been a joyous occasion.

Just when Ramya was about to give in to her feelings of rejection, someone caught her eye in the distance.

"Oh my God! It's Deepa!"

"Who?"

"Deepa, my friend from Maryland! I stayed with her and her wife in New York before I came to Nigeria the first time. I reminded my mom about Deepa in my email."

Ramya jogged over to the other side of the room to say hi, bracing herself for the outpouring of love she was about to receive from her oldest childhood pal. Deepa turned at exactly the wrong moment, and Ramya just narrowly missed tapping her shoulder. Deepa and Audrey disappeared into the crowd before Ramya could catch them.

"Nooo! Why do I always miss her?"

"Attention!" a booming voice said.

She spun around to the stage area and saw her father, who had picked up a microphone and was waving his hands.

"Everyone, please find your seats at the tables. We're about to start the program."

Ramya walked back over to Juliet, who had torn off paper signs on two chairs that said "Reserved."

"Ramya, I couldn't find our names. We didn't have place settings."

"It's okay, stay positive. There must be an explanation."

The temperature of Juliet's body was like fire, which Ramya knew meant Juliet was really angry. Ramya had no words to cool her down.

"Thank you everyone for coming. I know this is a long way to travel for a birthday party," Ramya's father said.

Several guests nodded. Many of them leaned forward; Ramya guessed because they appreciated her father had acknowledged their effort. He had always had a talent for speaking in front of crowds. That was one of the few things Ramya admired about him.

"How come? How did he not acknowledge you first?" Juliet said.

"I guess he wants to end by introducing the guest of honor?" Ramya said with a forced half smile, convincing neither of them.

"Gathered in this room are more than two hundred fifty guests who came from more than five countries. We're so grateful you could make it," her father continued.

"Wow, that's a lot of people. Why don't I recognize anyone except Deepa and Audrey?"

"I'm not surprised," Juliet replied.

"We couldn't let today pass by without honoring our daughter," her father continued.

A breath of air escaped Ramya's throat. She felt Juliet's body temperature cool slightly and her body language soften. Those were the precious words Ramya needed to hear. She estimated her parents had remembered her birthday one out of three years, and those remembered birthdays were never met with a concerted effort. One year, they had handed Ramya a $100 bill in a plain envelope. Ramya never spent the bill; it was too valuable.

"This is the first time they have planned anything for me," Ramya whispered.

"I'm happy for you, baby. You deserve to be celebrated."

"To mark our daughter's thirty-second birthday, we decided to come here to the Burj Khalifa, which she had always wanted to see. We never made the time," her father said.

The guests let out a collective, audible "aw."

"What does that mean? I'm right here." Ramya said.

"My wife still emails Ramya, all these years later. In fact, she emailed Ramya the plans for today. We pray that she joins us from the heavens."

"What does that mean?" Ramya screamed again.

Ramya was so confused. She turned to face Juliet.

"What is wrong with my father? Juliet, are you ok? Do you feel sick?"

"Ramya, are we supposed to be here?"

"What do you mean? Of course, it's my birthday party."

"Baby. Ramya. Listen to me. Look around you. Why does everyone look sad? Why is your friend Deepa crying? Why hasn't anyone said hi to us?"

Only then did Ramya turn to face the guests. Most were dressed in white, the traditional color of Hindu funerals. Juliet was right. Many guests, including a normally stoic Deepa, were crying. She looked up at her mother, who hadn't made eye contact with her. Only then did she notice her mother's face had aged a lot since they had last seen each other; the dark circles under her eyes extended down to her cheeks. Her mother's skin was so ashy that it glistened as a steady stream of tears poured down her face.

In the background, Ramya heard her father's speech continue.

"Ramya was a one-of-a-kind person. She had big dreams. When young people are ripped from this earth…"

"What kind of sick joke is this? I can't hear any more of this shit. Juliet, let's go!"

Ramya turned back to Juliet, who slowly turned to face her. Except it wasn't Juliet, at least not how Ramya knew her. From memory, Ramya could trace every line and curve of Juliet's face, but the Juliet before her was disappearing, like a backward time lapse of a hyper-realistic pencil drawing. The color slowly drained and the lines that Ramya knew became barely visible. Ramya tried to replace the lost definition with her memory; even that was fading.

She tried to grab Juliet. Their hands slipped right through each other. A wailing noise came over a loudspeaker and Ramya cupped her hands over her ears.

"Do you hear that!?" Ramya screamed.

Juliet, or what was left of Juliet, sat completely still, unresponsive to Ramya's words. Ramya looked around and saw everyone else was still fixated on her father's speech. Ramya must have been the only person who heard the noise. The room started to flicker, first pixel by pixel, then square by square, and finally in its entirety. It disappeared like the LED lights of the Burj Khalifa.

"Juliet!" she screamed again into the total darkness.

In the distance, her photo and the garland reappeared. A Hindu priest was chanting and splashing drops of holy water. Ramya felt like she was watching the priest through a screen that was a mile away.

"Oooommmm," the priest said.

Ramya lost control of herself, and her eyes were forced to stay open as her body was catapulted to right in front of the screen. A movie started and soon, Ramya was inundated with so many awful scenes—Beth jumping from the patio of the gay bar in Cape Town and Sarah jumping after her. Their mangled bodies lying motionless on the concrete below. She saw Carl's and his father's plane crash the day after Carl's university graduation, their family crying uncontrollably next to their caskets. Then she saw the guy from the airport climb on top of a bridge railing before jumping out into the ocean.

Ramya shook uncontrollably as she saw Chiamaka get electrocuted from plugging in the television. Unlike what Chiamaka told Ramya had happened, this version showed a teenage Juliet walking into the sitting room and discovering her sister's dead body. The screen then jumped to Faiza, who was walking across the London Bridge when a man came running up from behind. He stabbed Faiza in the heart; she bled out quickly. Ramya was even upset as she saw Johannes, Juliet's ex-boyfriend, drink himself into oblivion, dying alone in the street from alcohol poisoning. The movie ended with Lynne, whose house was blown up in a ground attack during the Rwandan genocide. She died alongside her husband and two children.

They were dead.

"All of them, they're dead," Ramya said.

The screen disappeared and Ramya was forced to keep following the sound of the *Om*. She regained control over her body, but no matter which direction she ran, she found herself back in the classroom at the scene of the shooting. The different shades of red still lay thick on the floor. Her coffee had been knocked over and was swirling in a pool of her blood nearby. Ramya heard the EMTs faintly at first, their voices growing louder with each word.

"Victim number fourteen is female, early twenties, blonde hair, wearing a green dress! She's unresponsive and not breathing, over! Victim number fifteen is female, early twenties, brown hair, wearing a blue shirt. She's unresponsive and not breathing, over!"

Ramya looked to the right and saw herself. She remembered she told the guy at the airport how she had dyed her hair brown. Her favorite blue shirt was stained in red at the hip, where she had been shot. Soon, the EMT would realize she was the sole survivor. Except he kept going.

"Victim number sixteen is…"

She walked closer to her body, this time brushing back her own hair. Ramya was shocked and panicked to see that behind the tuft she was missing a chunk of her brain, which looked like the same color as the bright crimson floor. Her mouth was fixated in a gut-wrenching scream, as though she knew she was going to die.

"Ramya?" she heard a voice say.

Turning around, she saw Megan, who like Ramya's body on

319

the floor, was missing a part of her head.

"Hi, Ramya. It's good to see you. Come here, come sit."

"Megan? What are you doing here in Dubai?"

"Ramya, we're not in Dubai."

Megan motioned around her, and Ramya looked out of the window. Instead of the skyline of Dubai, Ramya saw the unwelcome and familiar rural Virginian landscape. The classroom hadn't come to her; she had come to the classroom. Megan pointed to an empty chair and Ramya involuntarily sat down beside her. The EMTs continued lifting victims onto stretchers. Ramya knew they couldn't see Megan or her sitting and watching them like a play in the theater.

"Megan, what's happening? Why am I here? How are you still alive?"

"Oh, Ramya, I'm so sorry. I saw scenes from the life you thought you had lived. It was beautiful."

"What do you mean, thought I had lived?"

"Oh, Ramya. I'm so sorry," Megan repeated.

Ramya wanted to cry, but her eyes wouldn't allow it. She wanted to collapse to the ground, but her legs wouldn't allow it. She wanted to go deaf, but her ears wouldn't allow it. She couldn't bear to hear a truth she had long feared, one that she knew Megan had been sent to explain.

"I don't believe you. This must be another dream. I'm stressed about seeing my parents. I'm stressed about Juliet meeting them."

"Ramya…you've never met Juliet. She was never with you."

"How is that possible? I've spent the last year falling in love with her."

The back wall of the classroom suddenly went dark, and Dr. Pillay's office appeared, only it wasn't how Ramya remembered. Instead of the crisp details she recalled, the office was blurry and spotty, like a hazy memory. Ramya was floating in one corner across from Dr. Pillay, who was also floating. Juliet was not there. The recording from Ramya's group therapy session with Juliet played. She heard herself and Dr. Pillay conversing. Straining to hear, Ramya thought the recording picked up a distant echo of Juliet's voice. She wasn't sure.

"If Juliet wasn't there physically, she must have been on another level. A part of us must have met?"

"It doesn't matter, Ramya, because none of it really happened."

"My life after the shooting…none of that was real? I didn't survive?"

"No, Ramya. We didn't. We only experienced what it meant to survive."

"We?"

Megan told Ramya about how she too had thought she lived on the earth after the shooting, unaware that those around her had also died or were in between realities. In Megan's version, there were two survivors in their French class.

"Remember Stephen?" Megan asked.

"Yes, of course. He sat close to me that day."

"We had just started dating a few weeks before the shooting."

"I didn't know that. Did he survive? I thought I saw he…"

"No, he was like us. But I didn't know. Neither did he."

"So, you two…" Ramya started.

"Yes. I remembered in class you were always talking about how you wanted to travel the world, Ramya. You had big dreams. But me? All I wanted was to be a French teacher and a mama. Stephen and I, we thought we recovered from the shooting together. Then we thought we got married and had a baby. I was pulled away just like you were today, on the night of our son's first birthday. I never saw Stephen again. My son never existed."

The wailing noise had returned, faint at first.

"How long were you and Stephen together after the shooting?"

"Seven years? Five days? Four months? I don't know. Time doesn't work the same way for this, Ramya."

The loudness of the noise increased, and Ramya felt her head shaking.

"Does she exist? Juliet?"

"Yes, in some reality. Maybe her body is alive, and her mind is not."

"Will I see her again?" Ramya asked.

"No, Ramya. This life, your life, ended in this classroom," Megan said.

The noise grew to an unbearable volume. Ramya's head felt like it was splitting apart. Just when the pain became unbearable, it became worse. She felt like pieces of her brain were ripping through her skull.

Her memories were disappearing—so many good memories. She had not gone to graduate school in New York City. She had never travelled to Africa. She had never worked for the UN or landed her dream job at a tech company. She had never come to terms with being gay. She had never found love. She had never met Juliet. She had been ripped from this earth before she had a chance to find happiness. The remnants of her body had been cremated and spread out over a river in Virginia. Since her death, her mother had periodically sent emails to her old account as a means of catharsis. Her parents regretted not really knowing who she was.

Finally, Ramya was transported one more time, next to Juliet on the bus to Ghana.

"Should we listen to music together?" Ramya asked.

"That'd be nice," Juliet replied.

Juliet continued to sing along as Ramya felt her body slip away.

Her spirit had wandered the earth for what felt like ten years in search of her soulmate, her Juliet. She wasn't sure in what reality they had met or why they had been given this year together. As quickly as Juliet had appeared in Ramya's alternate life, Juliet faded from her view. Ramya knew it was time she returned to her place of death. She watched the EMT zip the body bag over her. A mere idea of what she could have been was all that remained.

CHAPTER THIRTY-FOUR

 Juliet

 February 8 (last year)

 Ghana

"ADMINISTERING 5 CC'S, doctor..." Juliet heard someone say.

Her eyelids felt heavier than car doors and it took a few attempts to let in light.

"You can come in now," she heard the person say.

"Ramya," Juliet whispered, her throat on fire.

"Oh my God, Juliet! You're awake, praise Jesus," Sylvia said.

Juliet felt her friend's hand press against hers. The warmth gave her strength, and she forced her eyes open wider. A pale blue curtain surrounded her on two sides and a harsh light shone down from behind Sylvia. She was in a hospital.

She tried asking what happened. Her throat was too dry. Swallowing felt like eating glass. Sylvia understood and gently raised her head so she could take sips of water.

"My friend, wetin dey happen here?" Juliet whispered.

"You were in a bus accident coming into Accra, Juliet. They rushed everyone to this hospital. The travel company had my number and called me," Sylvia replied.

"Abeg, when did this happen?"

"Three days ago. You've been unconscious since."

Juliet was disoriented. It had been nearly a year since she left Ghana. She was last in Dubai, on her way to immigrate to America.

"Where's Ramya?"

"Who be that? Who is Ramya?"

She closed her eyes again. Surely this was a cruel joke. When she looked back at Sylvia, she saw her friend had a small baby bump again.

"Wey your pikin?" Juliet whispered.

"My friend, our first child isn't due for another five months."

"Where is Chiamaka?"

Sylvia gasped, the expression on her face now scared.

"Oh Juliet...your sister, God rest her soul. Chiamaka has been gone for many years."

The memories returned to Juliet. She had been seventeen years old when she discovered her eldest sister's body. Chiamaka had been electrocuted by a faulty wire when she tried to plug in a television. Juliet remembered that's why Mummy had disconnected the electricity from the family house.

Sylvia helped Juliet sit up, and she burst into tears.

"This can't be happening."

"Juliet, please rest. You must have a concussion."

"Sylvia, please borrow me your phone."

"Juliet, you need to rest. You go get strong, Juliet."

"Your phone, abeg!"

Sylvia heard her desperation, and finally reached into her purse. As Juliet took the phone, her hands were shaking profusely. Her neck cracked painfully, and she used every bit of strength she had to force her fingers to move. She clicked on the phone browser, which took a few seconds to load.

"The connection is slow here in the hospital. I've been by your side a lot. So has my husband. He kept asking how this happened to you," Sylvia said.

"Thank you, my friend."

The voices in her head now made sense, though nothing else did. There was only one way for Juliet to confirm what was reality. Slowly, she typed three words she had searched a dozen times after Kenya: Ramya Durga Virginia

All the results came back with the same story, but a different result than she had read,

> *A mass shooting occurred in*
> *Virginia, claiming the lives of*
> *32 people. Among the victims*
> *was 22-year-old Ramya Durga,*
> *a native of Richmond.*

She looked at the dates of the articles. Ramya had been dead for nearly ten years.

Juliet went mad that day. She had never cried so hard or so long. The nurses and doctors in the hospital threatened to sedate her, which only made her scream louder.

"Do it! Sedate me, abeg! Make I go see my Ramya again!" she shouted, over and over.

No amount of pleading changed the Google results for Ramya's name. Every number Juliet dialed for Ramya connected her to a stranger or to static. Sylvia had never heard of Ramya, and Juliet could not convince her friend otherwise. By her third waking day, Juliet heard Sylvia discussing with the doctors the possibility of putting Juliet in a facility to treat psychological disorders. Juliet, who according to Sylvia had never completed a semester of university classes, knew what those disorders meant. She forced herself to stay quiet.

"How you dey, Juliet?" Sylvia gently asked the next morning.

"Better. Borrow me your phone, Sylvia."

"Juliet, Ramya is not real."

"No no, I want to call Ifeoma, my sister," Juliet assured.

Sylvia agreed, handing Juliet her phone and excusing herself from the room before Ifeoma picked up.

"Juliet? How your side? You dey ok? Sylvia don call me yesterday," Ifeoma asked.

"I'm okay, my sister. How your side? How is Daddy?"

"His dementia don progress, Juliet. He go slip in and out."

Juliet heard the exhaustion in Ifeoma's voice. Ifeoma, who had given up her tailoring business and moved back to the family house to take care of Daddy after Mummy died two years ago. Juliet usually tried not to ask Ifeoma for favors given the circumstances. Today, she was desperate.

"Abeg, Ifeoma. Make I talk to him. Please."

Juliet heard Ifeoma shuffling across the room to hand Daddy the phone. His breathing was heavy at first, and Juliet waited for him to catch his breath.

"Daddy?"

"Hmm?"

"Daddy, it's me. Juliet. How your side?"

"I'm fine. Who be dis?"

"Juliet, Daddy. Your daughter."

"Hmm…Juliet. How your body? How is Ramya?"

Juliet's breath caught in her throat. She silently sobbed, afraid of alarming an impatient doctor or nurse.

"Daddy, you know Ramya, abi?"

"Mmm, that Ramya na nice girl. Make you hold onto her, Juliet."

"I will, Daddy. You take care, you hear? I go see you soon."

She hung up the phone before losing herself to another crashing surge of tears. Whether in this life or another reality, Juliet knew her love for Ramya had existed. There was no psychological disorder to explain away her truth, but there was no truth she psychologically felt safe to reveal. This was for Juliet and Daddy to preserve, not for those around her.

Sylvia and her husband graciously paid for Juliet's hospital bill the day of the accident. Juliet was embarrassed, but grateful, for she knew most hospitals would not treat a patient without first getting the money. Juliet might have died without Sylvia's generosity. The first few days after she was released from the hospital, Juliet thought that might have been better.

Her friend insisted Juliet stay in Ghana for as long as she needed to recover. The doctors used a big word—atrophied—to describe her muscles. Three days in one position was enough for everything in her body to become useless, and it took Juliet two weeks to relearn how to walk. Like a young baby, she spent hours coaching her legs to hold her weight. Sometimes she fell on the floor of Sylvia's sitting area, which she saw looked nothing like what her mind had created while she was in the coma.

The recovery gave Juliet too much time to think and to mourn the loss of a relationship she now knew had never existed, at least not in this reality and on this earth. Three days in her body had been a year in her head, and Juliet remembered everything.

"Juliet, na wa. You dey speak more like an Americana these days," Sylvia remarked.

"My brain is different after the accident."

"How come? The concussion?"

"The growth. I can't explain it."

By late February, on the day Juliet had thought Ramya asked her to be exclusive, Juliet was restless. She had been in Sylvia's house for weeks and needed to do something to honor Ramya, and to try to move forward.

"Sylvia, no vex, borrow me fifty cedis? I want to go somewhere."

"No wahala, Juliet. Here, take."

Juliet sifted through her broken suitcase and its contents, thankfully finding her makeup bag intact at the bottom. Slowly, she dressed up. Although her going-out ritual didn't bring her the same pleasure, she still admired herself in the mirror when she finished. She was beautiful, and though it had not happened physically, she knew someone had once loved her inside and out.

Outside for the first time in days, the setting sun was bright enough to blind her eyes. A taxi pulled up and Juliet told him her destination:

"The Movenpick Hotel, please."

She hesitated.

"Sir, is the Movenpick Hotel a real place?"

"Yes of course, ma'am. It's the nicest in Accra."

"Okay, take me there."

Unlike Sylvia's house, the Movenpick was exactly how Juliet remembered. She found the same bar where she first met Ramya and walked up to their table.

"Can I get you something, ma'am?" the waiter asked.

"Yes, two mojitos."

"Are you waiting for someone else?"

"I am. But she's not coming."

The waiter looked confused, nodding his head anyway and walked away to get her drinks. When he returned, he said,

"That madam over there has paid already."

He pointed across the room at a sophisticated-looking woman. Something in Juliet's mind told her they had already met. The woman walked calmly up to Juliet, as though she had been waiting for her.

"I spotted you from across the bar," the woman said.

"Sorry, do I know you?"

"I'm not sure. Something told me we were meant to meet.

329

My name is Margaret. I'm an investor and I'm looking for new talent."

"Eh? I'm not a…" Juliet started.

"Not like that! I am an investor in the *fashion* industry. I am on a West African tour to discover new artists. I noticed your dress. Did you make it?"

Juliet looked down at herself. She had purposely worn the same dress as in the Tinder photo Ramya had complimented.

"Yes, I did," Juliet replied.

"Wonderful! That's what I was hoping. Your accent though?"

"I'm from Lagos."

"You are? Perfect! That's my last stop. I'll be there in three weeks. Will you be back? Could you bring me samples of your clothes? We should talk business."

Margaret handed Juliet her card and sent her a calendar invite for their meeting. As soon as Margaret left, Juliet took out the new phone Sylvia had bought her and Googled Margaret's name.

> *Margaret Juma, 52, is*
> *reinventing the continent's*
> *fashion industry,* said an article
> in Forbes Africa.

Margaret was who she said she was. Everything—the business, the investing, the scouting for talent in West Africa— was real. Juliet sat back in her chair and took a big sip of her mojito. She looked around the bar, admiring the patrons and her place among them.

Finally, it was time to go home, and Juliet accepted Sylvia's last gift of a flight back to Lagos. She spent the loneliest week of her life in her apartment, mourning her love and trying to piece together her former existence. The day of her meeting with Margaret arrived, and Juliet grabbed her suitcase containing the best outfits she had ever constructed.

"Banana Island," she told the taxi driver.

Margaret's temporary office was just a few blocks away from where Juliet remembered collecting her precious new iPhone from Ramya's colleague. Juliet nearly passed out from the pain in her heart as she lumbered up the stairs to the office building.

"You're welcome, Juliet. Thank you for coming," Margaret said once Juliet was inside.

"Thank you, madam. I brought my stuffs."

Juliet watched Margaret sift through her clothes portfolio, periodically answering questions about why she chose certain materials, styles or accents. She imagined what it would have been like to have her life champion, her Ramya, waiting for her outside. The feeling was overwhelming and Juliet nearly succumbed.

"You are very talented, Juliet. I would love to work with you. But may I ask, you seem very sad. Are you ok?"

"Thank you, madam. Honestly, no, I am not. I lost someone very close to me recently."

"Oh child, I am so sorry. Nothing can replace that love. I'm sure they would be proud of you today."

"Yes madam, she would have been."

Margaret showed Juliet to a side room, where a lawyer met them to discuss the details of a contract. Juliet was overwhelmed with the options and was grateful the two professionals in front of her explained things slowly. She walked out of the office with her signed copy and Margaret's promise of a bright future.

Margaret walked with her to the main junction and prepaid the taxi fare for her to go home.

"I'm lucky to have met you, Juliet. We will do wonderful things together with your vision."

"Thank you, Margaret. Thank you for taking a chance on me."

Nearing the end of the workday, the Lagos traffic was heavy on the way home and forced her car to completely stop on the main bridge. Juliet turned her head in both directions, the familiar divide between traditional Lagos on one side and new Lagos on the other. She told the driver she needed some air and excused herself to walk over to the edge.

Staring at the vast expanse of her city, Juliet knew nothing would ever replace the love she had felt for Ramya. Nothing would ever compare. Somehow in that other reality, Ramya and Juliet had empowered each other, and therefore Juliet would never be the same in this reality.

"Ramya, love. I wish you could come back to me. Please come back to me, love. And if you can't, I want you to know that I will do more than survive. I go carry you in my heart, and I go thrive," she whispered.

ACKNOWLEDGEMENTS

I want to start by thanking my incredible wife Cybel Emmanuel, who has permanently changed my life for the better. Thank you for giving me the courage to write this story. The most beautiful outcome of surviving in this world is being with you.

Thank you to my brother Kiran Kumar, who has been one of my greatest champions since we were kids and a vocal advocate of all womxn and LGBTQI people for decades. Equitability would reign with more people like you.

Thank you to my parents Latha and Ashok Kumar, who supported me through my darkest days following the *Virginia Tech Massacre*. While I was not physically injured in real life, what I endured could have easily broken me. I am where I am today because of you.

Thank you to Salem West, Paula Martinac, and Nancy Squires of Bywater Books for taking a chance on this important story and for helping me deliver its messages with nuance. And to Selden Grandy for the cover design.

Thank you to the friends, workshop participants, and writer's group participants who gave me their valuable editorial opinions. You've helped me shape this story.

And finally, I want to acknowledge the victims of the *Virginia Tech Massacre*. There is nothing that justifies the ways your lives were impacted. You, your families, and us, your friends, deserved so much more.

ABOUT THE AUTHOR

Mala Kumar is the author of the 2014 novel, *The Paths of Marriage.* *What It Meant to Survive* is her second novel. Her op-eds, interviews, and essays have appeared in *The Guardian, The Advocate, TechCrunch, USA Today,* and *India Abroad.* In her professional life, Mala is a global leader in tech for social good. She lives in New York City with her wife. Visit https://malakumar.com for more information about her writing and work.

Bywater Books believes that all people have the right to read or not read what they want—and that we are all entitled to make those choices ourselves. But to ensure these freedoms, books and information must remain accessible. Any effort to eliminate or restrict these rights stands in opposition to freedom of choice. Please join us by opposing book bans and censorship of the LGBTQ+ and BIPOC communities.

At Bywater Books, we are *all* stories.

We are committed to bringing the best of contemporary literature to an expanding community of readers. Our editorial team is dedicated to finding and developing outstanding writers who create books you won't want to put down.

For more information about Bywater Books, our authors, and our titles, please visit our website.

https://bywaterbooks.com